FLEET OF GHOSTS

BOOKS BY TAYLOR ANDERSON

DESTROYERMEN: SCOUT CADRE

Fleet of Ghosts

THE ARTILLERYMEN SERIES

Purgatory's Shore

Hell's March

Devil's Battle

Inferno's Shadow

THE DESTROYERMEN SERIES

Into the Storm

Crusade

Maelstrom

Distant Thunders

Rising Tides

Firestorm

Iron Gray Sea

Storm Surge

Deadly Shores

Straits of Hell

Blood in the Water

Devil's Due

River of Bones

Pass of Fire

Winds of Wrath

DESTROYERMEN:
SCOUT CADRE

FLEET OF GHOSTS

TAYLOR
ANDERSON

ACE
NEW YORK

ACE
Published by Berkley
An imprint of Penguin Random House LLC
1745 Broadway, New York, NY 10019
penguinrandomhouse.com

Book design by George Towne
Maps and schematics by Taylor Anderson

Library of Congress Cataloging-in-Publication Data

Names: Anderson, Taylor, 1963– author
Title: Fleet of ghosts / Taylor Anderson.
Description: New York: Ace, 2026. | Series: Destroyermen: scout cadre; 1
Identifiers: LCCN 2025038356 (print) | LCCN 2025038357 (ebook) |
ISBN 9780593641606 hardcover | ISBN 9780593641620 ebook
Subjects: LCGFT: Fiction | Alternative histories (Fiction) | Science fiction | Novels
Classification: LCC PS3601.N5475 F58 2026 (print) | LCC PS3601.N5475 (ebook)
LC record available at https://lccn.loc.gov/2025038356
LC ebook record available at https://lccn.loc.gov/2025038357

Printed in the United States of America
1st Printing

The authorized representative in the EU for product safety and compliance is Penguin Random House Ireland, Morrison Chambers, 32 Nassau Street, Dublin D02 YH68, Ireland, https://eu-contact.penguin.ie.

To all the Armed Forces of the USA,
past and present,
in this 250th year of American Liberty.

USS *WALKER* (DD-163)

1946

*** Specifications**

Class-Wickes (Little)

Displacement--1200 tons

Length--314'4" Width--31'8"

Draft--9'4"

Speed--32 Knots

Armaments:

Main

4X4"-50

8X21" Torpedoes

Secondary

4XType 96 25mm AA

4X.50" 6X.30"

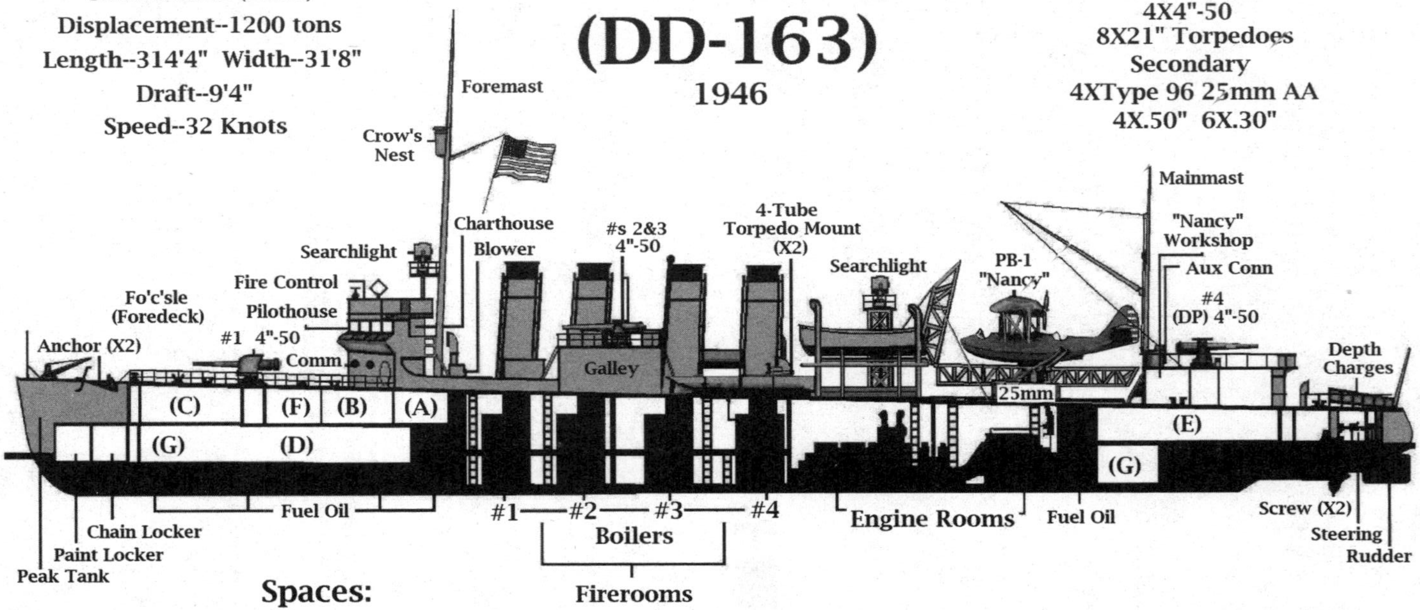

Spaces:

(A) Captain

(B) Officers

(C) Chiefs/Warrants

(D) Fore Crew

(E) Aft Crew

(F) Wardroom

(G) Storage/Magazines

* New Construction "Walker-Class" DDs have similar specifications but are 4-5 knots faster and 150-200 tons heavier

Ship Recognition Silhouettes

LDT BETTINO RICASOLI (DD)

USS WALKER (DD-163)

LDT ENSEIGNE GABOLDE (DD)

IJN SHONAI (CA)

LDT ELSASS (CA)

USS TEXAS (BB-35)

PRINZ EUGEN (CA)

USS SAVOIE (BB)

LDT FRANCE (BB)

USS FITZHUGH GRAY (CL-1)

LDT SUFFREN (BB)

USS IMPERO (BB)

THE ISLANDS VARIOUSLY KNOWN AS RAROR, OGYGIA, AND CAPRONA

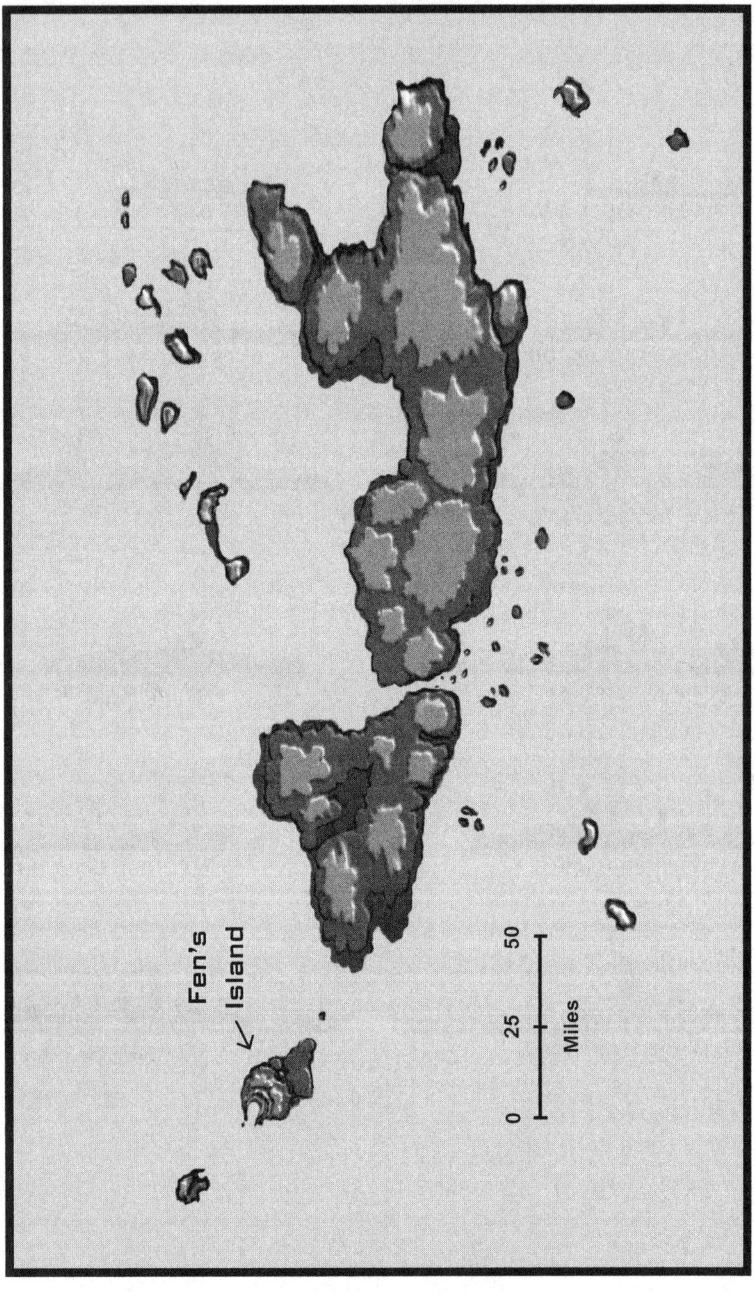

FEN'S ISLAND

(Ships not to scale)

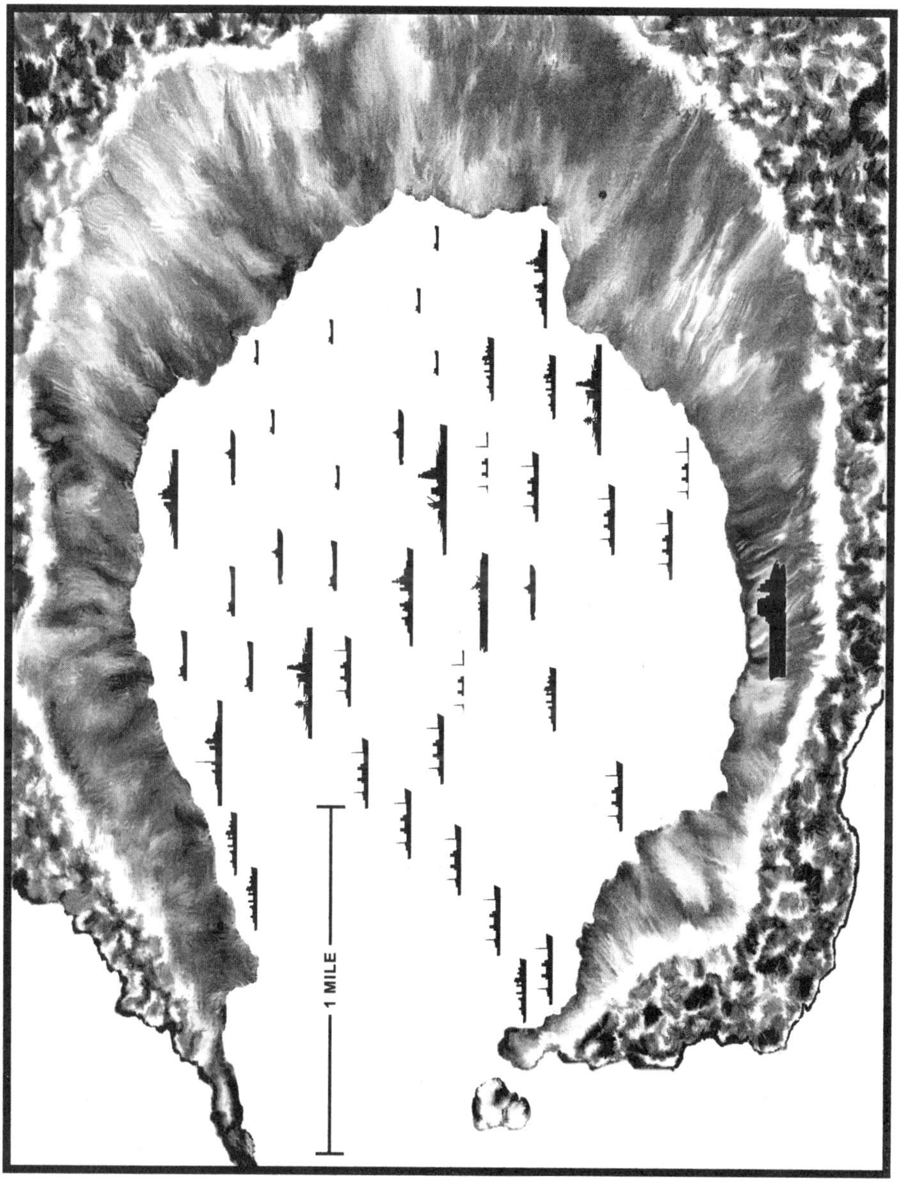

FLEET OF GHOSTS

OUR HISTORY HERE

By March 1, 1942, the war "back home" was a nightmare. Hitler was strangling Europe and the Japanese were rampant in the Pacific [having] seized Singapore and Malaysia, destroyed the American Pacific Fleet and neutralized their forces in the Philippines, conquered most of the Dutch East Indies, and were landing on Java. The one-sided Battle of the Java Sea had shredded ABDAFLOAT: a jumble of antiquated American, British, Dutch, and Australian warships. Its destruction left the few surviving ships scrambling to slip past the tightening Japanese gauntlet. For most, it was too late.

With several other refugees, I managed to board an old American destroyer, USS Walker, *commanded by Lieutenant Commander Matthew Reddy. Whether fate, providence, or mere luck intervened,* Walker *and her sister* Mahan, *their gallant destroyermen cruelly depleted by combat, were not fated for the same destruction which claimed their consorts. Instead, at the height of a desperate action against the mighty Japanese battlecruiser* Amagi, *commanded by the relentless Hisashi Kurokawa, they were . . . engulfed by an anomalous force, manifested as a bizarre, greenish squall—and . . . swept to another world entirely.*

I say "another world" because, though geographically similar, there are few additional resemblances. It's as if whatever cataclysmic event doomed the prehistoric life on "our" earth millions of years ago never occurred, and those terrifying—fascinating—creatures endured, sometimes evolving down wildly different paths. We quickly discovered "people," however, calling themselves "Mi-Anakka," who are highly intelligent, social folk, with large eyes, fur, and expressive tails. In my ignorance and excitement, I promptly dubbed them "Lemurians" based on their strong (if more feline) resemblance to the giant lemurs of Madagascar. (Growing evidence may confirm they sprang from a parallel line, with only the most distant ancestor connecting them to lemurs, but "Lemurians" has stuck.) We just as swiftly learned they were engaged in an existential struggle with a somewhat reptilian species commonly called "Grik." Also bipedal, Grik display bristly crests and tail plumage, dreadful teeth and claws, and are clearly descended from the dromaeosaurids in our fossil record.

Aiding [Lemurians against the Grik,] we made fast, true friends who needed our technical expertise as badly as we needed their support. Conversely, we now also had an implacable enemy bent on devouring all competing life. Many bloody battles ensued while we struggled to help our friends against their far more numerous foes, and it was for this reason I sometimes think—when disposed to contemplate "destiny"—that we survived all our previous ordeals and somehow came to this place. I don't know everything about anything, but I do know a little about a lot. The same was true of Captain Reddy and his US Asiatic Fleet sailors. We immediately commenced trying to even the odds, but militarizing the generally peaceful Lemurians was no simple task. Still, to paraphrase, the prospect of being eaten does focus one's efforts amazingly, and dire necessity is the mother of industrialization. To this day, I remain amazed by what we accomplished so quickly with so little, especially considering how rapidly and tragically our "brain trust" was consumed by battle.

In the meantime, we discovered other humans—friends and enemies—who joined our cause, required our aid, or posed new threats. Even worse than the Grik (from a moral perspective, in my opinion) was the vile "Dominion" in South and Central America. A perverse mix of Incan/Aztecan blood-ritual tyranny with a dash of seventeenth-century Catholicism flavoring technology brought by earlier travelers, the Dominion's aim was similar to that of the Grik: conquest, of course, but founded on the principle of "convert or die."

I now believe that, faced with only one of these enemies, we could've prevailed rather quickly, despite the odds. Burdened by both, we could never concentrate our forces and the war lingered on. To make matters worse, the Grik were aided by the madman Kurokawa, who, after losing his Amagi *at the Battle of Baalkpan, pursued a warped agenda all his own. And just as we came to the monumental conclusion that not all historical human time lines we encountered* exactly *mirrored ours, we began to feel the malevolent presence of yet another power centered in the Mediterranean. This "League of Tripoli" was composed of fascist French, Italian, Spanish, and German factions from a "different" 1939 than we remembered, and hadn't merely "crossed over" with a pair of battle-damaged destroyers, but possessed a powerful task force originally intended to wrest Egypt—and the Suez Canal—from Great Britain.*

We had few open conflicts with the League at first, though they seemed inexplicably intent on subversion. Eventually we discovered their ultimate aim was to aid Kurokawa, the Grik, even the Dominion, just enough to ensure our mutual *annihilation—removing multiple future threats to the hegemony they craved at once. But their schemes never reckoned on the valor of our allies or the resolve of Captain Matthew Reddy.*

Excerpt from the foreword to Courtney Bradford's
The Worlds I've Wondered
University of New Glasgow Press, 1956

The Great War was over at last. What had started, from the perspective of my Destroyermen friends, as a localized conflict between the rather felinoid Lemurians and the semi-reptilian Grik in the Java Sea and Indian Ocean, expanded into a near-global war between the Grand Alliance, composed of those displaced sailors, Lemurians, the Republic of Real People (populated by humans, Lemurians, and Gentaa), the human Empire of the New Britain Isles, and the NUS on one side, and the Grik Empire, human Dominion, and League of Tripoli on the other. The conflict ultimately tested the Grand Alliance to the limit, but with what might be seen as Pyrrhic victories over the Grik in Africa, and the "Doms" and League in the Caribbean and South America, an uneasy sort of peace was achieved.

The Grand Alliance was both spiritually and materially exhausted, ready for life without war, and began to tend somewhat toward isolationism as its members coped with the monumental changes the war had wrought on its various cultures. Unfortunately, even though they'd "won" the war, none of their enemies were entirely destroyed. Die-hard tribes of Grik warriors continued to challenge the Celestial Mother, now also a member of the Grand Alliance, for supremacy in Africa. Factions of the Dominion, including its vile leader Don Hernan, maintained their twisted ideology in the inaccessible vastness of South America. And the League of Tripoli, stung yet still dangerously powerful, merely retreated to its conquered home in Mediterranean and European waters to brood. Low-grade conflict persisted with all these factions and a "phony" or "cold" war festered with the League in particular, which remained more than happy to influence and encourage other rebellious groups.

Excerpt from Courtney Bradford's
Journal of a Gentleman Adventurer
University of New Glasgow Press, 1963

PROLOGUE

***USS* SCOTT**
SEPTEMBER 1946

The vast Pacific, or "Eastern Ocean" as Lemurians still called it, rolled endlessly and unbroken in all directions under great, puffy, pure white clouds. The sea beneath them was a deep, striking purple, starkly contrasted by a bottomless gray-blue tinged with silver where the sun stroked the waves. It was a fine, beautiful day for sailing, only the mild, quartering current preventing perfection, and USS *Scott* streamed along under a tower of canvas, her sharp hull foaming the sea around her.

Scott had been the first of her class, an improved wooden-hulled sailing steamer of 1,800 tons, named in honor of a fallen sailor who, as it turned out, hadn't precisely *fallen* after all. No one was more embarrassed by that than Tony Scott himself when he was discovered, not only alive but ruling as "king" of a North Borno tribe of human and Grik-like Khonashi. In any event, originally a frigate (or DD), USS *Scott* was 210 feet long with a 40-foot beam and had begun her gallant service to the American Navy Clan and the Grand Alliance as a formidable warship, earning numerous battle stars she was still entitled to fly embroidered on her flag. Quickly rendered obsolete for the battle line, however, she'd been reconfigured and redesignated an AVD, or seaplane tender. When the war was deemed "over" after the defeat of the Grik and Dominion, and the armistice with the League of Tripoli after the cataclysmic Battle of St. Vincent in the Caribbean, USS *Scott* and others like her were sold out of service.

Buyers got a very good deal, especially naval reserve personnel, who paid only a fraction of what the ships were worth. *Scott* in particular was just a few years old and had been well maintained. With her original sailing rig restored, she was a respectable sailer, and after the removal of all but one of her primary weapons and with no aircraft or catapult aboard, she could carry a heavy, profitable load. The only catch was that she retained her own reserve status as well, now designated an AVD-R, which meant she and her crew could be called back to duty if needed. This had happened a couple of times but wasn't much of an inconvenience. Once, she'd been slightly diverted to perform a search and rescue mission for a missing aircraft, finding the aircrew alive on an island. Another time she'd been called on to refuel and repair another floatplane that developed a fuel leak. A modest tank of gasoline for such purposes was always carried aboard and topped off on request at any port with American Navy Clan facilities.

Running under sail alone with her screw propeller freewheeling (the drag slowed her noticeably, but using the engine was expensive in fuel, and she was in no hurry), *Scott* was bound for Scapa Flow in the Empire of the New Britain Isles (where the Hawaiian Islands should be), from the Filpin Lands with a full load of ship turbines and aircraft engines. The voyage should take roughly two months. At Scapa Flow, she'd load another cargo bound for the Enchanted Isles (the Galapagos), which was another Imperial possession. Twenty-two days out of Maa-ni-la, most of the trip had been like today—easy sailing on relatively calm seas. There'd been a few hard rain squalls but no dangerous winds. Captain Morsey, an expat "Impie" (Imperial) who'd joined the American Navy Clan and served with distinction, rising to full lieutenant during the war, reckoned the weather should hold most of the way this time of year.

A young Lemurian apprentice seaman named Fen-An-Raar was busy on the fo'c'sle, sitting cross-legged on the deck by himself. He wasn't unpopular, he just needed the space to stitch a worn spot on a large flowing staysail draped across his lap. Fen was from the Filpin Lands himself and had enjoyed a brief visit with his mother while there. He was glad to be away, however. Her constant gentle nagging to stay and find a job in Maa-ni-la—on dry land—was understandable but grew quite tedious. He *was* very young after all, barely thirteen, and still pretty small. The average Mi-Anakka or "Lemurian," thusly dubbed by the great Courtney Bradford due to their vague resemblance to lemurs (though most other people just called them 'Cats), stood about 5′2″ and Fen hoped to reach that lofty altitude himself someday. At present, he was only 4′6″. He still had a chance. His three older brothers had all been taller than average.

Unfortunately, two of his brothers had been killed in action in the Navy. The third still lived, riding a savage me-naak with the 3rd Maa-ni-la Cavalry impossibly far away in Grik Africaa. Doubtless, that was another reason Fen's mother wished he'd make a life ashore. But his greatest ambition was to follow his other brothers into the Amer-i-caan Navy Clan, preferably aboard one of the sleek new destroyers still being built in Maa-ni-la and Baalkpan. Fen had a long way to go. Not only was he too young to join the "active" Navy, it presently preferred veterans who wanted back in or sailors with long experience. This in order to strengthen its ability to quickly train raw recruits if they were suddenly needed again.

The precipitous drawdown that followed the "end" of the Great War had resulted in an Alliance-wide labor glut and economic recession, mainly due to the vast numbers of ground troops mustering out. Some members of the Grand Alliance were transitioning easier than others, exploiting wondrous new technologies, but a lot of traditional occupations were probably gone forever, and even some of the new industries were shaky. As far as Fen knew, only the shipyards and aircraft factories still operated at anything like their wartime capacity (the League still enjoyed a significant material advantage), but there was no telling how long that could last.

Fen felt lucky to have a job aboard *Scott*, doing what he wanted and indulging in his love for the sea. Then again, long, dangerous voyages across the great Eastern Ocean weren't as popular as other routes. Even without a war, there were many hazards, from gigantic mountain fish and gri-kakka to the wildly malevolent cyclones called "strakkas" that boiled up to unimaginable size and strength in this seemingly infinite sea. But that meant Captain Morsey, who Fen much admired, couldn't be quite as choosy about his crew. *Scott*'s wartime complement had been around two hundred and sixty officers and sailors, but only about forty were really needed now. This was a mishmash collection of Impies for the most part, some naval reserve Lemurians, and even a few former "Dom" sailors from the Dominion.

Fen didn't much trust the latter. One of his brothers had died fighting Doms. Another died fighting the League at a place called the "Lake of Life," of all things. The former Doms serving on *Scott* seemed genuinely friendly and happy to be free, however, a few even a little friendlier than Fen was comfortable with, but he never had trouble with them. The only problem he seemed to have with anyone aboard came in the person of a junior officer named Lieutenant (JG) Ames, who seemed to feel required to lord it over everyone under him. It was rumored he'd once been with the Honorable New Britain Company, many of whom had been sympathetic to the Dominion. Yet Ames had supposedly performed well in the war, and Fen trusted his captain's judgment in officers. That didn't mean he trusted Ames. The man just *looked* disagreeable, with chaotic brown hair and a scruffy beard, narrow eyes and a beak-like nose. And he always had a disparaging remark about Fen's "blotchy" brindled fur, his somewhat extra-fluffy tail, and his bright yellow eyes most of all. Fen could take a joke, but Ames had a mean streak and *never* joked. His abuse of Fen never went beyond verbal, however. The little Lemurian was a diligent, willing worker and something of a mascot to the rest of the crew, not to mention the captain himself.

"Better wrap that up, lad," came a gruff, not unfriendly voice from behind Fen. He turned to look up at the looming figure of Handy Allen, the ship's chief boatswain's mate, or "bosun." As a naval reserve ship, rank structure and designation aboard remained the same as when she was in active service. A veteran of the Imperial Navy, Chief Allen was a good man, a good leader.

"Ay, Chief, just finishing up," Fen replied, grinning and blinking cheerfully. With 'Cats, a grin was a grin and a frown was a frown, but their faces weren't otherwise very expressive. Many thoughts and emotions were conveyed by the cant of their ears and position of their tails, but mostly by rapid, involuntary blinking that was difficult for other species to catch. "Sorry I haave took so long," Fen added.

Allen held out a hand. "It's not that, lad," Allen assured. "Ye work harder than any two others. It's just that with the watch change, we'll be alterin' course as well. They'll trample ye, adjustin' the sails."

Starting to gather his work, Fen looked up again. "Changin' course?" he inquired.

Others were assembling on the fo'c'sle and Fen quickly identified almost all the ship's officers: Captain Morsey and his XO, the Lemurian Lieutenant Jun-Soraat from the Republic of Real People, and even Lieutenant (JG) Ames. The only one missing was the engineering officer.

"Aye," said Captain Morsey, nodding down at Fen even after he straightened. "Stand easy, lad. No reason ye should'nae hear." Ames scowled, clearly disagreeing. "What?" Morsey asked, looking at him curiously. "I'll tell the whole crew soon enough. They've a right tae know." He took a breath. "You gentlemen first, o' course." His gaze touched everyone present, even Fen. "We got a coded transmission a short time ago." He shook his head. "I'll never get used tae these new, modern wonders. But the message directed us tae steer southward toward Respite Island an' investigate some very strange doin's. Seems that some time back, maybe a month or two or more—the message did'nae say—one o' them big, four-engine flyin' boats, a 'Clipper,' they call 'em, was on the monthly run down tae Respite when she saw—whatever it was that was seen—far tae the south o' there."

"We *must* go to Respite Islaand?" asked the Lemurian Lieutenant, frowning. "Thaat's a serious diversion and will put us significaantly behind schedule. We were in no hurry before, but there may be penaalties."

Morsey shook his head. "We've been reactivated fer the duration at Navy rates, an' that'll cover the terms of our shippin' contract as well. Nothin' tae worry about in respect tae that."

"Activated," Ames grumbled unhappily.

"It will be a long way, then?" Fen blurted, suppressing his excitement. He'd never seen Respite Island before.

"Aye," Chief Allen said absently. "But what're we lookin' for? What did the Clipper see?"

Captain Morsey shrugged. "Some kind o' great bloody flash o' light, like an explodin' volcano, they say. Must o' been bloody huge." He paused. "I told ye this happened some time ago, aye? Well, a pair o' civilian ships set out from Respite tae investigate an' did'nae return. No word from another vessel that went lookin' fer *them* either." He shrugged again. "Even two ships in company could o' met the same natural fate. A third comin' later . . . Why, that raises the specter o' foul play, does it not?" He scratched his chin. "'Course, none o' the investigatin' ships had wireless sets, an' it might be whatever they went lookin' for was farther than anyone thought."

"Or it wasn't anything at all," Ames muttered.

Morsey looked at him. "Aye, could be. But my understandin' is we're tae focus on search an' rescue more than seekin' strange lights on the horizon." He gestured at the single 4″-50 gun on a dual-purpose mount on the fo'c'sle behind them. It was the only armament *Scott* still carried. "But if there *has* been unpleasantness of some sort, we *do* have a wireless set—an' that."

Fen felt a surge of concern and blinked uncomfortably. Whistles blew as Chief Allen's bosun's mates began summoning all hands on deck and sending them to their tasks. The officers turned to head aft and change the ship's course. Chief Allen, expression thoughtful, was last to leave.

"Why send us?" Fen asked. "If someone expects trouble, *Scott* isn't really a waarship anymore."

Allen paused and regarded him. "They *wouldn't* send us if there was anything better nearby." He looked fondly around at the ship, his home. "An' she might surprise ye. That one gun alone can destroy anything we'd ever met before the war." He grinned. "An' 'warship' 'er no, *Scott*'s the closest Navy Clan asset an' it's our job." He chuckled. "I know you've always wanted in the Navy, lad, so welcome to it for the now."

USS *Scott* plunged southward with an even more favorable wind, though the current turned against her and actually slowed her progress. Fen didn't quite understand that—how the ocean flowed in different directions like rivers or why the big Clippers could fly straight from the Filpin Lands to the New Britain Isles, but *Scott* had to sail so far north of that line.

"It's the same with the wind, Fenny," admonished Fen's best friend, Waldo Dhar. From the Imperial Island of New Ireland, Waldo was a gangly kid, only slightly older, who worked in the engineering division. "Winds change about a bit more frequently," Waldo allowed, "but generally settle back to a reliable direction, for whatever time o' year it is."

Being from the Filpin Lands, Fen wasn't raised in a traditionally nautical clan, but wind made sense to him. He could feel it. "We could go straight from one place to another with the engine, true?" he asked. "Just like a . . . aar-plane. A destroyer could do that," he added wistfully.

"Aye," Waldo confirmed. "An engine is a wondrous thing to be sure, an' I predict we'll be usin' ours a bit more."

Waldo was right, and *Scott* soon proceeded under sail and steam combined, eventually raising the exotic, earliest outpost of the Empire of the New Britain Isles at Respite Island. It was a strikingly beautiful place of steep forested mountains, scenic shores, and a fine harbor protected by extensive but treacherous reefs. *Scott* took on a pilot, who led them safely through, and Captain Morsey called on the normally affable but increasingly concerned Governor Radcliff. There was no new information, and after a single night's stay, during which *Scott* took on provisions and topped off her fuel bunkers, she sailed south once more—into seas only rarely traveled.

The Empire of the New Britain Isles had experienced an exploratory phase that started about a century earlier, mapping new lands bordering the Pacific, even establishing outposts and colonies here and there. The most extensive of these was on the West Coast of North America and then down on the Enchanted Isles. Conflict with the Dominion had limited access to Central and South America, but only the amazing Pass of Fire, a natural passage between the Pacific Ocean and Caribbean Sea, had remained entirely unknown until recently—at least in the Northern Hemisphere and equatorial latitudes. Conversely, almost nothing was known of the Great Southern Ocean.

Numerous Imperial expeditions *had* been sent to investigate, and a couple ultimately confirmed that the "Drake Passage" between South

America and Antarctica was probably almost always completely blocked by ice. But voyages to investigate other regions either met with tragedy before much was discovered or never returned at all. Roughly fifty years earlier, the Imperials essentially gave up looking, and most gazed to the south with a near superstitious dread.

Farther west, Lemurians had circumnavigated the continent they called "Austraal," but it wasn't recorded if they went any farther. It was unlikely they had. Frankly, their Borno-centered civilization had been convinced—again, until recently—that they'd slide off the world if they did. They didn't think the earth was flat and were insulted by the implication, but down was down, damn it. One of the oldest Lemurian accusations of stupidity was "He thinks he can stand on the bottom of the world." That remained an insult, now ironic and directed at those refusing to contemplate new notions. In any event, even as the Grand Alliance combined all their charts of the known world, many large gaps remained. The southern Pacific was one of the biggest and it was into this vast region that *Scott* now sailed.

The first few islands *Scott* encountered were small, bleak, uninhabited atolls that actually had names given by mariners from Respite, but then came a two-week stretch with no land sighted at all. This started raising questions. "How far could the Clipper even *see* a flash o' light?" Waldo asked Chief Allen, who poked his lower lip out and arched his brows.

"Damned if I know. Farther than us. I guess it depends how high they were flyin'."

"An' maybe how bright the flash was, yes?" Fen prompted.

"That too, I reckon. *Can't've* been much farther, though. No matter. Skipper don't care as much about what brought the missin' ships a'lookin', compared tae the fate o' their crews. Their long absence implies somethin' happened to 'em, an' minus any debris, the best bet is we'll find 'em at some island attemptin' repairs. So, as much as wallowin' derelicts, islands is what we seek. No point sailin' all the way down tae the ice, however, so the skipper means tae wear west a ways tomorrow an' steer a new course parallel tae the one we took down. We're just one ship an' can only cover so much sea with each sweep. We'll follow the current west."

"How long will we keep that up?" Fen asked.

Allen scratched his stubbly chin. "No idea. Our cargo won't spoil, so as long as we have water, food, an' fuel, I reckon."

"Land!" came a cry from the lookout high on the mainmast.

"Where away?" roared Captain Morsey from aft. He was standing by the double-wheel helm just forward of the mizzenmast.

"I see it!" Fen cried excitedly, rushing to the rail in front of the starboard foremast ratlines, tail whipping behind him.

"Yellow eyes," growled Lieutenant Ames darkly, standing nearby, as if Fen had an unfair advantage. He did in a way. Lemurians could both see and hear much better than humans.

"I wish I could see like you, Fenny!" Waldo exclaimed with a hooded look at Ames as he shouldered in by his friend at the rail.

"Aye," laughed Chief Allen. "Need me some spectacles just tae see as good as I once did. Maybe next time we stop at New Britain . . ."

The lookout shouted the bearing down and the captain gave the helmsman a slight course correction. Smoke at the top of the funnel fumbled for a new direction and Chief Allen stepped back from the rail and called for adjustments to the sails. The island grew up out of the sea over the next few hours, getting larger and more promising as a possible refuge for the missing ships. Nothing was visible on their current heading, but the wooded, mountainous nature of the place might conceal a protected anchorage on the other side. The closer they came, however, the clearer they saw yet another island, even larger than the first, perhaps fifteen or twenty miles beyond it.

"We'll take in the sails if ye please, and proceed on the engine," Morsey shouted at Allen through a speaking trumpet. "Leadsmen forward, and extra lookouts into the foretop. Keep a sharp eye out for breakers an' shoals."

"Aye, aye, Cap'n," Allen shouted back.

Respite Island was surrounded by extensive coral reefs and this place might have its own. The first island, at least, certainly did, and *Scott* was forced to slow to a crawl and pick her way through treacherous waters in order to view the leeward side. Colorful, raucous seabirds and lizardbirds found her then, swooping through the rigging and shitting on the deck. Some snatched at morsels churned up by the ship's screw, but these were occasionally snatched from the sky in turn by voracious undersea predators with the same idea. A good beach eventually revealed itself on the island, relatively well protected, but no ships were seen. Of course, the island was fairly large and there might be other places for ships to land farther around the curving shore. They'd explore it further before moving on, but the other island was quite clearly much larger and more attractive to ships in distress and requiring forage and repairs. Captain Morsey wanted to inspect it first.

"Looks like it used to be a vol-caano," Fen observed. Almost half the visible land mass ahead was dominated by a tall, steeply conical mountain, but the top and western side looked almost as if it had been sheared off and it tapered more gently down a long, rugged slope to the sea.

"Aye," Chief Allen agreed, returning to stand by the little 'Cat. Waldo had left for his watch below. "Still is, I reckon. A big one."

"I wonder if that's what the Clipper saw? The vol-caano goin' off," Fen said.

Allen frowned. "Hard tae say from here. Ain't smolderin' 'er actin' much upset, an' I don't think it's gone off recent. The slopes're all covered with trees."

Allen's initial appraisal came under suspicion the closer they approached, however, and more of the "blown-out" side of the island came into view. Captain Morsey and Lieutenant Ames had joined them by then, scrutinizing the dense foliage on the slopes with their Imperial spyglasses.

"Well, there's been a fierce fire over there, up along the peak at least," Morsey observed aloud. "Another two points to starboard," he cried back over his shoulder before looking at the leadsmen in the chains. "What's our depth?"

"We're out of the shoals now, Cap'n," one man replied. "No bottom with this line."

Morsey grunted. "Deep here. I don't doubt both o' these islands are volcanic." He pursed his lips, looking back through his glass. "But even with the signs of a fire over there, it . . . doesn't *look* like the aftermath of an eruption. The broken slope is badly scorched, but doesn't look recently *disrupted*, if ye know what I mean?"

"That was my thinkin' too, Skipper," Allen agreed. "Looks more . . . I don't know, like God took a blowtorch tae the trees along the crest o' that ridge runnin' down tae the west."

Morsey was nodding. "I wonder. If the wall of the crater blew out or collapsed on that side of the island, whenever it happened, it might've left a large anchorage, open tae the sea." He glanced at Chief Allen. "Whether we find the missing ships or not, this could be a significant discovery on behalf of the Grand Alliance."

Scott steered yet farther west as she neared the island so she could pass to seaward of the looming headland, waves crashing on jagged stones. A new infusion of screeching lizardbirds joined those that hadn't left, and some were much larger, almost the size of "Grikbirds" or "dragons." Morsey considered having small arms issued, but these fliers seemed hesitant to approach too close. Just as well. Unlike similar creatures they'd encountered, these had tall colorful crests that actually looked like part of their skulls. They also had long sharp beaks instead of toothy jaws, which looked ideal for snatching fish.

"Bottom's coming up," the leadsman warned. "Ten fathoms," he added.

"Slow to one-third," Morsey shouted aft. They were getting close to where the ridge disappeared into the foaming sea, about a quarter mile distant, and would soon cross over it if it extended unbroken under the waves.

"Six fathoms."

"Can't go any slower here or we'll lose steerageway," Morsey said aside to Lieutenant Ames.

"No sir," Ames agreed. "Perhaps we should turn away," he added, somewhat anxious.

Morsey looked as if he was considering it but shook his head. "No, not yet."

"Three fathoms!"

Morsey frowned. That was only eighteen feet and *Scott* drew twelve.

"Lookouts?" he shouted upward before gazing to port, gauging where they should cross the underwater crest.

"I think we're over it, Cap'n," a man shouted down. "We just passed over a lighter spot below."

"Leadsman?"

"Five fathoms, sir," came a relieved-sounding voice. They might have wireless communications, but if they struck and damaged the hull, they were a long way from any potential assistance.

Morsey nodded. He was a careful skipper and hadn't considered that much of a risk, he was a majority owner of *Scott*, after all. He was inwardly relieved all the same. Almost immediately after passing the headland and crossing the underwater ridge, the sea became significantly calmer. Just as important, Morsey's speculation was immediately proven correct: the entire western side of the mountain, indeed the whole island, had been blasted away at some point in the past, creating a surprisingly large bay many miles across. He was already observing it with his glass, starting by examining the distant, hazy "southern ridge" that seemed to mirror the one now astern.

"Fifteen fathoms, sir."

Morsey grunted. "Keep callin' the depth, if ye please," he said, but looked at Chief Allen with a grin. "I was right. A fine anchorage, I believe. I wonder how well protected it is." Turning to gaze more deeply into what was so obviously a gigantic volcanic crater, he adjusted his glass and grunted again. "Several miles deep, at least. I would'nae've wanted tae be anywhere near when this place blew itself apart." He paused. "But it wasn't a recent event. The inner slope of the crater is covered with deadfall trees, it seems. Thousands of 'em, but deep green grass as well." He frowned. "Though the *trees've* been dreadfully scorched, and not long ago."

Fen was squinting. "Look down on the waater, sir!" he urgently pressed. "Within the aarms of the bay, there are *ships*!"

"Indeed?" Morsey asked, redirecting his gaze. The afternoon sun was sucking a thick, humid, fog-like haze off the water inside the crater, obscuring their view of what lay there.

"Is it the ships we're lookin' for?" Chief Allen asked excitedly, shading his eyes and squinting hard, but Captain Morsey was lowering his glass, an expression of shock spreading across his face. "Ah . . . no," he said distractedly. "I don't know," he quickly added. "They may be here, but there are . . . others as well. They're . . ." He stopped. "I have no words. Mr. Ames," he continued brusquely, "do you see it too?"

Lieutenant Ames collapsed his glass with a sigh. "I'm afraid so, Captain Morsey," he said, tone suddenly very formal.

If Morsey noted it, he didn't react. "Then please be so good as tae compose a report of our discovery at once. Directly to High Admiral Jenks, I should think, and have the operator send it in code." He fished a key up out of his shirt, where it hung around his neck. "This'll open the code safe in my quarters."

Ames didn't move except to retrieve a whistle from around his own neck and blow a long, harsh call.

"Mr. Ames?" Morsey asked, anger rising. "What's the meaning of this?"

Men started running around on the deck, just a few, but they began shoving other men and the few 'Cats aboard around. Scuffles and angry shouts broke out and then there was a shot. Wide-eyed, Morsey, Allen, and Fen looked back at Ames and saw that he'd produced a small semi-automatic pistol.

Ripping the key away from Morsey, Ames spoke with an entirely different voice, as if he weren't the same person at all. "I'm afraid I can't follow that order, Captain Morsey, and regret to inform you that you must consider yourselves prisoners of war in the custody of the League of Tripoli."

"He's a goddamned Leaguer!" Allen spat. "A *spy*!"

Ames bowed his head slightly and began to reply, but the fighting increased and there were a number of shots and screams. "I would prefer to avoid unnecessary bloodshed," he said over the tumult. "But I don't have a great many men on board. Most are former Dominion soldiers," he stressed with added menace. "All are armed, however, and will do what they must to compel obedience."

"I'll never surrender my ship," Morsey seethed, "and you can go to the Devil!" With that, he lunged at the renegade officer, and the small pistol, a

Beretta Modello 1934 in .380 ACP, barked twice. Captain Morsey groaned but carried Ames down to the deck, landing heavily on top of him. "Save the ship, Chief Allen," he gasped, struggling to keep Ames pinned and the pistol pointed away from him. Allen was savagely kicking the trapped officer in the hip and ribs while Fen went for the pistol. It went off almost in his face, leaving his sensitive ears feeling like he'd just been stabbed in them. He got hold of the pistol, though, and small as he was, his hands and arms were incredibly strong, like all his race, and he wrenched the pistol away. "Here, Chief Allen," he cried, tossing the Beretta at him.

"Good lad," Allen said, catching the weapon and glancing quickly at it. He was familiar with the Baalkpan and Maa-ni-laa Arsenal "1911s" and figured it worked much the same. "Stay with the skipper. I'm bound for the armory. Use that voice o' yers tae spread the word."

No matter how high-pitched a Lemurian's ordinary voice might be, they could harness certain frequencies that carried quite a distance. Fen used that now, shouting, "*Scott* sailors! To the aarmory! Get weapons and defend the ship!"

Captain Morsey was still grunting, still fighting to control Ames, and Fen took an instant to survey the scene around them. It didn't look good. At least a dozen men were down on the deck, many lying in pools of blood. A number of others were huddled together by the rail, covered by a likely enemy. Fen thought he recognized one of the "overly friendly" former Doms pointing another small pistol, and most of the fighting now sounded belowdecks. Gazing farther aft, he noted there was no one at the helm. Looking forward, he could see the far side of the bay much closer now, but more immediate still was something . . . some sort of complicated *structure* jutting out of the sea and *Scott* was steaming straight toward it.

"Caap-tain Morsey!" Fen cried out, turning back to look, just as Ames shoved the feebly resisting man off him. Morsey had clearly been shot, but now an ornate dagger hilt projected from his chest. "*Murderer*," Fen seethed at Ames. He lunged for the dagger, pulled it from his captain's chest, and coiled to spring at his enemy.

There was a terrible crash forward and the whole ship lurched sickeningly, flinging everyone off their feet. A crackling, crashing sound came from above and topmasts, spars, rigging, and flapping canvas plummeted down in a rush, smashing into the deck all around. Men squealed in agony and terror, crushed beneath falling debris. Steam roared from the funnel as someone, friend or foe, vented it away from the engine.

Jumping back to his feet, tail whipping with fury, Fen prepared to leap at Ames once more, but the Leaguer, propping himself up, merely smiled enigmatically and waved an admonishing finger before pointing back behind Fen. Hesitantly, Fen turned. A pair of his former crewmates were pointing pistols at him while two others supported the unconscious form of Chief Allen between them. The bosun's hat was missing and blood matted his hair.

"I couldn't care less what happens to you, *animal*," Ames said harshly, stressing the last word, "but I will need the cooperation of this ship's surviving crew, particularly now that she is damaged." He shrugged. "They may be less likely to help me if I have you killed, and then I shall be forced to choose examples to make from among *them*. All quite tragic and pointless, don't you agree?"

Fen hesitated just a moment, looking around. The proud former frigate was dead in the water now, wallowing away from whatever she struck. The bowsprit was a shambles and the forward bulwark over the portside headrail was smashed in. The object they hit looked bent, so it must've been metal of some sort. *Iron*, he thought with surprise, based on the reddish rust color and the red cloud of rust dust still drifting away on the wind. *We struck a mast or something protruding from a sunken iron ship*, he suddenly realized. Scanning the big bay for the first time from truly within it, he saw rusty iron ships all around. More were sunk, only their upperworks standing clear in the shallows, and others rode low and listing in the water. Some, to his amazement, lay shattered and crumpled either partially or entirely onshore. A fair number, however, just as rusty as the rest, seemed to float perfectly normally at anchor and, most stunning of all, some were absolutely enormous and many were quite obviously warships, bristling with gigantic guns.

"Ah, now you see why this discovery is even more important than your captain imagined," Ames chuckled, "and why absolutely *nothing* will prevent me from securing it for my superiors."

CHAPTER 1

BAALKPAN, BORNO
NOVEMBER 1946

The big four-engine seaplane, a PB5-D "Clipper," blue on top and white on bottom, roared into a banking descent over the glittering, bustling Baalkpan Bay. The Mi-Anakka city of Baalkpan, roughly where Balikpapan, Borneo, would've been, had grown from a quaint, if populous, early iron-age equivalent Lemurian "land Home" outpost on the densely jungled island of Borno into a thriving, industrial, frankly overcrowded metropolis in barely five years. Its character had changed just as dramatically and few who hadn't witnessed its transformation would even recognize it now.

When the elderly war-torn US Asiatic Fleet destroyer USS *Walker* first steamed into Baalkpan Bay in early 1942, she'd escaped the overwhelming juggernaut of the Imperial Japanese Navy on another world but had dropped right into an existential war against the marauding semi-reptilian Grik alongside her crew's new Lemurian friends. Back then, nearly every dwelling and structure onshore had been built on stilts or incorporated trees to achieve the necessary elevation to protect their inhabitants from local predators. Now those dreadful creatures had been pushed back from the sprawling, expanding city, and preexisting structures had been built "down" to the ground. Nearly all new construction was free-standing.

Now that the Great War—ultimately against far more than the Grik—was technically over, civilian commerce in the bay was coming back to life. It even retained some traditional aspects, supporting the gigantic seagoing Homes, which were floating mobile cities themselves, in exchange for the meat and oil of huge gri-kakka (plesiosaurs). Seagoing Lemurians had hunted those beasts throughout recorded history and gri-kakka meat, fish, wild land game, and now captive-raised animals of all sorts were in high demand to feed Baalkpan's growing population. With the widespread and increasing use of petroleum, one might've thought there'd be little demand for gri-kakka oil these days, but not only was it still used for cooking and lighting, it was a superior natural lubricant. Above all, every boiler in the city and along the waterfront that powered a vast array of machinery, from pumps, cranes, compressors, lathes, mills—whatever—had switched back to gri-kakka oil from petroleum. The smoke stank worse but was easier on the lungs.

That was important because Baalkpan's heavy industry was still booming, still largely devoted to shipbuilding, aircraft manufacture, and technological experimentation and development. This mitigated against the economic crunch the postwar drawdown imposed on many of its fellow Homes and allies, not to mention employing many veterans. And Baalkpan could afford it. Not only were more and more of its industries in private hands, veterans pooling their unspent pay to form corporations, but the things they produced—those ships, planes, weapons, fuel, radios, and conveniences as simple as light bulbs—remained in high demand all over. Most other Homes in the Union, with wartime industries of their own that were easily adapted to civilian pursuits, benefited as well. A few, like Sular on the island of Saa-Leebs, had been under extremely misguided, even traitorous leadership, and hadn't done much to benefit their postwar economies. They were suffering now. But even the great seagoing Homes still had a commercial purpose that allowed them to continue plying the seas *as* Homes as they always had, now even as far as some of Baalkpan's allies, such as the Empire of the New Britain Isles and Republic of Real People.

Both those nations arguably already had a greater industrial capacity than Baalkpan, perhaps even combined with the Filpin Lands, and were increasingly involved in military and tech development as well. But Baalkpan was the capital of the "United Homes," or simply "The Union," which was a new and diverse republic that included nearly every land mass from the Filpin Lands to Indiaa and Malaysia south to Austraal, as well as a large number of those seagoing Homes, all of which enjoyed representation in the Union Assembly. And despite no longer being the most populous city in the Grand Alliance, or even the largest economy, Baalkpan's senior membership and still somewhat central location ensured that it remained the headquarters of that far-flung association of cooperative military powers, with members as far away as Africaa to the west and the Americas in the east.

Leveling off for its approach to the buoy-marked zone strictly reserved for seaplanes, the powerful, reliable, but ungainly-looking aircraft touched down on the water and ponderously rumbled and shuddered to a stately, spume-spraying taxi speed. The pilot cut the two inboard engines and proceeded to maneuver toward shore, where the new seaplane docks and terminal building had replaced the old fitting-out pier. The earliest of several "new" fitting-out piers was just across a basin where the oldest and still biggest dry dock had been constructed. It had been vastly updated and improved, of course.

A 'Cat line handler climbed out of a hatch on top of the plane's fuselage and raced barefoot out on the reinforced centerline behind the engines on the broad portside wing to hurl a rope to a gathering of uniformed Navy 'Cats on the dock. As soon as they caught it and began heaving in, the plane's outboard engines slowed to a popping idle. Another rope flew out of the gunner's/observer's port in the waist. When it was expertly seized and drawn in as well, the pilot finally cut the remaining engines. Their rumble was replaced by the voices of 'Cats chittering in their own language to coordinate bringing the high hatch on the plane up to the dock. Moments later, the hatch swung open and a round grinning face with wide inquisitive eyes emerged, blinking under the hot, humid sunlight and looking about with an expression of wonder. Stepping quickly out on the dock, he straightened a long-tailed bright yellow shirt, hitched up his white, somewhat oversize trousers, and plopped a wide-brimmed straw hat on his head to protect his balding red pate from the sun. Grasping his hands behind his back, he anxiously bounced on the balls of his feet and waited for his companion to join him. After many unlikely adventures and a longer absence than most, the one-time Australian petroleum engineer on another world, hobby scientist and naturalist, frequent ambassador and occasional general—once briefly even an admiral—Courtney Bradford was "home" at last.

"Oh, do hurry, Mr. Cook," he scolded back into the plane. "I can't wait to explore the city anew! So much has changed!"

Marine Captain Abel Cook, tall and slender and dressed in his blues, struggled through the hatch with his *and* Courtney's seabags over his shoulders. He'd just been a kid when he came to this world, not aboard *Walker* or USS *Mahan*, but "evacuated" from Surabaya, Java, in the old submarine *S-19* with a bunch of other children of British diplomats and Dutch officials. Like those aboard the two destroyers, and ultimately several other ships and planes, they never reached their destination. All the children in *S-19* wound up serving in the war—as soon as they were old enough—but young Abel Cook and Nathaniel "Nat" Hardee, both now barely twenty-one, had especially distinguished themselves. Abel had even reached the rank of major in Colonel Chack Sab-At's Marine Raider Brigade, but like so many others who wanted to remain "regulars," especially in the Marines, he had to take a rank cut. It was in fact widely rumored that Chack's Raiders would be reduced to a single active regiment, and General Pete Alden's beloved 1st Marine Division would effectively become a brigade because Marine contingents for all Navy ships would be drawn from it.

And the Marines and Navy had it better than most of the "peacetime" Allied forces because they belonged directly to the "Ameri-caan Navy Claan" under the high chieftainship of Captain Matthew Reddy. Though subject to the authority of the Chairperson of the United Homes, Safir-Maraan, Matt Reddy remained a head of state in his own right. And besides being partially financially supported by the other clans in the Union, for the benefit of everyone, the Navy Clan had its own source of revenue in the oil-rich island of Tarakan, among a few other possessions. Matt Reddy used his clan's financial windfalls to maintain, upgrade, and expand the fleet, and take care of his people, of course.

"There won't be time for exploring, Mr. Bradford," Abel patiently reminded. "We're expected to report directly upon arrival."

"Nonsense," Courtney huffed. "They can't have been serious about that."

Abel nodded down the dock toward the terminal. "I believe they were, and it looks like they sent a welcoming committee to impress that upon us."

"Hmm," Courtney grumbled, glancing at the collection of 'Cats and men in Navy whites and tie-dyed Marine combat smocks. "Perhaps you're right, Mr. Cook. They do look like they're waiting for us, and rather impatiently at that." He smiled. "But I'm sure you outrank them. You can direct one of them to handle my bag!"

Courtney and Abel, both relieved of their burdens, were escorted through the terminal to the teeming street beyond. This one, like all streets servicing the waterfront industrial quarter, had been hard paved, and a paalka-drawn coach was waiting to carry them to the Great Hall. Paalkas probably resembled moose more than anything, with longer forelegs than rear, and an even more disapproving gaze. Few horses had been imported to Borno from the Americas yet and paalkas—themselves imported from the Filpin Lands—remained the primary beasts of burden. The very heaviest loads were increasingly shifted by machinery so the troublesome "brontasarries" were rarely used anymore.

Unlike the rest of the city, little had changed immediately around the Great Hall, which had long since become a vast shady park. The whole area had been cleared to become the training ground for the first army raised to defend the city but was now a hallowed cemetery. The Great Hall itself had once been supported entirely by the stupendous Great Tree of Baalkpan, the only full-grown example of a Galla tree anywhere besides Madagascar. (Madagascar was also—probably—the ancestral home of all Lemurians.) But the Great Hall had finally been built down to the ground, like so many structures, and upward as well. This to accommodate the many additional purposes to which it had adapted. The high chief of Baalkpan still theoretically dwelled there, sharing it with the Union Assembly Chairperson, but since the advent of the Union, that had been the same person. The last chairman had been Alan Letts, USS *Walker*'s former supply officer, who'd been assassinated along with a number of other officials and a great many civilians by an escaped League prisoner and some malcontents from Sular. The highly admired General Queen Safir-Maraan, from B'mbaado, had succeeded him by acclimation. The level below her Hall was devoted to "Department" offices, including that for War, and the one for Strategic Intelligence, where they were headed at present. The entire ground floor was the Union Assembly room. Other offices and new multistory embassies had risen to surround the venerated park.

Exiting the paalka-drawn coach, Courtney and Abel were politely conducted through the spacious, empty Assembly room and up one of three sets of stairs. At the top was another young 'Cat Marine, who led them down a corridor. At the end was an open window with actual cloudy glass in it (the very best glass was still reserved for ships and planes), but also a partially open door under a hand-painted sign that read, INTELLIGENCE.

"Oh dear," Courtney said with a chuckle. "'Intelligence,' is it? I fear we've come to the wrong place."

"You may be right," came a bellow in a much stronger Australian accent than Courtney's. "But here's where yer wanted. Get in here, both'a ya. Bloody damn flight schedule had ya here last night."

They stepped into a large dark wood office with an electric fan laboring in front of another open window behind a long desk. The fan could do nothing about the humidity, but it pulled fresh, shaded air into the room and moved it about. Two men and a tall, gray Lemurian stood up from behind the desk as if they shared it. Maybe they did. It was certainly large enough. Just a couple of folders were on it at present. Two people were also there, rising from a pair of the half dozen chairs and stools across from the desk. The chairs were for humans. Lemurian tails made them uncomfortable and they much preferred cushions, but stools would do.

Abel Cook quickly came to attention, recognizing all those in the room and their lofty positions. The one who'd spoken was Henry Stokes, a former Leading Seaman aboard the Australian light cruiser HMAS *Perth*, sunk along with the American heavy cruiser USS *Houston* in a furious night action against the Japanese on another world. He came to this one as a POW in the hold of the hellish Japanese prison ship *Mizuki Maru*. Wiry and bearded, with little formal education, he still looked and acted more like a well-dressed ruffian in his Imperial-style weskit, knee breeches, and tall brown boots than one might expect of the Director of Strategic Intelligence for the United Homes. His sharp, native intellect, cunning, and life experience had trained him well for his post.

Standing on his right was Doocy Meek, Stokes's colleague in the service of the Republic of Real People, in southern Africaa. He was an older, burlier man, also bearded, who'd ironically come to this world as a prisoner of war as well—a British merchant seaman taken aboard the German passenger liner turned commerce raider SMS *Amerika* before his ship was scuttled. That was in a previous war, back in 1914, and he and numerous other involuntary passengers of *Amerika* had been treated infinitely more gently by their German captors than Stokes and his fellow survivors were by the Japanese in 1942. Finding themselves all "here" together, everyone aboard *Amerika* jointly cooperated with their new countrymen—human, Lemurian, and Gentaa—in the Republic. They weren't the first to do so. The Republic's geography practically ensured frequent infusions of displaced refugees and their technology over the ages. *Amerika* helped bring it into the early twentieth century.

Standing in front of one of the chairs in immaculate whites, grinning and shaking his reddish-brown-haired head while he leaned slightly forward, hands on hips, was Captain Brad "Spanky" McFarlane. He wasn't tall or heavily built, but his personality always left people with the impression he was bigger than he was. Having started on this world as USS *Walker*'s engineering officer, he was now Matt Reddy's "XO," not just of the fleet, but the whole American Navy Clan. Currently overseeing naval construction and innovation at Baalkpan, he was also commodore of the "Home Squadron." Abel briefly wondered how big the squadron was. He hadn't seen much of a military nature moored in the bay.

The two Lemurians who greeted Abel and Courtney were probably even more revered among the panoply of heroes of the United Homes.

The first, still standing by Stokes, was the ancient Aryaallan General Muln-Rolak. Before the late war, Rolak had inarguably been the greatest, most experienced Lemurian warrior alive. Of course, warlike Lemurians had been exceedingly rare back then, and the only ones known at the time were Rolak's people at Aryaal (Surabaya, Java) and their equally belligerent neighbors on the island of B'mbaado. Even then, warfare between the two competing kingdoms had long been somewhat stylized and ritualistic. Warriors died in battle, sometimes very bloodily because the fighting styles with edged weapons were wickedly lethal, but the wars themselves were often small, limited affairs with narrow aims. Rolak himself had once referred to them as "war as play." All that changed after the Grik came and Rolak no longer enjoyed war.

The much younger 'Cat present, with brindled fur under mottled green-and-brown Marine combat dress, was none other than Abel's much admired commanding officer, Colonel Chack-Sab-At. He'd once been a rather extreme pacifist on *Salissa*, the seagoing Home of his birth, but changed just as much as his great ship. Even as *Salissa* had been given engines to replace her huge sails and was rebuilt into the Grand Alliance's very first aircraft carrier—she still remained on active reserve status while training naval aviators from the Empire and NUS in the Caribbean—Chack had grown into one of the Alliance's best battlefield commanders. His brigade was still in the Caribbean as well, on Martinique Island, but Chack was home on a long overdue leave, visiting his mate, who just happened to be Safir-Maraan, Chairperson of the United Homes.

"Oh, stand easy, Mr. Cook. You ain't on parade. Sit. Both of you," laughed "Spanky" McFarlane, moving to shake their hands before dropping back into his chair. Hands were shaken all around, with big grins and exclamations of greetings. Abel hadn't seen Chack since he'd been detached to accompany Courtney, but Chack seemed more "himself" than the last time they were together, his amber eyes less intense and haunted by battle. Stokes bellowed for refreshments, and a trio of 'Cat clerks or secretaries brought pitchers of iced fruit nectar and Imperial tea. The technology to make plentiful ice was just one of the myriad advances with more than just military applications that had been widely embraced.

"Now, Mr. Bradford," Stokes continued when mugs were poured and the servers had departed, "first, I'm bloody glad ta see ya. Safir's been askin' for ya every damn day—she'd be here now, an' Cap'n Reddy an' Pete Alden as well, but they're across the strait on Saa-Leebs. I expect they'll host a reception tomorrow evenin'. S'posed to be back by then. But for now, I want a quick account o' yer look at the, ah . . . *incident* in the Shogunate of Yokohama."

The Shogunate was a colony in "Japaan" composed of emigrants from the Filpin Lands, along with hundreds of Japanese sailors who'd come to this world aboard *Amagi*, *Hidoiame*, and *Mizuki Maru*, and it was a firm member of the Union. Right at the climax of the war, however, during the naval battle near St. Vincent Island, there'd been something described as a gigantic explosion half a world away, near where Hiroshima would've been. And a few days later, there'd been another, about where Nagasaki should be on the world the Japanese came from. Fortunately, considering the widespread blasted and charred nature of the coastal forests the first local investigators discovered, both regions had been virtually unpopulated "here."

Deeply involved in negotiating alliances, trade, and technological exchanges, as well as spheres of influence and terms of occupation in the Dominion after the war, Courtney hadn't been immediately free to visit the scene. Ravenously consuming every report he could get, however, he began formulating a theory and asked Steve Riggs, the "Minister of Communications and Electrical Contrivances" to cobble up and deliver a device capable of detecting X-ray and gamma radiation. That was one thing the young radio and electronics hobbyist turned Navy tech wizard had never tinkered with, but he'd been drawn to the "wow" factor of measuring radiation and cosmic rays and fortunately read enough about it to understand the principle. While other kids his age loved comics, he was a nut for *Popular Science*, *Scientific American*, *Radio-Craft*, and, of course, *Astounding*. He'd built a machine he'd thought would work and sent it to the Filpin Lands for Courtney to pick up.

Stokes gestured around. "Most'a us've read yer report, but not all. An' it may have a bearing on the main *other* reason yer here."

"And why we asked you here before you could even have a naap," said Rolak, blinking amusement. "Or waander off, chasing a bug."

"I protest, sir," Courtney said, smiling a little wistfully. "My desire for a new 'Corps of Discovery' to explore this fascinating world without constantly being required to shoot at someone has been thoroughly shattered. In the near term, at least," he stubbornly qualified. "In the meantime, I shall continue to do my duty."

Abel wondered if Courtney saw Spanky and Stokes exchange meaningful glances.

Courtney continued. "As you doubtless know, Mr. Cook and I spent several uncomfortable weeks tramping about and examining the environs of both, ah, 'incidents' as you called them. Though time had passed and ground cover foliage was regrowing, it remained quite clear that both areas had been subjected to a tremendous release of fiery energy that left scorched, denuded trees in their countless thousands lying on the ground and radiating outward from some central point. And the radius of destruction was truly stunning. More miles than we could pick our way through on the ground, through all the deadfall. An aerial observation shortly after the phenomenon estimated the circumference at more than twenty miles." He glanced at Stokes. "I'm sure you're familiar with that already, as well as the fact no crater or any indication of a volcanic explanation was seen."

He paused and looked doubtful. "That alone wouldn't rule out a natural cause. It may have been something like what occurred in a remote region of Russia early in the century, near a river called Tingusta or Tungista—something like that. I remember they thought a giant meteor struck there, or perhaps exploded in the sky, causing an effect similar to what Mr. Cook and I observed. It was quite the sensation at the time and the source of great speculation. The remoteness of the site prohibited a timely investigation, however, and with the coming of the Great War—back home—it was quite forgotten. Then after the war, there was the damned Soviets, who wouldn't let anyone in." He frowned. "Though I *do* recall hearing of an expedition in the late twenties, early thirties, searching for meteoric iron, that was surprised not to find a crater there either." He took a breath and ran a hand over his balding scalp. "That said, as you know," he reminded again, "I don't think any pair of meteors struck the Shogunate of Yokohama."

Spanky cleared his throat. "Yeah. You said it was a bomb. Bombs," he corrected.

Courtney nodded, glancing at Abel. He'd shared his thoughts about this with his young aide, who reminded him so much of himself at that age. Abel was more . . . adventurous, of course, but possessed the same insatiable curiosity for all things. Courtney sighed. "I'll remind you all again that I'm no true scientist. I'm certainly not accredited as such in any field beyond geology and petroleum engineering. As I always say, I know a lot about a little and a little about a lot, but most of my 'scientific' knowledge, primarily focused on the natural world, has been hoarded as a passionate hobby, little more."

"Bugger that, Courtney," Stokes countered. "Yer the closest to a multi-discipline *practical* scientist we've got."

"Untrue," Courtney denied. "There are any number of people in the Empire, the Republic, even the NUS, who know more than I."

"'Bout *this* world, maybe. Parts of it," Stokes hedged. "An' yer the only one with a clue about the cuttin' edge, what was bein' dreamed up for the future where we came from." He waved away Courtney's objection. "Sure, men like Steve Riggs know about radar, even saw the set aboard the *Boise*, but he ain't been able to make one yet." He pointed at Spanky. "And *he'd* been all over the new 'gold plater' destroyers, an' we're gettin' there, but they ain't nothin' *new*, just better refined." He pointed back at Courtney. "*Yer* the only one on this whole earth who jumped to the notion the Yokohama blasts were bombs, then threw in enough language I don't understand to make me believe it."

A silence lingered a moment before Courtney sighed again. "It stemmed from my interest in energy, I suppose," he finally said. "Energy and"—he shrugged—"everything. I don't imagine one can truly understand anything in the natural world without a smattering of physics. It's the foundation of natural philosophy after all, clear back to Thales of Miletus, Aristotle, Plato, Archimedes . . ." Frowning at the blank or blinking expressions, he continued. "The futurist writer H. G. Wells was probably first to propose the idea of an atom bomb. He might've got the notion from Ernest Rutherford, though the latter only speculated on the raw energy available in tiny amounts of matter, or atoms."

Chack was looking around, ears forward, blinking curiosity. "Whaat's atoms?" he asked.

"Later, Chackie," Spanky said, smiling.

"No," said Rolak, his usual urbane tone somewhat annoyed. "Everyone here must understaand this—and I only just begaan to myself." He considered. "You've looked in a microscope at the Navy Claan hospital and seen the tiny bugs otherwise invisible even to *our* eyes?"

Chack nodded, still blinking.

"Aatoms are at least as smaall again and are the . . ." Rolak was blinking now, trying to decide how to describe it. Finally, he grinned triumphantly. "Aatoms are the tiny timbers or stones that build all things, even those little bugs!" He looked at Courtney. "Considering how lively those bugs appear, aatoms must contain a great deal of energy indeed!"

Courtney blinked back, but saw Spanky and Stokes both nodding agreement. "Ah . . . indeed. It's rather . . . wildly more complicated, but I suppose that will suffice."

Abel leaned over and whispered, "It will. Trust me. 'Simple' is definitely best." Everyone knew Courtney could go on for ages beyond what anyone could bear to listen to about the most infinitesimal point.

"Of course." Courtney nodded, now glaring back and forth between Spanky and Stokes. "Well, surely *someone* here has heard of Albert Einstein, Enrico Fermi . . ."

Spanky snapped his fingers. "Einstein! I heard of him. Smart Jewish gent with wild hair the Nazis chased out of Germany, right? Made all the papers. Said he was the smartest guy in the world."

"That may be . . . may have been," Courtney agreed seriously. "In any event, my latest obsession before, well, the usual 'before,' had been to read everything I could find by men involved in studying the energy derived through atomic fusion, and then the more promising if somewhat ominous fission." No one reacted and he plowed grimly on. "The latest I gleaned, shortly before our old war started, was that a fission 'super bomb' might be built fairly easily. I remain skeptical of that. All the most difficult and momentous projects are initially instigated by an enthusiastic pitch that 'it will be simple!' But I do believe it was possible in time, especially for powers such as the United Kingdom, United States . . . and

Nazi Germany. Perhaps even the Soviet Union and Japan," he added darkly. "All had the resources, and the process—though difficult and no doubt wildly expensive—had become rather deplorably well-known. Not by *me*," he quickly inserted. "But I believe the difficulty lay more in the preparation of the uranium fuel for such a device and determining the best way to do it."

"Uranium," Spanky said doubtfully, then lit up. "Stuff's 'radioistic' or somethin', right? That's why you had Steve Riggs cobble up that funny gizmo for you. To see if whatever hit Yokohama was a uranium bomb." He looked at Rolak. "It was a big damn thing, bigger that the X-ray machine in the Navy Hospital that we took out of *Savoie*. Took a whole cartload of batteries."

"Radioactive, and essentially, yes. And the X-ray machine was required for . . ." He coughed and actually stopped himself. "In any event, large and cumbersome as it was, Mr. Riggs's 'gizmo' worked well enough for us to determine that radiation was indeed present." Courtney beamed. "I've already submitted plans to him for a smaller, more convenient device that functions on a different principle . . ." Courtney stopped himself again, noting that everyone else had seemingly exhaled at once and Stokes was frowning.

"Radioactive . . . rays, of all sorts, are dangerous, right?" Stokes asked.

"They can be," Abel answered, with a glance at Courtney.

Now Rolak was blinking concern, the gray-white fur on his face surrounding a kind of frown of his own. "Raadio . . . rays? The invisible signals raadios send can haarm you?"

"No," Abel quickly assured. "It's more like the rays of the sun. You've seen how some humans get painful burns when they don't protect themselves?"

"Aah. Yes. Like our deeply mourned former chairman, Mr. Letts. A terrible thing not to haave fur—not thaat I agree with the common sentiment thaat it makes you humaans especially ugly," he hurried to declare.

"'Course not," Spanky said with a chuckle, "despite what you usually say." Rolak was right, though. Alan Letts had been famously fair-skinned and prone to sunburn.

Courtney cleared his throat. "The radiation produced by an atomic weapon would be *much* more harmful than sunlight. Initially, concurrent with the detonation of such a device, I expect it would be as deadly as the blast. But the lingering levels we detected in Japaan were already relatively safe. And lacking a crater, the bombs must've been exploded quite a distance above the ground, which would mitigate against deep contamination as well. The rains no doubt washed a great deal of it away."

"Rain," murmured Doocy Meek, commenting for the first time. "This 'radiation' can be washed off?"

"Yes. That's my belief, though like I said, it might depend on how deeply it's absorbed by different materials. Or beings," he added with apparent reluctance. "I fear there may be adverse effects upon those exposed early on."

Stokes produced a few sheets of thick paper from a shelf in the desk and started scribbling with a pencil from his shirt pocket. "I'll send a warning to the Shogunate to have any early visitors checked out," he explained. When he was finished writing, he set the pencil down, pressed his hands together on the desk, and leaned forward. "Sounds like a less attractive weapon all the time, but d'ya think there's any way at all we can make some of 'em?"

Courtney actually barked a laugh. "Good heavens, no," he finally managed.

"Hmm. Didn't think so." Stokes sounded disappointed. "I hope, at least, the same's the case for our enemies."

Abel answered since Courtney still seemed overcome by the preposterous suggestion. "No sir. None we know of, at least," he warned, reminding them that despite the world-spanning scope of the recent war, there was still far more of the world they knew absolutely nothing about, particularly inland on the continents, than they were familiar with. "Mr. Bradford thinks it's *possible* the League has similar, even greater knowledge about atomics than him, but the *theory* isn't really the primary limiting factor. From what little I know, the technological and industrial effort's beyond what our entire combined alliance could achieve. And League defectors have told us that, though they have significant material advantages over us in terms of modern ships, aircraft, even armored vehicles, they relied too much on that superiority at the expense of expanding their industrial base, which doesn't yet surpass our own. Of course, I'm sure they're using this time of peace to rectify that."

Everyone else believed that as well, that this peace with the League was ephemeral, only temporary. A kind of "phony war" like had existed where they came from between the United Kingdom and its allies and Hitler for a while even after the formal declaration of war. That was the main reason all the members of the Grand Alliance still dedicated so much of their industry to defense. "In any event," Abel continued, "we don't believe they can build atom bombs at the moment, or for some time to come."

Doocy Meek coughed and flattened the whiskers on his chin. "But that's almost beside the point. Nobody bombed the Shogunate o' Yokohama with a *pair* o' these magical weapons that no one we know of on *this* world can make. Did they?" It wasn't really a question.

Courtney shook his head. "No. Not only don't we know of anyone who possesses such weapons, there's no rational target where they were exploded." He paused. "On *this* world, at any rate. There's really only one possibility, and the rather extensive, curious debris we found at the blast sites furnishes certain confirmation."

"Debris? What debris?" Spanky asked, sitting up.

Courtney blinked confusion, much like a Lemurian would. "Why, all the shattered masonry and other architectural rubble we noted intermixed with the scorched, fallen trees," he explained. "I'm quite sure I mentioned it in my report."

"No," snapped Henry Stokes sarcastically, gazing at the ceiling support timbers overhead. "I would've remembered that tiny detail."

Courtney looked surprised and glanced at Abel Cook. The young officer held up both hands as if to say, "It was *your* report."

"I would've sworn . . . Hmm. Perhaps the pertinent page was mislaid by the telegrapher. Well, there *was* substantial debris scattered among—and sometimes *on top of*—the labyrinth of shattered timber, like some of it fell on the trees after they were blasted down. We even recognized the mangled remains of what must've been automobiles! I'm therefore in no doubt that *someone* deployed atom bombs against *someone else* in a different Japan, on an entirely different world, and some of the effect bled over to us here. On land this time, which is not only significant but also believed to be especially rare." Courtney's voice was gaining enthusiasm, which was equally likely to presage a profound revelation as a tedious and meandering dissertation.

"Whatever the most likely theories we have for such . . . 'transfer events' at present, even those that some of us have experienced, all seem to agree they must require the release of tremendous energy. The events currently in question, at least, seem to have been fueled by the power of atomic weapons. I'm *quite* sure I included *that* speculation in the report I transmitted from Maa-ni-la." He grasped his mug of iced juice from the desk and gulped down several swallows.

The others in the room exchanged looks of different sorts and Henry Stokes finally scratched his nose and cleared his throat. "Yeah, you did, which brings us to the main point o' this little meetin'."

"Indeed?"

Henry Stokes opened one of the folders and shuffled the pages in front of him. "Yeah," he said again with something like a glare across the desk. "Against my stated misgivings, Cap'n Reddy and Chairperson Safir-Maraan agree it's time to grant yer heart's desire an, allow the formation of yer 'Corps of Discovery.'"

Courtney seemed to have been struck speechless, a singular event in Abel Cook's experience, and could only stare back at Stokes with his mouth open. "That's wonderful news, Mr. Stokes," Abel said, then prodded Courtney. "Isn't it, Mr. Bradford?"

"I . . . Yes! By heaven, that's fantastic! I can't wait to get started! There are so many places and things that absolutely *demand* investigation. I don't know how I'll choose where to begin!"

"Actually, that's not gonna be a problem, Courtney," Spanky told him. Courtney stared back, flustered. "Sure, you're gonna get to do all them things you been itchin' to, but there's a catch. Always is. See, your Corps of Discovery'll be real as can be, like an agency devoted to scientific exploration for its own sake, which you'll do plenty of, but it's also a cover for you . . . an' certain others to do a little apparently innocent snoopin'. Maybe a bit more than snoopin' from time to time."

"That's quite a 'catch,'" Courtney grumbled. "If you'd said there were 'strings attached,' I'd counter that they appear to be anchor cables instead."

"Not a baad description," said Chack-Sab-At.

"Et tu, Colonel?" Courtney bleakly said.

"Yes," agreed Chack, who knew the reference. "And though I'm sympaathetic, this is something we need you to do." He gestured around as if including the city beyond the Great Hall. "The Dominion haad spies all around us, laargely posing as expaat Imperials. We still caatch them now and then. But with the faall of the Dominion, maany now serve the League. And who knows how maany expaat Leaguer defectors, all over the Graand Alliaance now, still secretly work for their old maasters? Whatever the reason, the League clearly remains better informed about whaat we're doing thaan we are about them."

"I'm no spymaster," Courtney objected, now glaring back at Stokes. "Even if I wanted to be, I wouldn't know how."

"You're much too well-known to go creepin' about anyway, Courtney," said Spanky, "but so are your . . . scientific proclivities. Any missions you lead, even if they have Navy Clan support, which I expect they usually will of necessity, won't have 'spyin'' written all over 'em. It'll be assumed you're goin' lookin' for what you *say* you are."

Courtney was silent again, thinking furiously. Finally, he spoke. "You may have a point—and I will always be pleased to serve the Union, Alliance, and of course, the Navy Clan." He released a sigh. "And I will be permitted to do some real exploring?"

"Yeah," said Stokes. "The Corps of Discovery will be real."

"Excuse me," said Abel, "but may I ask a couple of questions?"

"Sure," said Spanky.

"Of course," agreed Rolak. "I believe Caap-i-taan Reddy hopes you are willing to continue your aassociation with Mr. Braadford. If so, this haas a bearing on your future and caareer as well."

"Thanks, and I kind of suspected that, so still two questions." He thought for a moment before shaking his head. "I guess maybe just one bigger question after all. Why now, and what does this have to do with what we saw in Japaan?"

"I told you he was shaarp," chuckled Chack.

Henry Stokes nodded. "'Now' because we need it, and it's not just an admittedly beneficial but low-priority extravagance anymore. We're not doing too badly compared to some places, Sular, for example. They never established any industry to speak of and thought they'd rake it in by colonizing the places we liberated during the war. Use their support in the Assembly to skim off the cream for themselves. That didn't work. But now that the Sularans have cleaned up most of the corruption at the top, we need to promote more investment there. Might even have to do some ourselves, with Union and Navy Clan funds, so we have to keep an eye on the budget. That's just one example above and beyond ongoing expenditures." He arched both brows. "But the 'now' got even more pressin' when we got"—he glanced at Courtney—"the part of the report Courtney actually sent. The rest reinforces it." He cast his eyes at Rolak and Doocy, then continued.

"Seems there was *another* bright blast-flash on the horizon some months ago in the South Pacific. Respite Island is closest. But several ships that went to investigate never returned and now a vessel in the Navy Clan Reserve that was diverted to search for *them* is out of communication and considerably overdue. The 'Corps of Discovery' will be openly carried down to investigate by"—he seemed to be trying to suppress a smile—"a, ah, 'minor' Navy Clan asset. More specific orders and information'll come."

"Another question, then," said Abel. "Why not just openly send a Navy squadron down to check it out?"

"Because," Spanky said more somberly, "the damned League is suddenly actin' up around the Azores, performin' aggressive fleet maneuvers with some of their heaviest ships. More tonnage than we can do much about at the moment and they know it."

The armistice with the League of Tripoli specifically stated that the Allies would stay out of the Mediterranean, but any League ships caught west of the Azores would be sunk on sight. The problem was that that was very nearly an empty boast.

"We've been sendin' almost everything we have to face up to 'em," Spanky continued. "I'll be goin' east with Captain Reddy, flying out in just a few days." He nodded at Chack. "He'll be goin' with us to reassume command of his Raiders. Otherwise, I bet he'd go with you." Spanky took a breath. "So, you're it, for this sideshow in the Pacific."

"I hope it *is* a 'sideshow,'" Doocy said darkly. "Oh, I don't think the League can be responsible for the flash. We don't even know if it's truly related to the ones you inspected," he said to Courtney and Abel. "But the League has kept secret bases in Alliance waters before and we're talking about particularly remote and unexplored seas." He glanced around. "And the timing is certainly suspect. Ships go missing in our backyard right when the League is drawing our attention elsewhere . . . None of us foresee a serious threat to this inaugural mission of the Corps. We wouldn't send it, especially on the"—he looked at Stokes—"'minor' Navy Clan asset in question. Just don't take it for granted there are no enemies there."

Courtney bowed his head at the Republic snoop, then suddenly asked, "Can I choose a team?"

"Why . . . sure, I guess," said Spanky. "We've already picked a few people, hopefully not only smart enough to actually help you with science stuff, but for your security detail too. Like I hinted earlier, they may not always be just for security. Needless to say, you've worked with nearly all of 'em at one time or another. I think you'll approve."

"I appreciate that and understand the possible dual role requirement. But whether you've already picked him or not, I want Dennis Silva."

Chack laughed out loud and clapped his hands together. Rolak grinned. Stokes looked disapproving, however, and Spanky was incredulous. "That maniac? What the hell for? He can't *sneak* anywhere and'll have us at war with anybody new you might meet."

Courtney stiffened. "I reject that, sir. The man is . . . impetuous, but if you'll recall, he was involved in most of the covert operations we engaged in during the late war, and his accomplishments then and when simply performing his customary duties in combat were nothing short of"—he appeared to contemplate the best description—"Homeric," he finally supplied in a satisfied tone.

"Oh, for God's sake," Spanky objected, spluttering. "Suicidal, you mean. Oh, sure, he's a damn hero. No question. And he's handy in a fight, but he's a *nut*!"

"I reject that as well," Courtney persisted. "And he *can* 'sneak.' I've seen him. So has Mr. Cook"—he glanced at Chack—"and the colonel as well. They collaborated quite often."

Chack had covered his eyes and was heaving slightly, clearly attempting to conceal continued laughter.

"Besides," Courtney went on, ignoring the Lemurian, "it sounds as if the Corps of Discovery will generally be operating openly."

"That's just the thing," Stokes said dryly. "There's no guarantee there'll be enough action to keep Silva entertained. I believe we're all aware how much trouble he can be when he's bored."

Chack exploded with laughter.

"I say, Colonel Chack!" Doocy Meek scolded. "This is serious business!"

"I . . . I know. I aapologize. It's just"—he grinned at Courtney and Abel—"I sure wish I could go with you. I miss my old friend very much right now!"

"Indeed," Courtney told him with a smile. "Perhaps you can join us another time." He looked back at Stokes and Spanky, in particular, and spoke in a level tone. "I have no illusions, gentlemen. I'm aware it can be argued that Mr. Silva is not a 'good' man in every respect, but he's the very *best* man to have at your back in a dangerous situation. He wanted this opportunity as much as I did when hostilities ended and was at least as disappointed as I by the delay. I feel I owe him this, and all other concerns aside, he's made something of a habit of keeping me alive during our previous associations. I shall rely on him to continue that habit."

Spanky puffed out his cheeks. "Fine. You can have him—if you can find him. Last I heard, he was in the Empire working on guns—as usual—and some crackpot scheme to do something about all the damn snakes on Martinique."

Of all the places they'd been on this world, few serpents of any sort had been encountered. Courtney had proposed they couldn't thrive because there were so many things that would eat them. Martinique, and possibly other islands, were the exception. Without natural predators, snakes had overrun the place.

Chack chuckled again, nodding and blinking. "I've heard about that.

I don't know whaat he's up to, but I hope it works. Maartinique will be a much better posting if it does!" he added with feeling. The League had established a naval and air base there during the war but the Allies had taken it from them. League infantry on the island, mostly fascist Spanish, were happy to give it up when their fleet was defeated. Mostly due to the snakes.

"He's still a 'regular,'" Spanky said, "technically on extended, open-ended leave. If you catch him, you can call him up." He frowned. "Come to that, puttin' him to work might be the best thing you can do for him. He's never been worth a damn without a war on, but nobody could say he doesn't pull his weight in a scrape."

CHAPTER 2

EMPIRE OF THE NEW BRITAIN ISLES
NEW IRELAND
DECEMBER 1946

"Eat?" came a hopeful, almost whispered chirp right next to Chief Gunner's Mate Dennis Silva's left ear.

"Shut yer stupid hole, Petey. Goddammit, you just ate a hour ago an' now we're sneakin'," Dennis Silva hissed back.

Petey was a colorful—mostly green and blue and a mix of the two—feathery-furry tree-gliding reptile-like . . . thing. Kind of a cross between a lizardbird and a flying squirrel. He couldn't really fly (under his own power, at least) but could glide an amazing distance from a lofty perch by extending thin membranes between his hind legs and—sort of—arms, steering with a long feathery tail. Like a parrot, he could mimic many sounds, including human speech, and actually understood an ill-defined number of words. Most amazing perhaps, he could even use a few words appropriately. Unsurprisingly, considering who he learned them from, they weren't all "appropriate" in every setting or circumstance.

The "perch" he most often chose these days was just under six feet high, drooped around the back of Dennis Silva's neck like a sweat rag atop the man's broad muscular shoulders. Silva stood taller than that of course, but Petey rarely launched himself from the top of the big man's scarred, burr-cut head. That usually got him tossed in directions he hadn't meant to go. Why Silva, who was probably capable of more casual violence than anyone in the Grand Alliance, put up with Petey at all remained a mystery to most. But despite his reputation, Silva wasn't *really* a monster, not entirely, and was only middling huge. Sure, he had powerful muscles, but nothing disproportionate. He generally resembled any other strong, well-exercised, prime-of-life "shell-slinging deck ape," just on a larger scale.

There was no denying he had an intimidating presence, though, and was always conspicuously well armed, even off duty. He'd been caught unarmed a time or two and, just as bad, "empty." He was deeply paranoid about that ever happening again. Dressed in his usual dungarees, boondockers, and canvas leggings, he wore a web belt festooned with his trusty, hard-used 1911 Colt in a flap holster, a razor-sharp 1903 Springfield bayonet in a scabbard (for a fighting and hunting knife), four twin magazine pouches for the Colt, and—as always—a battered 1917 Navy cutlass. The weight of all that was supported by shoulder braces. His primary weapon at the moment, however, as he crept slowly down a narrow trail on the Imperial Isle of New Ireland (which he still thought of as Oahu) through chest-high grass, was his newest "project gun," a big lever-action rifle chambered for the same .50-80 black powder cartridge still used in frontline Allied infantry rifles.

In spite of all that, probably nothing was quite as scary as his face, at a glance. A decidedly unwholesome-looking, sweat-soaked black patch covered his ruined left eye, and that side of his face was liberally and brightly scarred against otherwise dark tan skin by the same spattered bullet fragments that "knocked out his headlight," as he called it. Uncountable other scars were hidden under a wild sun-bleached blond beard that, combined with the eyepatch and the weird parrotlike creature on his shoulder, gave him a distinctly piratical flair. Strangely, when he exhibited his gap-toothed grin, it could either reinforce or shatter that first savage impression, depending entirely on his mood. The actual expression wasn't that different, but the intent behind it was obvious at once.

"Eat *now*," Petey sulked.

"We're both gonna *get* ate if you don't shut yer flap," Silva growled back.

"*You'll* get ate," came a sudden soft, strangely accented voice from the deep grass beside them to the left. "He'll just run a'ay."

Petey flinched in alarm, but Silva thumped him on the head and snorted, outwardly unsurprised by the appearance of his friend. "Hey, Larry. Expected you sooner."

"Larry," or "Lawrence," as he was better known and frankly preferred, eased out onto the trail. He was a Tagranesi (Sa'aaran now), a race closely related to the Grik, their once mortal semi-reptilian enemy. He had the same long toothy jaws, wicked claws, and long rigid tail. The biggest differences were his orange-and-black tiger-striped crest and plumage (Grik were predominately gray or dun with dark contrasts), and springing from an island race rather than a continental one, he was smaller than most Grik as well. Lawrence was different in other more subtle but interesting ways, such as the fact he spoke nearly perfect English and Lemurian, marred only by his somewhat awkward speech due to a physical inability to say words requiring lips. When he couldn't simply rephrase things with easier words, he tended to skip sounds he couldn't make. He habitually filed the claws off his right thumb and two opposing fingers so he could more easily handle cartridges. Currently dressed in a tie-dyed Marine combat smock, he carried a single-shot, breechloading "Allin-Silva" rifle-musket, which remained the standard Allied infantry weapon.

The first of these rifles had been .50 caliber muzzle-loaders with a medium-fast rifling twist to stabilize heavy-for-caliber minié bullets. Silva had copied the Allin "trapdoor" conversion design with which he'd been intimately familiar as a country gunsmith before joining the Navy. This allowed existing weapons in the field to be modified into breechloaders capable of firing the same powerful .50-80 black powder metallic cartridge Silva's new repeater was chambered for simply by dropping in a new barrel and hammer. Later versions were built as breechloaders from the ground up at the Baalkpan and Maa-ni-la Arsenals. To better cope with the threat of the League, more up-to-date combat weapons were in the works, designed for modern high-pressure cartridges like .30-06. But the .50-80 might forever remain popular with civilian hunters, perhaps even the military, for its potency against medium-large predators. A few of Silva's brutal "toys" were sufficient for the very biggest predators, but even he didn't much enjoy shooting those. That was something in itself, because Silva dearly loved to shoot things. He'd even shot Lawrence the first time they met, understandably mistaking him for a Grik, but—weirdly—they'd been inseparable ever since.

"Little shit wouldn't get far from *this* hungry booger," Silva continued lowly. "All he could do is glide to the ground, an' there ain't no trees close by. He'd get rooted up an' ate like a bug!"

"Good riddance," Lawrence said, and Petey hissed at him.

"See anything ahead?" Silva asked.

Lawrence nodded. "Our quarry is near, 'ut so are two hu'ans and a 'Cat, thrashing along, too loud. I think they're looking us, 'ut our quarry is likely to catch they."

"Dammit. Humans and 'Cats out here? What for?"

Lawrence shrugged his narrow shoulders.

"Recognize anybody? Ruinin' our fun, I don't care if they *do* get ate if we don't know 'em."

Lawrence shook his head. "I couldn't get too close or the quarry catch La'rence's scent. It's gonna catch theirs, though. Go get they soon."

Silva knuckled his eyepatch. "Dammit. Okay. Guess we gotta save their stupid asses." He arched the brow over his dead eye. "But maybe we can use 'em as bait while we're at it. Take us back overlookin' a clearin', if there is one, a little ahead o' where you seen 'em. Keep us off-wind o' the booger, though. I got a score ta settle with him," he added grimly.

Lawrence nodded briskly and darted back off the trail to the left. Silva followed, with Petey clucking disapprovingly by his ear. They moved much quicker, even without a trail, making more noise as well. Lawrence stopped frequently, however, raising his long snout and testing the wind. It wasn't strong, but even Silva knew it was enough to carry their still rather stealthy sounds as well as smells away from the beast they sought. He was surprised by these unknown visitors, however, and suspected Lawrence was right and they were looking for him. But not only did very few people even know where he was, Lawrence said there was a 'Cat with them. Most 'Cats were seafaring folk, even those that lived on land, but that only made them extra careful on unfamiliar shores. Silva couldn't imagine a Lemurian, *any* Lemurian, just tromping along with the wind through grass over their head.

Lawrence stopped again, then pointed at an angle to the right. "I think it's clearer ahead, that 'ay," he breathed.

"You're the one with the super snoot," Silva reminded with a slight chuckle. "Lead on."

Lawrence nodded seriously and took off again. Moments later, they came to the edge of a more substantial clearing than Silva had expected, the tall grass sheared low. Several partly denuded trees stood here and there, all having been fed on by some huge herbivore. Lawrence had done the largest share of the scouting for the business endeavor they'd been engaged in and Silva hadn't seen this place. He saw the strangers almost at once: two men, one taller than the other, and a short female 'Cat. All wore camouflage smocks and the taller man had a rifle over his shoulder, but they were just strolling along about ninety yards away to the left as if they didn't have a care in the world.

"Never seen such dismal dumbassery," Silva objected, and as if to reinforce his judgment, a thunderous, squealing roar erupted from the tall grass to the right. "An' there he is," Silva stated matter-of-factly, barging past Lawrence into the open, setting his feet, and raising his big rifle to his shoulder. A huge dark blur exploded from the grass like a four-footed freight train with the throttle wide open. It first came in view about sixty yards away, almost straight ahead, parallel to the wind from them, but straight downwind of the strangers who were clearly the target of its wrath. Silva had already fired and levered his rifle three times before the taller newcomer even had his weapon off his shoulder.

Boom! Shink-shak. "Shit!" Silva had snapped when the first round threw up a cloud of dust just behind the charging beast. *Boom! Shink-shak.* Another cloud of dust exploded, this one behind the thing's shoulder. *Boom! Shink-shak. Whop!* came the sound of a slug pounding the thing in the belly, and it arched its back and screeched but didn't slow. *Crack!* came the first shot from the taller stranger, but the bullet whined away, probably hitting the thick sloping bone of the monster's skull. It was almost on them, but Silva took an instant longer with his fourth shot, muzzle leading the killer beast just so . . . *Boom!* With an ear-shattering squeal, the thing cartwheeled head over heels and crashed down right where its prey had been standing. It would've crushed them all for sure if they hadn't scattered at the last possible instant.

Shink-shak! Silva ejected another spent case and chambered one to replace it. "Whew!" he boomed happily. "That'll get the blood pumpin'! An' them idiots over there ain't as stupid as I thought. Waited right to the end before boltin'. Booger would'a had ta spin an' come back to run 'em down. An' with 'em all separate, they might'a put more holes in it. Still . . ." he started to add, voice less exuberant. "C'mon, Larry. Let's see who's here."

"Eat! Goddamn!" Petey cawed, now standing on Silva's shoulders and staring greedily at the huge mound of meat in the distance.

The tall man was easing carefully closer to where it lay, still breathing loudly, chest and belly heaving, but it couldn't move. Silva's last shot had broken its neck, right behind the narrow bony frill at the back of its head. Silva was surprised to see the shorter man and female Lemurian trotting toward him while the tall man fired six quick shots from a 1911 into the beast at his feet.

"Well, lookie there!" Silva said, picking up his own pace. "I'll swan, if it ain't young Fred an' Kari!"

Kari-Faask used her momentum to launch herself into his arms, wrapping hers around his neck. Silva grabbed the 'Cat with his left hand, holding his rifle to the side. Petey screeched and jumped over on Lawrence, who cursed and tried to pull him off and throw him. Petey's claws had curled into the fabric of his tunic, however, and wouldn't let go. He was absolutely terrified of being on the ground in strange territory.

"Why, *Loo-tenat* Kari-Faask!" Silva exclaimed in a mock scandalized tone. "Ain't dignified at all for officers to go snatchin' on to lowly CPOs like me!"

"I don't care!" Kari said, grinning and blinking happily. "I haaven't seen you for more thaan a year!"

Fred Reynolds had slowed and now approached at a walk, grinning also. "We found you!" he proclaimed triumphantly. "Hey, Larry! Still hanging around this maniac?"

"Like a tick," Silva said.

"I don't know 'hy—the reason," Lawrence agreed.

"Sure you do, you overgrown gecko. You'd die o' boredom with anybody else."

"I could, I guess," Lawrence accepted dolefully.

Kari slid down from embracing Silva and gave Lawrence a hug as well. As always, he received it awkwardly but with evident pleasure.

Petey made an exasperated sound and jumped back on Silva's shoulders. "Eat!" he insisted.

"You will," Silva said impatiently, gesturing at the monster he'd killed as they all started walking that direction. "We gotta take that devil apart pretty quick, an' you can have all yer favorite mushy parts. He likes *lungs*, for some reason," he said aside to Kari, rolling his eye. "God knows why."

"He just likes to 'lay in they," Lawrence scoffed.

"He eats 'em too," Silva defended, then tilted his head to the side. "But yeah, he does like to play in 'em. Nasty little dumbass."

Nearing the huge carcass of what was essentially a gigantic hog, Silva quickly recognized "Gunny" Arnold Horn looking down at it. He'd thought that was who it was, even at a distance. Black-haired and bearded, Horn was as tall as him and nearly as stout. Ironically, considering how long they'd known each other—back in Shanghai before their "old war" started—and the fact one was Asiatic Fleet Navy and the other emphatically a "China Marine," they'd only ever fought each other once. By all accounts, that titanic drunken brawl was a draw, leaving them both bloody and briefly unconscious. But Silva had lost his "favorite" upper front tooth, and Arnold Horn still carried it pierced by a leather thong around his neck as a trophy. It also served as a handy reminder of one of his toughest (if still somewhat hazy) battles and a ready prop with which to mock Silva.

Perhaps most ironic of all, the two men had revived quickly enough from their one fight to evade the Shore Patrol and plunge into further joint adventures that made them fast friends. One of those escapades apparently reached epic, near mythical proportions that might've resulted in their being decorated—if not for the international repercussions that could've gotten them shot. Most suspected they'd done something to "inconvenience" the Japanese on the other side of Soochow

Creek during the Battle of Shanghai in 1937. Whatever happened, they only occasionally referenced it obliquely, like an inside joke, and never fully explained it to anyone.

Horn was gesturing at the giant dead beast with his 1911. "You used us as *bait* for that . . . whatever the hell it is!"

Silva shrugged. "Sure, sorta. We didn't invite y'all out here—didn't know you were comin' a'tall—an' I expect you'd'a got thrashed by the booger if we weren't already after 'eem." He kicked the huge wire-haired mound of dead meanness. "We knew about where he was holed up an' was puttin' the sneak on 'eem. Larry seen ya an' we intercepted him on his way ta get ya." Silva grinned beatifically. "All's well that ends well, right? As for what it is, why, this here's New Ireland's version o' 'rhino pigs,' like them around Baalkpan, in Borno. You seen plenty o' *them*," he reminded.

"Looks different. Bigger too," Kari-Faask noted. "Stinks worse," she added, waving a hand in front of her very feline-looking nose.

"More horns," Fred Reynolds agreed.

Borno "rhino pigs" actually were a species of pig that ran in packs and looked like bigger, heavier razorbacks, complete with obsidian-sharp tusks protruding from their mouths behind their snouts. The only obvious difference was a single forward-curved horn with a sharp leading edge on top of their skulls, and the big boars tended to top out at about half a ton. As they were primarily grazing and rooting omnivores, the horn had clearly evolved as a formidable defense against even larger predators that understandably craved their succulent flesh. This beast was even bigger, built more athletically for speed, and boasted twin horns and a narrow frill protecting the top of the neck.

"Yep," Silva granted. "These devils, the boars, anyway, is mostly like rhino pigs in every important way, but more likely ta chase shit down an' eat it instead o' just rootin' it up. This one in particular." He paused. "You gotta *swear* you won't steal me an' Larry's business idea . . ."

Horn grunted and waved, and Fred and Kari both laughed. Horn was a "lifer," with no interest in anything other than being a Marine, and Fred and Kari were fliers, period. "If you ever need paartners to spot things from the air, we're the ones you waant," Kari said, "but we aren't cut out for chasing giaant pigs on foot."

"Hmm. Well, I wouldn't mind any o' y'all for partners," Silva mused, rolling his eye at Horn. "Even the jarhead, I guess. But this is a 'get rich quick,' likely one-time scheme. I doubt it'll be a growin' concern." He stopped and glared at Larry. "What're you doin' just standin' there with yer pointy face hangin' out? Get busy cuttin'. Meat'll spoil quick in this heat."

"I all'ays get the shitty chores," Lawrence grouched at their visitors, drawing his cutlass with resignation. He'd use that to hack through the thick, protective case on the beast.

"I shot 'eem," Silva piously proclaimed. "Gotta do yer part, little buddy. Besides, with all yer claws an' such, yer better at this part than me." He looked back at Kari. "We been trappin' these boogers, shoats mostly, 'specially smaller sows. Those're the ones we keep, anyway. Can't just *trap* the shoats, 'o course, but we part out the big ones an' sell 'em for meat. Ain't much money in that part, but it finances the rest. Keeps us in beer an' tobbaccy."

"Why do you want the little ones?" Horn asked.

Silva grinned. "Cuz they ain't no bigger than a ordinary pig. Ain't too big an' scary ta ship!"

"Ship *where*?" Horn persisted.

"Why, to Martinique Island, o' course. There'll be a young boar or two along—things breed quicker'n bunnies—an' the sows'll be squirtin' out young'uns right an' left, two or three times a year!"

Kari was blinking confusion at that, and Silva understood. They hadn't found proper rabbits yet, or anything nearly as helpless and inoffensive.

"Pretty damn fast," Horn translated for her before looking back at Silva. "You know? That isn't . . . the stupidest idea you ever came up with."

"I know!" Silva agreed enthusiastically. "I've had *way* stupider schemes than this! Martinique can be a helluva base, for ships, planes, the works—if we get rid of the goddamn snakes." He gestured at the bihorn rhino pig. "These things'll gobble 'em up like worms!"

"Yeah," Horn nodded with evident admiration. "Not much else for 'em to eat there either. Have to start killing the pigs pretty quick—"

"—which'll provide ready meat for the garrisons!"

"Until *all* the snakes run out," Fred said.

"Never happen, if the pigs get thinned enough," Silva said. "An' neither of 'em'll be a nuisance, by then." He shrugged. "Hafta keep the airstrips fenced off, I expect."

Horn was nodding. "I confess. It sounds like a good plan. Bound to be a catch somewhere."

Silva frowned. "Yeah, well, the biggest 'catch' is, fast as they breed, one shipment's about all it'll take." He suddenly kicked the beast again, savagely this time. Lawrence was already swiftly cutting on it and Petey had hopped over, waiting impatiently for scraps to snatch. Both jumped, surprised. "An' *this* big bastard was another one. We had about forty good shoats rounded up in a sturdy-built pen. Had overhead protection too, so Grikbirds couldn't get 'em. Wild survivors from the war, I reckon. But *this* evil shit came in the night an' busted it all up, loosed whatever shoats he didn't kill or eat . . ." Silva was getting worked up now. "God-DAMMIT!" he shouted, kicking the corpse yet again. "Me an' Larry put *real* work in this project an' this horny bastard ruined it all. We'll hafta start all over now," he simmered. "This killin' was personal." He paused, brows pinching. "An' that sorta killin' . . . ain't as fun as it used to be," he confessed.

"Jesus, Dennis," Horn consoled him, instead of objecting—as one might expect—to the fact Silva could be a killing fiend at times. Especially since he'd learned to consciously limit collateral damage when he could, his capacity for imaginative violence was actually an asset to the Navy Clan and Grand Alliance. But the last time it got "personal," when his dear friend Sister Audry was killed, he'd nearly lost himself. His few true friends shared an understanding that, in the right (or terribly wrong) circumstances, they had to be prepared to put him down like a rabid Grik. He'd even want them to.

"You shouldn't take it personaally," Kari objected, blinking at the carcass. "He waas just being the waay he waas. Same as you." She paused. "And as it haappens, you maay not haave to 'staart all over,' at least not right awaay. Leave your project be for a while. Give it a rest. Come baack to it fresh and haappy again." She chuckled, whipping her tail. "Even if someone else haas the same idea, they won't haave the guts to pull it off!"

Silva looked at her, then Horn and Fred. "So. I reckon we're fixin' ta get to it then. How come somebody sent you out here to find us. Heads up, Larry. Here comes the pitch."

Kari and Fred looked at Horn and he cleared his throat. "Mr. Bradford's finally got his 'Corps of Discovery,' Dennis," he said. "Everybody knows you wanted in on it if it happened, and Mr. Bradford specifically asked for you."

If Horn and the others had expected an enthusiastic reception, they were disappointed by Silva's frown. "So that's what this is about. They want me to hold Courtney's hand while he stares at bugs an' chases lizards around. Prob'ly catch shit an' hold it down while he draws pictures." He grunted. "I'd'a jumped at it in a second a year ago. I needed it then, to be around people an' stay busy, but"—he glanced at Larry, who'd stopped cutting to listen—"maybe I ain't in the mood no more," he added in a lofty tone.

"Honker shit!" Lawrence declared, referring to a kind of domesticable bipedal swamp bird with a face like a duck and a hollow crest on its head that made its cries sound like a long, drawn out fart.

"Honker Shit!" screeched Petey.

"Shut up, you," Silva told him.

"There'll be more to it than just chasing bugs," Horn assured. "Intelligence gathering, maybe even a little . . . direct action, from time to time, with scientific discovery and exploration as a cover."

"*C'mon*, Chief Silva," Fred urged him temptingly. "It'll be fun!"

Silva pursed his lips. "Who all's in?" he asked.

Horn gestured at the youngsters with him. "Us, that I know of. Mr. Cook too. Some others I'm not sure of yet."

"How about Pam?" Silva asked bluntly.

Nurse Lieutenant Pam Cross was an earthy, saucy, even acerbic young woman from Brooklyn who'd hopelessly loved Dennis Silva for years. The thing was, Silva was just as hopelessly in love with her—most likely. Only she probably knew for sure. He didn't. They'd "been together" off and on numerous times, but their personalities clashed so epically that they never could seem to *stay* together long.

Horn hesitated. "Well . . . yeah. She jumped at the chance. She'll assist

Mr. Bradford, but also be ship's surgeon on the, uh, 'transport' we'll use for the first mission we've already got."

"She aalso joined on the condition thaat you *not* be invited," Kari said slyly.

Silva harrumphed. "Zat so? Well, I reckon I *gotta* go now, to keep my eye on her." He looked at Lawrence. "Hear that? I guess we're in. I'll help you finish that, but I reckon we'll just take what we need for supper back to camp." He raised his brow at Horn. "You ain't still a officer, are ya?"

Horn shook his head. He'd been the acting gunnery officer aboard USS *Savoie* at the Battle of St. Vincent Island due to some peculiarities the captured League dreadnought shared with the old USS *New York*, which he'd once served aboard. "Nope, it's just 'Gunny' again, thank you."

"Swell. Tomorrow morning's soon enough, right? We got a fair stash o' beer I don't wanna leave to waste. Guess you can help me an' Larry clean it up. Bar-be-kyoo pig an' beer for supper!"

"What about us?" Fred asked.

"Ain't proper for officers ta get awash with us lowly, sweaty enlisted types," Silva proclaimed with mock seriousness, and Kari made a rude noise.

Soon, they were walking through the tall grass once more, Petey contentedly gnawing a large gobbet of bloody flesh while they made their long trek back to Silva and Lawrence's camp. Lawrence and Horn both carried heavy burlap-like bags full of more meat over their shoulders.

"Got a question, Dennis," Horn huffed. The humidity was bad enough to make it hard to breathe.

"Spill it, Arnie," Silva replied.

"That gun you shot this critter with"—he tugged on the sack—"another one of your inventions?"

Silva shook his head. "Just another shameless copy. I ain't so good at conjurin' up brand-new ideas—I ain't no John Browning, God bless 'eem—but if I ever looked at somethin' a lot, workin' on it, I generally remember how it's made. Just gotta look at the pictures in my head." He hoisted the big rifle. "This'd have the Winchester Repeatin' Arms Company after me like flasher fish if they had lawyers on this world. Guess they'd hafta sue the Imperial Small Arms Manufactory on New Scotland too. That's where I made it, an' they're makin' more. It's prob'ly a little too close a copy o' Winchester's 1876 model. Not as strong as a 'eighty-six, but plenty big an' strong enough to handle our issue fifty-eighties. *Way* less complicated, for me anyway, and the fastest-shootin' repeater I ever played with."

"I want one," Horn said.

Silva snorted. "What about your 'holy' 'oh-three Springfield?"

"What about it? It's still better for long range and I never said I'd ditch it."

Silva laughed, then sobered. "I'll see what I can do. Got a question for you, though. What's this ship that's taking us on our little trip? I hope it ain't one o' them shitty Impie cruisers."

Horn hesitated and Kari released a short chuckle. "Well," Horn finally said, "she *is* an old warship, but more of a school ship now. Courtney's going aboard in the open, with a declared mission that even a relatively harmless school ship can handle, but part of our 'cover' will be that we're the instructors for a bunch of 'cadets' aboard her. That's a real job, by the way. But it seems the League is acting up around the Azores and all the first-line ships are heading there. There's nothing new for us to use anyway."

"Shit," Silva grumped. "I hate to miss it if another real war lights off with them bastards."

"I doubt that's very likely," Fred opined. "They may still outweigh us on the water a good bit, but we've got the edge in Naval Air."

"But if they're packin' a bunch o' kiddies aboard our ship, we won't get to go anywhere an' do anything *really* fun at all," Silva complained.

"I wouldn't worry about that," Horn said, then smiled. "And I think you'll approve of our ship."

CHAPTER 3

EMPIRE OF THE NEW BRITAIN ISLES
SCAPA FLOW
NEW SCOTLAND

Good God a'mighty!" Silva exclaimed. "She's *beautiful*!" They'd arrived at the primary Imperial Navy base at Scapa Flow, New Scotland, and taken a Filpin Lands–built MTB (motor torpedo boat) across the water to the massive Imperial shipyard. They'd first passed a cluster of newly completed Impie protected cruisers, and Silva wasn't the only one with a low opinion of them. Brand-new, they were currently laid up "in ordinary" while plans were evaluated to convert them to something else hopefully more useful and survivable. Next came the Imperial fitting-out docks, and they'd seen some familiar, heartwarming shapes. United Homes shipyards at Baalkpan and the Filpin Lands were pushing forward with what Spanky McFarlane referred to as "gold plater" destroyers, based on his recollections of the Sims and Benson-Livermore Classes he'd been intimately familiar with. They were superior to the old "four-stackers" in every way: bigger and heavier, with a more usefully arranged and better-protected main armament, and faster as well, with four high-pressure boilers trunked into only two stacks. A major innovation was the staggered separation of their two engine rooms and two firerooms, better preserving the ship's mobility from a single hit at the junction of two compartments.

But the newest Impie destroyers, six currently in the water and completing with six more building, were their first attempt at anything "modern" and were still largely copied from the first four-stacker DDs made in the United Homes, which in turn had been patterned after USS *Walker* and USS *Mahan* themselves. Just beyond those, however, was another shape, painted light gray instead of the "standard" Allied dazzle scheme, that was as familiar to Silva as the back of his own hand: USS *Walker* herself. The Empire of the New Britain Isles had always been a maritime power, and the Governor/Empress Rebecca Anne McDonald was anxious to achieve technological parity with her allies, not to mention their mutual enemies, but they had to start somewhere. And outdated as they were, ships like *Walker* were still useful. She and her sisters, or more appropriately daughters, had proven that convincingly against the might of the League.

But as Silva had noted with delight, USS *Walker* was tied to another pier by herself, practically aswarm with workers (mostly Lemurians who'd come from the Union for the purpose), completing the final touches of a lovingly comprehensive overhaul and refit. There was no question it was her, both because of the bright new paint and tall black-edged white numbers standing proud above the waterline on her bow: 163. Silva had known she'd been towed here, the farthest anyone dared in the condition she'd been in after her last action, but hadn't expected the resurrection of her shattered hulk to be a priority for anyone. But *Walker* and her people had been a big part of virtually every success in the recent war, and he'd badly underestimated her value as a unifying, defiant symbol in the face of overwhelming odds to the United Homes, and indeed the Grand Alliance.

"Beautiful," Silva said again, voice suspiciously husky. "Last time I saw her, after the fight with *Leopardo* on Lago de Vida, she was steamin' on one fireroom, the other was flooded, an' there weren't much o' anything left standin' on her flush deck. Now look at her! Why, she's purtier than I ever seen her in the Philippines before the war—the one with the Japs—kicked off."

"And practically brand spanking new," Fred Reynolds fondly agreed. He'd once been the youngest crew member aboard her and loved her as much as Silva. "Oh, she's got maybe twenty percent of her original hull plates—about all that didn't have holes in 'em, mostly below the waterline—and they're still pretty washboarded. But even those have all been reriveted."

"She *does* look good," Lawrence appraised. "Gooder than I saw her last. A lot less dangerous to get on," he added pointedly. There might've even been a touch of pleasure in his tone. Lawrence got attached to people, but very rarely things. There were a few exceptions to that. He still carried the long brass-barreled flintlock pistol Silva took from the assassin, Linus Trulove, and eventually gave to him, but despite springing from a seafaring race himself, he wasn't keen on ships. He much preferred fighting on land. That didn't mean he wasn't sensible to what USS *Walker* meant to others.

"I swear," Silva declared, then paused, glancing at the MTB's Impie skipper. "We're headed straight for her." He gazed back at his companions. "Y'all takin' me an Larry for a closer look?"

Gunny Horn laughed. "Sure, dumbass. Close as you like. *She's* our transport!"

"Dumbass!" Petey crowed triumphantly.

The MTB rumbled up to the dock, smoke coiling from the exhaust on the transom. Line handlers scurried to tie the boat off. Silva was the first to climb up into the late-morning shadow of *Walker*'s nearly straight-up-and-down bow, pausing a moment with his left hand on his hip, right hand balancing his big repeater on his shoulder while he took in the sight. 'Cats up on the fo'c'sle, bustling around the anchor hoist, peered down over the top cable rail.

"Brow's this way, Chief Silva," Gunny Horn said, joining him and gesturing farther onward.

Silva looked at him and blinked. "I know where the goddamn brow is," he drawled sarcastically, referring to the wooden ramp-like gangway piercing the solid rail just behind the ship's forward superstructure. "But why so formal all of a sudden, Arnie? I can't remember the last time you called me 'Chief.'"

"Because, as of now"—he gestured up at the 'Cats—"in front of anybody watching, we're back on duty. As a matter of fact, you need to get properly turned out as soon as possible. We took the liberty of shifting all your crap aboard before we went looking for you." The United Homes Transient NCO and CPO Barracks on this very base had been listed as Silva's and Lawrence's "permanent" address.

"Took a lot for granted, didn't you?" Silva grumped.

"No," Horn replied. "I'm glad you're here voluntarily, and I know Mr. Bradford will be too, but Captain McFarlane, even Captain Reddy, said we could shanghai you if we wanted."

"Like ta see ya try." Silva gestured at himself. "An' how come I gotta change? I might smell a tad ripe, but I've done my duty dressed—an' smellin'—like this more often than not."

"That won't work on this assignment. Not day-to-day. You remember the part I mentioned about *Walker* being a school ship now? You have to set an example. Skipper'll insist."

"You do need to get clean," Lawrence agreed judiciously. "I do too."

Silva shot him an annoyed look. "Who *is* the skipper?" he asked. "I know it ain't Cap'n Reddy. He's waaay too busy ta take up schoolmarmin' now. Specially if the Leaguers are actin' up!" A look of horror appeared on his face. "Goddamn, I hope it ain't Spanky!"

Horn chuckled. "It isn't Mr. McFarlane," he reassured, "but . . . you aren't far off," he added cryptically. "Point is, the cadets we'll be in charge of have already had some training. Most are already aboard, learning the ship, while they help with the finishing touches. Not only are they pretty sharp, top of their classes to rate this cruise, but most are the kids of prominent members of the Alliance. We *know* some of their parents, capiche? Maybe most important from a political standpoint, those who do well, from all over the Alliance, will be enlisted or commissioned as ensigns or petty officers directly into the American Navy or Marine Clan for a six-year hitch. *Walker*'s going to be the graduate school for the military leadership of the whole Alliance, while helping ensure our clan keeps its support and we keep getting the best and brightest. At the very least, it'll help all our respective forces get on the same page and stay there so we can work together more smoothly in the future."

"I hadn't thought about that part," Fred confessed. "Sounds like a good idea, though."

"I hear there's plaans to expaand the prograam," Kari put in, "by integrating our laand force Maarines, like Chack's Raiders, an' Navy Aviation too, using Aahd-mi-raal Keje's *Salissa*." She blinked a little sadly. "Big Saal is really too slow and vulnerable to remain a frontline caarrier once our new ones caan replace her, but she caan keep training the next generation."

Horn nodded but looked at Silva again. "Just as important as all that, those of us in Mr. Bradford's 'Corps of Discovery' have to keep our cover. He'll have his 'own' people openly working for him, but as far as anyone not on his team is concerned, anybody watching, or even anybody on board," he warned, "we're here to lead our divisions and 'polish' the youngsters. Period. That's the only job we let on about to anybody, see?"

Silva frowned. "I still ain't convinced. With the League raisin' a fuss, we're really gonna be wastin' poor ol' *Walker* as a baby carriage for wet-nosed kiddies? Wastin' *us*?"

"Two things, Chief Silva," Horn began to explain, all amusement gone from his voice. "First, even you should understand that 'poor old *Walker*,' while obviously not useless in battle, has certainly seen her share of it. More than her share, and nobody's anxious to risk her like that anymore. She's more important as a symbol, an example, than just another tin can for the enemy to shoot at. And her current role, our role aboard her, will help prepare that new generation I was talking about to take other ships like her, and better ones soon, back in the fight. Second, what we're going to be doing, besides what everybody knows about, is important too. I guarantee it."

"Swell, swell," Silva said, waving at him. "I get it. So I'm still chief gunner's mate to a buncha scrawny-ass snot lickers." He nodded at Fred and Kari. "I reckon they're in charge o' the aviation division. But what's Larry gonna do? An' what's your job?"

"Lawrence will help you, as usual, but he'll help me too. Like I said, we're training Marine cadets as well, and who better to demonstrate some of the fighting techniques of Grik—and other things like them—and how to overcome them? That'll be his official job, anyway." He grinned again. "And while I, and some others, will be polishing those Marine cadets, my other job will be performing the duties of your boss"—his grin got even bigger—"as 'acting' gunnery officer again."

"You lyin'—" Silva began, but Horn held up a hand.

"No, I told the truth. It's just 'Gunny' this time, and 'acting' is the operative word. That's the part of the job I can do that you can't." Horn's expression turned smug. "You can't even *pretend* to be an officer."

Moving along, they reached the gangway and paused again, looking at the whole ship. USS *Walker* had been rebuilt to varying degrees several times over the course of the war. The most comprehensive refit probably occurred after she actually *sank* after the Battle of Baalkpan, though later repairs might've gone even deeper. None had left her looking like she must've when new, way back in 1919, but this one might've succeeded. Except for those few washboarded plates, she no longer looked slightly wrinkled and, well, *bent* like she had for so long. Her lines were sharp and clean, and all four of her tall funnels stood straight and unpatched. The splinter shield protecting her number one 4″-50 on the fo'c'sle had clearly been replaced entirely, no longer battered and dented and sitting somewhat askew. The bridge structure sat square as well, with new clear glass in the pilothouse windows, gleaming in the late-morning sun. Silva smiled to see all the icons, representing everything from Japanese planes and ships to those of the Grik, Dominion, and finally the League—with numerous weird caricatures of Grikbirds and other strange things mixed in—painted on the side of the pilothouse under the bridgewing. It would take quite a while to count all the small hash marks beside each symbol.

The amidships deckhouse / gun platform was raked slightly upward aft once again to compensate for the rapid decrease in freeboard of the flush main deck that tapered down dramatically closer to the water at the stern. New four-tube torpedo mounts had been installed alongside the aft funnel, and new gun tubs protected the heavy antiaircraft armament that had replaced her aft torpedo tubes on either side of the seaplane catapult. The aft deckhouse (which always looked like an afterthought to accommodate otherwise forgotten necessities) enclosed the machine shop, torpedo storage, and, not least important, the aft crew's head, and was also where the auxiliary conn was sited, as well as the number four 4″-50 gun. Silva noted that this weapon still stood on the only dual-purpose mount *Walker* had been provided with, even after all her "daughters" were equipped with them.

"She does look fine, don't she?" Silva exclaimed with satisfaction as they finally strode to the top of the gangway.

At a glance, it was apparent more than half those aboard were human or Lemurian "younglings," the humans wearing blue or white dungarees, the young Lemurians in kilts. All wore "fatigue tops" (basically T-shirts) and white canvas "dixie cup" hats. Most were following older, taller versions of themselves, human or Lemurian, around in clusters, being set to work on various tasks. Others were assisting humans in the grayish coveralls that Imperial "yard apes" preferred. All were busy either helping complete final touches to the ship or receiving supplies for the upcoming voyage that were swayed aboard by dockyard booms and rushing to stow them as directed. There was quite a racket, ranging from shouted commands and chittering younglings, to deafening metallic banging from somewhere forward. Silva was actually used to the ship being overrun with short people. Adult 'Cats weren't much bigger than early teen humans and he was taller than most human adults. The fact that almost everyone was even smaller than usual was a little disconcerting, however.

There were exceptions. When they all paused to salute the Stars and Stripes fluttering from the halyard on the mainmast astern, then the strikingly tall ebony-skinned young human who met them at the side of the ship, Silva arched his brow over his good eye. The kid, maybe thirteen or fourteen, judging by his boyish face, was as tall as he was! When they'd completed the ritual of announcing themselves and asking permission to board, the youngster, wearing a web belt with a holstered 1911 around his slim waist, solemnly returned their salutes and granted their request.

"Say, son," Silva blurted impulsively, "I reckon yer a Repub—I mean, from the Republic o' Real People, an' I ain't met a lot o' folks from there, but you look mighty familiar." He grinned. "An' yer height's kinda distinctive too. None o' y'all have names on yer T-shirts, but you wouldn't be kin to a even taller fella named Bele, would ya?"

The corners of the youngster's lips twitched slightly. "Prefect Bele is my father," he said. "Welcome aboard, Chief Silva." A full smile struggled to escape. "You made an impression on him as well."

Silva grinned. "Is that so? Well, I won't embarrass ya by askin' if it was positive, but I'll say up front without wigglin' that yer pa's a helluva fighter, a helluva man. What's he up to these days?"

Horn cleared his throat. "Um, this is Cadet Philan Bele, but he's on duty, Chief Silva. You can swap war stories later."

Silva grunted and eyed his friend. "Aye, aye, yer noxiousness." He winked at young Bele. "See ya later, son."

"Yes, Chief Silva."

"Is the skipper aboard?" Horn asked.

"Not at present, Gunnery Sergeant," Cadet Bele replied. "But you are expected, as are a number of other officers and division chiefs. I was told to pass the word that there will be an informal"—his eyes flicked to Silva—"but mandatory reception in the wardroom at 1800 hours. The captain and Mr. Bradford will both be there."

"Swell," Horn said, then turned to Silva. "Go ahead and look around. I know you will, and you might as well do it before you get cleaned up. You better be presentable by 1800, though."

Silva sneered. "Is that a *order*, Gunnery Sergeant?"

Horn sighed and shook his head. "No, just good advice. Trust me."

Silva grunted, slightly mollified. Then he cocked his head to the side, listening to a muffled diatribe aft, and his tanned face suddenly lost all its color. "What the hell? C'mon, Larry. I may be half deaf, but I've either plumb lost my marbles, or I'm hearin' the grouchy, gravelly wailin' o' the fattest ghost that ever was."

"I'll stay here," Lawrence protested. "I don't like ghosts."

"C'mon, dammit. It's just comin' from under the amidships deckhouse, 'round the galley." He paused and frowned. "*Right* where the nasty bastard's spook'd haunt us too!"

Horn grinned but hid it. Fred and Kari looked at each other in alarm but moved to follow Silva as he started weaving purposely through the surprised work details. He was careful not to knock anyone over, but his pace was determined. Moving into the shade of the amidships gun platform, passing the starboard ladder upward, his eye sorted a short, scrawny "snipe" out of the cluster of shorter shapes lining up at a stainless-steel counter attached to the side of the ship's galley. He immediately recognized the snipe and wasn't even surprised to see Chief Isak Reuben, king of all the snipes on this world, his long-sleeve blue shirt somehow just as filthy as always, ranting at someone through the galley window in his reedy, raspy voice.

"What the hell *is* this slimy shit?" he demanded, smacking the counter and bouncing a sloshing bowl resting on it. "Looks like some kinda goddamn *okra soup*! Smells like it too, with a turd floatin' in it, but I'm damned if I'll taste it!" He crossed his skinny arms over his narrow chest. "An' you ain't feedin' it to these here kiddies, neither. Poor little bastards been workin' just as hard as real people—the grown sort, I mean—an' you'd have 'em eatin' some nasty swill that'll screamer more weight off 'em than it puts on. What the hell's the matter with you? How're they s'posed to get any bigger like *that*? What's wrong with a honest *sammitch*, fer God's sake!"

Silva had to stifle a laugh. "Same ol' Isak," he said. "Maybe a touch bolder than I remember, but still the weirdest little creep in the Navy. Not a bad wrench, I'm told," he added for the benefit of the gawking youngsters.

Isak threw a dismissive glance at him and sniffed. "Heard they was off lookin' fer you. Hoped you might'a gave some bush booger the ragin' screamers by now."

"Good ta see you too, Isak," Silva laughed, but then he heard the ghost voice again, drifting out of the galley.

"Which there ain't no bread for sammitches 'cause these useless 'kiddies' o' yers they assigned me didn't make any yet. An' it ain't okra." A slight pause. "Was that that damn maniac Silva? Feed it to him."

Silva pushed Isak aside and stared into the galley, shocked enough that even he couldn't speak for a moment when a massive, ugly, tattooed form with a dirty apron stretched around his protruding belly lumbered into view. "Earl Lanier," he finally managed. "Yer *dead*, damn you," he added, blinking his eye as if it would banish the unwholesome image. "I *seen* you dead, laid out with the rest after that hit on the galley at St. Vincent!"

Earl Lanier, who it clearly was—despite all Silva's blinking—merely grunted and shrugged. "So?" he said. "Maybe I *was* dead for a while. Don't much remember."

"I do," Silva adamantly assured. "I got conked on the head so there's gaps here an' there, but you were dead as hell. I know what dead looks like, an' you were layin' there, bug-eyed, tongue pokin' out, shit yerself dead!"

Earl shrugged again. "What can I say? Must'a got over it." His expression turned furious. "Not that it nearly didn't matter. I don't remember this part either, thank God, but I heard the silly bastards actually *threw me over the side*—took two fart bags to cover me," he inserted proudly, "an' they'd weighted me down with my beloved Coke machine, which wasn't even damaged." He shook his head. "Good thing it wasn't heavy enough ta sink me, an' I took to wigglin' around. They fished me an' my Coke machine both back out before the flashies could get me. Next thing I knew, I woke up with a heap other wounded on a 'Cat flattop."

"I heard about that," Fred and Kari chorused.

"I didn't," Silva said, shaking his head again. "I swear, Earl. That's the damnedest thing. But what're you doin' here? What about your bar back in Baalkpan?" Earl and a 'Cat called "Pepper" had a thriving saloon/café there named the Castaway Cook. Most people, including Earl, referred to it as the "Busted Screw."

"I still got my share," Earl said, "but when I heard they was fixin' this ol' girl up . . ." He looked away and affected a casual tone. "This is my home. Only one I got."

Isak tapped the bowl of green goo. "Should'a left him in the water."

Silva, Lawrence, Fred, and Kari continued working their way aft, where the two fliers inspected "their" aviation division. A seaplane was already on board, a late model "Nancy," but it had been disassembled and placed in storage where spare torpedoes would normally be. (*Walker* would only sail with the fish in her tubes, and two of those were inert practice torpedoes for training purposes.) Fred and Kari's own personal aircraft, an older-model Nancy they preferred, sat on the dock in a cradle and would be hoisted aboard before they left.

Other, less recognizable things were arranged in crates, ready to be swayed aboard as well. Some probably contained scientific equipment that Courtney Bradford had procured—specifically optics, which the Imperials were the best in the Alliance at making—while he and Abel Cook visited important friends and greeted other members of their Corps of Discovery as they arrived. The optics included a pair of what were probably the finest microscopes in the world, the biggest telescope he'd be allowed to bring, and a number of ordinary spyglasses strictly for the benefit of the ship. He'd even negotiated the donation of some new binoculars the Impies were making in exchange for a promise to recommend their acquisition by the Navy Clan.

Of more dubious utility were a large number of collapsible steel cages of various sizes Courtney had commissioned and planned to inhabit with live specimens of new species he hoped to find. On the other hand, these preparations and others of the sort, as well as the assembly of cadets from all over the Alliance and the newly created "Corps of Discovery" was happening quite openly. It was no secret whatsoever all the acquisitions and personnel were going aboard USS *Walker*, the new Navy Clan school ship.

Although some of Courtney's team, himself included of course, were celebrities of a sort, the cadets got the most public attention. A large percentage of these youngsters were, quite frankly, war orphans. Most of the human children and Lemurian younglings practically raised in the various new naval academies were. Some still had a single parent but very few had both. Those who did were either from here in the Empire or the faraway Republic of Real People. These parents, either the local variety or those who'd accompanied their cadets from elsewhere in the Alliance, were reassured by the clearly nonbelligerent nature of *Walker*'s first voyage in her new role. Especially given the rising tensions with the League on the other side of the world that had accompanied the departure of Imperial Navy ships or the few Navy Clan vessels still passing through. That *Walker* was technically just as well equipped to defend herself as she'd always been was actually a source of further relief, not less. She might not be steaming off to confront the powerful League, but she was—again, quite openly—headed for unknown seas.

Imperial and Union counterintelligence assets, working together in the Isles (the spies watching all the known and suspected spies), saw no evidence their targets suspected there was any more to it. The enemy understood that *Walker* was an icon and they didn't seem at all surprised the Alliance wouldn't want to risk her in potential combat again. The same was true for Courtney and Cook's visits with high-ranking Imperial officials. It was common knowledge they were close friends of High Admiral Harvey Jenks and even Rebecca Anne McDonald, the Governor/Empress herself. (Some spies on both sides even knew there might be something more than friendship between the Governor/Empress and Abel Cook.) But their visits inspired little speculation, which left them free to discuss all sorts of things beyond scientific exploration.

Silva's friends eventually went below to start sorting out their quarters, and he finally worked his way forward, amiably nodding at cadets who didn't seem to know what to think of him. Making his way through the lower bridge structure beside the comm shack, he stepped out through the hatch and onto the fo'c'sle where, all alone for the moment, he approached the number one gun. Walking around in front of it, he grunted satisfaction when he saw the new, crisply rifled liner in the barrel, but also the expected markings that proved this was in fact "his" number one gun, not a replacement.

Laying his hand on the sun-warmed steel, he gently caressed it. "Hey, babe," he murmured softly. "Remember me? I'm back."

CHAPTER 4

Silva found Lawrence arranging his few possessions in the space reserved for them in the chief's quarters forward of the wardroom. Lawrence had already taken the top bunk because he'd fit in it better and didn't mind jumping up in it. Besides, once when they'd shared such quarters before and Lawrence thought to get Silva's goat (whatever that meant) by claiming the bottom bunk first, his big friend never even argued. Not only did that ruin the whole point of the exercise, Silva made a point of stepping on him every time he climbed—noisily and awkwardly—in or out of his rack. Worse, nearly every time Lawrence woke up, one of Silva's dirty socks was draped over his snout. He quickly suggested they make a trade.

Petey hopped down in the little sink in front of the single mirror and cawed, "Eat Water!"

Silva snorted and turned the tap to drip before dumping his own seabag out on his rack and rummaging through the contents, selecting a khaki shirt by holding it to his nose and shrugging. The shower in the chief's head was occupied, and the noise and voices in the passageway implied there was a line, so Silva pulled off his T-shirt and wadded it up in a laundry bag before wetting a towel, much to Petey's annoyance, and wiping himself down with it.

"Feels good," he said, turning to let the breeze from an oscillating fan play across his scarred and tattooed torso. "Never had a fan before. They spared no expense on the luxury o' our accommodations, did they?"

"Electric 'otors are getting easier . . ." Lawrence agreed, then assumed that frustrated expression, almost like a snarl, that he got when it was going to be hard to say what he wanted. "'Ore o' they getting . . . 'uilt."

Silva nodded. "More o' *ever-thing* that makes life easier's bein' made these days. Not havin' ta spend every minute an' every speck o' metal makin' ships an' bullets anymore." He frowned. "I guess that's a good thing—least as far as fans go." He pulled on the shirt, then bent and opened a thick cardboard box in his pile. Inside was his best "chief's hat," which Chief Bosun Gray had left him, and he took it out and put it on. He hardly ever wore it and would probably only appear in a much-battered facsimile after this.

Lawrence turned off the tap when Petey started playing in the water, and the little tree glider hissed at him. "One o' these days, I going to eat *you*," he grumbled quietly.

Petey shrieked and leaped back on Silva's shoulder, dampening the fresh shirt. "I just oughta let him too," Silva agreed with a laugh, thumping Petey on the head. "C'mon, Larry. Hurry up an' get dressed an' let's go ahead on to the wardroom. Maybe there's coffee."

Lawrence held up a white kilt in one clawed hand and a combat smock in the other. "Is I in the na'y or 'arines today?"

Silva sighed but nodded emphatically at the tie-dyed Marine garment. "That one. God knows, with Mr. Cook comin' an' Gunny Horn already aboard, we got plenty o' Marines runnin' around, but damn, you look silly in a skirt."

They'd both soon discovered yet another Marine already waiting in the wardroom. Like much of the rest of the ship Silva had inspected—he hadn't looked at engineering, of course—the wardroom appeared virtually new. Fresh white paint was on the bulkheads and cabinets, and no orange rust stains or streaks were visible. The deck was still roughly the same medium dark green, but none of the nasty, cracked, scorched, and smelly linoleum remained. Its primary purpose was to make the steel deck slightly less slippery, but in its place was some kind of thick, hard, clearly durable paint, probably mixed with sand. Identical paint, sans sand, now covered the long wardroom table, intended to do double duty as an operating table when necessary. The same (or similar) lighting arrangement was suspended above it, capable of being lowered down closer to a patient. What caught Silva's attention at once, however, was, sitting at the table and sipping from a mug, a man he'd completely forgotten existed.

"I'll be damned if it ain't Corporal Miles!" Silva exclaimed. "Not that I've thought o' you more than a time or two in the last few years, but when I did, I figured you were dead."

Another former "China Marine" who came to this world in *Mizuki Maru* with Gunny Horn, Ian Miles *wasn't* Silva's friend. Average size, dark-haired, and probably smarter than was good for him, he'd been something of a barracks lawyer at a very grim time for the war effort. He'd been so bad, in fact, when Spanky McFarlane sent him on a mission with Silva into the wilds of Madagascar, he'd actually left it up to Silva whether or not to bring him back. He hadn't, in point of fact, but not because he did anything to him. Everyone had something of an epiphany on that trip, searching for more Lemurian allies (Madagascar was their ancestral home) against the Grik. Not only did they—amazingly—find strange human descendants of the same people who founded the Empire of the New Britain Isles half a world away, they discovered that not all Lemurians were friendly. Others were, however, and were having a very hard time with the Grik. Corporal Miles learned at last how truly monstrous the Grik really were and chose to remain with the "good"'Cats they encountered to help them against their ancient enemy.

Eventually styling himself a "colonel," Miles coordinated arms and supply shipments to the beleaguered natives, human and Lemurian, and helped lead them to victory against the increasingly isolated Grik. The war finally over, he was given the choice of remaining a colonel, even ambassador, in the swamps and jungles of "Mada-gaas-gar," or coming out as a sergeant. He was a little bitter about that, thinking his work wasn't appreciated, but jumped at the chance to get out. Knowing he was available, it was Horn himself who recommended him for the Corps of Discovery. Horn didn't much like the "old" Miles he'd known, but the man had demonstrated unsupervised competence and gained a lot of experience surviving and fighting in a deadly wilderness on a shoestring.

"No, I'm not dead, not yet," Miles replied before leaning back in his chair and regarding Silva with a strange expression. "Gunny Horn told me it might get left up to you whether I stay that way. Again," he added sourly. "I take it I'm on probation of a sort." He quirked his lips. "They're not sure I can play well with others."

Silva shrugged. "Never was much good at that myself." Drawing a cup of coffee, he moved to sit on a new padded wooden chair at the wardroom table across from Miles. "One thing I *did* hear was you did some good work with them Shee-Ree 'Cats after we split up. I don't see us ever bein' pals, but you do yer job"—Silva grinned—"whatever that winds up bein' for any of us, an' I'll watch yer back if you watch mine. Deal?"

Miles nodded. "Fair enough."

Lawrence sat sideways on another padded chair next to Silva while he and Miles compared adventures, amusing himself by occasionally feeding a cracker to Petey, watching the pile of crumbs grow on his big friend's shoulder. It wasn't long before others began filing in, filling coffee cups and choosing little snacks from the countertop on the starboard side of the aft bulkhead and the center passageway. There'd never been a hatch there, but now a finely finished and ornately carved door had replaced the old green curtain. Other doors now separated the chief's quarters forward, for that matter, as well as the captain's stateroom—the only accommodation with direct access to the wardroom.

Gunny Horn and then Fred and Kari were the first to join them, talking animatedly about how gently "their" plane had been hoisted aboard and secured to the catapult. Of course, they were both clearly excited just to be back aboard "their" ship and their glowing description of her current condition generally matched Silva's appraisal. Chief Bosun's Mate Carl Bashear, another old companion, came in with Isak Reuben, almost pushing the little guy who still managed to look scruffy in clean khakis.

Silva's eye widened. "Why, hidy, Carl. Still ain't snatched you up for a officer yet, I see."

"Never will," the fireplug-shaped CPO swore. "Same as him"—he gestured at Isak—"or you, for that matter."

"Never, by God," Isak affirmed. "This ol' girl wouldn't never recognize me with shiny jools on my collar," he added darkly. "Some of us got the *jobs* o' officers," he continued morosely. "All the goddamn paperwork o' engineerin' officer fer me, but I hear the idea is for us ta rotate them *kiddies* through as officers, with us tellin' 'em what ta do." He released a long-suffering sigh. "Just as well ol' Gilbert never lived ta see it."

Gilbert Yager had been Isak's half brother and another quintessential "snipe," but was killed in *Walker*'s last fight on the Lago de Vida.

Bashear canted his head at Silva. "Surprised you didn't die of boredom without a war on. How'd you survive without somebody to kill?"

Silva affected an "aw shucks" expression as the aft door opened again. "Been killin' lots o' rhino pigs an' other nasty boogers. Ain't the same sense o' satisfaction, mind, but between that an' stayin' to myself for the most part . . . it keeps me from killin' every idiot I come across."

"You staying away from people is probably best for all concerned," said Surgeon Pam Cross, stepping into the wardroom with the Lemurian Lieutenant Commander Tab-At, better known as "Tabby" to her friends. Pam was no taller than Tabby and her face, framed by short dark hair, had a natural wholesome beauty. It was somewhat at odds, at present, with her Brooklyn-accented sarcasm and decidedly bitter expression. If Tabby took note, she gave no sign, blinking something like joy. Only the fact she was an officer, *Walker*'s new XO in fact, kept her from rushing over to hug her friends. She did quickly join them at the table. Pam held back, finding a place to lean against the counter.

"Hi, doll," Silva tentatively called to her with his version of a gentle smile.

"Don't you *dare* 'doll' *me*, sailor," Pam snapped with an angry sneer, prompting a short, uncomfortable silence. Understandable, since the last some of those present knew, Silva and Pam were finally "together," practically married, it seemed. Their relationship had always been volatile, however, so there was probably little surprise that things had come unglued.

Silva started to speak but caught himself, apparently deciding this wasn't the time or place. He'd have to try to sort this out, though, or his time aboard *Walker*, or even in the Corps of Discovery, was going to be a trial, to say the least.

A door to port of the passageway opened and two men and a 'Cat walked into the wardroom from the captain's stateroom. The Lemurian wore yet another Marine combat smock. A third man followed. Clearly, the stateroom had been expanded if four people could even fit in there.

Tabby jumped to her feet and shouted, "Aattention on deck!" when the third man, taller than the rest, appeared.

Everyone sitting on a chair or stool quickly rose. Even Pam straightened her posture while Commander Rolando "Ronson" Rodriguez, USS *Walker*'s new captain, blushed a little and waved at them with a self-conscious grin.

"As you were, all of you." Stepping past those who entered with him, he moved toward the head of the long table, still gesturing for everyone to sit. He didn't. "I think everyone here knows me," he began with a wide smile beneath the luxuriant signature mustache extending just a little past his upper lip. He'd lost most of the rest of the hair on his head when it caught fire during the Battle of Baalkpan (earning him the nickname of "Ronson," after a brand of lighter), and he'd kept the rest of it shaved ever since. Like most of his surviving shipmates from *Walker*, *Mahan*, *S-19*, and now other ships as well, he'd risen steadily in the ranks, ending the war as XO on USS *James Ellis*, then acting captain on *Walker* herself after "*Ellie*" was torpedoed and her captain, Perry Brister, killed. It had in fact been largely due to his and Tabby's and Isak Reuben's efforts that *Walker* wasn't lost as well.

"And I'm sure you all know Mr. Abel Cook," Captain Rodriguez continued, nodding at the young officer, "and some of you know these other people too." He gestured at the ones who came in with him as they took their respective seats. "For those who don't, I'll introduce them directly. First—" He paused and aimed a stern look at a couple of cadets acting as mess attendants bringing in another tray of appetizers. "That'll be all," he pointedly told them and they scurried out of the room, closing the door behind them. "Sergeant Kaik," he addressed the Lemurian Marine, "please check and make sure the passageway's clear."

"Ay, sir," the 'Cat replied, jumping up and doing so.

"Swell," Silva grumbled at Horn. "*Another* Marine."

Kaik blinked something at Silva before proceeding to peer out through the open portholes along each side of the wardroom as well, likely ensuring no work parties were hanging over the side or listening from the dock. "All clear, Cap-i-taan," he finally reported before taking his place by the door. He'd hear if anyone else approached.

"Sergeant Kaik-Sar *is* yet 'another Marine,'" Rodriguez confirmed, lifting a brow at Silva. "Late of the First Marines, in fact, and most recently General Pete Alden's personal aide. Like a few others of you here, I'm told he was getting bored with the peace. I asked him to double-check that we could talk freely because, with the exception of Courtney Bradford, who"—he cleared his throat wryly—"hasn't yet joined us, those of us here at this moment are the only ones aboard with any knowledge of the"—he paused—"the *dual nature* of the Corps of Discovery, and why—besides the obvious—it's accompanying this first voyage of USS *Walker* in her new role. In regard to the first of those subjects, I'd like to introduce you to, um, 'Optio' Jack Meek." He indicated the other man who'd been in his quarters. "As his no doubt fictional rank implies, he's from the Republic of Real People and is officially here as its representative and observer. There are a number of Repub cadets aboard. He'll also, officially, serve as our comm officer, so calling him 'Sparks' Meek shouldn't raise any eyebrows."

Jack Meek stood, and for the first time, most of those present really looked at him. He was average size with short, dark hair, and had a very ragged and impressive scar down his face, from forehead to chin. He saw people staring and smiled. "A Grik foot claw," he explained. "Ruined my looks." Even as he spoke, his accent went . . . from something else to a close approximation of Rodriguez's mild southwest Texas drawl. "I don't need to be an officer," he added. "Maybe better if I'm not."

Silva barked a laugh. "He's a snoop!"

Meek bowed very slightly. "Among other things. I was most recently with Legate Bekiaa-Sab-At. That's where I got this." He pointed at the scar. Everyone knew Bekiaa's reputation. If he'd been with her, he'd seen some fierce fighting.

"So," Miles probed, "is that supposed to prove you can fight—or survive getting stepped on?"

"That's enough, Sergeant Miles," Captain Rodriguez scolded.

"Yep, still a asshole," Silva mouthed at Lawrence.

The captain continued. "Lieutenant Meek is also the son of *Ambassador* Doocy Meek, who's best pals with Henry Stokes. Besides that, he comes with the highest . . . electronic gizmo . . . recommendation of Steve Riggs."

Grasping his hands behind his back, Rodriguez proceeded. "Anyway, as far as anyone else is concerned, this ship is practically a holy relic of the founding of the United Homes. She's a 'show the flag' ambassador and still the honored flagship of the Grand Alliance, all while serving as a floating academy to advance the careers of some of the Alliance's brightest naval prospects. This is a school ship now, first and foremost, and our job—even those of you in the 'Corps of Discovery'—is to make officers and senior POs and NCOs out of the kids we're taking on. We'll put the finishing touches on skills they've already learned the basics of while showing them the reasons for a lot of the traditions of the United States Navy and the American Navy Clan that they've been soaking up in classrooms." He paused. "A lot of these kids'll go straight back to school, but the oldest and best'll leave for new ships as midshipmen or petty officer strikers." He glanced at Silva again. "Not everybody's cut out to be an officer."

There were a few chuckles as he looked at the faces staring back. "All that said, *Walker* has always been and will remain a ship of war, and it's up to you—and others aboard—to make sure her crew is ready to fight if it has to."

"We're takin' little *kiddies* out ta fight?" Isak's reedy voice demanded incredulously.

Captain Rodriguez shook his head. "No. Not deliberately. And in spite of what I just said, on the surface, our primary scientific mission sounds like pretty straightforward investigation. We're going to check out some weird flashes, maybe big blasts, like those that hit the Shogunate of Yokohama." He dipped his head at Abel. "Mr. Cook went and looked at where they happened, along with Mr. Bradford, and can tell you more about them." He chuckled. "Just as well Courtney's not here. He'd go on for hours. In a nutshell, though, Mr. Cook and Mr. Bradford think the blasts—they *were* blasts—leaked over from another world close to the, ah, 'frequency' we're on, or some such . . ." He shook his head. "I've never understood any of that. But it wasn't a direct attack on us. And even if it might've been really bad to be there when they happened, they didn't find anything that should be hazardous to us, after the fact. *If* the incident we're going to investigate was the same sort of thing," he qualified, rubbing his nose. "That said, we're also going to look for some ships that went missing, one of which was Navy Clan Reserve."

He looked around. "Our secondary mission is almost purely exploratory, and is probably the part that Courtney's most excited about: to locate a very large island that's known to be down in those seas." He looked at Abel. "Again, you can ask Mr. Cook for more details on it, but apparently the Impies found it themselves—named it Ogygia—during their 'age of exploration,' and what they found is pretty much what shut that part of their history down." He nodded at some of the surprised expressions. "Yeah. We've even got a pretty good idea where it is from old charts the Governor/Empress gave us, but it's considered a pretty dangerous place. I'm sure Mr. Bradford'll want to romp all over it, but my orders are not to explore it, not with a ship full of kiddos. We're just supposed to find it if we can and map however much of the coast we have fuel for." He looked back at Isak. "See? Ought to be a cinch. And let me be clear: we won't *ever* look for a fight. Not with the cargo we carry." He shrugged and ended wryly, "But all of us know that doesn't always matter. Fights have been known to find *Walker* whether she's looking for them or not."

CHAPTER 5

A purple-orange smear sharply defined the high dark mountains to the east, beginning to stretch across the cool morning sky and finally competing with the dockside lights illuminating a crowd of spectators and dignitaries already gathered there. A bugle, having sounded reveille an hour before, now called the ship's company to assemble on the dock. Everyone had been expecting it and the gangway thundered under the stampeding feet of one hundred and eighty young humans and 'Cats (almost twice USS *Walker*'s original complement), who quickly formed by watches. They'd already been assigned their initial divisions, but the idea was to rotate many of them through every division during the course of the voyage. There'd be exceptions for those showing a special talent or preference for critical occupations like engineering, gunnery, torpedoes, navigation, or quartermaster's duties, but even those who were bound to be Marines would get some practical ship maintenance and operation instruction. Just as Navy Clan sailors had often been called on to carry small arms ashore, Marines usually manned the secondaries, especially antiaircraft (or anti-Grikbird) armaments on Navy Clan ships and had to be able to fill in on main battery weapons when needed.

In any event, despite the arbitrary nature of the cadet formation, division chiefs or officers took their accustomed places, calling the cadets and about half the regular veteran crew of forty or so lined up behind them to attention. Captain Rodriguez, Governor/Empress Rebecca Anne McDonald, and Captain Abel Cook, all in their finest uniforms, strode out in front of them. Courtney Bradford followed, dressed in stylish, if somewhat rumpled, Imperial civilian attire consisting of coat and weskit, fluffy cravat, and knee britches and boots. Regardless of his vaguely disheveled appearance, there was a wide smile on his ruddy face.

"Hand salute!" barked Chief Bosun Bashear when the bugler, standing atop the aft deckhouse with several of the "regular" crew, sounded "To the Color" as a sailor briskly hoisted the Stars and Stripes, still the flag of the American Navy Clan, up the mainmast halyard. "Order . . . arms!" Bashear concluded, the first sunbeams of the day brightening the colorful streaming flag. A lot of the traditions and regulations in Captain Matthew Reddy's Navy Clan had been tweaked somewhat. Not least of these being, by necessity, females in the service. There hadn't really been a choice at first because, quite frankly, they'd needed the numbers. Ultimately, since most of the Allies they gained already used females in combat roles to various degrees, it just became "normal," even to die-hards like Silva, Isak Reuben, even Matt Reddy himself. Nobody knew what Captain "Ronson" Rodriguez thought about it all, but he was a stickler for the traditions that remained, different or not.

"At ease, cadets," he said loudly, voice strong and firm. "As you know, this is the big day that many of you have worked so hard for," he smirked. "Some a little harder than others, but that'll change." This was meant as praise for those who'd been here awhile, helping with preparations, and a shot at a few cadets who waited for the very last minute to report. The selection process had left plenty of time for all to come early, even those farthest away, and they'd been encouraged to do so. The crisis in the Azores might've disrupted shipping, but the big flying boats always had deadheads and the cadets had priority for space on those flights. Rodriguez continued. "Today we shove off for the next phase of your education. Not only will you put a lot of what you've learned to this point to use, you'll probably pick up more each day that we're out than you would in a month of classes." He shrugged and grinned. "And some will seem to contradict what you already *think* you know, guaranteed. I'm not saying your schooling's been wasted, it's just that as important as 'reading' and 'hearing' is, 'doing' is the best learning there is. You're here to *do*."

His grin grew a little. "Some of the . . . more pampered or refined among you might be a little surprised by the . . . *tone* of this phase of your instruction, but bear in mind you're training for an extremely hazardous occupation and all your teachers *here* are real sailors with hard-won experience in combat on an unforgiving sea. It's not their job to patiently reexplain all the basics you had to learn to get here, or kiss your boo-boos and make 'em better." His grin vanished, expression turning grim. "They have orders to be just as unforgiving as the enemy and the sea, so you don't make stupid mistakes that get you or your shipmates killed. That said, they were chosen as your instructors because they're the best at what they do." His gaze strayed to Isak Reuben and his lip twitched under his mustache. "No matter how unlikely that seems. The point is, when—not if—you get an ass-chewin' like you never imagined, wait for the smoke to clear and *ask* for help to get better. They'll give it. None of them are here just to make your lives miserable." Examining the reaction to what he'd said reflected on the young faces before him, he saw both trepidation and confidence on the shiny human ones and nervous or determined blinking on those covered with fur. He hesitated at the sight of Silva's amused expression, standing with that dopey lizard on his shoulder. "Not most of them, anyway," he amended. "They'll test you, though. They'll push you, pull you, shout at you, cuss you—hell, they might even prank you. That's part of the life. Don't tell me you don't prank each other already. None of 'em are supposed to *hurt* you, though, any more than each other, see? Don't put up with that. You're subject to—and protected by—the same Navy regulations they are, so if any of you wind up with a genuine beef over the way you're treated, take it to your division chief or officer. If they're the source of your problem, take it up with Lieutenant Commander Tab-At." He gestured at Tabby. "But I better not hear you went whining to her because somebody hurt your feelings."

He paused a moment, looking around, then gestured aside to a petite, almost elfin young woman with tightly braided golden hair in an impeccably tailored but otherwise unadorned Imperial Navy officer's uniform.

Taking a step back, he said, "That's all from me for now, so listen up to our gracious host here, Her Majesty Rebecca Anne McDonald, Governor/Empress of these New Britain Isles."

With a shy smile at Abel Cook, whose arm she'd hooked with her own while she stood there, the young woman stepped forward, smile growing and firming. Quite a few of those present were her subjects and they bowed their heads respectfully. Lemurians from the Union and Republic stamped their feet and polite applause otherwise prevailed to honor the popular leader.

"Thank you, Captain Rodriguez," she said, voice surprisingly strong for her size. There was also a confident, commanding tone that Silva called her "pixie potentate" voice, which annoyed her, but she loved Silva like a wayward older brother and couldn't stay angry with him. "We live in a dangerous world," she said, addressing her audience now. "A world full of dreadful threats from terrible beasts and even more monstrous enemies." She raised a hand to reference the old ship behind her. "And before the arrival of this storied vessel and her gallant crew, and the advent of our glorious alliance, all our peoples had to face this frightening world quite alone. In many cases, we were not even *aware* of potential friends across the globe. Having all now joined together, we're much stronger than the sum of our parts. Together, we utterly defeated some of our most ancient, ruthless enemies, and threw others back on their heels."

Still smiling, she gently shook her head at the enthusiastic response and it quieted when she resumed. "Yet many threats remain. Some are known, but there are doubtless others we know nothing about. This world is vast and mysterious, after all, still largely unexplored by us. There was a time when my people attempted to learn as much about it as we could, but we were frightened by some of what we found. For generations, it was the policy of the Empire to *hide* from the wider world, falsely secure in our belief that we could cope with the threats we knew about and stubbornly ignoring whatever transpired beyond our view." She shook her head again. "Ultimately, even the menace we knew proved to be more than we could handle alone, and the deadly consequences of our happy insularity were brutally driven home. Never again," she stated flatly, with fierce determination. "We *must* explore beyond the horizons of our knowledge, not only marking the hazards we discover but the opportunities as well. Together, our Grand Alliance has the strength to do that with confidence, but in peace or war, it *will* be tested again."

Her smile turned warm and inviting. "Which brings us to you. You are the best and brightest of students from all over the Alliance—from the newly founded Scapa Flow Naval Warfare Academy right here on this island, to the Baalkpan Home and Advance Naval Training Center in the United Homes, to the Alex-aandra Scholla Belli in the Republic of Real People. I'm sure others will attend in the future, and the future is what we are building. All of you will serve an enlistment in the American Navy Clan, which helps protect us all, but many of you will then take what you learn to the navies of your homelands, entering their service as experienced leaders. This voyage will be your first step on that path and I wish you the very best of luck!"

There were cheers this time, quickly silenced in the ranks by growls from the chiefs, Bashear's admonishment rising above the others.

"Stuff it, you buncha shit stains. Who said you could open your faces? Look like a buncha baby lizardbirds squawking for their mamas to puke a fish in your mouths!" A silent pause ensued before Bashear hastily added, "S'cuse me, Majesty."

Few of these kids had ever been spoken to like this before, not even those who'd been here awhile already, working under Carl Bashear. Apparently, the real training truly was about to begin. Silva chuckled at Lawrence, standing beside him. "Ol' Carl sounded like Chief Gray just then! I miss that tough ol' bastard."

Lawrence was shaking his head. "Gray 'as scarier," he hissed.

Silva frowned and nodded. "Yeah, he was."

A grinning Courtney Bradford stepped forward to speak. "Now," he said eagerly, "that is very well, I'm sure, but as you all know, this isn't just a training cruise. What a dreadful waste that would be. No, as Her Majesty alluded, this is also a historic voyage into the unknown, the inaugural operation of the Corps of Discovery, and we have a *real* mission ahead of us, of investigation and exploration! I'm sure you're all as excited as I am."

Captain Rodriguez touched Courtney's elbow from behind. Glancing back, Courtney saw him making a wind-it-up gesture and harrumphed. "Well," he said, disappointed, "I was asked to keep my address short, for the moment, and I shall. Time and tide wait for no man, as they say, and I suppose we should get on with it. I *shall* speak more with you all later." He smiled at the cadets again. "In any event, I hope you're all as proud to participate in this endeavor as I am. We're going to have *so* much fun!"

Bosuns' pipes and whistles shrilled and the cadets made for the gangway with the chiefs herding them along with strikingly unkind words and tones.

Abel stepped over to the Governor/Empress. "Well," he said lowly, "I'm off again, it seems."

Rebecca nodded. "It was nice to have you here. Even if just for a few days." She pursed her lips. "It will always be this way, you know. That's why . . ." She waved it away. They'd discussed all this before.

"Maybe not *always*, Your Majesty," Abel told her. "And even if so, what's strange about that?" He managed a tentative smile. "If you wanted some highborn, noble, stay-at-home stick-in-the-mud, you could've already picked one. Lord knows I've seen enough of them sniffing around while I've been here."

Rebecca's lips formed an impish smile. "Perhaps I'm just waiting until you leave."

Abel smiled back more broadly. "No," he said, hopeful as always, but maybe a little more confident than before. "You're waiting until I come back." Grasping her hand, he bowed over it and kissed it. Looking deeply into her eyes as he rose back up, he finally turned for the gangway and strode briskly up it.

"Be careful, Abel Cook," he heard her say.

"So long, li'l sis," Silva said, stepping up behind Rebecca.

She turned and grasped him tightly in a hug.

"Shove off, doll!" Petey shrieked indignantly.

Silva thumped him on the head. "Shut up, you!"

"He learned that hearing Dennis and Surgeon Cross argue," Lawrence confided in her.

Rebecca snorted a laugh, but her eyes were swimming when she looked up at Silva. "Please take care of Abel," she murmured.

"Sure, Sis," Silva consoled, patting her on the back. "Always do."

"You chopped off one of his fingers!" she said accusingly. That was true enough, but Abel had been infected by a singularly insidious plant thorn at the time and would've died without the timely amputation.

"Yeah. See? Always do," he repeated, patting her again, but seeing Pam Cross waiting to say farewell to the Governor/Empress, he cleared his throat and stood back. "Well . . . so long." Abruptly, he and Lawrence departed up the gangway.

Bashear was blowing his bosun's pipe between calls for "All hands, all hands, make all preparations to get underway!"

Two boilers had already been lit, and a gray haze of smoke and a wisp of steam were rising over the tops of the two forward stacks.

"Engineerin' division, muster aft!" came Isak's reedy voice. "Whichever o' you munchkins is in it today," he added with a growl. "Crazy way ta run a ship, switchin' ever'body around. Yer either born a snipe or you ain't. What am I gonna do with a buncha born *deck apes* in my spaces?"

"Call the special sea and anchor detail, Chief Bashear," Tabby cried.

"Aye, aye," Bashear replied, then looked suddenly lost. A kind of chaos was already erupting all over the ship as a weakness in the new arrangement suddenly manifested itself. While most of the cadets were aware of what division they were supposed to report to, few had been assigned to the various standing details within them yet.

"We gotta watch this," Pam chuckled to Rebecca, standing with Courtney now.

"Many of the permanent crew are just as new at this as the cadets," Courtney observed, also amused. "They will learn just as much, I suspect. It's easy to forget the little details that one considers common sense or second nature." There was a great deal of shouting now as this oversight began to be addressed.

Rebecca turned to face Pam and took her hands. As short as Pam was, the Governor/Empress still had to look up at her. "I take it that you and Dennis are fighting again," she said.

Pam shrugged, frowning now. "Same long fight. It just gets interrupted now and then." She sighed. "Sometimes I love the big dope so bad it breaks my heart, but then he does somethin' . . . an' I hate his guts enough to make me sick. So . . . I'm pretty much miserable all the time an' I can't keep from makin' him miserable too."

Rebecca nodded at the gangway. "I suspect he feels much the same. Perhaps you both need more time away from each other. Why go on this trip?"

Pam rolled her eyes at Courtney. "*He* said Dennis wasn't goin'."

Courtney coughed and looked startled. "I beg your pardon, my dear. When I approached you about participating, Chief Silva hadn't even been *found* yet."

"You said he wasn't comin'," Pam said, accusing him directly.

Courtney shook his head, expression the picture of innocence. "He wasn't at the time."

"But you knew he would," Pam pressed.

Courtney pursed his lips, then nodded. "I suppose I did, if he could indeed be located." He paused, regarding her gently. "But so did you, my dear." Turning to Rebecca, he bowed to her. "Farewell, Your Majesty," he said, then turned to go as well.

"Y'know, he's probably right," Pam confessed, a little bitterly. But forcing a smile for the diminutive ruler, she said, "So long, Rebecca. Take care."

"You as well, and God bless you. I look forward to your return." She paused. "And despite my rousing words, I do hope you don't find anything *too* interesting!"

Stepping aboard the ship and energetically mounting the stairs to the pilothouse, Courtney stopped on the shiny new wooden deck strakes intended to keep water from sweeping the watch standers off their feet in heavy seas. He beamed benevolently around at the bustling activity. "Permission to come on the bridge?" he inquired.

Captain Rodriguez tossed him a grin. "Sure. Make yourself at home, Mr. Bradford." He nodded at a carafe on the glass-covered chart table. "There's coffee. The real stuff," he added significantly. They'd subsisted on a vile, brown, green-foamed brew called "monkey joe" for a long time before they beat the Grik on Madagascar.

"Might there be any tea at all?" Courtney asked, disappointed, even though he'd been the one who discovered the precious beans in the first place. But real tea was available here in the Empire.

Rodriguez playfully narrowed his eyes at him. "Maybe in the wardroom, but I'll remind you this is still an *American* Navy Clan ship."

Courtney cleared his throat. "Of course. Well, thank you," he said, selecting a cup. "Don't mind if I do." Filling the cup, he blew on it before taking a sip, eyes following the various watch standers taking their places. Only a few of these were cadets at this point, and then only ones who'd been here awhile. One tiny female 'Cat was in the talker's position and others were on the bridgewings by the torpedo directors, stationed as lookouts, but one young Lemurian stood beside the EOT, or engine order telegraph. "The yard did a lovely job on the grand old lady," Courtney observed appreciatively. "The last time I was aboard, the spot where I am standing had been blasted entirely away. I can't see the slightest evidence of that now."

"The Impies in the yaard helped a lot," Tabby agreed, "an' we couldn't haave done it without their faacilities, but most of the work was done by our own people." By that, she meant Union or Navy Clan personnel.

"You were a bit battered yourself, if I recall," Ronson pointed out. That was true as well. Courtney had actually taken the wheel at the height of the Battle of Lago de Vida. Many others had died and Matt Reddy himself was nearly killed.

"Good as new." Courtney smiled, patting himself. "But I was evacuated back to the fleet at Martinique. You were the ones who brought her in later, barely afloat."

"Still under her own power," Tabby said proudly.

"And you had the conn," Captain Rodriguez reminded her with a smile. "Are you ready to take her out?"

Tabby blinked. She'd been *Walker*'s engineering officer a long time and would've been happy to remain so indefinitely. It was Captain Reddy who finally decreed it was time she move up the ladder, and he personally appointed her as *Walker*'s XO. Of course, that left the problem of what to do with Chief Isak Reuben. Painfully insular and antisocial, he wasn't a natural leader. He'd grudgingly accepted becoming a senior petty officer because he truly was a gifted engineer and he'd slowly evolved the ability to—tediously—pass his great knowledge on to others. He and his dead half brother, Gilbert, had been Tabby's own mentors, after all. But he wasn't any more suited to being a commissioned officer than Silva, for wildly different reasons. So he'd basically be the old ship's *acting* engineering officer for as long as he wanted to be. Just as well, since it would be easier to pull a hermit crab out of its shell without hurting it than permanently pry Isak out of *Walker.*

Tabby could sympathize, feeling much the same herself, and maybe even more like an impostor in her new role as XO. She was confident she could handle much of the job okay, but remained extremely nervous on the bridge. Considering all the effort it took in the past just to keep *Walker* going, she'd never spent as much time there as she should, and her navigation and ship-handling skills had been sorely lacking. Thankfully, Ronson Rodriguez was a good, patient skipper as well as a friend and had been working tirelessly with her. Looking at him now, she gulped and nodded, confident she could indeed "take the ship out," though she still had little notion of how she'd ever *fight* her, if she had to.

"Ay, Cap-i-taan," she said forcefully. "I haave the conn."

"How exciting!" Courtney exclaimed.

What a goose pull," Silva groused to Lawrence as they went out on the fo'c'sle, dodging confused, running younglings being chased by their instructors. About three times as many kids as would be required for the detail were clogged around the anchor hoist, probably wondering why they'd even been herded there since neither anchor was actually out.

"I don't know 'goose.' Is it like these younglings not kno'ing things us thought they did already?" Lawrence asked.

"Ah . . . sorta," Silva chuckled. "Actually, though, I ain't sure they don't know more about what we're doin' than us, just now. Remember, besides this bein' *Walker*'s first cruise as a school ship, it's Ronson's first command." He grinned. "Tabby's first time as XO too, an' *everbody's* figurin' out you can't do shit without a watch bill!" He paused, observing one of Bashear's Lemurian bosun's mates roaring at the gathering forward, pushing younglings into place. His lower lip protruded. "Then again, nothin' wrong with a crash course in 'Holy shit! We gotta DO somethin', no matter how confused we are!' I bet that's the big idea."

Silva's suspicion seemed to be confirmed when Tabby leaned out on the starboard bridgewing, ignoring all the chaos, and bellowed fore and aft, "Single up all lines!" Lemurians had a way of making their voices carry astonishing distances and she didn't need a speaking trumpet, at least while the ship was stationary.

Silva's grin got bigger. "C'mon," he said, heading aft. "Let's go throw our own wrench in the works!" Passing through the hatch on the front of the bridge structure, he continued on through the gaggle of kids running around like chickens, though most gave him a wide-eyed berth. "Up there, Larry." He pointed at the top of the amidships deckhouse gun platform where two of the ship's 4"-50s were mounted, one to port, the other starboard. Spotting the tall Black kid named Philan Bele towering uncertainly over the other younglings with an almost desperate look on his face, Silva laid a hand on his shoulder. "You like guns?" Silva shouted over the growing roar of the nearby blower.

"Uh . . . yes, Chief Silva."

"Swell. Round up some o' your pals that ain't doin' nothin' yet an' meet us on the number three gun, on the double!" Silva gave the lad a feral grin. "There's a League cruiser bearin' down!"

A panicked expression flashed across the youngster's face and he whipped his gaze out toward the mouth of the bay before realizing what Silva intended. "Aye, aye, Chief Silva!" he cried, cheeks burning at his own gullibility. Silva nodded, then sprinted up the stairs to the top of the platform.

Lawrence was already there, examining the weapon. "Looks good, Dennis," he said approvingly. "They . . . re'air all the da'age."

Silva was looking the gun over too. The last time he'd seen it, the mount was a wreck and all the recoil cylinders were shredded by shell fragments. "Looks good as new," Silva decided, taking a moment to gaze around the ship from their elevated position, watching the chaotic activity everywhere slowly coming under control. Planned or not, other division chiefs were doing the same as him, seemingly snatching groups of cadets at random and throwing them into impromptu tasks. Even as he and Lawrence watched, the starboard-side torpedo mount was slowly training out over the side, and Fred and Kari were waving and shouting unheard at another cluster of kids around the seaplane catapult.

Young Bele clattered up the stairs leading a pack of kids ranging in size from just shorter than him to a pair of female Lemurians who barely came up to Silva's belt. All wore determined expressions, however.

Silva sighed. "Jeez. What a nonsensulous aggregation. Who'd you bring with you, Cadet Belly? That's yer new name, by the way."

Another flash of embarrassment touched Bele's features, but he pointed at a tan boy near his own height with somewhat spiky dark hair. "Samuel Jenks. He's from here in the Empire, and is the son of . . ."

Silva stopped him. "I bet I know, an' don't give a shit. Welcome aboard, Sammy," he said, and it was the other boy's turn to blush.

Philan Bele went on to name the other kids he knew: male and female Union 'Cats called Kaan-Dis-Ar and Haan-Ara, who Silva promptly dubbed "Candy" and "Hanna." Then there was another Imperial named Daniel Baker and a female human from the Union, actually an "expat Impie gal," named Susan Raj, who quickly became "Danny Boy" and "Susie." Bele didn't know the others who'd followed him, but they provided their own names, all of which were whimsically changed or modified. Finally, the smallest of the 'Cats, a female from the Filpin Lands, proudly identified herself as Maarik-Fas. Silva was pretty sure he knew her kin as well, but immediately christened her "Monkey Fish." To everyone's surprise, she actually "kakked" a laugh and clapped her hands with glee. "I haave a Naavy nickname!" she said, blinking rapidly, tail swishing with pleasure.

Lawrence gaped at her, jaw hanging slightly open, then said somewhat apologetically to the other kids. "He all'ays calls things di'rent than they are. He . . . can't not do it."

"You're one to talk," Silva replied airily. "You can't even say your *own name* right."

"Can too. *Laa'rence*," he said defiantly.

"Just call him 'Chief Larry,'" Silva instructed his audience. "He ain't really chief o' nothin', except bein' a pain in my ass an' the most Grikish-lookin' critter aboard. Helluva fighter, though," he added truthfully. "But he likes it, an' it'll prob'ly keep him from eatin' ya."

The youngsters exchanged uneasy glances when Lawrence opened his mouth to object, displaying all his frightening teeth, but he was interrupted by Tabby's voice blasting back from the bridgewing: "Take in the stern lines!"

Almost immediately, the deck under their feet started to shudder and Silva and his new students turned to face aft. "Rudder'll be hard left, now," he explained. "Port screw's windin' up, its thrust aimed at the dock, pushin' the stern away." Even as they watched, dirty brown water churned under the port propeller guard and *Walker*'s low, cramped stern did indeed begin to shift. Silva grasped a stanchion and turned to Lawrence, beaming. "The old girl's back to life, little buddy." There was genuine emotion in his voice and his good eye looked a little moist. Cheers erupted on the dock, where a larger crowd had gathered to see them off, many of them relatives of the young cadets, waving tearfully. "I'll swan," Silva murmured.

Gunny Horn and Abel Cook had joined them, followed by another pack of younglings. "I saw what you were doing up here and it looked good to me," Horn said. "Kind of silly to add to the chaos by assembling the Marines at this point, so I'll run these kids through a drill on the number two gun, to port."

Silva waved at him. "Goddamn, Arnie. Just quit talkin' a second, will ya? You're ruinin' the moment."

"Goddamn!" Petey squawked scornfully at the Marine.

With the old destroyer's stern now angled about thirty degrees away from the dock, the port engine stopped and the rudder centered up.

"Take in the bow line," Tabby shouted forward, still quite audible. Moments later, the deck rumbled again when both screws bit, easing the ship aft. When she'd backed a safe distance, a little rudder started twisting her tail back to port while the turbines stilled once again. Then, after she'd drifted around parallel with the dock, about a hundred yards out, the rudder swung to the right and the turbines spun up. There was just the slightest groan in the fibers of the ship, a far cry from her previous rattling gasp as her sternway was arrested, and she began moving forward and away from her berth. Very quickly, the stern was crouching down and the water of the harbor was curling away from the long, narrow length of the hull and peeling off into a wide, frothing V.

Silva was grinning like a kid, the rising breeze whipping past his damaged, weathered face. "Damn! I've missed this ol' bucket."

Horn cleared his throat. "Yeah, I get it, but this ain't a pleasure cruise."

Silva nodded but retorted, "Speak fer yerself." Turning to the tall Black cadet from the Republic, he pointed at the number three gun and barked, "Are you familiar with this weapon, Cadet Belly?"

"Yes, Chief Silva. We trained on one at the scholla."

"Swell. You're gun cap'n. Throw a crew together an' show me what you got for a combat drill in local control." He ostentatiously peered out to starboard, choosing an imaginary enemy. "Make it snappy, though. See that little fishin' boat headin' for the mouth o' the bay? *That's* the League cruiser, an' it's barely fifteen thousand yards!"

With that, Silva and Lawrence simply stepped back to watch. Bele looked a little hesitant for a moment, but his expression quickly firmed when Silva made a "get on with it" motion, and Bele began placing his fellow cadets in the various positions around the gun. Not surprisingly, he put "Sammy," the second tallest, in the pointer's "bicycle" seat on one side of the gun but didn't interfere when the shortest, "Monkey Fish," determinedly snatched a life vest and threw it on the trainer's seat and hopped up on it, quickly testing how freely the windage wheel turned. Though it was usually the pointer's job, Silva wondered how she'd stomp the foot pedal "trigger" with her short legs if the need arose. Bele seemed to hesitate again. "There are no sights," he said simply. "Should I appoint sight setters?"

Silva waved. "Up to you. That's always best, o' course, but believe it or not, *glass* telescopic sights get damaged from time to time." There was just a hint of sarcasm in his tone. "An' sometimes you flat don't have time to adjust 'em proper even if you got 'em, so the whole pointer, trainer, sight setter team has to learn ta calculate windage an' elevation on their own an' shoot from the hip."

Bele frowned. "That's not what we were taught."

Silva blinked. "What *were* you taught?"

Monkey Fish spoke up. "Our instructors pounded it into us thaat pointers and trainers must *never* deviate from the laateral or verticaal sight adjustment made by the setter."

Silva mockingly clapped his hands. "Very good. Right out'a the manual. But there's fire an' iron flyin' through the air an' nothin' but blood spatter where yer sight setter stood. You ain't even got a splinter shield on this gun. You gonna stop fightin'? Call time out an' wander around in circles with yer thumb up yer ass? You can get mighty dead that way, an' so can yer ship an' all yer pals. I seen it," he added darkly, then arched the brow over his good eye at Bele. "So, what're you gonna do, *gun cap'n*? Fight with what you got, or stand around waitin' for what you don't?"

Bele quickly directed the others to those positions he could fill with their limited numbers, doing away with the shell man and other handlers, then paused and regarded Silva with the slightest upturn of his lips. "The number three gun is as ready as I can make it, under the circumstances," he formally reported, "but I have no choice but to wait for *one* thing I don't have." Silva cocked his head to the side and Bele continued. "Without ammunition, should I proceed to engage the fishing boat/cruiser with simulated sounds and harsh language?"

Silva laughed out loud. So did Lawrence, in his weird scratchy way. Even Petey imitated the sound, whether he had any idea why or not. Gunny Horn glared across the deck from where he'd begun performing more formal instruction and Dennis Silva laughed even louder. "Yep, yer Prefect Bele's boy, all right." He motioned the youngster to carry on. "Leave the harsh language to us geezers fer now, for appearance's sake. Just say, 'Boom!' when yer pertendin' ta shoot."

Released from the dry dock where she'd been virtually rebuilt from scrap, then unbound from the pier where she'd been lovingly and painstakingly lavished with all new and rebuilt equipment during her lengthy fitting out, USS *Walker* rapidly picked up speed, steering for the mouth of the harbor and the wide, mysterious sea beyond.

CHAPTER 6

RESPITE ISLAND
***USS* SCOTT**

The hull hadn't been significantly damaged by *Scott*'s collision with what turned out to be a steel cargo crane on a sunken vessel of some kind. *Scott* was Lemurian-built, the last class "frontline" wooden-hulled warships built in Baalkpan and Austraal, and even with her classic late nineteenth-century lines, her purely Lemurian diagonally reinforced and cross-laminated construction made her a very tough ship. Her masts, spars, and rigging did suffer extensively, however, and her surviving crew, now prisoners in their own ship, labored at gunpoint to make essential repairs. That required that she linger in the vast lagoon with its amazing occupants longer than the traitor, Mr. Ames, was happy with, and he grew increasingly short-tempered. There was nothing the prisoners could do; they were all working as hard as they could, but they did get a very good look at the wonders on display—not that they could do anything about that either. One mystery was solved, at least. Two of the missing ships they'd searched for were lying at anchor, also in the custody of their League-Dom captors, and both their small crews had been moved to *Scott* to make them all easier for their outnumbered guards to watch.

Neither of those ships had wireless sets, however, and Ames hadn't been able to report having had to take USS *Scott* and the significance of a Navy Clan ship, reserve or not, in this place. The third missing ship, also captured, had departed for a League "base" somewhere a few weeks before. No matter how savagely Ames ranted, nothing could be done for *Scott*'s wireless set either, hopelessly smashed when the falling aerial yanked it across the comm shack and shattered more vacuum tubes than they had replacements for. Eventually, with a minimal sailing rig restored (*Scott* wouldn't have the range on her engine alone), she hoisted her anchor and made for Respite Island to secure supplies for more comprehensive repairs—and wireless parts in particular, if available.

Now, with *Scott* lying at anchor within the complex barrier reef at Respite, the ship's new commander had gone ashore to dine with Governor Radcliff, as was expected, and spin a tale of tragedy and disaster. He'd relate how *Scott* never found a trace of the missing ships and was herself nearly wrecked on an unsuspected shoal, the falling debris sadly crushing her captain and other senior officers on deck. He'd also do his best to discourage any further search of the bleak, "empty" region.

The sailors remaining loyal to the Grand Alliance had been required to work the ship but were now secured in the dank cable tier up forward on the orlop deck. With *Scott*'s bulky cargo still aboard, there was no space for them in the hold. Packed in with the mildewing cable like grawfish, they felt the motion and heard the sounds of the vessel being warped in alongside the fueling pier and taking on supplies, water, and the spare masts and spars required to restore her rig. Even at the height of the war, Respite was somewhat out of the way and was never a really busy port. No other ship was waiting now and there'd been no reason to shift away from the pier, but Ames had *Scott* hauled back out over her anchor to remove any temptation for her people to escape. That was practically impossible for the nearly thirty men and 'Cats, including surviving crew from the other ships, with only a single oil lamp for light and the hawsehole for the anchor cable for fresh air.

It might not be impossible for one of them, though.

"Now's our only chance, lads," murmured Lieutenant Jun-Soraat in his careful English. The Lemurian from the Republic was the only officer left and spoke quietly in case anyone was listening beyond the locked door that kept them confined.

"Aye," agreed Chief Allen, looking at Fen with a mix of fondness and hope.

"*What* chance?" Waldo scoffed bitterly but quietly. Fen's friend wasn't taking any better to captivity than anyone. "How are we going to get out of here?"

"*We* aren't," said Jun.

Allen nodded at Fen. "Sometimes bein' small is an asset. Only a nipper his size'll squeeze through the hawsehole. If he makes it ashore, he can warn the guv'nor, maybe even fetch assistance quick enough tae rescue the rest of us."

Fen felt a thrill at the chance to do something to save his friends. No one believed their captors would let them live when their usefulness was at an end. His excitement was quickly followed by horror, however. "The fish will get me!" he objected. Everywhere he'd ever been, ever heard of, nothing could survive the voracious flasher fish in the water for more than a few moments. He thought he might fit through the hawse, but the fish would surely eat him.

Jun was shaking his head, blinking and smiling. "That's just the thing," he said, "they won't."

"He's right, lad," Allen assured. "I've been here to Respite many times, an' this anchorage—inside the reef, mind—is the only place in all the world where flashies are few enough that a man can actually survive in the water."

Another sailor, off one of the other ships, was nodding. "He's right. I'm from here me'sef. Flashies avoid the fierce surf o' the reef."

"Aye," agreed another man. "Once when I was here, me an' me mates played in the shallows like fishies." He snorted. "Strangest-seemin' thing I ever done!"

The first man looked over at Allen before glancing back at Fen. "'Course, we'll haf'tae *float* the wee bugger with somethin'. I don't reckon 'e's ever learned tae swim. Who would?"

It was a tight fit and Fen nearly panicked, thinking he was stuck at one point, but naked and slick with foamy Lemurian sweat, he finally squeezed past the coarse anchor cable in the hawsehole and almost popped out the other side. Then he *did* panic because he almost fell in the water below before his tail wrapped desperately around the cable and his clawlike fingernails dug in. Gasping, he just hung there a moment.

"Go on, Fen," Allen softly encouraged him through the hole. "I know it don't seem natural, but it's safe as can be. Me word on it, lad. Here. I'm pokin' yer britches through after ye. Don't drop 'em. They're all ye'll have tae float ye."

Someone had come up with the notion of tying knots in Fen's pants legs, suggesting they'd float him if he grasped the open end. He imagined that was so. It was a lot more believable than what they told him about flashies in the bay. But why would they lie to him? Their fate was tied to his and he was pretty sure they liked him.

Reaching up behind him, he firmly grasped the breeches and managed a shaky reply. "I'm going," he assured them. "Just give me a minute, will ya? I've never been in 'wild' waater before!" All Lemurians bathed, almost religiously. Their sweat dried stiff and uncomfortable in their fur. They habitually used tubs, however, or running water showers, and were warned against "wild" water from infancy. Fen supposed all people were. He'd occasionally bathed in the sea alongside the ship if a sail was sunk in it, supported by a boom with a weight in the center. That was actually considered somewhat adventurous. Most often, they were hosed down on deck with water pumped—and by definition, somewhat filtered—from the sea. He'd never imagined voluntarily getting in unprotected water, however.

"Very well," came Lieutenant Jun's comforting voice. "Take your time, within reason. Aand don't splaash about. Aafter you're in the waater and supported by your breeches, point yourself at the pier and start kicking. Try to keep your kicking underwater if you caan."

"I'll try," Fen replied, beginning to creep down the slanting cable. "Maker," he muttered to himself, "I don't waant to die. An' I *really* don't waant to get eaten!"

Just a few feet over the water, Fen finally allowed his tail to uncoil and turned around. Grasping his breeches in his left hand, still tightly clutching the cable with his right, he looked back up the way he came. Someone was still watching him, blocking the meager light of the lamp through the hole he squeezed through. He was breathing fast, probably loud enough to be heard by anyone on watch on the fo'c'sle above, but he couldn't help it. It was almost pitch-dark. There was no moon and only a few lights marked nearby ships. There were a couple of relatively bright lanterns on the dock, but even with Fen's excellent night vision, only reflected starlight revealed the black surface of the water.

"Maker protect me," he prayed once again before letting the cable slide through his hand, lowering him slowly into the warm salty sea. Warm or not, he shivered with terror as water lapped up to his chin, expecting the first agonizing bite at any instant. He wouldn't survive but a handful of them. He'd never yet witnessed a sea battle and the horrors people faced when their ship went down in seas already baited with blood, but he'd heard stories. And he'd seen plenty of flasher fish, of course, with their terrible teeth and jaws. Everyone, his people included, caught and ate the things themselves. But he'd personally watched the frantically roiling water when offal of any sort was cast into it, and he knew the cause.

His tightly woven canvas breeches were bobbing beside him, the upper legs just above the deep V-cut for his tail holding air like he'd been told, and nothing had bitten him so far. *Maybe the locals spoke the truth?* he thought, with the first hint of relief. Still, it took a supreme effort of will to release the anchor cable and float free. Clutching his breeches with both hands, close to his face, he turned toward the dock and began gently kicking his feet. Right at water level, his objective looked farther than it had and he could see the boat that Ames had taken ashore. He noted with alarm that a couple of men had remained with it, talking to another man above them on the dock, probably a guard or watchman. Busy or not, the fueling pier and warehouses and tank batteries behind it needed *someone* to keep an eye on it all.

Fen couldn't just go over there, though. The man on the dock might be sympathetic—or not. *He could be another traitor,* Fen realized. *Even if he isn't, there's only one of him.* Looking from side to side, he turned a little away, toward a darker area of the dock, and started kicking harder. Even then, his progress seemed excruciatingly slow and he began to wonder if he was fighting the tide. *Tide or not, I'm not made for swimming,* he thought adamantly. Still, he *was* making progress, nothing had eaten him yet, and he urged himself onward to where he dimly saw a line tied to a cleat on the dock trailing off into the water.

A new sound came to him over his suppressed but still heavy breathing and he saw a small freight wagon drawn by a pair of honking burros pull up to the dock. A figure jumped down and strode out onto the timbers, bootsteps sounding loudly.

"How is the tide?" a voice asked the lone watchman. With another thrill of fear, Fen recognized it as Mr. Ames.

"Ebbin' soon, sur," replied the man he addressed.

"Are my boatmen still present?" Ames asked. "Or have they run off to the alehouse?"

The other man chuckled and tilted his head toward the water below. "No, sur. Both still here. We just been gabbin' an' passin' the time. You still plannin' on sailin' tomorrow?"

"Aye," Ames agreed, stepping closer to the man and casting his gaze about. His eyes passed right over Fen but never saw him in the gloom.

"Ain't steamers wonderful things, sur?" asked the man, somewhat wistfully. "Ye can sail whenever ye like, no matter the tide, nor even the wind."

"Quite amazing," Ames agreed, just before casually pulling a knotted line from a pocket of his boat coat. As quick as the peck of a lizardbird, he whipped it around the watchman's neck and wrenched it savagely tight. One of his men scrambled up from the boat and helped choke the life from the watchman, twisting him around while Ames leaned away, garrote over his shoulder, actually lifting the poor, flailing man off his feet. "I believe we'll be using the tide after all," Ames said, voice slightly strained but still conversational. "We have to sail at once," he continued, obviously to his companion now. "That damned old man, Governor Radcliff, is sharper than you'd think at first. I don't think he quite bought my story. I expect we'll have visitors before morning. Best if we're already gone."

"They'll squeal like a dragon with a broken tooth," the other man warned, "an' they'll be at us from the air with the dawn. They have a few flyin' machines, y'know."

"Not many," Ames said confidently, "and I've already insured they'll be taken care of by local . . . friends."

Fen was concerned about the reference to "friends" but didn't know what the rest of that was about. He'd made it up under the dock, now hanging from the dangling line, and there he waited nervously while the traitors quietly lowered the body of the watchman into the water. That done, they descended into the boat and shoved off, rowing briskly back to *Scott.* Fen remained just as anxious to get out of the water as he'd been since he got in, but couldn't risk discovery now. He felt confident no one would catch him even if they saw him, but as casually as Ames murdered the watchman, Fen feared he'd react violently toward his comrades if his escape was quickly discovered. He'd certainly accelerate his departure, and Fen hoped to rouse a rescue and recapture *Scott* before she set sail. Still out of the light of the lanterns, as soon as he judged the boat far enough that he wouldn't be seen, he climbed up on the dock and scuttled into even deeper shadows before starting to unpick the knots in his breeches.

He might as well have run naked. Though Lemurians were uncommon on Respite (ironically far more so than their small, apparent 'cat' cousins that jumped ship from the earliest Imperial visitors) and as likely to draw as much attention naked as clad, there wasn't anyone around to see him on this stretch of dock. From a practical standpoint, without the belt he'd forgotten, his wet breeches kept falling down and slowing his progress. Bare feet flapping on the cobbles on the road beyond the warehouses and tank batteries, he finally managed to catch up with the only person he saw: the man driving the very wagon that returned Ames to the ship.

"Wait!" Fen cried. "Wait!" he repeated louder when there was no response.

The man on the wagon seat drew in his reins and the burros brayed indignantly. "Who's out there callin' at me? Show yerself, damn ye. I'm armed!" cried the driver.

Fen ran up alongside the wagon, prepared to sprint away. Frightened as he was, Ames's reference to "friends" wouldn't allow him to dismiss the possibility this man was a traitor as well. He'd already claimed he was armed.

"My name is Fen-An-Raar, of the Reserve Union Steamer USS *Scott.* I pray you're a loyaal subject of the Empire because the maan you delivered at the dock was not!" Fen gasped out. "I swear thaat if you're in league with him, I'll see you haanged!"

The driver was older and somewhat portly, with a beard the same color as his burros. If the shock he exhibited at the sight of a soaking wet Lemurian shouting accusations of treason wasn't genuine, he was the greatest actor in the world. "The hell you say!" he bellowed in protest. "An' what the hell are *you* doin' out here, sneakin' in the dark an' scarin' water out o' peaceful folk earnin' a few coins on a fare?" He narrowed his eyes. "Yer one o' them 'Cat critters, ain't ye? A Laroomian! Who the hell're you tae speak tae me like ye done?" he demanded, hotly glowering.

Fen caught his breath. "My aapologies, sir," he offered quickly. "But your recent fare is an enemy agent who haas taken control of our ship, USS *Scott*. Her crew are all prisoners aboard her. I escaped by swimming ashore. We must inform Governor Raadcliff at once! They're going to sail tonight and we'll lose our chaance to rescue my friends."

"Take ye tae the guv'nor," the man grouched doubtfully, looking Fen up and down. "Ye look like a fur clot in a drain." He took a deep breath. "But that don't matter if yer tellin' the truth, I reckon. Hop up here beside me, but keep yer distance. I don't need a soakin'—an' by God, ye smell like wet death!" His eyes went wide as Fen hopped up and settled on the bench. "Worse every instant!" he exclaimed, leaning away from the young wet Lemurian, who was blinking embarrassment.

"I aapologize again," Fen said. "My comraades and I have not been able to maintain our customary hygiene."

"Aye, weel, p'raps the guv'nor'll at least pay the fare for another trip up the hill tae the palace." He spanked the burros with his reins and they roared their displeasure. "Gotta feed these grumpy buggers."

What was only a couple of miles as the lizardbird flew took the teamster's burros the better part of an hour to heave his cart back up the long, winding, often switchback road to the governor's palace near the summit of the highest point on the island. Increasingly impatient, Fen was repeatedly tempted to jump down and run the distance himself, but considering his half-starved condition, he doubted he'd make it any quicker. Then, when they finally arrived, it was only the relative rarity of Lemurians on Respite and Fen's anxious insistence (and obvious harmlessness) that gained him admittance to the "palace" (more like a large, comfortable villa), under escort by dubious guards. An elderly gentleman in a surprisingly colorful housecoat and slippers, identified simply as the governor's factor, launched a rapid-fire, skeptical interrogation of the bedraggled young Lemurian but was almost immediately usurped by a short, broad, energetic older woman with iron-gray hair. She'd boisterously appeared wrapped in a voluminous, shapeless robe while Fen was retelling his tale once again.

"I have him, Mr. Jacobs," she insisted. "It sounds as though there are venomous fiends on the loose in our midst."

"You *believe* this nonsense, my lady?" the factor asked, surprised.

The woman glared at him. "Of course I do! *Look* at the poor little thing! How many starving, destitute Lemurians do *you* know of, lurking about on our island? It's quite obvious he has suffered—and what could he possibly hope to gain by bearing a false tale to us here, at this time of night? I would thank you to alert the guard commander at once! That ship must *not* sail."

What appeared to be servants were beginning to arrive, and she directed them to ensure that "Mr. Radcliff" had managed to "wake himself entirely" and bring blankets and refreshments to the parlor. Finally resting her gaze on Fen, she conjured a strained smile in spite of the damp stench he'd brought with him. "Come, my dear. My name is Emelia Radcliff, and we shall make ourselves more comfortable while you deliver your message to me and my husband, the governor. He will be along momentarily, I'm sure. He had just gone to sleep, you see, and is quite the lethargic riser no matter what time it is."

Wrapped in a blanket, likely more to protect the furniture from him than anything else since he was now practically dry, Fen had ravenously gorged himself from a tray of things he hardly even looked at while Emelia Radcliff looked on and tutted. Now he was drinking tea, holding the cup with shaking hands and just beginning to realize he was free and safe when Governor Radcliff stepped into the parlor. The governor's equally shapeless robe left him matching his wife in dress as well as general shape. He was a little taller, however, with lighter skin and pure white hair. His smile was just as welcoming and solicitous as his wife's, though his keenly intelligent eyes reflected more anxiety.

"Good evening, young . . . fellow," he greeted, moving straight for a tray of brandy glasses a servant had poured. Fen had politely declined an offered glass and suspected no one had any idea how young he was. "No, don't stand," Radcliff commanded as Fen moved to do so. "Mr. Jacobs briefed me on your tale while I dressed and, um, revived myself. You must be quite exhausted. Dreadful! Dreadful! An Alliance ship and all her people in the hands of our enemies!" He looked at his wife. "And to think we hosted the fiendish architect of this atrocity here in our very home!" He shook his head. "I wasn't impressed with the man and suspected some sort of strangeness associated with his story. Remarkably convenient that he was the only remaining officer," he muttered, "and why not allow his people ashore and perform his repairs here?" He shook his head. "Quite obvious now."

"I disliked him immediately!" Emelia proclaimed. "His table manners were atrocious, his conversation dull and evasive."

"Quite right, my dear," the governor conceded. "You suspected him of something nefarious at once. I *saw* you do so, heard it in your tone. I planned to have the guard visit his ship in the morning."

"Yes sir," Fen said, leaning forward. "He—Ames—guessed you would. I heard him tell one of his men thaat they must sail without delaay." He paused, then added, "This just after they killed a maan on the dock. A waatchmaan, I think."

Radcliff frowned back at Emelia. "Despicable. Well, orders have been sent to the guard, and the harbor patrol is alerted as well." He sighed. "I only hope we're not too late. The one disadvantage to living at the top of this lovely mountain is we're so distant from the heart of the city and the bay. Ordinarily, I consider that an advantage. And the daily drive down and back is so relaxing. Sometimes I ride, which is quite exhilarating and good for the constitution!" Emelia cleared her throat and the governor caught himself. "Your pardon," he said. "I'm amazingly easily distracted these days. We do have a telegraph now, of course, an operator here on the grounds, but . . ." He held out his hands. "The warning was quickly sent, but we don't exactly practice for situations like this and I fear the response will be somewhat . . . disorganized. How I *wish* we had a few Imperial or Navy Clan ships in port!"

Fen stood; he couldn't stop himself. "Sir," he said earnestly, "it is of the *utmost* importaance that *Scott* be stopped from sailing. I told you about our caapture and the people aboard, the faact the culprits serve our enemies in the League . . . But I haaven't yet told you whaat we *found*, whaat Ames and the League will do anything to keep us from reporting—and they'll surely use against us if they caan!"

Windows in the wall separating the parlor from the veranda overlooking the beautiful bay a couple of miles and roughly a thousand feet below suddenly shuddered, accompanied by a dull, rumbling roar. Governor Radcliff and his wife stood and paced quickly to the largest window and gazed down at the city by the bay, quickly followed by Fen and a pair of servants, Fen still clutching the blanket around himself.

"The harbormaster's office!" the governor gasped. "My God, they've blown it up!"

The blast that destroyed the rather large building near the center of the dockyard at the edge of the city had left a billowing cloud of firelit smoke and dust roiling up in the night. Just then, they saw a jet of fire out on the water that briefly illuminated the source: what was unmistakably the single 4″-50 gun mounted near the bow of the suddenly malevolent shape of USS *Scott*, steaming for the convoluted, reef-tangled mouth of the bay. The gun could only have fired at something else in the darkness. That "something" quickly revealed itself when five orange flowers of flame lit up the side of a small two-masted ship, one of a pair of harbor patrol vessels that doubled as pilot ships when visitors needed to be led through the reef. This one was a swift little brig, armed with ten muzzle-loading 6pdrs, which she'd just unleashed on her attacker.

Another flash lit the night farther down the dock, erupting in the midst of a cluster of small floatplanes bobbing in the water. A nearby gasoline tank exploded as well, pouring flaming fuel into the water among the floating planes. A second bright spear of fire lit *Scott*'s deck and a reddish light snapped to life against the side of the little brig. An instant later, the gallant little ship's powder stores must've been ignited because a brilliant yellow-white flare scattered the patrol vessel across the bay.

"They're escaping," Fen breathed.

"Quite boldly and murderously so," Governor Radcliff grimly agreed.

Fen looked at him. "We must send out waarning at once! Caall any Navy ships in the area down on them!"

Radcliff shook his head. "That's quite impossible, I fear. First, with the League demonstrations around the Azores, little remains remotely close enough to reach us in time to find them. Second, and most insurmountable," he ground out, "the wireless communication office shared the harbormaster's building."

Fen looked at him and blinked. "But . . . the aerial maast stands atop this very mountain! I saw it when we came through before. I assumed you had a traansmitter here."

Radcliff ruefully shook his head, with another sidelong glance at his wife. He cleared his throat. "Such an assumption is entirely understandable, since we *do* have a telegraph and a small team of operators here, as I said," he sighed. "But all these electrical wonders are very new to us. The telegraph was longer established, and we would send messages down the mountain by wire to the transmitter, which is connected to the aerial up here . . ." He raked his white hair back with his fingers. "Mrs. Radcliff has quite often suggested . . ."

"*Quite* often," Emelia inserted emphatically.

"Yes. Well. She has frequently proposed that we acquire exactly that sort of additional apparatus necessary to equip the palace telegraph office with a wireless transmitter of its own. I can assure you that we shall do so now," he added resolutely.

"But . . ." Fen began, astonished. "You mean there is *no* other wireless traansmitter on the *entire island*? How soon will we be able to reestaablish communications with the rest of the Alliaance?"

Governor Radcliff had to think about that. "It's always possible a suitably equipped ship will suddenly arrive, unexpected. Otherwise, it will be perhaps a week before the monthly Clipper flies down on its regular run."

Still stunned, Fen pressed. "But won't anyone notice when there's no word from here for thaat long?"

Now Emelia looked a little uncomfortable. "Perhaps," she said, "but one of the things we Respitans love most about our lovely little island is precisely how isolated it's always been from, well, everyone. I shouldn't be too terribly surprised if our silence didn't excite much concern for a while."

CHAPTER 7

USS WALKER

The little blue-and-white floatplane rolled inverted and dove at the ship steaming at high speed down below. With its five-cylinder radial bawling and the wood-and-fabric airframe thumping and rattling as it picked up speed as well, the plane's nose began bobbing slightly as if sniffing to determine the best angle of attack, or indeed predict what evasive maneuvers the target would make in the coming seconds. And truth be known, there actually were a discouraging number of seconds for the ship to evade the attack. Regardless of the skill of the pilot, slow, relatively obsolete seaplanes made suboptimal dive bombers, especially when their strike was fully expected, in daylight. Skill—or luck—could always crack the odds, however, and just as the suddenly sprinting target heeled sharply to starboard and the roaring seaplane flared out of its steep dive, pulling up and away, a dark object tumbled free from under the single broad overhead wing and swiftly plummeted down. A roiling gray cloud erupted on the deck right behind the racing ship's bridge, and machine guns opened up on command, sending tracers chasing the fleeing low-flying attacker.

"Goddammit!" roared Chief Bosun's Mate Carl Bashear, voice almost cracking with fury as the "smoke" from the "bomb" streamed over him. "Look at the mess they made of my topsides!" he bellowed, coughing now.

"Cease firing!" Silva shouted at his cluster of defenders on the amidships gun platform where they'd been feeding and firing three faithful copies of M1919 water-cooled .30 caliber Browning machine guns mounted on rail pintles. The weapons quickly chattered to a smoking stop. He coughed as well and rubbed his eye when the rapidly diminishing plume swept across him and his charges. It wasn't really smoke of course, nor had an actual bomb struck the ship. What Fred Reynolds and Kari-Faask quite definitively hit them with, dropped from their "Nancy" floatplane, was nothing more lethal than a canvas mattress cover filled with charcoal ashes from the galley stove that ruptured on impact. It's possible it could've hurt somebody if it landed right on them, but injuries do happen in training. Far more dangerous had been the real bullets fired from the machine guns in response, but these were directed at a target sleeve the Nancy was towing a considerable distance behind.

Brushing ash off his arms, Silva shook his head. "That would'a took out the forward fireroom, maybe the bridge. Might've even sunk us."

"We couldn't stop it," Philan Bele defended. In the week since they steamed out of Scapa Flow, he'd assumed increasing moral authority over firming up the "gunnery division," and though he hadn't been shooting himself, he was speaking up for the other kids who looked to him for leadership. "We couldn't shoot until you told us, and all we had were thirty cals anyway."

Silva took off his hat and whupped it against his leg to knock the ash off, watching as Carl Bashear directed "damage control," making up all kinds of terrible scenarios for the kids to cope with. He would've done that whether the ash bomb hit or not, but his voice likely held more authentic fury than it would have if it missed.

Abel Cook had been watching the drill and now said, "You couldn't very well shoot at the aircraft as it attacked." He smiled. "And the actual hit will be on the head of whoever was conning the ship. Your gun's crews showed acceptable proficiency, in my view, and will be judged on whether there are any holes in the target sleeve or not."

"Holes," said Petey, seeming to agree, voice very solemn.

They were currently steaming on the numbers three and four boilers, which vented their exhaust into the aft two funnels, but a deep hollow roar whooshed up from within both forward stacks and a gout of steam propelled a thick black cloud of soot from their tops. In spite of their speed, there was a following wind and much of the soot settled heavily on the deck.

"God a'mighty," Silva guffawed, even as Bashear raised his voice in renewed fury: "Oh, that creepy little bastard!"

"Looks like you'll need a damage-control party down in the forward firerooms, Carl!" Silva called gleefully down to Bashear.

"What haappened, Chief Silvaa?" asked Maarik-Fas, who Silva had called "Monkey Fish" until he realized it didn't bother her. Now he just used her real name, but she'd been one of the 'Cats actually on a gun.

"I never seen it myself, but maybe ol' Isak *does* have a sense o' humor after all—that, or he's genuinely pissed that somebody let a bomb of any sort hit where it would'a clobbered one o' his be-loved boilers." He snickered. "Bet he heard it hit, or somebody told him right quick. Either way, he blew tubes in the forward boilers, which"—he waved—"does what you seen."

"I'd say he was simulating damage while registering his discontent," Abel agreed.

"Well, he's started it now," Silva said solemnly, gesturing down at Carl Bashear, who was already sending a runner toward the bridge as he hastily assembled another detail.

"'At's he going to do?" Lawrence asked.

"Same thing *I'd* do, I bet." Silva grinned. "Declare a casualty in the aft firerooms an' shut down Isak's fuel from the deck valve. Starve the lit boilers."

Abel was shaking his head. "I'm beginning to wonder who the children on this ship really are."

"Gotta teach these kiddies the *important* shit too," Silva piously declared, "like the holy an' immemory-able tradition o' rivalry 'tween deck apes an' snipes!" He waved over at Gunny Horn and Ian Miles, who were supervising gunners on the port rail. Fred and Kari's plane had one more "bomb" and it would approach from that side next. "Hadn't even got started on *Marines* yet."

"Children," Abel repeated with a sigh.

"I never thought we'd be flyin' around *aaskin'* ta get shot aat!" Kari-Faask shouted indignantly through the intercom connecting her rear observer/copilot position to Fred Reynolds's seat up forward. It was a lot easier to talk than it used to be, when they had to shout at each other through a speaking tube, and that with the little plane's center-mounted engine on the wing up above and between them. Their plane had a few of the advancements made during the war and wasn't one of the very earliest models with an in-line liquid-cooled engine, but it certainly wasn't one of the newest. Not only were the latest models still in service, Fred and Kari believed they had more to go wrong with them. True or not, they'd gotten a good deal on this aircraft, still new in the crate, and secured an agreement that if something happened to it (not a long shot by any means, considering how many planes they wrecked during the war), it would be replaced.

"It *is* a little weird," Fred agreed philosophically as he urged the plane to climb against the drag of the long sheer fabric sleeve it was towing. Much like a giant wind sock, the thing wasn't heavy but there was a lot of surface area exacting a stiff penalty. "Just be glad we're not towing a target raft behind the motor launch for the big guns to shoot at! Does it look like anybody hit the sleeve?" he asked.

Kari squirmed around to look behind them before dropping heavily back in her wicker seat. "How the hell aam I supposed to tell?" she demanded. "It's still baack there, so they didn't shoot it apaart."

"Well . . . we gotta give 'em a couple more chances. Who knows how they'll tell who *did* hit it—if they do." Struggling higher, Fred looked around, taking in the view. The sky was a clear, gentle blue, with only the slightest hints of white streaks here and there, and the horizon was sharply defined by the deep purple sea all around. Utterly alone upon it, for as far as Fred could see, the narrow blue-and-haze-gray shape of USS *Walker* steamed boldly along, drawing a frothy silvery-white line with her wake. It stirred his heart to see the old ship he loved so much, that he'd grown into a man aboard, moving with such apparent good health and vigor. Especially since the last time he had this view of her, she'd been a creeping, smoldering wreck. He suspected Kari felt the same. "Hold on," Fred told her. "Here we go again!"

They weren't as high as they'd been on the previous dive and Fred was approaching from the port quarter as if to make a glide bombing attack. He'd never do such a silly thing for real, of course, and they'd probably never even make it to the release point if they were taking fire on the run in, but this exercise was as much for the bridge crew as the gunners, teaching them how to maneuver the ship under attack from the air.

"Get ready, Kari!" he shouted. She'd be the one to actually drop the ash bomb on his command, and he intended to peel back away to port so the gunners on that side would have a chance at the target as well. The wind whipped over him, around the small glass windscreen in front of his cockpit, as the shallow dive finally allowed the little Nancy to reach something near her usual cruising speed. Aiming a little forward of the bridge on his angling approach, he thought he saw the ship start to twist her tail a little and begin to turn away.

"Wrong again," he muttered to himself with a small predatory smile. He and Kari had seen the black smoke of the boilers blowing tubes after the first "hit" and knew if they managed another one, Chief Bosun Carl Bashear would probably have a stroke. As always, everything seemed to speed up the closer they came to the target, and just a few hundred feet up and outboard, he shouted at Kari to "drop!" An instant later, he felt the weight of their "weapon" fall away and snatched the stick and kicked the rudder left, almost sliding into his turn. Nancys weren't known for their speed but could be improbably maneuverable in experienced hands. For just an instant, the target sleeve seemed to pause in midair before whipping after the plane once more, almost directly away from the ship.

Kari was squirming in her seat again to watch the sack of ashes arc down. "Daamn! We miss! But *near* miss, right alongside. We would'a opened seams . . . Wait, whaat the hell?"

Fred felt the rudder pedals buck under his feet and the stick jerked in his hand.

"Muzzle flaashes! Muzzle flaashes! They shoot too soon!" Kari screeched.

"I think they *hit* us!" Fred shouted back.

"Yaah!" Kari roared furiously. "They shoot the goddaamn *tail* haaff off!" Like that of many Lemurians, Kari's otherwise excellent English bent a little when she got excited—or enraged.

Fred craned his head around to look for himself and saw shredded streamers of the red-and-white-striped fabric that covered the control surfaces whipping behind them. "Shit," he said, before redirecting his attention forward, gently experimenting with the rudder and elevator. The plane seemed to obey, but the response was mushy. "Jettison the target. We don't need anybody *else* shooting at us and I want it off our back. As soon as you do that, get on the horn and declare an emergency. I still have some control and I'm setting us down right now while I do."

The wounded aircraft leaped forward when the target sleeve fluttered away, but it also became less compliant. Fred figured it was something like a kite losing its tail. All the while, Kari kept ranting, even after she contacted the ship.

"Those little *shits* shoot up our plane! Me an' Fred's *own* plane, not the Naavy's! Yaah, we cut the taarget loose! Is you stupid? We gonna laand wit a sea aanchor on our aass? No, we ain't comin' baack around! You *is* stupid! We laandin' right here, right now, before the goddaamn tail faalls off! You gotta come get us—an' somebody better praay to the Maker those stupid shits din't shoot no leaks in our plane!"

Despite Fred's concern and general agreement, he couldn't help but chuckle at Kari's tirade—which brought it down on him, of course.

"Whaat you laaffin' aat, you silly hoo-maan? This plane's haaf mine, you know. You laand it gentle, no craack it up worse thaan it is!"

"I'm *trying*, Kari," Fred told her patiently, voice a little strained as he fought controls that were rapidly becoming less responsive as the wind-tattered fabric left them. "Quit bitching and crank the wing floats down!"

"I *aam*!" Kari snapped back.

Gauging the distance to the water, Fred briefly considered the irony of how often he and his Lemurian friend had been in scrapes like this, usually wishing they had a lot more altitude. The only blessings this time were how calm the sea was and how low they already were. "Hold on!" he yelled, trying to flare out right over the water, but the nose didn't want to come up anymore. He heaved even harder back on the stick. Bumping and bobbing, ever so slowly, the blue, boatlike bow of the plane crept up toward the horizon, and feeling more than seeing the proximity of the wave-tops, he cut the throttle to slow the plane practically into a stall. With a spine-compressing thundering boom, the crippled Nancy slapped down on the water, swiftly wallowing to a near stop. Taking a deep breath, Fred mashed on the left rudder pedal to try and turn back toward the ship but detected no response. Unbuckling his straps, he twisted around up on his knees in his seat to look past the spinning prop, Kari, and the tail back behind her. He blinked when he saw that the wooden framework of the rudder was entirely naked now, and only one elevator had any fabric left.

Leaning back down, he cut the ignition and fuel to the engine and waited while the prop wound down and jerked to a stop. "Wow," he said, staring at the tail again.

"All you caan say is 'wow'?" Kari demanded incredulously.

Fred shrugged his shoulders, attention now drawn to *Walker*, just a couple of miles away, steaming swiftly toward them. He grinned back a little weakly at his friend. "Wow," he repeated.

Walker hove to with the little seaplane bobbing in her lee. A motor whaleboat was launched to stand by while the Nancy was hoisted from the water by a boom on the mainmast, Kari standing on top of the wing holding the cable she'd affixed to the lifting points. Water streamed across the deck as the plane swung inboard to be placed on a wheeled truck instead of the catapult. No longer required to stand by for safety reasons, the whaleboat grumbled off to find and secure the target sleeve.

Once the plane was secured, Fred climbed out of the cockpit and Kari jumped down from the wing to the deck. Blinking furiously, fur frizzed and tail arched belligerently, Kari looked like an overcompressed spring about to slip loose and launch.

Tal-Eraas, chief of *Walker*'s small air division, intercepted Kari before she could storm right over to where Silva, Lawrence, and Gunny Horn stood, surrounded by a cluster of their cadets. All looked extremely nervous in the face of her obvious wrath and Horn was holding yet another much smaller 'Cat, almost suspended by the scruff of his neck.

"Is thaat the stupid shit thaat almost shoot us down?" Kari almost screeched, pointing at the little Lemurian in Gunny Horn's custody.

"Stupid Shit!" Petey shrieked gleefully. That was his very favorite combination of words.

"I waant you to throw thaat idiot over the side, right now," Kari snapped at Horn.

Horn shook his head with what appeared to be regret. "Can't, Lieutenant," he replied in his most reasonable tone. "It might take a few minutes for the flashies to find and eat him out here in the middle of nothing, but they would. Eventually." He shook his head. "Ridiculous as it seems, like the skipper said, Navy Clan regs apply to these little scamps, same as us." He gently shook the miserable culprit.

"He could've killed us," Fred reminded, tone more measured but still angry. "I guess—I hope," he added with a glare at Horn, "the little guy got a little trigger happy?"

Horn nodded. "He opened up before I gave the command." He ventured a small smile. "They counted your second bomb a hit, by the way. You should've heard the yelling from the bridge. Tabby popped her cap."

"Swell," Fred said, pointing at Horn's prisoner. "But what're you gonna do with *that* little assassin?"

Silva rolled his eye. "What're you bitchin' about? The little scudder actually hit you, prob'ly shot through the target to do it durin' that fancy turn you made. Didn't hit *you* on purpose. Hell, I bet I been shot more often on accident than I ever was deliberate, like." He conked Lawrence in the head with his elbow. "I know ol' Larry has. So what? You got shot down again. Woop-te-do. Far as I know, you two hold the record for survivin' that. Oughta be gettin' good at it." He waved at the plane. "Looks like it to me. Hell, *this* one'll prob'ly fly *again*."

Captain Rodriguez, Chief Bosun Bashear, and Courtney Bradford had pushed their way through what looked like half the crew and cadets now gathered in the vicinity of the aft searchlight tower. Most of the talking stopped when Ronson glared around, the only voices coming from forward where the motor whaleboat was being recovered. "Well," he said, "that exercise was a fiasco for sure." He rubbed his face. "And I'm a little surprised, since everybody's been shaping fairly well. Just expecting a little too much too soon, I guess."

"Nonsense," Courtney proclaimed, gesturing around. "All these youngsters have already been through more 'basic training' than most of our crew replacements ever had during the war. If anything . . ." He paused, considering. "It may be possible you haven't yet pressed them hard enough, simulating that accelerated, high-stress training that worked so well to keep all our combined navies prepared for combat." He rubbed his hands together. "Why, when the Kaiser put me in charge of the Republic Fleet, I drilled my ships' crews quite mercilessly, I assure you!"

Rodriguez nodded, still a little mystified by how Courtney wound up a temporary admiral. Weird enough if it had just been for show, to demonstrate solidarity in the Alliance, but it wasn't. He hadn't actually commanded any of the ships in his powerful squadron in action, of course, but he had been in charge of their movement. Probably because of his intimate knowledge of Captain Reddy's overall strategy . . . "Maybe," Ronson finally agreed, "but these're kids and we aren't at war." His tone firmed. "And we just had a serious accident."

Courtney arched one of his caterpillar brows. "Accidents happen all the time, Captain, in peacetime and war." He paused in thought before continuing. "And regrettable as they are, they often serve to heighten awareness and prevent more and worse accidents down the line. And as for being at war . . . are we not? I doubt there will ever be actual peace between us and the fascist League." Courtney managed an encouraging smile for all those present before gazing back at Ronson. "Press them, Captain. Young they may be, but not so much younger than many who served in the war. There will be more accidents, no doubt, perhaps even more serious than this, but you do no one any favors by going easy on these cadets. Not them, not us, and certainly not the Navy Clan and Grand Alliance."

Ronson was nodding again. "You're right, Mr. Bradford. As usual." He grimaced, suddenly sure that Courtney Bradford had been a pretty good acting admiral. He raised his voice. "Right," he said, "from this moment on, we're kicking things into high gear." He looked at Bashear. "We'll revise the watch bills to proceed under wartime condition three—a third of the crew on watch at all times and half the weapons manned. I'd go to condition two, but we still need time for instruction. And all drills will be performed as if our lives depend on them—and they might." He pursed his lips at Kari, who was still steaming. "I'm sorry about your plane, Lieutenant. Damage doesn't look too bad, but we'll have to dismantle it for repair and we still need you flying."

"We'll be shootin' the *big* guns at you next!" Silva chortled.

Ronson glared at the big man but continued speaking to the young aviators. "That means you guys'll have to fly the ship's plane after we haul it out and put it together. In addition, I want you both to start switching off, taking the air-minded cadets up with you."

Kari was taken aback. "But . . . I'm not the flier Fred is," she said doubtfully.

"You *are* checked out in the newer ships like we've got aboard, right?" Ronson asked.

"Sure she is," Fred assured.

"Then that's settled."

"Not quite," Kari disagreed, glaring at the little 'Cat that Gunny Horn had finally set down. The young Lemurian cringed. "Whaat about him? He gonna get punished?"

Ronson waved the question away. "That's up to you. Seems that his . . . exuberant negligence had the most effect on your division."

Kari narrowed her eyes. "Chief Eraas? You just got a new 'volunteer' for all the shit jobs in the air division, but most especially to re-cover the control surfaaces on me an' Fred's plane. He'll haappily work on thaat in addition to whatever you or anyone else caan think of for him to do." She glared at the unfortunate 'Cat. "Isn't thaat right, cadet?"

"Ah, ay, ay, Lieutenant Faask!" the miscreant swiftly replied, before mumbling, "I like the air division anyway."

Fred's eyes widened. "Is that so? What's your name, kid?"

The response was almost intelligible.

"Speak up, sonny," Silva said, leaning in.

"Speak Up!" commanded Petey.

"Ah . . . Aalak-Maraan," the youngster reluctantly confessed.

"Any relation . . ." Captain Rodriguez began.

Courtney interrupted him. "Why of course! I know you!" He looked around, beaming. "This is a . . . nephew, I suppose, of our esteemed Chairperson, Safir-Maraan! I believe the proper Bm'baadan/Aryaalan term is 'sister-' or 'brother-son.' Adopted sister in this case, if I'm not mistaken, since Safir-Maraan is not only an orphan but an only child." The importance of blood relationships in the now combined East Jaavan kingdom could be somewhat wildly schizophrenic. Safir-Maraan was still queen there, in addition to being Chairperson of the United Homes, but battle injuries had made it doubtful she and her mate, Chack-Sab-At, would ever leave a natural heir of her body to the throne, so she had to adopt a blood relative to provide one. What all that meant at the moment was that the awkward youngling who just shot down Fred and Kari's plane was next in line to the throne of Aryaal and B'mbaado.

"'Course he is," Horn mumbled. "Shit."

"Shit," Petey philosophically agreed.

"Makes no difference," Captain Rodriguez decreed. "This isn't a pleasure cruise for the aristocracy. Fact is, the high-ups in our alliance have almost all set the example of leading from the front and we've lost"—he glanced at Aalak—"or nearly lost a whole bunch of them, including his aunt." He looked around at the many watching faces. "So he'll endure his punishment detail, just like any of the rest of you will, no matter 'who' you think you are. Clear?"

For a moment, except for the rumble of blowers, the rush of exhaust from the nearby stacks, and the freshening wind, there was no sound.

"Clear?" barked Gunny Horn.

"Ay, aye!" came the shouted response from every cadet, human and Lemurian.

Rodriguez finally nodded before turning to the various gathered instructors. "Good. We've wasted enough time. Carry on."

"Right," Silva called. "While we're just wallowin' here, let's put the motor launch an' target barge over the side. We'll exercise the main battery"—he paused, considering—"right after chow!"

"Chow!" Petey emphasized. "Eat!"

Silva winked at Fred and Kari. "Then, soon as they get the other plane put together, we can do some high-level antiaircraft practice with the aft, four-inch-fifty on the dual-purpose mount!"

"So, you are a prince of some sort, correct?" Samuel Jenks asked Aalak-Maraan. To his credit, he kept his voice cordial—and low enough—not to be heard much beyond his close, now trusted, circle of friends standing in the chow line under the amidships deckhouse.

Aalak blinked rapidly, looking around, probably expecting more verbal abuse. "Yes," he finally ventured guardedly. "I haave no say in thaat maatter. But no one could deny me my desire to join the Naavy Claan! The Maraan family name has estaablished a traadition of service, aafter all," he defended ironically.

"Most certainly," agreed the towering—compared to Aalak—Philan Bele. "As have virtually all our families." He nodded at Samuel, the small female Lemurians Haan-Ara and Maarik-Fas, then the male 'Cat Kan-Dis-Ar, as well as Daniel Baker and Susan Raj. They'd all been virtually inseparable since that first day and not only bunked in close proximity in the forward berthing space, but had also managed to "rotate" through their various assignments together. Bele believed their instructors did that on purpose to help them build comradery. Especially since their little group represented nearly every power in the Alliance. He thought he'd seen other such groups of companions broken up or remixed and suspected it was done to keep factional cliques from forming. That and simply so younglings from the wildly diverse races, even species, could get used to each other. There were vast physical, even cultural differences between them, but all were equally qualified or they wouldn't be here, and this had been stressed from the start. It was up to each cadet to discover their own unique strengths and weaknesses and focus on what they were best at. If one persisted in striking for a rating they just weren't cut out for, for whatever reason—size, smarts, temperament, it didn't matter—

there'd be no accommodations or dispensations. A cadet might try again after they grew or studied more, but nobody would finish this voyage with a rating they didn't earn.

"Well . . . yes, I suppose thaat's true," Aalak conceded. "Though I may be the only aactual 'prince.' And the knowledge of thaat faact among . . . some others aboard, haas caused me a measure of . . . discomposure."

Bele's naturally agreeable expression turned grim. "You have been bullied?" He looked around. "By whom?"

Aalak waved it away. "It doesn't matter. I haave been trained in an ancient Aryaalan fighting style that would allow me to defend myself quite ably regardless of my size—if it ever came to that—I assure you." His tone left no doubt of his confidence. Still, there was a tentative note in his voice when he resumed. "My . . . staatus . . . haas made for a notably solitaary experience on this voyaage, however, when I haad expected something quite different: all the tales I haave been raised on of the fellowship among sailors and waarriors . . ."

The group of friends were looking at each other and it was with the clear agreement of all that Samuel spoke for the rest, gesturing at them. "Let us try to help fix that," he said, proceeding to introduce the others, each stepping forward to shake hands. A genuine smile, confirmed by pleased blinking, was growing on Aalak's face.

"Quit screwin' around out there!" came the indignant bellow of Earl Lanier through the serving window over the stainless-steel counter. "Who's next, damn it? Yer holdin' up the line!"

Aalak now blinked mortification when many of the kids behind him laughed and he saw he was next. Hurriedly, he advanced his tray to be filled.

"Oh, it's you," Earl grumped down at him, pointing with his ladle. "*Heard* about you. You're the kid who enjoys shootin' our own flyin' officers out'a the sky!"

There was more laughter and Aalak seemed to shrink even smaller while his new friends instinctively turned to defend him. It wasn't necessary. Through a chuckle of his own, Earl continued loudly, "'Course, I seen the target sleeve, an' it looked like to me that you was the only one who hit *anything*. After all the lead the rest o' them useless bastards threw at the *whole damn ocean*, that's pretty funny, you ask me." Dumping something unrecognizable (but that actually smelled pretty good) on Aalak's plate, Earl poked his jowly face through the window and scowled at the other cadets. "C'mon, you bunch'a walkin' bellies! Get it before I throw it to the fish!"

Philan Bele led them all down the companionway to the forward berthing space, and they arranged themselves around the table rigged out between lines of racks, four high, and they sat on the footlockers for benches.

Aalak had followed and now joined the unlikely little band, sliding his tray onto the table. "Is this all right?" he asked.

Samuel shook his head. "Sit where you want. Anywhere there's room." He grinned. "You might want to avoid sitting too close to Maarik, though. She's an amazingly messy eater!"

The only one at the table smaller that Aalak, Maarik casually blinked disdain and directed a rude hand gesture at the tall Imperial, causing laughter around the table. Soon, the space began to fill with other cadets and their banter, but Aalak and his friends focused on wolfing their food. They got up (or were often still up) before dawn, depending on the watch bill, and exercised a lot through the day. Everyone was always hungry.

"So," Bele finally began as he wiped his plate with a piece of orangish bread. He stuffed it in his mouth and started chewing, but he was looking at Aalak. "What's your primary interest and who is your favorite instructor?"

Aalak looked around, expecting more ribbing, but ultimately shrugged and took the plunge. "Aviation," he said guardedly. "I waant to fly. Not lumbering seaplanes, but fighters—not thaat Lieutenaants Faask and Reynolds are not excellent teachers or exaamples," he hastily added. "Their war record is quite remaarkable. And they are still so young! But I once saw a P-40 fly—Maker, such power!—and Bull-Baats are as close as I caan get." The latest Allied fighter aircraft were monoplanes with an enclosed cockpit and double-banked air-cooled radials and were a far cry from the earliest efforts. Officially designated "P-5 Nighthawks," but almost universally referred to as "Bull-Bats," few had any idea they bore a striking (if shrunken) resemblance to the Curtiss P-36 on another world. That wasn't surprising. Two operational P-40Es remained on this world and they'd evolved from P-36s themselves. Their lines and airframes had been as shamelessly copied in wood and fabric as possible. P-5s still had fixed landing gear and couldn't compete one-on-one with some of the modern aircraft the League was known to possess, but more powerful versions with retractable gear were in the works.

Bele was nodding, perhaps a little wistfully. "I would have liked that myself," he confessed but gestured at himself. "Unfortunately, it is . . ." He grinned. "*Expected*—with good reason—that I will grow still taller than I am now and the only aircraft I'd fit in are those big 'lumbering seaplanes.'" He took a breath. "It's gunnery, for me. Perhaps a command one day."

Samuel tilted his head at his friend. "He's *really* striking for lookout. He'll sight the enemy twenty miles away, from any part of the ship!"

Everyone laughed again and Aalak found himself loosening up.

"I think we are all aiming for a command someday. Of something," said Susan Raj, pursing her lips. "I'm for engineering, though, and Chief Reuben"—she shook her head—"I think he is the strangest man I ever met. It is an open secret that he is attracted—they call it 'sweet on'—Boilermaker First Class Sureen. He even called me that name by accident, so she is certainly on his mind. They say he and his brother were called "mice"—and he does look like one—and he seems hardly able to talk. He *could* be *such* a good teacher because he knows *everything*," she continued more enthusiastically. "I bet I still learn more from his grunting and pointing than I ever did in the classroom."

"He is very strange," agreed Daniel Baker in his upper-crust Imperial accent, eyebrow arched. Everyone, even Aalak, nodded somberly.

"They all are," said Maarik-Fas, tiny voice matching her size, but there was sincere frustration in her tone. "They are all heroes, laarger-than-life, but seem so much more . . . ordinaary than I ever would haave expected. Sergeant Miles led Shee-Ree rebels against the Grik in the wilds of our ancestral home on Madagascar, but seems so maatter-of-faact about it all, haardly referencing any of his experiences during our smaall-aarms training. And Gunnery Sergeant Horn! Certainly one of the great heroes of the Baattle of the St. Vincent, yet toward us, he is just a maan with a sometimes distaant gaze."

"The only one who truly frightens me is the XO—Commander Tab-At," Samuel confessed. "She barely even comes up to my chin yet is more intimidating than Chief Bosun Bashear!"

"That's because your focus is ship-handling," Bele pointed out. "Something she readily confesses she is still learning as well, so she is just as strict on us as she is herself, I suspect." He looked at Maarik-Fas. "Commander Tab-At came up through engineering as well."

A few of the other officers and chiefs were discussed, as well as Courtney Bradford and Abel Cook. Courtney's general enthusiasm drew amusement and Susan confessed she was "sweet on" Abel. She received a good bit of ribbing for that, but none was intended as hurtful, much to Aalak's surprise.

Courtney and Abel stirred new speculation on the nature of the adventure ahead, but Bele brought them back to the previous subject when he said, "It is Chief Silva and his . . . reptilian friends I find the most difficult to fathom." He looked around. "My father was a prefect in General Kim's Army of the Republic during all its great actions from the plain of Gaugala to the Battle of the Locks." He took a long breath. "He told me he never met a more ruthless and deadly—he used the term 'warrior'—in his whole life. With the possible exceptions of his Legate Bekiaa and her cousin Chack-Sab-At," Bele qualified. "Yet despite his clear knowledge of *Walker*'s great guns—and any sort of small arm—Chief Silva strikes me more as . . ." He paused, looking around as if searching for a description. "It's hard to describe," he complained. "I suppose the best I can do is to say that he reminds me more of *us*—a mid-age youngling—than a celebrated war hero of the Grand Alliance."

Samuel was nodding. "Indeed," he agreed. "And I believe his irreverence of any authority aside from my Governor/Empress or Captain Matthew Reddy himself would be the most striking if he did not demonstrate even more for himself and his accomplishments! It's like nothing he has ever done is more important than whatever prank or scheme he recounts!" Samuel seemed genuinely bothered by this.

Bele managed a small smile. "To be fair, he *has* given us some very good ideas"—he nodded at Aalak—"to avenge the slights to the newest member of our own little division."

Grins and amused blinking spread around the table and Maarik-Fas clapped her hands together. "I like the one with the little burning boats floating under the 'craapper' seats!"

Just then, static squawked in the speakers mounted on the fore and aft bulkhead of the berthing space and a bugle began urgently blaring the "general quarters" call. There was only the slightest hesitation in the space, long enough for a few exchanged glances, before everyone erupted up from their benches, headed for the passageway aft and the companionway just beyond it. Most swept up their trays, empty or not, and dumped them in a bin as they went, but a few got dropped or spilled, and whoever had the mess detail that day would have some cleanup ahead of them. Once on deck, under the forward superstructure, most of the kids quickly donned life jackets and helmets before scattering for their next duty station. Aalak's new friends each gave him a grin and a pat on the back as they dove through the forward hatch to the fo'c'sle together and, with just a trace of reluctance, he headed aft. He was actually looking forward to duty in the air division, but hated for this first taste of real fellowship aboard to end.

CHAPTER 8

Move it, move it!" bellowed a Lemurian bosun's mate under the amidships deckhouse, gazing at an Imperial watch. "Get you lazy aasses to you stations! We could be under attaack!"

Aalak dodged running figures, nearly all of whom were considerably taller and could've knocked him flat to the deck. Passing the starboard torpedo mount and aft searchlight tower, both of which had young sailors climbing them, he finally reached a different kind of chaos. *Walker* had a pair of twin 25mm antiaircraft gun tubs in front of her aft deckhouse where the number three and four torpedo mounts used to be. These were being manned and prepared to the accompaniment of harsh shouts for them to hurry. In between them, however, where the seaplane catapult stood, other harried figures were racing to finish bringing all the parts for the "spare" plane out of what also served as the torpedo workshop. Others waited impatiently to shove the dismounted wings and fuselage of the damaged aircraft through the enlarged hatch its replacement was emerging from. With so much going on in such a small place, and with no idea what to do, Aalak saw Lieutenant Reynolds standing in a strange bubble of calm by the winch under the lifting boom on the mainmast. Relieved that it wasn't Lieutenant Kari-Faask, who'd acted *much* angrier at him, Aalak made his way to the aviator.

"Sir!" he said, smartly saluting. "Cadet Aalak-Maraan, reporting as ordered!"

Fred Reynolds smiled and sketched a salute in return. "No need for that," he said. "Here, just step over by me."

Aalak looked anxiously around. "But . . . what should I be doing?"

Fred chuckled. "For now, staying out of the way. Like me. You show me some air and I'll fly in it, but fixing busted planes is more Kari's thing."

Very quickly, all of *Walker*'s various stations, at least those Aalak could see from where he was, started reporting that they were "manned and ready," but an annoyed-sounding Kari-Faask called to a talker stationed on the auxiliary conn up on the aft deckhouse that the air division was still busy exchanging aircraft.

"Good thing for you this is just a drill," Fred said aside to Aalak, and the young 'Cat blinked a question at him. "If we were going into action right now, we'd have to throw *both* our planes over the side," Fred elaborated archly. "If we can't fly it off, we throw it off. Can't have a plane, and its fuel tank in particular, out on deck in a fight."

Aalak looked down. "I'm sorry," he said.

"I know," Fred acknowledged, grinning again, but the grin swiftly faded. "But 'sorry' doesn't cut it, or bring your friends back when they die. You didn't hit our plane on purpose, even Kari knows that, and accidents happen when you train hard. You gotta do it, though, and hope the consequences for training accidents aren't as bad as they'd be in battle." He looked at Aalak again. "And whatever other accidents you may have in your life, I bet you won't have that one again." His grin returned and Aalak was pretty sure it was his natural expression. "Neither will most of those around you when it happened, seeing how mad Kari got." He shrugged. "Everybody goofs up, especially under pressure. I have, lots of times. I don't think I've goofed up in ways that would kill me"—he glanced at Kari, still directing the stowing of their injured aircraft—"or somebody I care about more than once, though." He scratched his chin. "So I guess, in a way, some accidents are good, as object lessons. Even when people get hurt—or killed—they might save more lives in the long run." He shook his head. "Sucks for whoever the 'example' was and whoever screws up that bad. Especially if they aren't the same person. And I don't just mean the punishment, which is part of the lesson too. It's the living with hurting or killing somebody by accident. That'll torment you forever." He took a deep breath and shook his head again. "I'm a crummy philosopher, Kari'll tell you." He nodded up at the amidships gun platform. Just about everyone was in their positions now, ready for whatever the general quarters alarm could've prepared them for, but cadets now manning the number three gun were excitedly training out to starboard.

"C'mon," Fred said, moving over by the starboard gun tub and shading his eyes with his hand. "Wow," he said.

Aalak had much better eyes than any human, but not the height to see what Fred and a growing number of others were looking at. All he could see was a green-gray mound in the hazy distance, like a small island, barely distinguishable from the sea. He suspected what it must be, however. "Is thaat a . . . mountain fish?" he asked, voice full of wonder. He'd never seen one of the titanic creatures. His people, from B'mbaado and Aryaal, were some of the few Lemurians who had little to do with the sea before the Great War.

"Yeah," Fred replied. "Scary damn things."

"Are they really big enough to threaten a seagoing Home? Or air-craaft caarrier?"

Fred glanced down at him. "Yeah, I've seen some that could do that, and just about any of 'em could crunch *Walker* like a shrimp." That wasn't as effective an analogy as it might've been since some of the closest adult "shrimp" analogs on this world were the size of a full-grown dog—which there weren't any of at all, as far as they knew. Aalak got his point, however, and Fred continued. "There doesn't seem to be many of 'em—mighty territorial, according to Mr. Bradford—and they eat most of the little ones themselves. I haven't seen hardly any since the Battle of the Pass. You might've heard a lot of 'em got killed there." His tone sounded regretful.

Aalak was nodding, tail swishing behind him. "They helped us win the baattle, didn't they?"

"Kind of," Fred hedged, tilting his head to the side, "but it's not like they set out to. That was an 'accident' we sort of caused on purpose. And nobody imagined so many of the humongous damn things would die."

Aalak gazed at the distant beast, apparently simply basking on the surface as *Walker* steamed past perhaps eight or ten miles away. As huge as mountain fish were (called "leviathans" by both Repubs and Impies), averaging roughly two hundred tails—or yards—in length, no one really knew exactly what they looked like in life since so little of them could be seen above water. Aalak had only ever seen rather fanciful illustrations, likely drawn from beached corpses at low tide. It was known that Courtney Bradford longed for a better observation, yet even he'd admit the water was too hostile for any realistic attempt. This one seemed utterly unconcerned by their proximity and that made Aalak wonder.

"I aapologize for asking so maany questions, but may I ask another?"

"Sure," Fred replied. "You're here to learn and I'm supposed to help you, I guess." He sounded a little self-conscious about that.

"I understood thaat only aactive sonar—appaarently somewhat painful to them—would reliably prevent them from attaacking a ship sailing through whaat they view as their territory?"

Fred nodded. "Yeah. That, or sometimes cannon fire. Big noises, anyway. They don't like 'em. Ordinary machinery noises might even provoke an attack. Same reason we darken the bronze screws on new ships—to keep those gigantic-ass sharks from chomping on 'em like fishing lures. But that means we gotta run our active sonar all the time, which can reveal our position to other listeners."

Aalak was nodding. "Like submaarines."

"Right," Fred said. "We know the League has one. At *least* one," he added. He didn't mention the *U-112*, a large former League submarine now in Allied service. That remained a carefully guarded secret, or so it was hoped. "But that's why the whiz kids in Maa-ni-laa came up with these super-low-frequency whistles, or something, they put on the hulls of our ships. Pretty easy to make, once they figured out how, and found the right frequency, of course. I don't know how they did it since it's too low for even our best sound men to hear. The gizmos—they call 'em 'rumblers'—must work, though, and either mountain fish don't like whatever noise they make or it just doesn't bother them. Either way, they leave our ships alone. At least while they're underway," he qualified.

His and Kari's damaged plane now secured, he gestured to where the division was preparing to assemble the other one and lift it up on the catapult. "You better go over and pitch in before Kari sees you loafing." He chuckled. "Ask her what she wants you to do."

Courtney Bradford was on the starboard bridgewing with a pair of his new binoculars. He was making appreciative noises while he observed the distant wonder, completely in the way of the cadets who'd manned the starboard torpedo director. They were milling about somewhat helplessly at the moment and Abel Cook gestured at them reassuringly. "Stand easy," he said lowly. "I guarantee we won't be shooting at it."

"The air division will be ready to launch the replacement aircraft in fifteen minutes, says Lieutenant Faask," related the young female cadet from the Empire serving as bridge talker, the helmet, headset, and microphone on her head looking ridiculously oversized. Her expression was resolute and serious, however. "Otherwise, all stations report 'manned an' ready.'"

"Very well," said Captain Rodriguez, with a glance at the large chronometer mounted over the pilothouse windows. He pursed his lips. "Not as quick as yesterday, but not terrible. Especially considering the fiasco aft."

"I say, Captain!" Courtney exclaimed, with a glance back over his shoulder. "I don't suppose we might steer just a *little* closer to the target?" The mountain fish had been designated a target ever since it was sighted and Courtney had fallen into referring to it as such as well, regardless of the fact he'd never countenance using it as one.

Rodriguez sighed. "No, Mr. Bradford," he began patiently, "I don't think so. The 'rumblers' on the hull are still as much theoretical as not and it isn't our job to test 'em to failure."

Courtney made a moue. "Perhaps not," he conceded. "Mr. Cook, please make another note: this specimen seems of roughly average size but is decidedly *green* in color. Quite striking. And I don't believe it's simply festooned with weed." Raising the binoculars again, he resumed his examination of the great fish. As usual, he'd casually used poor Abel as a kind of personal secretary, but the young officer didn't mind. Though a seasoned, veteran Marine, Abel was almost as interested in the natural world as his mentor and actually smiled fondly at the much older Australian's back.

"Of course," he said, and he would later on, adding the observation to the journal he kept in his quarters, even though the cadet quartermaster was even now making note of the fact in the log.

"Thoughts, XO?" Captain Rodriguez asked Tabby, who'd remained on the bridge during the drill to observe instead of taking her own proper battle station on the aft deckhouse, at the auxiliary conn.

Tabby blinked grudging acceptance, tail twitching slightly. "It waas okay, I guess," she conceded, "but I got no idea, up here, how the engineerin' division manaaged—not thaat it got a test."

Rodriguez was shaking his head. "Engineering's not your job anymore, XO," he said, stressing her new role. "It's Isak's." He smiled. "But we'll pull a drill that'll shake 'em up belowdecks pretty soon, and you can go down and watch. How's that?"

Tabby seemed to contemplate that a moment before her large eyes narrowed slightly and a predatory grin spread across her face, revealing long sharp canines. "We'll haave 'em cope with something serious," she said, clearly imagining all manner of horrible engineering casualties. "We got the fuel for another high-speed run or two? Aside from those scheduled," she asked.

Captain Rodriguez matched her grin and nodded. "Sure. Or we can mix 'em up. It's just about time to practice a torpedo attack, anyway. We'll get up to speed, let 'em shoot off the practice fish, then take a simulated hit. I like it."

"Let's do it at night as paart of a general surface action, complete with main baattery fire."

"You really want to throw the works at the kiddos," Rodriguez observed. His grin faded a little. "I guess it's time, though." He suddenly frowned. "Pam Cross won't like it. If there's one thing she hates worse than tending people wounded in battle, it's patching up training injuries—and there's bound to be some. Hopefully just a few cuts and bruises, mashed fingers and toes—and tails." He took a breath and his expression hardened. "Tough. I don't know what her deal is, whether it's just another fight with Silva or what, but she's had a crummy attitude this whole trip, so far." Pam Cross was well-known for her wisecracks and could cut her victims to the quick. "Sometimes it's funny," Rodriguez confessed, "but she hasn't shut it off since we left Scapa Flow and it's getting hard to take." He looked at Tabby. "You two are pals, right?"

Tabby blinked something that roughly translated to "sort of."

"Well, see if you can squeeze it out of her. And not just the cause, but her manner. She at least needs to tone it down a little. I prefer a more cheerful wardroom!" Turning to the pilothouse at large, he raised his voice and said, "Secure from general quarters. Resume condition three."

Though normally steaming at a sedate and fuel-miserly twelve knots over the next few days, a more urgent and advanced "wartime" curriculum was increasingly implemented. Ordinary ship maintenance and operation procedures, along with scheduled fitness and small arms and fighting instruction, were frequently interrupted by progressively more urgent and challenging combat and disaster drills. And despite the obvious toll this was taking on the young cadets in terms of stress and exhaustion, even the occasional inevitable injuries, accidents that caused those injuries, along with general foul-ups, were growing less frequent, not more so. Much sooner than most expected, *Walker*'s student crew was beginning to achieve what many would consider sufficient proficiency for operational service.

They hadn't started from scratch, of course, and those cadets most likely destined for specialties in the engineering division had been especially advanced in regard to theory, though Isak continued to demean them as "bilgewater scum floaties"—whatever those were—and unfit for the exalted renown of the title of "snipe." Even he had to reluctantly admit that if "one o' them shifty deck apes thows me over the side," his students *might* somehow manage to make the ship go.

Roughly halfway to Respite Island, loping along on a moderate sea under a low gray sky, the insular little academy on board the heroic old ship was first brushed by the broader events that would ultimately change the nature of their voyage entirely. Standing by the chair bolted to the forward, starboard side of the bridge, Captain "Ronson" Rodriguez rested his elbow against its back, gazing out at the fo'c'sle and the white-capped sea beyond. No one expected a storm, not even the first lieutenant, a rather dour, very stoic 'Cat named Daanis, who'd actually undergone some "Sky Priest" training in his youth. Like most who stuck with it, not as many these days, Daanis had picked up an uncanny "feel" for the weather. The wind was surely rising, however, and so was the sea, causing the motion of the ship to increase. Ronson watched packets of spray falling back to spatter the crew of gun number one as they secured the weapon, the only one with its own splinter shield.

"Captain," came a voice from behind him and Ronson turned to see "Lieutenant" Jack Meek had joined them on the bridge and now stood with a message form in his hand. It was obvious that's what it was because the paper had a yellowish tinge and Mr. Meek didn't look happy at all. For an instant, Rodriguez thought he knew how it must've been for Captain Reddy so many times when he got bad news this way—a feeling that somehow combined the opposing sensations of freezing mercury and molten lava flowing down his back. He cleared his throat.

"Whatcha got, Sparks?" he asked, remembering to use the occupational "cover name" Meek had agreed to. Wordlessly, the Republic snoop handed over the page. Rodriguez read it twice, the first time quickly, then more carefully the second time. Blinking, he looked back at Meek. "You confirmed this? It definitely came from Respite Island?" There'd been no communication with their destination since they set out.

Meek nodded. "I did," he replied. "It's for real. You'll remember I reported that the Clipper sent word that comms were down on Respite and they needed a whole new set?" Meek lowered his voice. "There was a priority code attached to that request." He nodded at the message form in Ronson's hand. "Then that came in, in the latest code that Respite wouldn't have if another Clipper hadn't immediately flown it down with the new equipment."

Ronson looked back at the page, then passed it to Tabby, who quickly began reading as well. "Okay," he said, then lowered his voice. "This could change things. Maybe a lot. Go around, inform Corps of Discovery personnel and others in the know that we'll have a meeting in the wardroom"—he glanced at the chronograph—"at seventeen hundred. Nobody else," he added unnecessarily. "If anybody asks, tell 'em we're cooking up a secret surprise drill." Looking at Tabby, he finished, "We were *going* to, after all." He paused. "And let me know immediately when there's any other response to this." He motioned at the message, suspecting there would be since the coded report would've gone out everywhere, even being repeated and passed along to the Allied high command all around the world. "Query anything that even remotely seems to reference us because God knows what they're going to want us to do about it."

"Aye, sir," Meek acknowledged, and after a short hesitation, he turned to clamber back down the stairs, aft.

Rodriguez caught Tabby's gaze. "Jesus," he murmured.

"Maker," Tabby agreed.

Neither spoke about their suspicion that the innocent-young-cadet-training focus of USS *Walker*'s voyage had come to an end.

CHAPTER 9

MARTINIQUE ISLAND
THE CARIBBEAN

Martinique Island, the former League marshaling point in the Caribbean, had become one of the American Navy Clan's very few land possessions, joining only Tarakan Island in the Makassar Strait (where much of its fuel oil, gasoline, and frankly revenue was produced), Midway Island (a critical replenishment depot), and San Diego Bay (gifted by the Empire of the New Britain Isles). All those other territories were in the Pacific. Now, not only did the Navy Clan need a base in the Atlantic, Martinique had the largest cemetery for Navy Clan and United Homes sailors and Marines in the region. Captain Matthew Reddy, still Commander in Chief of All Allied Forces (CINCAF), and High Chief of the American Navy (and Marine) Clan, hadn't gotten involved in the postwar squabbling between the Allies over spoils, territories, and spheres of influence, but made it clear to all that the ownership of Martinique—and all the "salvage" there—wasn't negotiable. Nearly all that salvage, sunk or afloat, had been captured by his clan, after all.

Every friend was welcome, however, and all the Allies contributed to the construction and operation of the growing facilities that were turning the picturesque island into the biggest, most strategic military base in the hemisphere. There were already four large airstrips (two had been built by the League and since repaired after being bombed into uselessness), and another naval base had been built on the west side of the island at what some wag (possibly Dennis Silva, who was prone to such things) had dubbed "Frog Bay." This had been necessary because the original League naval base at what would've been "Baie du Galion" on another world had been choked with wrecks, either damaged or destroyed in place, or towed there after the Battle of St. Vincent Island. It was quicker and easier in the short term to build a new base at Frog Bay than rebuild the one the League began, and the first priorities had been a dry dock, repair yards, and the obligatory seaplane base, of course. That initial dry dock hadn't been much more involved than the first one Matt's destroyermen built at Baalkpan, basically a dredged-out cove with one of the great seagoing Homes flooded down across the mouth of it and all the water pumped out.

The first ships to use it were destroyers with damage below the waterline, but even while those repairs were underway, the "cove" had been lengthened and widened. When the "mudhole," as the only relatively "dry" dock was known at the time, was big enough and clear, a new member of the Navy Clan, the German cruiser *Hessen*—which had defected from the League (in which the Germans were *very* junior partners) but suffered underwater damage when a nearby ammunition ship blew up—was the first larger ship to go in the "pit." (Another common term for the dry dock.) Like the League of Tripoli itself, *Hessen* was another anomaly that clearly came from a different—other—earth than USS *Walker*, since no ship of her class was ever completed where Matt and his people were from. The closest analogies they were aware of had been Deutschland Class "panzerschiffe" like *Admiral Graf Spee*. Actually an improved "pocket battleship" herself, with steam turbines instead of diesels and six 11″ guns, *Hessen* was quickly made seaworthy again and became a valuable addition to Matt Reddy's fleet.

Other damaged cruisers had been swiftly patched, either in the mudhole or by divers in new, *very* protective hardsuits, and the American Clan light cruiser (CL) USS *Fitzhugh Gray* had been returned to full service. The two most heavily damaged were sent to better facilities at San Diego Bay or the Enchanted Isles, where the Impies had built their own forward dry dock. These included the Gray Class USS *Maa-ni-laa* (CL-2) and the Italian-built Trento Class prize, USS *Adige*. This was done for several reasons. First, both were so badly damaged that it was a toss-up whether it was truly practical to repair either one. Second, a trio of new CLs had recently been completed in Baalkpan and Maa-ni-la. Essentially improved Gray Class ships with four stacks and similar dimensions (440′ × 45′), they had more armor over their engineering spaces and magazines. That increased their displacement by a thousand tons, but the greater efficiency of their new superheat boilers and improved engines actually made them faster than *Fitzhugh Gray*. Only two of these ships had been planned, but a third had been laid down in Maa-ni-la at the height of the war "just in case." High Chief Saan-Kakja was like that.

In any event, the continuously increased space in the mudhole was desperately needed to fix serious damage to the Navy Clan's two repairable battleships, USS *Savoie* and USS *Impero*. *Savoie* was a French-built Bretagne Class superdreadnought that originally belonged to the League but came into Navy Clan possession by a rather violent and convoluted path. At roughly 544 feet long and 88 feet wide, armed with seven (another story) 13.4″ rifles and numerous secondaries, and displacing about 25,000 tons after repair and refit, she'd been the most powerful ship in the Allied fleet at the Battle of St. Vincent—and drew perhaps more than her share of fire from the League battle line. Under the command of the Imperial High Admiral Jenks (with Gunny Horn in charge of fire control), she'd pitched it back hard, giving as good as she got. But riddled with holes from shellfire and torpedoes, she barely made it through the fight.

The former RM, now USS *Impero*, was a Littorio Class Italian-built battleship about 790 feet long and 107 feet wide. Armed with nine 15″ rifles in three triple turrets, a dozen 6″ secondaries, a veritable swarm of antiaircraft weapons, and displacing almost 46,000 tons, she was huge on a whole other level, just a couple hundred feet short of a Lemurian seagoing Home. It's probable that if she'd been at sea for the fight off St. Vincent Island, none of the Allied ships could've survived and the war would've ended quite differently. Fortunately, though, as one of the newest and most modern ships in the whole League Navy, she'd only participated in the operation to intimidate the Allies and been deemed "too valuable to risk" on the sortie to bombard the NUS city of Santiago, Cuba, which ended with the battle that wrecked most of her consorts.

Meanwhile, she'd been at anchor at the League base on Martinique when a combined air and sea assault hit her with torpedoes, and along with everyone else left there, she'd been obliged to surrender. Now *Savoie* had been out of the mudhole for four whole months and even her topside repairs were almost complete. *Impero*, however, though virtually undamaged above the waterline and with all her fighting ability intact, had been in the pit ever since. Granted, the facilities at Frog Bay remained rather primitive, but it was clear she would've proven just as stubbornly difficult to fix anywhere.

"Is it just because she's so . . . damned *big*?" Brad "Spanky" McFarlane asked Walbert Fiedler, who'd found new employment as the coordinator for all the construction projects on Martinique. The first former League convert to the Allied cause, Fiedler had been the German pilot of a Ju-52 trimotor transport sent to ferry League representatives to the unlamented Hisashi Kurokawa and his faction of Japanese sailors who'd technically aided the Grik in the war, but mostly pursued the wild ambitions of the maniacal Kurokawa. Already disgusted with the excesses of the fascist League in the Mediterranean, not to mention the attitude of the more numerous and powerful Italians, French, and Spanish toward their German "partners," it didn't take much prodding for Walbert to change sides rather than support the nightmare represented by Kurokawa and the Grik.

Since then, he'd been a helpful analyst with crucial insights about the League's capabilities and almost single-handedly—at first—recruited most of the defecting crew of *U-112* into the Navy Clan, without whom it might've been impossible to keep the big, powerful submarine in service. Together with that boat's skipper, Oberleutnant Kurt Hoffman, he'd also engineered the defection of *Hessen* and her crew. It was while he was pitching in as an interpreter and technical advisor during the big cruiser's refit that his skills, both practical and organizational, saw him installed in his current post. Walbert might've been "just" a pilot in the League, probably all he'd *ever* be, but the Grand Alliance, with its many races, ethnicities, even species, would happily make use of his advanced training as an engineer.

The only ones who still felt . . . a little weird about having "so many krauts—not to mention Japs—running around loose" were a few old *Walker, Mahan, S-19* sailors, and survivors of *Mizuki Maru*. All had—probably—come from the same world where they were locked in a death struggle with Nazi Germany and the Empire of Japan. It could be tough for them to remember that Walbert's Germany wasn't ruled by Adolf Hitler—Walbert didn't even know who that was—and had essentially become a client of the other members of the fascist Confédération États Souverains on the obviously divergent (at least post–World War I) world the current "League of Tripoli" came from. Speculation abounded on what had gone differently, but the most likely cause appeared to have been a farther-reaching Bolshevik Revolution and more militant European reaction to it. Frankly, though, none of that really mattered. Nothing from the who knows how many "old worlds" that leaked over here did.

"*Impero*'s size is certainly part of the problem," Walbert agreed, nodding back at Spanky and Matt Reddy himself, who, along with Colonel Chack-Sab-At and Henry Stokes, had arrived just that morning by Clipper after spending several days at nearly every layover they'd been forced to make on their long flight here. Each stop was essentially a state visit after all, and they did need to confer with the various leaders of the Grand Alliance, most specifically about what they could and would do in response to the League buildup at the Azores.

"She *is* godawful big," Matt observed quietly, rubbing his lip and looking down at the mudhole from a large, elevated office, built in the sturdy Lemurian way so the seemingly countless project supervisors could view as much of the growing yard and various undertakings as possible. Always conscious of his role and appearances, whether he liked either or not, Matt Reddy never appeared unshaven or untrimmed and usually wore immaculate whites. His self-appointed "CINCAF's Assistant," the peg-legged Filipino, Juan Marcos, saw to that. Not today. Juan had made the trip with him of course, but even he knew it was pointless to lay out whites for a visit to a worksite of this scope. Today, Matt stood ramrod straight in khakis just like everyone else but Chack, who wore a Marine combat smock. He was also the tallest one there, at a touch over six feet, just edging out Ben Mallory, who commanded the fledgling

Combined Allied Army and Naval Air Corps. It wasn't official, but some used the acronym CAANAC to get his goat. Apparently, caanacs were a kind of flightless carrion eater in the Republic of Real People that, like the skuggiks Ben was familiar with, were related to lizardbirds. He had nothing to say at the moment, taking in the size of the project underway. Even here, elevated about fifty feet and with *Impero*'s main deck just slightly above ground level, the top of her superstructure loomed up over them.

"It is the mud, you see," Walbert continued. "The sheer weight of the ship continuously presses the blocks underneath her ever deeper into the ground. It is concreted by ages of volcanic ash and coral, but remains saturated with seawater and somewhat loose. The ship . . . sags, I am afraid, and we have constantly had to dig down to repair the lowest buckled plates." He shrugged, and some of his assistants, mostly Lemurians, looked at each other nervously. "Of course, not only do those holes fill with water and have to be constantly pumped—we are *always* pumping," he sighed, "but the ship just settles even more, putting stress . . . well, everywhere."

Matt looked at him. They couldn't see any of what he was talking about from here. "Then why not float her? Take the stress off. I was told she was ready for that. What's left to do?" he asked, then smiled dryly. "I mean, besides paint."

"And don't forget painting the deck," Ben Mallory suddenly insisted. "That stupid diagonal red-and-white . . . barber pole paint job on her front and back decks is gonna get her bombed by our own fliers!"

Matt chuckled at that, but Ben was right. The strange paint scheme was on most of the League and all the Italian ships. It made perfect sense if they wanted to prevent being mistaken for the enemy by their own planes. Keeping it might even protect her from the enemy, but maybe not their own. "I'm sure her own crew can sort that out, after she's underway if need be, but what's left to keep her from doing that?" Matt pressed.

Walbert made a brisk gesture with his hands, like he was washing them, but when he spoke, his voice was confident. "She will float," he insisted. "She will leak," he hedged, "but she will float."

"How bad will she leak?" asked Spanky.

Walbert pursed his lips. "I cannot say for sure."

"Her pumps'll keep up, won't they?" Spanky pressed sarcastically, but Walbert actually hesitated before replying, somewhat reservedly, "I believe so."

"Jesus," Spanky barked, looking at Matt. "How bad do you think we'll need her?"

"That depends," Matt temporized. "Why so cagey, Walbert?" He immediately grimaced at his own inconsistency.

Walbert sighed again. "Do not mistake me. *Impero* truly is quite a wonderful ship in many ways. A fine prize indeed. And her machinery layout is almost as artistic as her lines."

Matt was nodding. There was no denying the great Italian battleship was pretty, in her way.

"But," Walbert cautioned, "we have had many problems, most entirely unexpected. As you know, she suffered significant torpedo damage aft, so much that had the water been deeper, she probably would have sunk. Her stern *did* sink to the bottom. This damage also practically destroyed the portside engine in her aft engine room and there is simply no practical way to restore it. The port inboard shaft was likewise badly warped, so she will be down to three engines and shafts at best."

Matt nodded again. That had already been known, and the screw on the shaft had been removed to reduce drag.

Walbert's face assumed a perplexed expression. "But, ironically, her rather . . . unusually designed torpedo protection system may have actually magnified the effectiveness of our weapons." Allied torpedoes were better than they'd been, arguably better than any *Walker* ever had in the world and war she came from, but they were still relatively unsophisticated, underpowered, and lacking in range. Equally ironic, it was the Japanese—and more recently Italian—members of the Alliance who were helping the most to alleviate that. Walbert proceeded to explain what he meant. "Instead of an external blister, which I'm sure you are familiar with, *Impero* has an *internal*, ah . . . 'tube,' essentially, running roughly the same length as the major armor belt"—he blinked—"which is composed of various surprising components, but is likely fairly effective. But the 'tube' was clearly intended to collapse and absorb the destructive force of a torpedo before it could open the inner compartments, and it might have done, to some degree. But the *execution* of the design may have spread the minor damage over a larger area and more compartments."

"More leaks than there would've been with just a giant hole," Spanky guessed.

Walbert nodded. "Possibly." He looked back at Matt. "All things considered, we chose to simply plate over the whole mess and make it as watertight as we can instead of attempting to restore it. That means there is no torpedo protection at all where the damage occurred." He paused. "And I do not know how many more seams will keep opening as long as she remains in that . . . *sumpf* down there."

Now Matt's expression was confused. "Sounds like you're telling me that whether she sorties or not, the sooner we float her, the better off she'll be?"

"I suspect so."

Chack blinked vague impatience. "So float her," he suggested.

Walbert saw Matt tilt his head as if to say, "Why not?" before he continued. "I had hoped to perform a final repair," he explained, "to the portside outboard rudder. You knew she has *three* rudders, did you not?"

Matt looked at Spanky, who was nodding, but shook his head. "No. Weird. Four screws and three rudders." He snorted, then said, "So?"

Walbert took a breath. "There is concern . . ." He glanced at his assistants. "The outboard rudders are behind the *outboard* shafts," he explained, "and the one to port was wrenched rather badly while the ship's stern was working against the bottom—with the tides coming in and going out . . ." Matt made a wind-it-up gesture. "Yes, well, despite the speed penalty of steaming on only three shafts, with the damaged rudder behind the only turning screw to port, *Impero*'s seakeeping characteristics will be . . . abysmal. And the corresponding drag . . ."

Matt was grinning. "Okay. So"—he shrugged—"cut it off. Patch the hole. Do whatever you need to, then float the damn thing."

Walbert looked scandalized. "It is actually a very innovative design," he defended, "not to mention the redundancy it provides, if the primary rudder is damaged."

"Kraut engineers," Spanky chuckled. "No offense," he added. "Actually kind of a compliment, and I get it." Looking at Matt, his next question was still aimed at Walbert. "So, how long to fix it?"

Walbert looked down. "Too long, if you do indeed mean to take her to the Azores."

"And all the while, she's settling in that pit," Matt prodded, eyes sweeping over the massive ship, watching sailors scurry all over her. Even while she was under repair, a crew, albeit far smaller than her original complement of something like two thousand, had been training to man and operate her. He looked at Spanky. "To answer your earlier question, I *do* think we're going to need her." It was his turn to sigh. "The League still outguns us at sea, by a lot, and the scout planes off the AVD pickets we've got watching the Azores report that the fleet they've gathered there is already bigger than the one we fought at St. Vincent." He pointed at *Impero*. "Hell, they've even got another one of *those*—without any holes in it." He shook his head. "If we just show up with *Savoie*, a small handful of cruisers, and *maybe* a dozen destroyers—which is all we can scrape up otherwise—they'll *laugh* at our armistice restriction doctrine of 'sinking anything they send beyond "their" waters,' and I expect we'll have to fight for sure."

"The Republic Navy'll be there, and we'll have a couple of carriers," Spanky pointed out. The Republic of Real People not only had several fairly well-armed capital ships they liked to call "battlecruisers," but had captured their own virtually undamaged League battleship, the *Francesco Caracciolo*, attempting to escape after the Battle of St. Vincent. Renamed *ResPublica*, the prize was the same vintage as *Savoie*, if more powerfully armed. Still, she was certainly no match for *Impero* by any measure.

"True," Matt said, "but this time it'll be the enemy who has the short logistics tail and all the fuel they need. If it comes to a ballroom dance that covers the whole floor"—he shook his head—"which we can't let it . . ." He stopped when he saw Chack looking at Walbert, blinking amusement. He was used to phrases like that, but the German wore a mystified expression. Matt managed a chuckle. "I mean a big battle of chase and maneuver." He gestured at *Impero*. "We'll have to keep 'em bottled up in port or face 'em when they sortie, and I think they'll be less likely to do that if she's sitting out there waiting. Our industry's more advanced than theirs. We might've gotten here later but had a lot less to start with and had to build up quickly. They had enough hardware from the start that they got lazy. Anyway, we can replace what we lose more quickly, at least when it comes to smaller ships. That probably won't last, but we still have the advantage. As long as they think we can hurt 'em real bad, even if they beat us, I don't think they'll risk a fight. Not yet. That may be the whole point behind their threat, after all—to see how we react." He took a deep breath. "Float her, Walbert. We have to show 'em we meant what we said."

Henry Stokes cleared his throat. "That raises another little detail that might bear on the 'point' behind this," he said, glancing at Walbert's assistants.

"Right," Matt breathed. "Sorry, gentlemen. This is a little above your grade. Give us the room, if you please."

Those men and 'Cats quickly bustled out of the large office, several grasping big rolls of paper, probably plans or drawings they'd brought for reference if they'd been asked for details. When the room was clear of everyone but Matt's party, Walbert, and Ben Mallory, Matt looked around at the curious expressions. He was the only one present who knew what Henry had to say.

Stokes cleared his throat again before he began, brow arched, tone wry. "As I said, there might be somethin' more to all this. Seems we finally got word of our missing reserve ship that went to investigate that new flash o' light that was seen, southeast o' Respite, and search for some other missin' ships as well."

"That was quicker than I expected," said Spanky. "*Walker* and Courtney already got there? I thought they were takin' their time, doin' training maneuvers on the way."

"*Walker* isn't there yet," Stokes said, looking at Matt, "but has now been ordered to *get* there as quick as she can." He turned back to the others. "It seems the reserve seaplane tender USS *Scott* did indeed locate at least some of the other missing vessels, but also made another bloody amazing discovery—what was practically a huge bloody graveyard o' ships. *Steel* ships," he stressed.

"Whaat *kind* of ships?" Chack quietly asked.

Stokes bowed his head slightly at the 'Cat for getting straight to the point. "All sorts," he said. "Big ones, little ones, sunk ones stickin' up, an' others still afloat. But a fair number seem to be rather large *warships* an' all are completely abandoned."

The silence in the room was profound, the only sounds now being muffled shouts and machinery noises in the yard.

"Somebody's goddamn fleet," Spanky mumbled.

Stokes nodded. "Yeah, but whose? An' right about where that bloody great flash o' light was seen."

Matt spoke up. "You all came to the consensus that the blast sites Courtney inspected in the Shogunate came from . . . atom bombs, was it?" He nodded to himself. "Atom bombs exploded on another world." He shrugged. "I can't imagine a bomb big enough to do something like that—leak across from one world to another!" he added skeptically, then snorted. "But I guess it makes as much sense as anything. Especially when Courtney reported these weapons somehow"—he waved a hand vaguely—"generated enough energy—or whatever it takes—to not only affect us here but create a . . . crossover event that actually deposited *debris* from their targets from that other world to this one." He motioned at Spanky, Stokes, and Chack. "You thought whatever was witnessed southeast of Respite was another one of those blasts, and that's one of the reasons we sent Courtney and his Corps of Discovery on *Walker*'s training voyage there. Looks like maybe it was," he said grimly. "And if one of those bombs could transport junk in one place, why not do the same with ships in another?"

"But whose?" Spanky repeated what Stokes had said.

Henry Stokes frowned. "I sent another team to the sites in the Shogunate, precisely to try to determine that," he said. "To examine the debris Courtney reported in better detail." He looked around. "Some of the ironwork in particular appeared to have Japanese markings on it. Stamped or cast," he elaborated. "And there were other signs that corroborated this."

Spanky scratched his head under his hat. "So you're sayin' some other version of our side"—his expression brightened—"maybe even our *actual* side, threw a couple of these bombs at the Japs?"

"It's . . . a possibility," Stokes conceded. "An' it could be that 'our side,' as you put it, used another one on a Japanese fleet somewhere." He frowned. "Or the Japanese used one on us."

"That's a chilling thought," Matt mused.

Chack was shaking his head. "I aam glaad no one *here* haas the ability to toss such terrible weapons around!"

"You said it, brother," Spanky agreed with feeling. He looked at Matt. "So now *Walker*'s gonna have a look at this 'ghost fleet'?"

Matt nodded. "Yeah," he agreed, "but there's a problem."

Spanky rolled his eyes. "Sure there is!"

"Yeah. What Henry hasn't gotten to yet is none of this was actually reported by USS *Scott*. Seems a young sailor aboard her managed to escape from some League and Dom pirates who *took* her when they put in to Respite for repairs and provisions, pretending to be her real crew."

"What the hell?" Spanky exploded.

"Bastards," Ben growled.

"What's more," Matt continued, "not only had these Leaguers already been at the site awhile, long enough to capture all the other missing ships, which implies they've got *another* secret base somewhere near"—a number of those had existed in various parts of the world, but especially in what would become "Allied waters," since before the war ever started—"but *Scott* shot up the anchorage at Respite and wrecked the transmitter there. That's why we're only now finding this out."

Chack blinked. "Thaat could mean . . ."

"Right," Spanky said. "The damn League *already* knows about all this—an' the buildup at the Azores is just a distraction while they pillage the ghost fleet in our own backyard!"

"That possibility can't be dismissed," Stokes agreed. He sighed. "Nor can their actions be ignored, for all the reasons we've already discussed. We *have* to confront them."

"But if any of the ghost fleet ships have more advanced technology than we do, the damned Leaguers'll get it!" Spanky exclaimed.

"And that's why *Walker* has to continue her mission," said Matt.

Spanky whistled, and Ben and Walbert both frowned. "A school ship full of kids?" Ben said doubtfully.

Matt sighed. "I don't like it either, but she's still a warship with some of our best people in charge."

"But still, Skipper . . . Those kids . . ." Spanky shook his head. "What can we send to help 'em?"

"Not much," Matt allowed. "Some second-line and reserve ships have already been diverted, but none were especially close. Respite's a little out of the way, remember. And all the operational first-line ships we have are already closer to here than there." His tone hardened. "Captain Rodriguez and Mr. Bradford have been ordered to take all reasonable measures to ensure the safety of the ship and crew, but they *must* attempt to secure the discovery."

"Sure, sure," Spanky conceded, then whistled again and shook his head. "But damn."

"We really don't know anything beyond what a frightened young sailor reported. I give him the benefit of the doubt when it comes to his ordeal and observations, but I can't imagine the enemy has sneaked any sizable force back into what we consider 'our' waters."

"They've done it before," Spanky pointed out. "More than once."

"Quite so," Stokes agreed. "But they could only come through the Pass of Fire or around the Republic in the south of Africa, both of which are under strict Allied control and observation." It was now known that a passage through the ice between Antarctica and the horn of South America was theoretically—briefly—possible on occasion, but would be even more nightmarishly dangerous than sailing against the tidal surge through the Pass of Fire. "So I don't expect a large enemy presence."

"Unless, like some of the others we found, it's been there all along," Matt said, troubled.

Stokes looked at him. "In which case it would've been perfectly placed to disrupt our efforts during the war." He shook his head. "No, I don't expect much more than what we know of: infiltrators who have taken over our own ships, like *Scott*, or perhaps posed as members of our Alliance on the countless steam and sail merchantmen that now proceed unobstructed through the Pass." He paused. "And it's not like *Walker* doesn't have a certain"—he smiled—"reputation. Even if these Leaguers are still there, it's entirely possible the young sailor's escape from the pirates made them clear out, fearing a larger response than we can actually make. I suspect *Walker*'s arrival alone will force them to withdraw."

"Fat chance," Spanky grumbled and everyone looked at him. He snorted and explained his skepticism with a question. "When has anything ever worked out like that?"

CHAPTER 10

USS WALKER

So that's the dope," said Captain Rodriguez, knocking the ash off his cigarette, one made with real Nussie tobacco, and gazing around at the others in the wardroom. Their responses were mixed.

"Say," said Silva, grinning widely, "now there's a chance for a fight, I like this trip a lot better."

"You idiot," Pam snapped. "Is that all you care about?"

Silva leered at her. "Not the *only* thing, doll."

Reddening, Pam very nearly exploded but quickly caught herself, glaring at Captain Rodriguez instead. "There's all these kids in the ship. Or have you forgotten?"

"Of course not," Ronson replied, suddenly angry himself. Pam Cross had a talent for raising people's hackles with fewer words than anyone he knew. Maybe it was just her tone? "That's about all I've been thinking about," he added, his tone hardening even more. "Except for the orders we're bound to obey," he reminded. "Orders straight from Captain Reddy, who wouldn't have given 'em if it wasn't important, an' who I *guarantee* hasn't forgotten there's a load of youngsters on board." He looked around at the rest of them. "This is a pretty big deal. We'd need to go flush these Leaguers an' Doms out, even if that's all this was. But these ships . . ." He shook his head. "No sense even speculating about that until we know more, but even if it was just a bunch of good, salvageable steel just sitting there, we have to secure it before the enemy does—or takes it from us by sinking it."

"Hear, hear," Courtney Bradford said, applauding by tapping his empty pipe on the green wardroom table top. "That concern struck me at once and you're the first to voice it."

Ronson tilted his head at Jack Meek. "He told me. Well, him and Mr. Cook." He nodded at Abel.

"Came to the snoops an' scientific fellas first," Silva needled Gunny Horn. "Guess we always focus on takin' or defendin' stuff, huh?"

"Ha!" Pam barked, pointing at Silva. "God only knows how many things *you've* destroyed to keep out of enemy hands."

Silva shrugged philosophically. "Maybe so, but that ain't always the first thing that jumps ta mind."

Pam visibly coiled to retort, but Ronson interrupted her. "You two lovers can fight all you want later. Let's stay on topic for now." He looked around again, gaze settling on Tabby. "What can Isak give us?" Isak Reuben was the only one "in the know" not present.

"Twenty knots," Tabby promptly replied. "Thaat'll get us to Respite the day aafter tomorrow."

"That's the best we can do?"

Tabby nodded. "On two boilers. Even then we'll be suckin' fumes. We light off another boiler, we'll only gain another six or seven knots an' won't haave the fuel to get there."

Ronson sighed deeply. "Very well. We all know what to do. Keep up the training." He reconsidered. "Pick up the pace however you can." He pointed his cigarette at Silva, Horn, Miles, and the Lemurian Marine Sergeant Kaik. "Gunnery, torpedoes, and small arms in particular." He frowned at Fred and Kari. "No flight training, I'm afraid."

"Just as well," Kari said. "These younglings got no feel for flyin'."

Fred rolled his eyes at his friend. "Like you did? And you weren't any older than some of them when you started either."

"Neither were you," said Ronson, grinning.

Fred's face colored. "I was a *little* older."

"I wasn't," said Abel Cook, rather pointedly. "I was *younger* than many of the trainees on board."

"That's true," agreed Ronson, expression now curious, "and I suppose you brought that up for a reason?"

"I did," Abel confirmed. "I understand that everyone here"—he smiled—"with the possible exception of Mr. Bradford, who knows better, is . . . reluctant to expose the children in this ship to any risk. My point is that there was always, *is* always risk associated with any voyage on the seas of this world." He nodded at Courtney. "And our mission concurrent with the educational aspect added another accepted layer to that. Now, I don't know how this new feature will affect our original purpose. I hope it turns out that we can settle this matter and proceed to examine the strange ships that have been reported and then go on to locate the mysterious land mass that Mr. Bradford most craves to visit." Courtney gave him a fond smile before Abel continued. "But I believe the argument has been made already that, during the war, many of our ships went into desperate action far less prepared than this one already is. So"—he took a long breath, gazing at Pam, then Tabby, finally Captain Rodriguez—"if it becomes indispensable that you do so, you must not hesitate to take *Walker* into battle, regardless of the risk to her crew, no matter how young it is."

The wind and sea continued to mount through the day, and the long, narrow destroyer began pitching and rolling worse than she had to this point in the voyage. As fast as her sleek hull shape made her, that and her flush deck also meant that *Walker* was a wet ship in any kind of sea, and Chief Bosun Bashear had lifelines rigged and screens placed over the few companionways that weren't shut and dogged. First Lieutenant Daanis, with his Sky Priest learning, remained firm in his opinion that the weather wouldn't turn bad, but "bad" can be a relative thing, and a number of cadets, regardless of their shoreside training and level of accomplishment, weren't prepared for such brisk and unexpected motion and the puke buckets in the berthing spaces began to fill. Misery of that sort has a tendency to beget more misery and aside from yawning, perhaps, puking might be one of the most contagious activities known. It wasn't long before nearly every belowdecks surface was practically awash with vomit.

"I'm going to die," groaned young Philan Bele, sitting on the edge of a rack with a bucket in his lap. "I *want* to die." To his mortification, the tall Repub cadet had been one of the first afflicted. The fact that his condition was now nearly universal was small comfort.

"You're not going to die," predicted Susan "Susie" Raj, dropping on the rack beside him, chewing on a sandwich she'd just retrieved from the galley.

Bele merely glanced at the food with the bite taken out before spewing in the bucket again.

"You are an evil girl," pronounced Daniel "Danny Boy" Baker. Though not feeling as bad as Bele, he didn't really feel good.

Susie waved her sandwich before taking another bite. "Whole stack of these up above," she said, chewing. "Mr. Lanier isn't cooking. Says it would be wasted effort, so he put these out in a basket on the counter." She looked at Bele. "It's lashed to the counter so it doesn't fall on deck and scatter the parts everywhere."

Bele made unpleasant, slightly echoey noises.

"He was going to make soup," she continued, "out of 'tomatoes,' he called them. The Nussies grow them. So do the Doms, and the soup is very bright red," she said cheerfully. When that didn't seem to have any effect, she added, "He was going to mix things in, to make it colorful and chunky."

Bele heaved.

"Evil girl," gasped Daniel.

A damp breeze wafted through the space and a few of the twenty-odd off-duty sufferers looked up to see Silva, Lawrence, and Petey stroll in, apparently oblivious to the movement of the ship and the stench.

"Lawsy, Larry!" Silva exclaimed. "Did you ever see such a fit o' mass pukery in yer whole lizardy life?"

"Ne'er," Lawrence somberly replied.

"Pukery!" Petey shrieked, jumping from Silva's shoulder and swooping down on the deck.

"Why, I expect if we had to fight right now, a one-legged skuggik could float up on a stick, board, an' take over the ship!"

"Shocking," Lawrence agreed.

There was virtually no response, though Susie was grinning, still eating. Silva winked at her. "Goddammit, Petey! Quit lickin' that up. What's the matter with you?"

"Goddamn!" Petey exclaimed indignantly, leaping back up to his usual perch. He'd been innocent, for once, of licking anything, though he had been sniffing a nearby puddle with interest. Silva's admonition had the desired effect on nearly everyone else, however, and the sounds of retching in the compartment redoubled.

"Ah, hell," Silva said. "Perpetual pukapalooza. Disgraceful. C'mon, Larry." He turned. "Let's go get some chow—an' get out'a here before we get painted." He paused in the hatchway and called loudly over his shoulder, "By the way, only time I'll ever warn ya—Gee-Kyoo'll sound in about"—he pulled an Impie watch from his pocket and glanced at it—"two an' a half minutes. An' if you don't beat yer last time—which was pitiful—we'll keep at it till ya do!"

Susie promptly shoved the remains of her sandwich into Philan Bele's view. "Want a bite?"

CHAPTER 11

RESPITE ISLAND

As First Lieutenant Daanis predicted, there was no actual storm, but the sea ran high for the rest of the day and through the night. And as Silva had warned, numerous drills were sounded regardless. If the performance of these drills never quite met the supervisors' standards, the cadets at least managed to competently man their designated stations, and the rampant seasickness did diminish. A few young sailors were genuinely too ill to do anything, but most either had something to think about besides their misery or were simply all puked out. The sea moderated the following day and appetites and performance improved. Just after dawn the day after that, the high hazy peak of Respite Island was sighted from the lookout in the "bucket" high on the foremast. By late in the forenoon watch, *Walker* was met by an old Imperial steam launch bearing a pilot who transferred aboard to help conn the ship through the treacherous, turbulent reef to the comparatively tranquil inner harbor. All the while, the old destroyer's rails were lined with gawkers taking in the exotic sights of the scenic, largely unspoiled island.

Lizardbirds and a surprising variety of "real" birds swooped and capered over the breakers in a riot of color. Many broke off to follow the ship through the one narrow navigable channel, squawking and fussing as they snatched at morsels stirred up in her wake. The city encompassing the anchorage, while expansive and holding the majority of the island's population, remained charmingly quaint and picturesque. Almost all construction had utilized native materials: timber and gray and black volcanic stone for the most part, which blended harmoniously with the exposed rocky crags, but also the deep green of the dense surrounding forest. And some of the architecture consisted of more ambitious, vaguely classical governmental or administrative structures.

Most of the gawking youngsters came from places that hadn't been terribly different a generation before, but few much remembered how they looked before the war had turned them into overcrowded fortified centers of industry. But the war had largely passed Respite by—until now, after it was "over"—and the evidence of destruction wrought by the rogue USS *Scott* grew more evident the closer they came to the harbor front. The people here were well aware of and much appreciated how blessed they'd been. Returning volunteer veterans made sure of that. So USS *Walker* was especially welcome for the protection she'd always symbolized ever since her very first visit a number of years before. Now she was obliged to slow to steerageway as shoals of small fishing boats and skiffs swept out to celebrate her arrival and the shore started filling with people.

"Where's the fueling pier?" Ronson asked the pilot, a short, portly young man who, despite his shape, had clambered aboard with the ease of a Lemurian.

The man frowned for the first time. "Ah . . . aye, I fear we ain't got one enow. Which them bloody damned pirates burned it up, didn't they?"

Tabby glared at the man. "Then, where are we supposed to refuel?"

The pilot shrugged uncomfortably. "Which ye'll hafta ask the guv'nor that." He pointed in the general direction of the commercial docks, currently occupied by a few sailing ships and one old Impie steamer. "I was told tae bring ye tae anchor just offshore, yonder."

"We're not to tie up?" asked Jack Meek, proving that if there'd been any instructions for when they arrived, he hadn't received them.

"Ah, no." The pilot's expression brightened. "P'raps it's so ye won't be overrun by islanders. Folk here are truly glad tae see ye."

Ronson frowned, glancing at Tabby. "That's swell, but it seems we ran our bunkers dry for nothing." He sighed. "We're already down to one boiler, but have Isak reduce fuel consumption as much as he can. Just enough steam pressure to maintain essential electrical power." Everything in the ship started with steam, including the generators. And they didn't just make power for lights and bilge pumps, but had to run the gyro, gun and torpedo directors, and myriad other things—even the pumps to move water and oil to make steam. "Sparks," he said to Meek, "get on the horn and see if you can find out, now we're here, what the hell we're supposed to use for fuel." He didn't have to tell him to code the transmission. Jack Meek hadn't sent anything in the clear. Looking back at Tabby, he said, "Pass the word to call the special sea and anchor detail. We'll drop the hook where the pilot tells us."

Shortly thereafter, USS *Walker*'s portside anchor splashed down in the calm, virtually transparent blue water of the bay, even while her starboard motor launch was swung out and lowered over the side. With Courtney Bradford, Abel Cook, Fred Reynolds, Kari-Faask, Pam Cross, Sergeant Kaik, Jack Meek, and Lawrence already in the boat, Silva pushed past a distracted Carl Bashear and slid down the falls into the stern and took his place as coxswain before grinning up at the sputtering bosun. Visiting a friendly port, Silva wore a minimalistic "dress" version of his "just in case suit," adding only leggings, pistol and web belt (completely encircled with magazine pouches), and his battered 1917 Navy cutlass.

"You used to be quicker, Carl," Silva taunted. "Gettin' old."

"Damn you, Dennis," Bashear hissed down.

Silva waved expansively at the boat. "Still plenty o' room." That was true enough, but Carl Bashear just shook his head. "Not with you drivin'."

"Suit yerself."

While wondering, as always, about the . . . mixed example Silva set for the cadets, Ronson pretended to ignore all this—as he should—and spoke to Tabby. "I don't know how long I'll be ashore." He waved generally upward at the peak of the looming mountain where the governor's palace was. "If I have to go all the way up there, it could take a while. Hopefully, I'll come back with good news. Or *some* news."

Tabby nodded and gestured around. "We gonna give these kiddies liberty?"

"Why not? Work out a schedule. Make sure they're supervised, though."

Tabby blinked amusement. In addition to its natural beauty, Respite was renowned for its ale shops. There was also a disproportionately large number of poor, formerly "indentured" females who'd come here from some of the more oppressive places in the Empire before Governor/Empress Rebecca McDonald's social reforms. Not only were they often unusually beautiful, they generally wore very little and dreamed of being carried away to more exciting lives. Many of the "expat Impie gals" in the west originally hailed from here. "But who's gonna supervise the supervisors?" she asked.

Ronson chuckled. "Good point." Tone now more formal, he said, "The ship is yours, Commander."

Equally serious, Tabby replied, "Ay, Skipper. I haave the ship."

Turning, Ronson grabbed the rope falls and slid down as well. Silva already had the engine burbling contentedly and soon the boat had been unhooked and was gently curving toward shore. There was no band waiting to welcome them, but there was an honor guard, all dressed in the island version of the old Imperial Marine dress uniform. Quite a few others in the cheering crowd were obviously veterans, wearing pieces of uniforms as well. Most were just happy or curious islanders (including a fair percentage of those scantily clad girls, contrasting profoundly with the shapeless, overdressed style of more affluent women). Smiling and waving, and in some cases staring, Ronson and his party made their way through the press to where, to their surprise, Governor and Emelia Radcliff were waiting on a streetcar-like carriage hitched to a dozen matching burros with feathery plumes on their heads. Silva actually barked an incredulous laugh at the ridiculous sight, but Ronson flashed him a cautionary glare before stepping forward and rendering a sharp salute.

"Captain Ronaldo Rodriguez, USS *Walker*, come to report, Your Excellency."

Governor Radcliff, dressed in the finest Imperial style of several years ago—long but lightweight maroon tailcoat and black cravat over a cream-colored weskit and knee breeches and dazzlingly polished black knee boots—stood in the carriage and excitedly waved a small golden baton that looked strikingly like a long chicken bone as he beamed at his visitors. "I remember you perfectly, Captain Rodriguez, as I do most of those with you! Emelia and I, all of Respite, are overjoyed by your arrival"—he smiled even wider—"and the sight of your iconic ship, of course. Welcome, welcome, welcome indeed!"

Courtney was dressed much like the governor, except in tan, with the addition of a wide-brimmed straw hat. He and Abel Cook moved forward to join Ronson.

"Ah!" Emelia exclaimed. "The inestimable and ever versatile Mr. Bradford!" She fluttered an intricately carved bone fan and smiled. "Or should I call you 'Admiral'?"

Courtney bowed deeply. "No, my lady. That was the briefest and most figurative title I ever had."

"That is *not* what we heard," Emelia firmly countered.

"Nevertheless, I come before you now as only the same amateur naturalist you first met." Courtney stood straight again and smiled as well. "Though perhaps now I am proud to be a schoolteacher as well."

"I guess you're aware that was the original purpose of our voyage," Ronson prompted the governor and his wife.

"Indeed," agreed Governor Radcliff, though the skepticism in his voice was fairly clear. "Come," he said. "Join us on the carriage. There's room for all," he added, which was true. With the exception of the portion of the carriage already occupied, the sides were open, with long benches facing outward. "We've arranged a short private reception in a suitably private venue here in the city," Governor Radcliff continued, then chuckled. "No need for a tedious drive up the mountain."

Ronson's relief was obvious. "Thank you, sir. Have I your permission to extend liberty to my ship's company?"

Governor Radcliff waved that away. "Of course, of course. I'll issue the invitation myself." Signaling to one of the horse-mounted guards surrounding the strange vehicle, he sent the rider down through the crowd toward where they came ashore.

"One other thing, Your Excellency," Ronson pressed, then paused as the governor regarded him with a knowing expression. "Fuel," he continued. "I understand the, uh, 'pirates' destroyed the reserve that's maintained here. Our bunkers are dry and we have to have fuel to continue."

Governor Radcliff's countenance darkened. "Yes," he confirmed, "considerable damage was done and a number of people were killed or badly injured. You cannot imagine how anxious I am for you to catch and punish the fiends responsible." He took a calming breath. "But I do have one piece of good news, at least in respect to fuel. The small monthly oiler that replenishes our supply could arrive any day. That is why the pilot had you anchor away from the dock, so the oiler could go directly alongside you when it does. I understand that another one, as well as some . . . miscellaneous other 'support' ships have been dispatched to assist you in your efforts, though it will be somewhat longer before they appear."

Ronson nodded. He already knew that whatever was available was being scraped together to join them, but he wouldn't wait. Whatever came would have to follow behind them.

Governor Radcliff clasped his hands together. "Now, do come along, if you please." He lowered his voice. "There is a remarkable young . . . person I want you to meet."

The reception took place in the Respite Assembly building, one of those somewhat classical structures complete with porous columns of dark volcanic rock. A few more local representatives and administrators were present to greet them but didn't stay long, promising to attend a more public reception for *Walker*'s officers that evening. After everyone in the more intimate group made themselves comfortable around a long, darkly stained wooden table in the conference room and refreshments were served (Petey was remarkable restrained in the presence of the dainty snacks provided, as long as Silva slipped him the occasional morsel), the young Lemurian seaman's apprentice named Fen-An-Raar was presented and quickly became everyone's focus.

Fen was a little shy and tongue-tied at first, being introduced to such relatively well-known heroes of the Alliance. He might've been somewhat uneasy in the presence of the very Grik-like Lawrence as well. He gradually collected himself, however, and repeated his tale from start to finish in an increasingly confident manner. Everyone seemed quite impressed, but then the questions began. Jack Meek started off, initially intent on establishing that Fen's story was true and the youngster was who he claimed to be, but was soon satisfied, and more questions came from the others.

"You're *sure* they were Leaguers and Doms?" Ronson asked.

Fen nodded and blinked, tail swishing. "They made no secret of it at all," he stated flatly. "Thaat was one reason Chief Allen and Lieutenaant Jun were sure they'd never release us, or probably even let us live."

"Bastards," grumped Silva. "You reckon this 'Ames' fella was in charge?"

Fen gulped. Lawrence was certainly frightening, in his toothy, savage way, but the one-eyed giant was the most intimidating human he'd ever seen. "Ames was in chaarge of us, but it seemed clear he answered to someone else in the region, wherever their 'base' is."

"And you have no idea where that might be?" asked Abel Cook.

Fen blinked regret and shook his head. "No sir, though we got the impression thaat, though it was inconveniently distaant, it waasn't . . ." He paused as if pondering how to explain.

"Not outrageously so?" Courtney supplied.

Fen nodded agreement. "Thaat was just the feeling we got."

"Why's that?" Ronson asked.

Fen blinked uncertainty. "Well . . . no one ever went ashore, thaat we could see, to forage for food or even water. Not even the prisoners from our ship or the others, who the pirates used for most of the labor, were sent. We never knew why. But doesn't thaat mean they couldn't be too far from someplace to take on provisions?"

"Makes sense," Ronson allowed, clearly impressed by the observation. "I wonder what kept them offshore?" he mused.

"What condition were the other prisoners in?" asked Pam.

"Some were okaay. Others were weakening. Some of those from ships they took earlier seemed in very baad shape, to me."

Pam's expression clouded. "Those"—she glanced at Silva—"bastards," she said, as if hesitant to agree with him about anything.

"The same enemy we have grown accustomed to," Courtney Bradford sighed. "Now," he said, leaning forward, "tell us more about what you saw—this 'ghost fleet' you reported."

Fen tried his best, but his only reference was other ships he'd seen, and he attempted to make comparisons. Given materials, he even attempted to draw what he saw, but his talents as an artist were lacking. All he could really do was confirm there were "many" rusty iron ships, some of which had what could only be very large guns. He'd once seen USS *Savoie*, and said a couple of the ships looked a lot like her, which caused the exchange of significant glances. "And some looked a little like *Waalker*," he finally added, as if just remembering, "but different too. A little laarger I think, with not as many smokestaacks." He paused and blinked shyly. "I haave seen *Waalker* several times in my life and saw her steam into the harbor. She looks even more beautiful than ever," he almost gushed.

Ronson smiled. "I understand you're from the Filpin Lands. She's had some work done since the last time she was there."

"I thought she was beautiful then," Fen said softly, wistfully.

"Said like a buddin' dee-stroyer-man," Silva pronounced with approval.

"Yes, well," Courtney interrupted, looking intently at Fen. "The question is, young fellow, are you sailor enough to read a chart and show us on it where we can find this island where all these ships were and your own was taken by our enemies?"

Fen regarded Courtney, suddenly blinking something like defiance. "No sir," he said. "I caan't show you on a chaart—*won't*, unless I must," he corrected, "but I caan *take* you right to it."

It took a few moments before the substance of the declaration broke through the boldness of it and Silva guffawed, startling Petey from his perch and sending him coasting to the floor. Lawrence snuffled some sort of laugh and Courtney blinked in surprise. Even Ronson displayed a small smile. Abel Cook and Pam Cross immediately nodded approval, understanding.

Still smiling slightly, Ronson inquired, "Are you attempting to *blackmail* your way on board my ship?"

"No sir," Fen quickly denied. "At least I don't think so." His tail swished swiftly and his ears laid back in embarrassment. "I don't know what 'blaackmail' means."

"It means what you're doin'," Pam said with delight. "You'll do this if we do that."

Fen blinked at her. "I thought that waas 'negotiation'?"

"Sorta," Silva gleefully agreed, then sobered. "But you don't usually get to do that with yer skipper."

"He's already an experienced sailor and has demonstrated admirable initiative," Abel told Ronson, then shrugged. "And *Walker* is currently serving as a school ship." He looked back at Fen and continued more seriously. "A school ship for cadets who, if they perform satisfactorily, will owe at least one enlistment to the American Navy Clan."

Fen's eyes went even wider than they already were. "I would be in the Navy?" he asked almost breathlessly.

Pursing his lips, Ronson nodded. "That's right. Subject to the orders of your officers."

Fen clapped his hands in excitement.

"It won't be easy," Ronson warned. "Sailor or not, you'll be behind everybody in your training and will need to catch up fast. Might even be tough to make friends who'll help you." He glanced around at the others. "Most had to work pretty hard just to get in the program and some might resent him just . . . dropping in."

"And some did little more thaan be born to the right parents," inserted Sergeant Kaik, speaking for the first time as he blinked something like resentment. Though he'd ended the war as General Pete Alden's personal aide, Kaik had fought through its most bitter battles with the First Marines. He deeply respected Pete Alden, but of them all, even Silva, Kaik probably harbored the least intrinsic esteem for officers in general, and especially those from the Empire and even the Republic, who had once been as likely to have purchased their commissions as earned them. That was less prevalent now, but it still happened.

"No problem," Silva said, eyeing Fen. "Little scudder's got spunk, that's sure. I'll take charge o' catchin' him up an' I know just the right cadets ta help him along. When we're all through here, I'll take him ta meet his new tutors when they come ashore on liberty." He chuckled. "I s'pect they'll all be together."

Ronson threw a quick glance at Pam, who only shrugged and nodded. Despite the destructive force of nature Dennis Silva could be, not to mention her own problems with him, even Pam had to admit he was—somehow—surprisingly good with kids, human or Lemurian. That was, in fact, one of the sources of her furious frustration with him. As far as she knew, only she and Chack ever heard a peep about Silva's childhood, how he lost both parents to the influenza and was raised by a brutally abusive uncle—who he ultimately killed. This left him unenthusiastic about the notion of becoming a father himself, though Pam remained as mystified by that as she was any number of his other attitudes and behaviors. Her inability to understand why she was still so crazy about him left her as mad at herself as she was him.

Looking back at Silva, Lawrence, and Petey—who'd stolen a little fruit tart of some sort before returning to his perch, where he proceeded to demolish it and string crumbs all over Silva's shoulder—Ronson sighed and leaned back in his chair. "Okay, it's a deal." He arched a brow at Fen. "But don't think you can pull any foolishness like this again. And not only do I expect you to show us"—he dipped his head at Governor Radcliff—"and anyone else who needs to know where we're going on a chart, I intend to test your ability to get us there, like you said."

"This here's Fen-An-Raar," Silva said, pushing the short, self-conscious Lemurian forward toward Bele, Samuel Jenks, Haan, Daniel Baker, Maarik, Susan Raj, and their new companion, Aalak-Maraan, who'd assembled together on the dock after coming ashore with a cluster of other cadets. A grizzled, veteran crew 'Cat was climbing up from the motor launch to join them. Silva waved him back. "I got these ones," he said. "Go on back an' fetch another litter for yourself." He looked at the other cadets, also a roughly equal mix of humans and Lemurians. "You bunch come closer. What's all this packin' up in separate groups? Yer all one crew, ain't ya?"

Bele leaned forward and whispered, "They're striking for *engineering*, Chief Silva."

Silva blinked his eye. "Oh. Well. That's different, ain't it?" He shooed the other cadets away. "Go latch on to Boilermaker Sureen over there." The young woman was already collecting another group of cadets out of a local boat that brought them ashore. "She speaks snipe better than me."

Regarding the smaller group that remained, Silva put his hands on his hips. "Fen may be little"—his eye passed over Aalak and Maarik, who weren't any bigger—"but he's a firecracker. No sense keepin' it secret now since I reckon you'll hear plenty from the locals, but one o' our old ships was took by a buncha bloodthirsty League pirates who then came here an' shot up the joint." Motioning at Fen, he continued. "This little fella was one o' her crew that got captured, but sneaked ashore to warn everybody." He shrugged. "Didn't help much at the time, but not only did he get the word out, he knows where them villainous bastards might be." Silva grinned. "Since it ain't much out'a the way where we're goin', Cap'n Reddy hisself invited us special ta hunt the devils down!" It wasn't the whole story, but Silva figured these kids would get that from Fen soon enough and had no doubt the whole crew would know before *Walker* left Respite in her wake. Just as well, he thought.

"You mean . . . we might actually get to see some action, Chief Silva?" asked Samuel Jenks, barely able to contain himself. Not everyone looked quite as eager, but all seemed game.

"I sure hope so," Silva said fervently. "Been too long since anything excitin' happened. 'Course, that means it's time we put some proper gun's crews together, all that sorta thing."

Bele and Jenks grinned at each other, but Silva pointed at them. "You two can't crew the same gun. 'Fact, I gotta bust y'all up on different guns 'cause yer the best I've trained." He chuckled at Aalak. "Aside from the Airedale you adopted. But Gunny Horn'll have his own list an' we'll put 'em together. Start trainin' all our crews *as* crews." He shook his head. "But that ain't why I brung you young Fen. He's a sailor already, but he's gonna need help catchin' up on just about ever'thin' else, startin' with bein' a *destroyer* sailor. In the meantime, when he ain't helpin' the quartermaster plot our course," Silva said airily, "we'll make him a hot shell man, or somethin'."

"I haave some . . . faamiliarity with the four-inch-fifty gun," said Fen. "There was one on *Scott*, after all."

Silva blinked at him. "Why . . . I reckon there would'a been, too." He shrugged. "We'll see what you can do." He turned back to the others. "Mainly, though, I know you fellas—an' gals—better than most, an' I've took note o' yer habit for takin' in strays." He grinned at Aalak again. "Point is, young Fen's signin' on for a reason, he's already been through a bit, an' I don't wanna hear about anybody who thinks he ain't fit ta be aboard tryin' ta push him around, see?"

All the youngsters in front of him were nodding back at him now, and Bele spoke for the rest. "Thank you for your faith in us, Chief Silva. We'll make sure Fen is welcome."

"Swell," Silva said, now looking around. "Say, I know a damn good grog shop. Several of 'em, in fact. Why don't we go put some suds up our nose?"

Lawrence spoke up warningly. "Younglings not su'osed to drink ale, are they?"

Silva looked surprised. "Why . . . I don't know. Some places they are. An' I never seen any 'Cat kiddies, er Impie young'uns fer that matter, de-nied a cup o' beer. Don't matter," he decided. "There's a place at the far end o' town right on a nice sandy beach. You an' me can drink an' watch 'em go a'swimmin' an' frolickin' in the surf!"

"Swimming!" Bele exclaimed in horror.

"Sure," Silva said. "Why not?" He leaned over and whispered at Lawrence. "That's the beach where them near nekkid Impie gals draw their fishnets up onshore, remember?"

"Believe it or not, you *can* get in the water here," Fen confirmed to the others. "I have," he added cryptically.

CHAPTER 12

The expected oiler arrived three days later and went straight alongside *Walker*, as directed. The ship was the *Uru*, named for a river somewhere, as all fleet oilers were, and it was one of the wooden-hull wartime-construction dedicated steamers with copper storage tanks. Like all Allied steamers, warships, or auxiliaries, *Uru* relied on oil to heat its boiler to power its triple expansion engine and turn its single screw, and the combination of oil-burning and wood construction had always given everyone the creeps. Especially in a ship that carried a lot more oil than it needed for itself. There hadn't been any alternative at first, before the Allies started building iron, then steel hulls, but the designs, and even more importantly, the procedures for operating and protecting them had been such from the start that ship fires had never been as much of a problem as people feared. Granted, when the ships burned, there wasn't much to do but abandon them and watch the spectacular show, but surprisingly few of them did.

Nevertheless, proper procedures were strictly enforced during the transfer of fuel and it took most of the day for the small oiler to fill *Walker*'s empty bunkers. After that, with all the essential apparatus stowed for the short trip to the fueling pier, which was still being rebuilt, *Uru* tied up where she could replace the destroyed storage tanks with herself until new tanks onshore could be built as well. At the same time, water and provisions had been floated out to the old destroyer and the cadets worked their tails off (whether they had real ones or not) to prepare the ship to depart the following morning.

Emelia Radcliff hosted a farewell ball at the governor's palace brimming with local dignitaries, and Ronson, Tabby, Courtney, Abel, Ian Miles, Jack Meek, Gunny Horn, Fred, Kari, and even Isak, very self-consciously escorting Sureen, attended in their best dress attire, whites for the sailors, blues for the Marines. Silva, Sergeant Kaik, and Pam Cross attended as well, also in their best, but they were primarily responsible for chaperoning a double handful of cadets. Lawrence refused to go and "get stared at" by the islanders, most of whom had never seen anything like him and that was probably just as well. Lawrence didn't really have a "temper" to lose, but Silva did and he likely would've lost it when his friend was almost inevitably slighted in some way. Of course, that left Lawrence free to look after Petey—which he hated. Whenever he was called on to do so, Silva was always about half sure that Petey would wind up eaten.

"This cloth is very uncomfortable," Fen whispered aside to Philan Bele, barely loud enough to hear over the chamber music and rumble of voices in the crowded, dimly lit room. He'd been outfitted in whites like all the cadets, and the tight-fitting tunic and tall straight collar were the most confining things he'd ever worn. He and the rest of the cadets had been presented to the governor and his wife, who both raved over Fen's new "dashing" appearance, particularly compared to the first time they met, but then all the youngsters were shuffled off into a corner out of the way under the watchful eyes of Sergeant Kaik and Pam Cross. Silva stood there as well, but as usual, his lone eye constantly roved all over as if searching for threats. There probably weren't any of those at the moment, aside from Respite society dames who were seemingly helplessly drawn to pet Lemurians for some reason, but that could certainly be awkward and his daunting glare discouraged it amazingly. Besides, he just couldn't help himself.

"Mine fits very well," Bele replied, then chuckled. "Of course, I'm skinnier than you, for my height." He glanced down at Fen. "Then again, you are fairly skinny as well, which, considering how you escaped captivity, might have saved your life." He gestured lower at the kind of kilt all Lemurians wore, regardless of sex or service branch, to accommodate their tails. "That looks rather comfortable, however."

"I suppose," Fen reluctantly grudged. "I'm just glaad our duty shirts aren't so tight." Daily dress was blue dungaree trousers for humans and blue kilts for 'Cats. Chiefs and above wore khakis. Loose-fitting T-shirt-like tops were otherwise universal, white for the deck division and gray for engineering, the latter so the unavoidable grime wasn't as apparent.

"I agree," confirmed the little female named Maarik-Faas, who seemed to have latched on to Fen. She snorted. "I don't know why we are here, though, if all we caan do is staand here. The music is weird and we caan't even go get any food."

"Seen but not heard," Silva proclaimed airily, surprising everyone, particularly Pam, that he heard the exchange. Silva was notoriously hard of hearing, though Pam was certain his deafness was at least partially selective.

"Why do you say stuff like that?" Pam demanded. "Just to hurt people's feelings?"

Silva looked back at her, blinking his eye. "Nope. Don't ever say things just to hurt folks on purpose, 'cept enemies, I guess." He arched the brow over his good eye at her. "What I say gets *took* hurtful sometimes, no matter how I mean it, an' it don't seem ta make any difference how well 'er how long *somebody's* known me," he added significantly, then shook his head and looked back at the crowd before grumbling, "What I just said was a figure o' speech, a observation on the way o' the world an' how life ain't always fair." He turned to gesture back at the cadets. "'Specially to young'uns." His one-eyed gaze found Pam's once more and seemed to pin her to the wall behind her with an instant's crushing glimpse of a lifetime of hurt and regret, and most surprisingly, a strange vulnerability. It vanished just as quickly, replaced by the usual carefree, gently teasing gleam she usually saw, but she was struck almost breathless by the fleeting intensity she apprehended.

Shit, she thought dismally. *That's why I can't just forget the big dopey jerk.*

The cadets were eventually released to mingle in small groups, always accompanied by Kaik, Pam, or Silva. And despite Governor Radcliff actually getting everyone's attention and reminding them that petting Lemurians was considered rude, a few of the smaller (frankly cuter) 'Cats had to endure the occasional pat or fleeting caress. Worse was hearing the violator excitedly gush to a companion how the fur felt, as if they weren't still standing right there. No one made a scene, however, until the grizzled Marine Sergeant Kaik felt someone stroke the fur on his head from behind. He spun around so quickly, with such a savage revelation of formidable canines even as he slapped his side for the cutlass that fortunately wasn't there, he elicited a shriek of stark terror from the malefactor: a somewhat puffy middle-aged woman in a dress that looked strikingly like the palace drapes. Losing her balance, the woman teetered alarmingly until a similarly dressed gentleman arrested her collapse. The calamity wasn't over, however, because what looked like at least three-quarters of her head, but was in fact an artistically sculpted and decorated bee-hive-shaped wig, had sustained the inertia she initiated and plummeted into a large crystal punch bowl. The resulting splash was all out of proportion to what a similarly sized heap of hair alone should cause, indicating that the density of the thing was more on the order of a woolly rhino pig turd (to which Silva later compared it, in mass as well as its suddenly soggy appearance). More shrieking—and hysterical laughing—erupted among the onlookers surrounding the explosion of punch that thoroughly inundated them. Utterly mortified, the woman snatched her streaming accessory and bowled her dripping way through the crowd. There was more laughter and some applause at the man who arrested her fall when he followed in her wake, expression a mixture of embarrassment and humor.

Few on Respite would've recognized it, but Sergeant Kaik was blinking what amounted to apologetic humiliation. But Silva stepped over and slapped him on the back, loudly exclaiming, "He didn't mean ta scare that big woman. Not a'tall." He grinned enormously. "But the sergeant here has been smack in the middle o' near as much killin' as me. I've heard that can put a fella on edge. Point is"—he ruffled the fur on Kaik's head, much to the Lemurian Marine's annoyance—"cuddly as they look, some 'Cats just ain't ta be petted." His grin faded just slightly. "Not ever."

There was another round of laughter, though it was somewhat

strained this time. Servants quickly arrived with towels, and the punch bowl and tablecloth were swiftly removed and replaced while the tone of the ball began to return to normal. "Generaal Aalden waas right about you," Kaik finally said to Silva, tone a little friendlier than it had been before. "You are a aasshole."

"That's right, Sergeant Kaik," Silva confirmed with conviction, then glanced at Pam, who'd followed him over, when he continued. "But assholery alone ain't always all it takes ta keep somebody from bein' a decent fella, otherwise." He patted Kaik on the back again. "Like you, I figger. Hell, near ever'body on this trip is a asshole, 'cept most o' the kiddies, the skipper, XO, Fred Reynolds, Kari-Faask, an' Mr. Cook. Even Mr. Bradford can be one from time to time. Ian Miles, Earl Lanier, an' Isak over there"—he tilted his head at the engineer—"was *born* assholes." He shook his head, looking at Pam again. "But I trust *almost* ever' one of 'em ta do the right thing when it counts; ta be 'good' when 'bad' rears up in front of 'em"—a slight frown touched his lips—"an' kill it."

Captain Rodriguez had been drawn by the ruckus and now approached through the crowd. When he spoke, it was to Silva, Kaik, and Pam. "Well, Chief Silva, you seem to have sorted that out in your usual . . . singular way. Well done," he complimented guardedly, probably much happier than he could show that no one had been killed. "Why don't you all show the cadets around a little more, about half an hour, then start them back down to the ship. I plan on clearing out of here as soon as I can myself. We'll all need some rest."

"We shovin' off at daylight?" Silva asked.

Ronson nodded, waving around. "All this has been a laugh, but we've still got serious business ahead." He lowered his voice. "Mr. Meek has been picking up transmissions we can't decode, which means it isn't anybody on our side talking to anybody we want them to, and the direction finder's pointing straight down the bearing we're headed. It's time we got busy."

Under the purple-gold sky of dawn, USS *Walker* crept up on her anchor and hoisted it high enough alongside to where the small anchor crane could be rigged out to hook on and swing it over to the billboard, where it could be secured. Cadets stood ready with hoses to wash the mud off the flukes. None came up from the coral sand bottom, but they went through the motions regardless, the rising sun festooning the spray with flickering rainbows of color. The ship was still moving slowly, the screws under the propeller guards gently roiling the water, but they churned it more vigorously as the sleek old destroyer rapidly picked up speed. Following in her wake and running flat out was the clunky steam-leaking launch, still serving as the pilot boat after *Scott* sank the real one. The sun was up entirely by the time *Walker* cleared the channel through the reef, dropped off the pilot, then stretched her legs to the southeast.

She couldn't stretch them too much since, though Fen was firm about the heading they should take, his island wasn't on the old Imperial chart and they only had a rough idea how far it was. His reckoning was based on how many days it took *Scott* to get there, and even conserving fuel, *Walker* was steaming twice as fast as the old former frigate could go. Ronson still worried, as always, about fuel. There was really no telling how long it would take the allocated replenishment ship to follow, and he had to balance his caution with the haste he'd been instructed to make. At least "the brass" was keeping him informed of the bigger picture. Things were heating up around the Azores, both sides having shot down a couple of each other's scout planes. On the plus side—perhaps—*Impero* had come out of dry dock, and she and *Savoie* had wheezed off to sea, accompanied by the cruisers *Hessen* and *Gray* and five "modern" Walker Class DDs. They'd be joined by Commodore Tassanna-Ay-Arracca's fleet carrier, USS *Madraas* (CV-8), and eventually by her mate, Keje-Fris-Ar, and his much slower—though larger—USNRS *Salissa* (*Big Sal*), which had been the very first Allied aircraft carrier converted from one of the huge seagoing Homes. Together, they could loft almost a hundred attack aircraft. More was on the way, and this didn't count all the necessary support ships. It was a formidable force, in theory, but no real match for what the League was already known to have at the Azores. The carriers might make a difference, but that confrontation was likely to come down to how big a price the League was willing to pay, and Captain Reddy was very anxious to learn what, if anything, events in the South Pacific had to do with it all.

Two days out of Respite, *Walker* crossed the equator. Unfortunately, in the opinion of many, there'd been no tradition of crossing-the-line ceremonies among Lemurians—the most seagoing folk on this world—nor had any such custom survived among other members of the Grand Alliance. Dennis Silva was particularly put out by this, forecasting doom at the hands of King Neptune, and he'd often attempted to kickstart the custom in the past, to no avail. Those who knew him were always extra vigilant for his imaginative gags, regardless, and he rarely missed an opportunity to spring one.

"What's Silva up to?" Ronson guardedly asked Jack Meek, who'd come on the bridge with Pam Cross and Tabby. These three were his "spies," a role that came naturally to Meek, he supposed. Rising from his chair, Ronson accepted the cup of coffee that Pam brought him with a nod of thanks.

Pam shrugged. "Bein' weird, as usual," she said in a long-suffering tone. "Right now, he's on the amidships deckhouse"—she gestured aft—"flyin' Petey."

Ronson blinked and coughed on his coffee. "He's *what*?"

"Flyin' Petey."

Ronson looked at Tabby, then back at Pam. "I know his obnoxious little lizard can glide pretty well, like a flying squirrel, but I didn't know he could fly."

"He caan't," Tabby confirmed. "Not by himself."

"Then . . ."

"When there's a wind, like now," Pam began explaining, referencing the prevailing wind and breeze generated by *Walker*'s own speed, "Silva flies the little bastard like a kite. Gives him a line to clamp in his mouth, throws him in the air, and runs the string out." She shook her head. "Petey seems to get a real kick out of it." She snorted. "I know the cadets are enjoying the sight."

Ronson frowned. "They're supposed to be practicing gunnery. Then small arms after that."

Tabby referenced the chronometer. "Aactually, it's time to switch over. Just a quick break while they do." She seemed amused. "Better he do this thaan something else," she reminded darkly.

"Don't just *assume* he isn't still planning to," Ronson warned, glancing at Meek. "Anything?"

"Nothing I've discovered, Captain."

"He's sneaky," Ronson emphasized, then, tilting his head slightly to the side, he said, "Wait a minute. How many of the cadets are watching this show?"

Tabby blinked. "Nearly all, I think. Most gathered aaft, lookin' up at Petey."

"And the *wind's* blowing aft," Ronson said, suddenly rushing out on the bridgewing, clutching his hat to his head. *Walker* was steaming on her aft two boilers, numbers three and four, and he got there just in time to see a great rushing gust of steam and a truly tremendous quantity of ash and soot erupt from the two forward funnels, much of which quickly settled to blanket the aft two-thirds of the ship, not to mention the staring cadets. Adding insult to injury, more white charcoal ash and steam belched out of the galley stove uptake, distributing more fine, gray dust on the unsuspecting victims. On the amidships deckhouse, where very little of the ash had fallen, Silva and Chief Bashear were laughing while Silva reeled Petey in. "By God," Ronson muttered, unsure whether to laugh or rant with fury, "Silva was just the diversion, the bait. He lured everybody out where Isak could blow tubes all over them—probably loaded the boilers with stove ashes Earl's been saving. And Earl threw water on his galley fire. They were *all* in cahoots!"

Meek couldn't prevent a smirk from forming on his scarred face. Courtney Bradford and Abel Cook were climbing up the stairs, looking over their shoulders, and Courtney had apparently heard what Ronson said. "Clearly, Chief Silva isn't the only one conscious of the importance of tradition." Smiling around at the others, he added, "And who better to spread them to than students under their influence, students who will help establish *future* Navy Clan traditions?"

"Well . . ." Ronson said, then hesitated. "The ship's a mess, but"—he finally grinned—"I can't believe Carl Bashear and Isak agreed to cooperate like this. Goes to show they can"—he chuckled—"for a good cause."

"Uh-oh," Tabby said. "Fred an' Kari are comin', covered in ashes, an' they both look pretty mad."

Still chuckling, Ronson waved it away. "*Somebody* probably should've warned them. They'll be mad about all the soot on their plane. It'll blow off the first time they fly."

Several more days passed with most log entries simply stating, "steaming as before." One exception to this was the sighting of another mountain fish, but either they didn't pass close enough to annoy it, or the rumblers on the hull really worked. And they started seeing more lizardbirds as well, larger ones mostly, which tended to venture farther from land or even commute from place to place. Fen was on the bridge, where he spent as much time as he did on the number one gun as part of Bele's crew, when the lookout in the crow's nest called down the sighting of an island on the horizon. As they drew closer, Fen began pointing out features he remembered. It wasn't the island they sought, but it was proof they were on the right course and getting close.

"We should start casting about up ahead, don't you think?" Courtney called in from the starboard bridgewing where he'd been watching the lizardbirds with binoculars.

"That's probably not a bad idea," urged Abel Cook, standing by Ronson. Gunny Horn was with them, having reported that an issue with the gun director was fixed.

Ronson frowned but nodded. "Yeah, probably. Making his decision, he called to the 'Cat cadet firmly clutching the big brass wheel. "Helm, come left to zero nine zero. Reduce speed to one-third," he added to the human cadet standing by the engine order telegraph, or EOT. Turning, he spoke to the talker. "Call the air division to prepare for air operations, starboard side. Lieutenants Faask and Reynolds to the bridge."

"Air operations starboard, ay!" the little female Lemurian bridge talker almost shouted. "Lieutenants Faask and Reynolds to the bridge." She'd opened the shipwide circuit, and her squeaky voice echoed loudly through the ship.

"Making my course seero nine seero!" the 'Cat at the wheel confirmed.

"All ahead, one-third," reported the boy on the EOT after shifting the big lever to the proper position and watching the pointer match it, confirming the order had been received and obeyed.

"My course is seero nine seero," the 'Cat at the helm finally announced, eyeing the compass binnacle in front of him.

"Very well," Ronson said, pleased. No cadet had yet conned the ship during a maneuver, even one as basic as this, and Ronson actually had Tabby do it more often than not. But cadets had been responsible for performing maneuvers ever since they left Scapa Flow. If the ship was still just a classroom, he probably would've let them take the conn for full watches by now. A minute or two later, Fred and Kari mounted the steps behind the bridge.

"We goin' flyin'?" Kari asked.

"One of you is," Ronson told them. "You pick. And choose a cadet for your observer." Fred and Kari looked at each other, clearly unhappy.

"Nonsense!" Courtney exclaimed. "*I* shall be the observer. Really, Captain Rodriguez, I've behaved myself amazingly well, not insisting that we steam closer to a mountain fish, or land on those islands we saw back closer to Respite. I shall not even demand that we spend time on this one"—he indicated the low dark green shape a few miles away—"because I *am* conscious that there are more pressing considerations, but don't forget there's still a scientific aspect to this voyage, and frankly," he said, lowering his voice, "I'm still in charge of the overall mission."

Ronson just shook his head. "That may be," he answered, just as low, "but scouting isn't your job and I won't risk you doing something someone else can do." He looked at Fred and Kari. "Same goes for you. I won't risk *both* my pilots when air recon later might make the difference between not only the success or failure of our mission, but the security of this ship and her people." He glanced back at Courtney. "*That* will always be my responsibility, mission or not."

"Even if the mission requires that they be risked?" Courtney pressed softly.

Ronson looked away. "Let's hope I don't have to make that call, but I'll be the one to do it." He turned back to Courtney. "And you aren't going on any joyrides before we even find out what the hell's going on out here. I'll get Captain Reddy to back that up if I have to, and you know what he'll say."

To Kari's feigned annoyance, Lieutenant Fred Reynolds won the toss (he cheated, refusing to show her the Impie coin with an unflattering image of Governor/Empress Rebecca McDonald on it before stuffing it back in his pocket) and climbed up on the catapult and into the forward cockpit of the PB-1F "Nancy" floatplane that replaced his and Kari's damaged D model. There was little difference in the basic airframe: a single broad wing over the boat-shaped fuselage, but the F model was more robust with a more powerful double-banked ten-cylinder radial that could push the plane up to 160 mph. And that was while carrying its crew of two people, two .30 caliber Browning-style machine guns and ammo, and up to six hundred pounds of bombs. The first production Nancy, the B model, had an in-line four-cylinder and could barely carry its own crew. Fred liked their D model the best, however. Its single-bank radial gave decent power and wasn't as heavy. The center of gravity on F models was too far back, in his mind, and made them trickier to fly.

Looking around at the nearby division members, the little 'Cat named Aalak-Maraan caught his eye. On a whim, Fred pointed and motioned him over. "You wanna fly?"

"Yes!" Aalak instantly replied.

"Whaat you take *thaat* assaassin for?" Kari demanded. She'd jumped up on the catapult as well, double-checking the plane—which Fred should've done himself, he realized, but Kari always did it and he'd simply grown to rely on her. *Maybe too much*, he conceded to himself.

"The little guy needs something to do." Fred shrugged and grinned. "He isn't much good at anything else. Maybe this is his purpose in life." He looked back at Aalak. "You know what to do?"

Aalak briskly nodded that he did, and he should in theory, having trained on the various duties of an observer/copilot. All except the copilot part, of course.

"Swell, jump aboard."

Excitedly, Aalak climbed up and into the aft cockpit, directly behind the prop up above. He would've gone up on the wing if they were going to hoist the plane out and set it in the water, but this would be a catapult launch. "Am I going to prop the engine?" Aalak nervously asked.

Fred shook his head. "Naw, this model has an inertia starter. More stuff to go wrong," he complained, but then conceded, "Pretty cool, though." He didn't add that Aalak was probably much too short and light to prop-start the engine in any case, and the mental image of the little Lemurian trying to, and just hanging there from the propeller, made him chuckle. "Just sit your ass down and strap in, for now," he ordered. "You know how to operate the coms, right? Put on the headset and goggles too."

Aalak quickly did so while a couple of other members of the air division, already on the catapult, inserted a crank into the fairing in front of the aft-facing engine and started briskly winding on it. A strange, high-pitched, moaning whine resulted that rapidly mounted in volume and frequency. He saw Fred talking to the huffing cadets, but his words were overwhelmed by the noise. At a motion from Fred, the cadets suddenly pulled the crank, and the whole plane gave a jolt as the prop suddenly jerked into rotary motion amid a roiling belch of white smoke. For a moment, Aalak could see the jerky rotation of the blades before they suddenly blurred into invisibility. A thrill welled up in him, quickly squelched when he saw Fred impatiently gesturing at him and pointing at his ears. Mortified, Aalak quickly looked down and switched on the intercom power, catching the tail end of what was likely a lengthy tirade. ". . . dopey little furball!"

"I—I aapologize, Lieutenaant. Can you hear me now?"

"Yeah. Okay. Look, they're gonna swing the catapult out and unlock us. You have to switch over to the ship's frequency—low power," he warned, "and inform the bridge. When I run up the engine, tell 'em we're ready to go, then switch back to me when they give us the word, got it?"

"Yes, Lieutenaant Reynolds."

Snapping the little pointed wooden knob over to the designated ship's frequency, Aalak plumbed his memory for the proper report and said nervously, "Ah . . . bridge, this is Cadet Aalak-Maraan, copilot of Long Nose Two, rigging out to staarboard and preparing to launch." Identifying himself as the copilot, no matter how ridiculous that was, gave him another thrill, as did the sudden motion of the plane and catapult moving.

"Bridge aacknowledges, Long Nose Two," a Lemurian voice responded. "Increasing speed now. Wind speed will be eighteen to twenty knots on takeoff."

Aalak switched back to the intercom circuit to report this to Fred, who said, "Yeah. Good. We'll rig out to thirty degrees, so it'll take some rudder to put us right into the wind, but that's just the way it is. Still better than taking off from the water. Usually gets us pretty wet." The catapult movement stopped. "Tell 'em I'm running up now."

Even as Aalak flipped back to the ship's circuit, the engine above and in front of him roared. "Bridge, Long Nose Two is ready to launch," he said.

"Ay, Long Nose Two. Staand by." A few moments passed before the voice came back. "Long Nose Two is clear to fly."

Aalak reported that to Fred, who only said, "Swell. Hold on." With that, Fred raised his hand out of the cockpit and waved at Chief Eraas. A moment later, Aalak felt like something slammed him in the back and was only peripherally aware of rapid forward motion because, as he realized to his horror, he'd closed his eyes. Popping them open, he gazed around only to see they were already speeding past the bridge of the ship just a few wingspans away.

"Wow," was all he could manage.

"Helluva kick in the ass, huh?" Fred laughed. "Zero to sixty in no time flat. The impulse charge that throws us off the ship gives us enough speed to fly unloaded by itself. But that's also why the air division spends so much time tightening stuff up on the planes."

Wind blasting the side of his face extending out from behind the little windscreen, Aalak was looking down as the Nancy swiftly gained altitude, rapidly leaving the shrinking ship behind. "I always waanted to fly," he said, "but never imaagined whaat it felt like."

"You're not gonna puke, are you?" Fred asked harshly.

"N-no, Lieutenaant Reynolds.

"Hmm. Well, what do you think?"

"Amazing. Just . . . amazing," Aalak gushed, a laugh in his voice.

"Fine," Fred replied with a tone of approval. A moment later, he added, "All the same, though, sightseeing is kind of part of our job, we have to make it count. We'll be over the island pretty soon. There's binoculars back there. You know how to use them?"

"Yes sir."

"Swell. Keep your eyes peeled for . . . well, anything. And don't forget to scan around at altitude either, even up above. Lizardbirds are aggressive and can get big enough to damage the plane. We're just fabric and wood, after all."

They flew around the island at about twenty-five hundred feet, gazing at the contrasting colors below: dark green interior; bright, almost white, sandy beaches with brilliant surf crashing on them. There were lots of lizardbirds, of course, most of them much lower than they were, and large shapes lurked in the water. Quite a few of these were plesiosaurs, long-necked creatures with flippers on fat bodies and fish-catching teeth bristling in long narrow jaws. They tended to move in V-shaped groups, corralling their prey as they went. Really big sharks seemed to loiter where the water went from light blue to dark, almost purple, where the flanks of the island plunged into the depths.

"I think we're drawing a blank here," Fred told Aalak. "Time to move along." Even at their relatively low altitude, other islands were visible in the distance, land that couldn't yet be seen from *Walker*. "Better report back to the ship, but keep the power low," Fred reminded. "Our signal will carry a lot farther from up here."

Aalak understood that but didn't know why it was so. That didn't much matter at this point and he complied. It was enough that he was aware that the more power he fed to the bulky radio behind the instrument cluster in front of him, the farther the signal would go. And there were times, like now, that they didn't want it going very far. Everyone aboard *Walker*, even all the cadets, knew their mission now had a new component that included the possible presence of enemies who they didn't want to know they were coming.

The Nancy gained more altitude, up to about forty-five hundred feet, and the distance they could see increased correspondingly. There were now at least three more islands in view. The nearest up ahead was even smaller than the first, much lower over the surface of the water and not as thickly overgrown. As they flew over it, they could more clearly see that it was in fact bigger, in a sense, in terms of how far the reefs and shallows extended. More sea life abounded, but there was no sign of habitation. The next hazy island was farther, considerably bigger and higher, and somewhat to the south. Cruising at about a hundred miles per hour, it took a little less than half an hour before they crossed the marching breakers below, aiming for the middle of the island. This was characterized by an ancient, thickly forested volcanic peak that appeared to rise up about a quarter of the distance underneath them. Overall, the place might've been as big as Respite.

"I see clearings!" Aalak exclaimed, gazing down through his binoculars. "Maybe some structures built in them."

"You don't say?" Fred replied with interest. "I'll go a little lower and circle back when we hit the far coast," he said. "See if we can figure out who"—he paused—"or what lives here."

"Okay," Aalak agreed, then focused his binoculars far ahead at the most distant island they'd seen. Now much clearer, it was even bigger than the one below and something about it jogged his memory. "Didn't Fen—the new 'Caat from Maa-ni-la—say the place where USS *Scott* was taken and where they saw all those ships had a kind of broken volcaano on one end of the islaand?"

"That's what I heard," Fred answered.

"Look up ahead," Aalak suggested. "The big mountain on . . . looks like the southwest side, looks kind of . . . sheared off at an aangle, doesn't it?"

Fred raised an Imperial telescope with one hand and stared. "Say," he cried excitedly, "I think you're right! Get on the horn . . ." He caught himself. "Belay that. You'd have to turn up the power to report it, and if there's somebody over there with a radio . . ." He shook his head. "No sense giving the bad guys a heads-up. Let's look over this island below us some more, then take our report back to the ship."

Suspecting Fred's decision was the wisest course, Aalak prepared to resume scanning around with his binoculars, but something in the corner of his eye drew his attention. Looking to his right, he blinked disbelief at the sight of another aircraft, considerably larger than the Nancy and painted predominantly green, seemingly just flying alongside and slightly behind them. A thrill of terror shot through him at the sight of something that absolutely shouldn't be there. Finding his voice, he shrieked at Fred, "Nine o-clock high, Lieutenaant Reynolds!"

Fred whipped his head to the side, and after the slightest instant's hesitation, his young voice practically squeaked, "Jeepers! It's the JAPS!" Instantly, he slammed the throttle to the stop and banked hard left into an inverted dive. "What're they doing?" he shouted, trying to be heard over the high-pitched, keening shriek. "Are they chasing us?" he yelled louder, but Fen was still screaming in terror. To be fair, Fred's voice sounded almost as scared as Aalak's.

For his part, Aalak was positive he would die. The strange aircraft frightened him, but then the radical, utterly unexpected maneuver made him sure that something that controlled their own plane had broken and they were now plummeting faster than he'd ever gone straight down at the ground. His scream was choked off by a gagging sensation when it felt like his stomach had jumped into his throat, but when Fred started pulling back on his stick, his stomach seemed to slam back down on his guts and he explosively vomited straight into the rushing wind, coating his goggles and the fur on his face. He couldn't scream then and he finally heard Fred's urgent shouting, but it took him as long as they swooped back up just above the wooded slope of the mountain below to respond.

"They?" he hacked. "I just seen one! But it kept flying straight when you dove—and turned me inside out."

"Sorry," Fred said, also gasping. "But I said 'they' because there were two guys in the plane. I saw 'em *lookin'* at us," he added with a shudder in his voice, head craning around in all directions. "Japs. Jesus. So much for our pleasant little joyride. We gotta get back to the ship."

"Should I make a report?" Aalak asked anxiously, wiping at his goggles with the rag he'd been told was to clean the oil from the engine off them.

Fred seemed to think. "Not unless they come back," he decided. "If they do, you can scream your head off because they'll probably shoot us down." He hesitated. "They already could have, easy. No idea why they didn't. It's not like they could've been confused about who we are." The white star with a red dot in the center surrounded by a blue roundel was quite prominent on their plane. "Just like it only took me a glance at their fat red meatballs. Jesus," he repeated.

"You waant me to keep looking at the ground at all?" Aalak asked.

"Hell no! Are you an idiot? As long as there's a Jap plane anywhere in the same sky as us, that's where you keep your eyes. Period!"

CHAPTER 13

"What did the plane look like?" Captain Rodriguez asked, frowning, as soon as the Nancy was secured back on board and Fred and Aalak climbed down on deck. They'd made a brief low-power report about their likely sighting of their objective and the reason they didn't go any closer as they approached for a landing on the water. Everyone had to wait to hear more while the special air recovery detail hoisted the plane back up on the ship, and Ronson, Courtney, Tabby, Kari-Faask, Jack Meek, Abel Cook, Ian Miles, and Gunny Horn were all there waiting impatiently.

"It was a 'Jake,'" Fred replied with absolute, dark certainty, using the American name for the Japanese Aichi E13A long-range reconnaissance aircraft. "All metal monoplane, sort of like a 'Kate,' but with two big floats. Dark green on top, white or gray underneath, black cowl, long cockpit, probably three seats—but I only saw two heads sticking up." He paused his description, which struck Aalak as remarkably thorough, considering how very few heartbeats Fred devoted to his observation.

"And you're absolutely *positive* the plane was Japanese?" asked Meek.

Fred looked askance at the Repub snoop. "With respect," he said, tone belying his words, "unlike you, I've actually *seen* Jap 'Jakes' before, back when they were dogging us all over the Java Sea, calling the whole Jap navy down on us!" He looked back at Ronson. "The skipper and a few others here would remember that too. But in case there's any doubt, the contrasting colors stuck out the most. One was the yellow leading edges on the wings, but what I never thought I'd see again and nearly made me piss myself was the big red meatballs."

"But the goddamn League ain't *got* any Japs, right?" Silva called from on top of the aft deckhouse, where he'd been supervising the "permanent" crew assigned to the number four gun, another 4″-50 on a dual-purpose mount.

Ronson glanced up, annoyed at the shouted interruption and amazed that Silva even heard them, but shook his head. "Not that I've heard."

"The Japanese were members of the alliance that the various League powers who wound up on this world had built on their old one," Courtney Bradford said doubtfully, "but they had no representation in the Mediterranean, or the mighty task force that was swept here to trouble us so." He paused, peering around. "Not to my knowledge. Am I correct in assuming there are no former Leaguers aboard who we might ask?" A moment of silence was all he needed before saying, "Indeed. I thought not." He looked at Meek, clearly conscious they were all still pretending he was just the communications officer. "I'd therefore suggest we send an immediate request—in code of course—that someone responsible for such things promptly ask our most trusted former Leaguers whether it might even be possible that they ever"—he glanced up at Silva with a vague smile—"had any Japanese."

Abel Cook was nodding. "It might also be helpful if they could arrange to fly at least one of 'our' Japanese down to Respite, where they can join one of the support ships that's supposed to follow us."

"An excellent proposal," Courtney complimented.

Ian Miles was scratching his neck, a perplexed expression on his face. "This seems like a lot of fuss over a single Jap plane. Chances are it wound up here the same way we did, right? Maybe it's all by itself. If it spots us and comes too close . . ." He shrugged. "We just shoot it down, right?"

"Two things wrong with that," Fred snapped, tone still somewhat belligerent, which was very unusual for him. Sure, he'd been scared very badly and was still a little hot that he'd been doubted, but mostly, he'd never much warmed to Ian Miles. Neither had Kari, who'd stepped up beside him. "First," he pointed out, with a look at young Aalak, "they had us. No question. I don't remember what guns a Jake carries, but they *are* armed. We were distracted and they could've shot us to pieces before we even knew they were there." He shook his head. "They didn't. Why not?"

"Maybe they didn't have any ammo," Miles speculated.

"But they *did* have the fuel to just swan around the sky and fly over to look at us? No way," Fred disagreed. "Not if they just 'wound up here the same way we did.'" He sighed. "I mean, I'm sure they did. They had to, right? But not today—or by themselves."

"He's right, Sergeant Miles," Ronson said resignedly. "And whatever their intentions, unless they actually attack us, I don't think shooting them down if we see them again is a very good idea."

Miles looked perplexed. "I still don't get it. It's just a scout plane. And they *were* Japs, right?"

Silva, Lawrence, and Petey had climbed down from the aft deckhouse and stepped up behind Miles, loosely followed by some of the cadets he'd been supervising. "I swear," Silva said. "As much as ever'body says you've th'own off yer old ways, you ain't wised up a lot." He rolled his eye at Gunny Horn. "He only ever made corp'ral on the China station, right? Not many things uselesser than a Marine corp'ral." He looked at Meek. "An' if Mr. Reynolds says he saw a Jake, he *seen* a Jake." Silva rounded back on Miles. "But the very *least little thing* a Jake would fly off of is a dedicated seaplane tender. They need a catapult—like we got—but Jakes're a *heap* bigger an' heavier than a Nancy." He arched the brow over his eyepatch. "An' what's the most *likely* thing ta carry one around? A goddamn *cruiser*, that's what. Maybe even a battlewagon. You wanna piss one o' *those* off?" He pretended to shiver, then held up his hands and looked at Ronson. "'Course, it *could* be, markins or not, they didn't know what ta make of a Nancy. Took 'em as much by surprise as the other way around. Then Fred peeled off an' gave 'em the slip so fast . . ." He shrugged. "They just went on with whatever they was doin'. Point is, though," he said louder, for the benefit of the cadets who'd crept closer throughout the discussion, "an' it ain't that long ago I learned this myself, you might get forgiven for shootin' a hole in somethin' on accident"—he winked his eye at Lawrence—"but you can't ever *un-kill* somethin', no matter how much you wish you could."

"Why, Dennis Silva!" Courtney exclaimed. "You've become quite the philosopher!"

Silva nodded somberly. "Had to, I reckon," he agreed, turning his attention back to the cadets. "That said, we gotta be ready to fight *whatever* we run into, whether it's a wooden-hulled League pirate or a goddamn Jap cruiser."

"Goddamn Jap Cruiser!" Petey declared and there were some chuckles.

"Gun's crews, get back to work!" Silva snapped, turning to move aft again.

Chief Eraas started yelling at the air division.

"Let's return to the bridge," Ronson said to those who'd accompanied him. "Please join us," he said to Fred and Kari.

"Should we talk openly even there?" Courtney asked. "Perhaps we should go to the wardroom instead."

Ronson tilted his head from side to side. "Nah, too hot belowdecks. Besides, I don't think it much matters that some of you have other jobs anymore, since *our* whole job on this mission has changed. No point or need to spill Mr. Meek's true occupation, but otherwise all of us are coping with unexpected things. None of that's a secret."

"What are your intentions, Captain?" Courtney asked, clearly suspecting Ronson might decide to call the whole thing off. His tone must've gotten through.

"Don't worry, Mr. Bradford. All concerns aside, it's even more critical now that we get to the bottom of things out here." He nodded over his shoulder at Fred. "And his transmission that it looks like we're barely a day away from our first destination—the place where Fen's ship was taken and the 'ghost fleet' was seen—means we might get a few answers pretty soon." He looked at Jack Meek. "I do want you to send the message Mr. Bradford suggested, however. I want *that* answer as fast as we can get it."

"Aye, sir," Meek replied.

"That might be the most critical answer of all," Courtney mused.

"We already know there's some sort of League presence in these waters. As reluctant as I am to admit it, yet another enemy might be more than we can cope with."

Ronson pursed his lips. "And I don't know if it's better or worse that a new enemy might be our oldest one of all."

USS *Walker* steamed on, circling wide around the island she'd been approaching, the crow's nest and fire control platform lookouts, just above the bridge, warned to be watchful for the shallows Fred and Aalak saw. The crew remained at a modified condition three state of readiness, with all of her still rather meager antiaircraft weapons ready and half her main battery crewed at all times. Obviously, additional lookouts were posted, with reminders to pay extra attention to the sky. Somewhat to Ronson's surprise, a response to Meek's query came back within the hour unequivocally confirming there had never been any Japanese presence in the Confédération États Souverains task force that became the League on this world. That somewhat expected verification left more questions than it answered, of course, but *Walker* and her people were the only ones who could answer them now.

Another surprise came later in the day as they approached the big island over which the unsettling aerial encounter occurred. This was in the form of a personal message from Captain Matthew Reddy himself, the Commander in Chief of All Allied Forces—who might be halfway to the Azores by now and certainly had other concerns—addressed to the whole ship and crew, cadets and veterans alike. It didn't reveal the Corps of Discovery had been tasked with performing possible covert activities, but it made clear he had confidence that his old ship, her officers and crew—of whatever status—would serve the interests of the Grand Alliance to the best of their ability. Reading the message aloud, over the shipwide circuit, even Ronson was moved by the conclusion.

"'Some of you might be a little nervous about the unexpected responsibilities you'll be operating under. A few might even be thinking you didn't sign up for this—hunting pirates with unknown resources, investigating a ghost fleet, and now meeting more possible enemies from another world, all on top of the ordinary hazards of exploration you'd anticipated. The fact is, however, this sort of thing is *exactly* what you can expect as officers and senior NCOs in the American Navy Clan: to face hazards of every imaginable, even unimaginable sort, to protect the peoples of our grand, sprawling alliance is what the American Navy Clan does. You might be starting a little younger than most, not all by any means, but you were better prepared to do so when you first went aboard USS *Walker* than any of the many scratch crews we were forced to throw together during the war. I'm sure, by now, you're much better prepared for the test ahead than most of those ships' companies of heroes ever were. Trust your veteran officers and the training they've given you, trust each other and the bonds you've formed'"—Ronson hesitated slightly—"'and trust USS *Walker*. She has never let us down.'" Ronson paused again before continuing. "Captain Reddy added that, in addition to the support ships already en route, they're scraping together whatever else they can find to send. We won't be by ourselves for long." He waited a moment longer and said, "That is all."

"That's enough," Pam Cross and Carl Bashear murmured simultaneously.

Tabby snorted at the obligatory comment.

Ronson looked at her. "No turning back. I didn't think so."

"It's wrong," Pam growled angrily. "We're *still* just a ship full of kids."

Young Fen-An-Raar turned on her, tail swishing, big eyes blinking indignantly. "Is *not* wrong!" he snapped, then quickly blinked apology and his voice softened. "It is not wrong," he said more carefully. "Cap-i-taan Reddy is right. I haave been aboard shorter than anyone, but I bet I'm already as well prepared as my brothers were, when one waas killed at the Paass of Fire and the other on the Lake of Life. Every cadet I haave met lost someone in thaat waar and is anxious to measure up," he stated. Apparently just realizing he'd spoken out of turn, he looked down at the deck strakes under his feet. "Please excuse my outburst."

"No apology necessary," Ronson told him. "Sorry about your brothers. I didn't know." It dawned on Ronson then that, as much time as Fen had spent on the bridge lately, he didn't know much about him beyond what he'd related about his recent experiences. "And you're right," he sighed. "Captain Reddy's right too, as usual. It's funny, you know? He never thought he was any good at motivational, prebattle speeches—that sort of thing—but whether he was or not, they worked. And what this one boils down to—" He waved the message form he'd read from. Jack Meek had cleaned it up, no doubt, after he decoded it, but the sentiment was classic Matt Reddy. "We're here, and we're all there is."

The target island, now frequently called "Fen's Island"—much to the young 'Cat's embarrassment—was visible as a hazy purple hump in the distance, but it would be close to nightfall before they could reach it without lighting off another boiler. Nobody was keen on opening the mysterious anchorage in the dark, and without a firm schedule for the arrival of the expected oiler, Ronson was against the profligate use of their limited fuel. He'd become a true destroyer skipper who, especially on this world with so many dangers, never knew when he'd have to steam at a sprint and was practically obsessed with his fuel state.

Instead of pressing on, he chose to make a cursory inspection of the big island they'd reached, steaming slowly along the north, then the northeast coast, while Courtney stood on the bridgewing, avidly gazing through binoculars, and Abel Cook sat on the number three gun's trainer's seat atop the amidships deckhouse, sketching some interesting features. It wasn't exactly a jungle island, in a dense undergrowth sense, and like other places—though what looked like classic palm trees existed—most appeared more like tall aspens with dark blotches on lightly colored bark, the dense canopy comprised of what looked more like giant fern leaves than fronds. Courtney cackled occasionally, calling for a cadet notetaker beside him to write down his observations of some winged creature he saw, or perhaps a fish that leaped in the surf. Fred and Kari had remained on the bridge and Aalak was called to join them, Courtney mercilessly interrogating him about the clearings he'd viewed from the sky. Fred saw them too, but hadn't glassed them. Aalak couldn't recall very much—the trauma of the strange plane and terrifying dive away had rather overwhelmed his memory—but he felt reasonably sure he'd seen structures or their remnants. This implied habitation, of course, but who—or what—were they?

"Bridge, crow's nest," came a young, hesitant call through the voice tube that extended all the way up to the cramped bucket-shaped cylinder high on the foremast. Most everyone preferred to use voice tubes over com circuits when the wind and machinery noises allowed. It was important that they practice with them in any event so they'd remember they were available if power was lost.

"Bridge, ay," called the female 'Cat cadet, reminding Ronson of an amusing confrontation that occurred a few days before. Lemurians of both sexes generally reached physical maturity younger than humans, but they also stayed smaller for longer before they finally "shot up" to their adult height. Even then, Lemurian females, like their human counterparts, rarely got as tall as males. Some never really "shot up" at all and remained pretty small their whole lives. Since only the very tallest Lemurian males could rival an average human in height, there were some occupations on a ship built for humans that the shortest 'Cats could never do well. But that was the source of a rebellion, of sorts, when a cluster of very small "'Cat gal" cadets made it plain they were tired of being disproportionately assigned as talkers.

Ronson was surprised and started to point out they were chosen for how smart they were and how critical it was to have smart, brave, and unflappable talkers in positions all over the ship, not just the bridge. What's more, they'd be exposed to all those stations and would be ready to do whatever they wanted when they got bigger. Tabby, Lieutenant Daanis, and Chief Carl Bashear quickly interceded, however, informing him they'd sort it out. They got together and promptly rearranged the watch bill, assigning complainants as shell handlers, paint chippers, and sweepers. A couple (with no interest in engineering) were sent down into Isak's murky domain, the hellish firerooms, and the one who objected most strenuously was condemned to go to Earl Lanier as a mess attendant.

That was the 'Cat now serving as bridge talker again.

"Looks like a lagoon opening up ahead, with a daark waater channel."

Ronson rubbed his chin. "Let's check it out," he decided. "If it looks like a suitable anchorage, we might as well use it for the night."

"Perhaps even dispatch a modest shore party?" Courtney casually called over his shoulder.

Ronson chuckled at his pretense of disinterest. "It's possible."

The lagoon, larger than was thought at first, perhaps a mile wide and as much deep, looked like a fine place to anchor. The most disconcerting thing, however, was the extreme depth of the water near the center—there was no bottom with the short lead the cadets were casting under Chief Bashear's supervision, and the long lead only found it at a hundred fathoms. Courtney excitedly proclaimed they must be steaming over an ancient volcanic crater. Ronson was less enthusiastic. Given the entirely unknown nature of the island (over which Fred and Aalak had encountered a Japanese aircraft), he hadn't wanted to anchor too close to shore. He didn't have any choice, however, and was ultimately compelled to ease *Walker* to within a couple of hundred yards of the beach before the bottom came up to a more convenient depth. His definition of that was the distance the motor launch should be able to cross, returning from shore at full speed, in the time it took to hoist the anchor and get the ship underway if necessary.

With the ship's motion halted, there wasn't even the slightest breeze. Exhaust gasses curled straight up in the sky from two stacks and the humid heat became brutally oppressive. This despite the fact there was barely two hours of daylight remaining when the anchor splashed down and the motor launch was rigged out over the side.

"Who's going?" Tabby asked Ronson as they stepped out in the open behind the bridge, looking aft.

"Courtney, of course," Ronson sighed, "but I want him to have plenty of protection. People he'll listen to," he added. "That means Silva, which means Lawrence too. Gunny Horn, Sergeant Kaik . . . Courtney will listen to them if they run into danger." He considered. "And Mr. Cook can make him see reason that might *keep* them out of danger"—he snorted—"not to mention get them back to the ship before dark."

Tabby blinked her reservations and spoke lowly. "Thaat's most of the 'Corps,' on top of bein' most of *the ship's* most . . . lethal protectors."

"Yeah," Ronson said, frowning, "but they're also the farthest ahead in the instruction of the cadets in their divisions."

"Which is one reason we can't send too many other permanent crew," Tabby agreed. "The question is, are we gonna let any cadets go ashore?"

"I'd rather not," Ronson confessed, "but that's part of what they're here for. To get real-world experience." He took off his hat and swept a hand over his bald sweaty scalp. "Guess I'll leave it up to Mr. Cook. He'll be in nominal command. Maybe a few kids to watch the boat or something like that."

Tabby suddenly barked a laugh and pointed, directing Ronson's attention to the round form of Earl Lanier, still wearing his greasy apron, lumbering purposefully out from under the amidships deckhouse toward the ship's side, assembling a new fishing pole as he went. A couple of put-upon-looking cadets on mess detail were following with buckets of galley scraps for bait. "It's good to see thaat *some* things never change," she chuckled.

Silva, Lawrence, and Petey, of course, emerged on deck below the bridge already wearing their "shore party suits" and armed with their personal weapons. Silva was wearing a khaki shirt, dungarees, leggings, and boondockers, as well as a "doughboy" style helmet on his head. Whether expecting combat or not, he liked the helmet for bashing through brush. He was carrying his new copy of an 1876 Winchester in .50-80 caliber, and a web belt harness supported a 1911 Colt .45, 1917 Navy cutlass, canteen, and plenty of ammo. His "belt knife" was a 1903 Springfield bayonet. Lawrence was in his usual Marine combat smock and had an Allin-Silva "trapdoor" rifle, also in .50-80. On his belt were Baalkpan Armory copies of the 1911 Colt and cutlass, and incongruously, his curious brass-barreled flintlock pistol hanging from a hook.

Silva paused in front of Earl and gave him a look. "Fatso," he greeted amiably.

"Headcase," Earl grumped back.

"I swear," Silva said, "here ya are, barely back from the dead, already courtin' yer doom. God knows what you'll hook, lurkin' down in the mysterious depths at the bottom of a drowned *volcano*."

Earl shrugged. "I like fish. You know that."

"*Ever'body* knows that," Silva scoffed. Originally from the vicinity of Pinedale, Wyoming, Earl Lanier had grown up avidly fishing the nearby rivers and streams for trout. "An' I get it," conceded the Alabama-born Silva. "Prob'ly the only thing about you I do, but I bet the only eatable fish that's ever swum under us has already got ate by sea monsters."

"Got Ate," Petey confided seriously.

Earl patted the holstered pistol at his side. "I catch somethin' scary, I'm ready this time."

"Pistol won't help ya if some toothy booger yanks you over the side."

Earl shrugged again. "Might help me shoot my way out of its belly."

Silva nodded sagely. "Could be. Worked for me once." That got the attention of the cadets, who stared slack-jawed. Silva pretended to ignore them, suddenly nodding at the fishing pole. "Why, Earl! You got a *reel* on yer pole!"

Earl proudly displayed it. "Yeah. Had it made on New Britain Isle."

"Looks swell," Silva admitted. "Well . . . good luck, an' so long."

"You goin' ashore?" Earl asked as Silva and Lawrence moved along.

Silva hefted his rifle. "Goin' a'huntin'."

"You're more likely to get ate than me."

"Naw. I plan on shootin' whatever tries *before* I get swallered."

"Asshole," Earl said.

"Shithead," Silva called over his shoulder.

Ronson, just up above them, heard the whole exchange and he chuckled. "Yeah, some things stay the same no matter what," he said aside to Tabby. "Thank God," he murmured.

CHAPTER 14

Silva was coxswain again when the launch shoved off from the ship. He and Lawrence were accompanied by Courtney, Abel Cook, Gunny Horn, and Sergeant Kaik, as Ronson predicted, and they'd been joined by the cadets Philan Bele, Samuel Jenks (both as tall as adults and having shown a proficiency with weapons), and Fen-An-Raar, who wasn't tall but had more than qualified with the small .45 caliber submachine guns known as "Blitzerbugs," with which all the cadets going ashore were armed. Blitzers were basically short, heavy, seamless pipes with a rudimentary pistol grip and buttstock and a twelve-inch barrel sticking out. They used Thompson SMG magazines and fired from an open bolt. Early models were full-auto only, but a selector switch and slightly better sights had been added, making them more useful for something besides simple suppressing fire. The last member of the shore party, probably without permission, was Pam Cross. She came sliding down the falls like a gymnast, burdened by her leather medical bag and Blitzer of her own.

"Hey, doll," Silva called cheerfully. "Skipper know yer comin'?"

"I guess he will soon enough," Pam snapped back with a challenging glare around at the others in the boat. She hefted her bag. "Nothin' goin' on aboard ship right now, an' at least one of you dummies is bound to hurt yourself."

No one objected to that, though Abel clearly started to speak before shrugging and shutting his mouth. No one said much at all for a while as the launch burbled across the still water toward shore. Even Courtney was relatively quiet as he fought to keep the wide-brimmed straw hat on his head against the breeze their movement created. He finally broke the silence as they neared the beach, however.

"There are a number of new flying creatures that none of us have seen," he observed. "I don't suppose anyone thought to bring a shotgun?" Some Allin-Silva rifles had been bored out and chambered for 20-gauge shot shells, and there were a few of those on the ship, but no one spoke up. "Damn," Courtney said mildly. "Perhaps we can get some specimens later. I simply *must* have my own fowling piece made!"

"Arnie's a good shot with that 'oh-three Springfield o' his," Silva pronounced with a grin at Gunny Horn. "He can shoot their heads off in the air!"

Courtney released an exasperated sigh. "How many times must I tell you that heads are quite often the most fascinating and distinctive parts? Chief Silva almost always ruins my specimens by shooting them in the head," he said aside to Abel Cook.

"*That's* the scary part with all the teeth, tryin' ta eat me," Silva countered defensively. "You see some little critter on the ground that you don't want holes in, we can sic Petey on 'em. 'Course, anything he brings up'll be pretty chewed an' slobbery."

"He 'on't gi' it to you any'ay," Lawrence warned.

"I'll bribe him with a cracker," Silva said.

"Cracker? Eat!" Petey exclaimed.

"Not *now*, stupid."

Silva throttled back closer to the beach and then threw the engine in neutral when the keel scrunched on the sand. Sergeant Kaik and Gunny Horn jumped down out of the bow into calf-deep water, looking into the meager surf for predatory fish, regardless how small, before spreading out and starting to scan the dense forest ahead. With no warning about the water, Silva killed the engine and everyone made their way forward out of the launch, finally dragging it a little way farther up on the beach before securing it to a mostly buried tree with the line.

"Whoa, Mr. Bradford," Gunny Horn said when Courtney acted as if he meant to simply stroll off into the woods. "Hold up here while we check the beach better."

"Really, Mr. Horn," Courtney began to object, but Abel told him, "It really is best to have a little patience, Mr. Bradford."

"But we have so little time before dark," Courtney complained to his protégé.

"Just give 'em a minute," Pam advised. "They do kinda know what they're doin'." She glanced at Silva. "When it comes to this sorta thing, anyway."

Gunny Horn and Sergeant Kaik went left, heading west, while Silva, Lawrence, and a silent but almost spastically watchful Petey moved east, all peering into the nearby forest or gazing at the sand they trod on. Silva kicked some up as he walked. "Looks weird," he said. "You know a lot o' this stuff is old seashells, ground up over ee-ons, right?"

Lawrence didn't have broad shoulders. They were powerful, but the bones and muscles were closer to a narrower upper rib cage. That meant he couldn't really shrug in the human way but managed to approximate the gesture by shortening his neck as much as anything. It looked kind of like a shrug. "So?" he asked. "And I don't know 'ee-ons,' or how they grind things."

"Never mind," Silva said. "It's just this crap looks more like busted-up crawdad or lop-ster parts than honest seashells. Way thicker an' bigger, though." He nudged a piece with his boot. "An' that looks like the tip off a hellacious big claw." He grunted, then added in a warning tone, "You remember them big spider-lop-ster critters, came gallopin' ashore on Talaud Island?"

"No."

Silva glanced at his strange friend. That only happened about four years ago, but sometimes he forgot that Lawrence was just—essentially—a different race of Grik; a species that physically matured very rapidly, but whose intellectual development took longer. That had made Grik warriors easier for their leaders to control, especially when the older ones were culled before they wised up. But even if Lawrence sprang from an entirely different race and culture, the now almost extinct Tagranesi, he'd only been about five or six years old when they met. Basically a teenager. And a lot of other things had been going on then, not least that Silva had shot him, they were taken captive by a rogue Imperial named Billingsly, and Talaud had later been utterly demolished by a volcanic blast. "Wouldn't o' thought you'd forget somethin' like *that*, but hell, I don't recall much from when I was that age, neither."

They'd moved along for another hundred and fifty or two hundred yards when Lawrence crouched down and pointed at some vague impressions that had been rendered unidentifiable by the surf at higher tide. "Tracks," he said.

"Yep," Silva agreed. "No tellin' what left 'em. Somethin' big, is all." Pausing to pull a pouch from his shirt pocket, he dug out an improbably large mass of Nussie tobacco, flavored with molasses, and stuffed it in his cheek. As always, he offered it to Lawrence who, as always, shook his head. "'Course, there ain't nowhere we've ever been that there ain't tracks o' *some* sorta big, scary booger, an' we can't tell nothin' from these." He tried to imagine where they came from, hoping to find intact examples higher on the beach, but except for the ten or fifteen yards of tracks they could see, they'd been too thoroughly erased. He spat a brown stream into one of the remaining imprints. "Hell with it. Let's go take Courtney for his stroll before he has a fit or bursts. You'll take point when we go explorin'?" he said and Lawrence dipped his snout. Not only was he a fine scout, his black-and-orange-striped feathery fur, combined with his camouflage smock, made him remarkably difficult to see. Silva would've thought the orange would negate that, but it didn't, for some reason.

"I'll scout, like all'ays," Lawrence confirmed.

Gathering briefly back at the boat, it was decided that Pam and Fen would stay to guard it. Pam probably only agreed because a brutal, humid heat practically gusted out of the forest and there was at least a meager breeze and shade from overhanging trees out in the open by the boat. Besides, Fen was particularly disappointed to be left and she liked the plucky little Lemurian.

Using his nose as much as his eyes, Lawrence led the rest off on a fairly well-worn path angling generally north-northwest, which Sergeant Kaik had found. The tracks on the sandy trail were as impossible to get a sense of as those on the beach, having obliterated each other. Lawrence mentioned that one of the scents he caught was "scroo-ee" but hadn't elaborated before pushing ahead with a peculiarly fluid gait.

"Little scudder moves like a chameleon when he wants to, don't he?" Silva murmured proudly to Gunny Horn.

"Chameleon," Petey gravely chirped, barely audible.

Horn glared at the tree-gliding lizard. "I swear, Dennis," he grumbled. "What's with you and all your pets? I don't mean Lawrence—not anymore," he hastily clarified before Silva could even frown. "But"—he shifted his Springfield off his shoulder—"I mean, yeah, at first, Lawrence was *like* a pet, but he took to you right off, even after you *shot* him. The Governor/Empress of the New Britain Isles thinks you're her big brother and Petey sticks to you like a tick. You never had trouble making friends with 'Cats." He gestured behind them. "And even these cadets . . . you scare the shit out of them, but I bet they'd follow you anywhere." He paused and added dryly, "And *I know* what a murderous bastard you are!"

Silva shrugged expressionlessly. "Must be my magnetical personality."

Horn snorted. "Somehow, I don't think that's it. You probably had packs of pups all around you growing up."

"Nope," Silva said, tone suddenly cold enough that Horn felt a chill despite the heat. "Never had a dog o' my own." When he finally spoke again, a couple of hundred yards farther up the trail, his voice had returned to normal and it was as if he'd never stopped talking. "I always wanted one, though. A dog, I mean. Larry made a pretty good substitute before he grew up into a *person*, not just the lethal lizardy monster we all love. As for little kiddies"—he shook his head—"I reckon they know their own. Pam says I never grew up from one 'cause I never got to *be* one when I was little. An' maybe I got a soft spot for 'em—way down deep where it don't show—an' feel kinda' . . . *called* ta look after 'em, see?" He clucked and spit a stream of tobacco juice. "I reckon that's one reason out o' maybe a thousand that Pam stays so sore at me."

"What? Why?" Horn asked. "She doesn't ever want kids?"

"Yeah, right," Silva groused. "*That* ain't it." He suddenly thumped Petey on the head with his thumb. "But to answer your quarter-mile-ago question, this lizardy little parasite's the only real pet I ever had."

"Parasite?" Petey seemed to ask, blinking.

"I wish you two wouldn't talk so loud," Courtney complained just behind them. "I can't hear the forest creatures over your confounded chitchat."

Silva stopped walking and held up a hand. "Hey, he's right. You hear that, Arnie?"

"What?" asked Horn.

"Nothin', that's what. No lizardbirds carryin' on, no nothin' at all just now." He lowered the lever of his big rifle enough to pull the bolt face back and double-check that he'd chambered a round. He had, of course, and Gunny Horn quietly opened the bolt of his Springfield for the same reason.

"You don't think Larry spooked everything quiet, do you?"

Silva shook his head, squinting his good eye and peering at what looked like a fairly substantial clearing up ahead.

"What is it?" Courtney hissed.

"Don't know. Maybe somethin' bigger than us that scares shit. Or a lot more o' whatever it is." He looked around. "Trees're thinner here. Let's spread out a little before we go rompin' out in the open, lined up like a buncha ducks."

"Where's Lawrence?" asked Abel Cook, who'd stepped up closer.

Silva waved ahead. "Out there, I reckon. Creepin' through that tall grass yonder. Bet he's tryin' ta find whatever it is that just gave us the shits." He motioned at the cadets and Sergeant Kaik, who were bringing up the rear, to ease out to the sides of the path.

Young Bele and Jenks looked understandably nervous but moved quickly enough, crouching behind the trees that Sergeant Kaik indicated. Silva and Horn crept forward a little, where they had a better view of the clearing, before taking a knee on either side of the trail. Courtney started to move up as well, working the bolt on his "personal" Krag-Jorgensen, but Abel Cook held him back, pushing him down.

"I object, Mr. Cook! I'm perfectly—"

"Quiet, Mr. Bradford," Abel hissed insistently. "You may recall that fighting whatever may or may not be out there isn't *your* mission on this trip!"

Courtney let out a breath. "Indeed," he said. "I suppose you're right."

Abel looked up at Silva and Horn. "What now?" he asked quietly.

Horn glanced at Silva, who smirked. "Can't stay here all evenin'. Might as well flush the pot." Putting his thumb and middle finger in his mouth, he produced a piercing whistle.

A few lizardbirds took to the air, but nothing else happened for a moment. Suddenly, much farther out in the clearing than most had expected, Lawrence jumped to his feet and sprinted several steps before dropping back down in the tall grass. No one but Silva had expected it, yet even he wasn't ready for the flurry of shots that rang out.

"Shit," Silva barked. "Larry already hates it when I use him for bait to get whatever's stalkin' him to jump to the chase so I can shoot it. He's *really* gonna be pissed that I got 'eem shot at."

Bullets were still chewing the grass where Lawrence went to ground, and Abel called out, "They'll cut him to pieces!"

"Nah," Silva said. "He ain't where they're shootin' anymore." Then he added, "I hope. All the same . . ." He looked meaningfully back at Abel, clearly waiting for him to do something.

Abel was the officer in charge, after all, and he nodded his understanding, took a deep breath, and shouted, "Commence firing! Target the muzzle flashes." These were fairly bright in the gloom of the woods around the clearing.

Horn raised his Springfield and fired, the roar of the .30-06 somewhat louder than whatever was shooting at Lawrence. Philan Bele and Samuel Jenks both opened up with their Blitzerbugs, firing controlled three- or four-round bursts like they'd been taught. Kaik popped up and fired his Allin-Silva, and Abel had moved forward between Silva and Horn where he could shoot Courtney's Krag. Now that they'd diverted the enemy's attention, bullets started throwing fragments of bark down on them.

"*There's* one o' the bastards," Silva said with satisfaction, spying what was clearly a human shape trying to move to a different spot. Raising his big repeater, he squeezed the trigger and the rifle boomed, throwing out a jet of flame and a white cloud of smoke. Quickly shucking the empty cartridge and chambering another, he tried to aim again. He'd have to wait. His ammunition was the same that Kaik's weapon used, the standard black powder infantry load, but Kaik was off to the side. Silva's smoke just hung there in the humid air, ruining nearly everyone's aim.

"Damn it, Dennis!" Horn objected.

"Hell, I'm sorry, Arnie!" Silva replied. "I was expectin' monsters, which is what I made this rifle special for. Didn't think we'd find a fight with somebody usin' *modern weapons*," he said significantly. "Should'a brung a BAR."

Young Bele cried out, and Silva looked in time to see the boy slap a hand on his arm, teeth clenched, but then he prepared to start shooting again and Silva grimly nodded approval. Someone must've hit at least one of their unknown enemies, however, because they became aware that there'd been a keening wail of pain for several moments. He suspected it was a Leaguer, maybe even one of the very pirates they'd been directed to find and stop. He didn't know for certain, though, and that started to aggravate him. Losing his patience, he suddenly bellowed, "Who the hell're we fightin', anyway? Identify yerselfs, goddammit!" There wasn't any response for a moment, which didn't really surprise him, but then there came some shouted words he hadn't been prepared for at all.

"Shageki o yameru!"

Silva and Horn looked at each other, wide-eyed. "Japs!" Horn gasped. "He said 'stop shooting'!" Raising his voice, he called to their companions, "Hold your fire."

"You sure?" Silva asked, eye narrowing.

"Sure, I'm sure. I learned more Japanese than I ever wanted to in China, and then when they had me prisoner."

"Yeah . . . but why should *we* quit shootin'? These're *wild* Japs, who shot at Larry for no reason. They ain't the friendly Japs we know."

"Who weren't always so friendly," Horn pointed out. "But these have to be the same ones who didn't shoot Fred and Aalak down, and now there's somebody telling *them* to stop."

The last was a fait accompli, since both sides had already ceased firing. Someone was still screaming, though. The same voice as before shouted out, "Americans?"

"Yeah. What of it?" Silva yelled back.

Horn glared at him. There was a rustling in the grass just ahead and Lawrence came crawling out of it. "You quit shooting," he scolded. "They *shot* I," he reported accusingly, gingerly touching what looked like a bloody crease in the fur on his neck.

"Sorry, little buddy. They got Cadet Bele too," Silva commiserated as Lawrence took a position beside him. "None o' that matters, though, 'cause they're Japs."

"I *thought* I scented Japhs earlier," Lawrence confessed. "I didn't trust the nose. Should ha' said, though."

"Don't worry about it. Surprised us too—but not as much as Arnie wantin' ta make *friends* with 'em."

"That's a damned—" Horn started hotly, but Abel interceded.

"That's enough! Quit bickering." He raised his voice to a shout. "Yes. Some of us are Americans." He hesitated. "Why would that make you stop fighting us?"

"Our war is over," came the shocking reply in good if somewhat strongly accented English.

"No shit?" Silva called. "Who won?"

"Shut *up*," Abel snapped at him, then shouted, "If that's true, why did you shoot at us?"

"We did not." The answer was now accusatory. "We knew you were coming and were looking for you, but we shot at a *monsuta* . . . a monster. You started shooting at *us*!"

"Now you're a monster, Larry," Silva told his friend. "Bullets first, then hurtful words."

"That was a friend of ours, a scout," Abel called.

There was no reply for a moment, then came the clearly skeptical response: "Apologies. We have met nothing like that creature that was friendly. We have injured. You will not shoot if we help them?"

"We will not," Abel carefully assured, stressing each word. He paused. "We have a doctor, a . . . medic nearby."

There was an even longer pause before the voice called back, "Yours is probably closer than ours. We would . . . thank you for his help."

"I'll summon her," Abel replied, then slowly rose to his feet. Silva and Horn stood up beside him, scanning watchfully across the clearing. Abel looked over at Cadet Bele and asked, "Are you all right?"

"Yes sir. Just a graze, I think. It hurts, though," he confessed.

"Good. We were lucky," Abel said with feeling, nodding at Lawrence as well. Lawrence wasn't acting like he *felt* very lucky, trying to press on his wound while Courtney held his hand away so he could look at it. Abel looked back at Bele. "You and Cadet Jenks run back the boat and stay there, if you please. Don't let your guard down either there or on the way," he warned. "Ask Pam Cross to dress your wound, if necessary, then hurry up to us with Cadet Fen. They should proceed under the same advisement of caution, of course." He glanced at Courtney, his expression a little anxious.

Courtney waved a hand. "No, I've nothing to add. You're doing exactly as I would. These people have a more advanced aircraft than we do, at the very least. They said, 'Our war is over,' and they were looking for us. I wonder what that means. Regardless, if we can manage to . . . cooperate with them in some way, it would certainly be preferable to fighting."

Silva grinned. "I bet Pam won't 'preciate bein' assumed ta be a 'he.'"

About a dozen men crept out of the woods surrounding the clearing, all in dingy whites with what might've been dark blue jumper flaps. A couple were wearing gray helmets, but most had white flat hats with a blue band. Each had an ammunition belt and bayonet, leggings, and a long-barreled rifle. Only one had what looked like a rumpled officer's hat perched on his head. Bele and Jenks had hurried off back the way they came, while the rest of them, all six, eased out in the open toward the men they'd just been fighting. When just a few paces separated them, the officer, obviously uncomfortable as he eyed Lawrence in particular, suddenly pointed at the lone Lemurian with them. "What is *that*?" he demanded.

"Why, that's Sergeant Kaik," Silva growled back. "*Another* friend o' ours. You ain't never met a Lemurian neither?"

"Not . . . anything like it as a *friend*," the officer harshly replied.

"That's enough, Chief Silva," Abel said mildly, calmly. "And this is one of those rare times when you *will* do what I say without argument."

Silva didn't even hesitate to reply, "Aye, aye, Mr. Cook. Just so long as these Japs don't get frisky—or turn out ta be pals with them League bastards. If that happens, me an' Arnie an' Lawrence"—he grinned—"an' Sergeant Kaik'll have ever' one of 'em dead before the first one even hits the ground."

"I know, Chief Silva," Abel said patiently, as if there wasn't the slightest doubt in his mind, "but I'm sure that won't be necessary."

The Japanese officer seemed taken aback, though his grim-faced companions didn't react. Apparently, he was the only one who spoke English. "We are most definitely not aligned with your League enemies," he stated, then suddenly smirked and gestured at the armed sailors to either side of him. "But your large oafish companion seems overly confident," he challenged.

Abel sighed. "I hope you'll trust me when I earnestly caution you that he isn't."

The Japanese officer snorted, but it wasn't a confident sound.

"Good heavens!" Courtney Bradford irritably exclaimed. "This is a momentous occasion! If you are not in league—ahem—with the League and their vile allies, that means you must come from the same world that we did." He paused and conceded, "Or one very much more like it than some. We believe this to be somewhat rare." The fact that the Japanese officer appeared to nod agreement encouraged Courtney to continue. "Ah! So you've seen evidence of this phenomenon as well! Marvelous," he enthused. "And you stated earlier that 'our' war is over . . ." He paused, catching the frown on the officer's face before giving Dennis Silva a meaningful glare. "Well, while I admit to being curious about the outcome, it has no bearing on us here and now and it only makes sense that we try to cooperate against what you've apparently determined independently is a common threat to us all!"

The officer appeared to contemplate that before barking a command in Japanese. All the sailors immediately lowered their weapons and stood . . . well, "easy" wasn't exactly right, but unthreateningly, at least.

Pam and Fen chose that moment to come trotting up, breathing hard. The officer blinked surprise at them both. Pam moved Lawrence's hand, which had unconsciously resumed pressing his wound, and peered closely at it. "In an' out, just under the skin. Worse than Cadet Bele's since the muscle will be bloodshot some," she conceded, "but some polta paste and a couple stitches'll sort it out." "Polta paste" was a potent infection-fighting analgesic fermented from the purple pear-shaped polta fruit. Distilled straight from the nectar, it was a popular recreational drink called "seep," but the curative properties of the paste were significantly better than sulfonamides. "Your weird fur has clotted it too much for me to even bandage it here," Pam complained. "Have to clean it up first, back on the ship." She looked at the Japanese officer. "Who're you?"

Everyone was suddenly a little embarrassed.

"I, ah, I am Lieutenant Chiba, of His Imperial Majesty's Navy cruiser *Shonai*."

Silva seemed to tense when he heard that, but Pam only said, "Swell. Where's your wounded man?"

The screaming had stopped and Lieutenant Chiba pointed in the direction Silva had shot his big repeater. "There are two. One is very bad, but they are both together now. Another man stayed with them." He said something in Japanese and a couple of sailors stepped forward. "These will take you there . . . but perhaps you might leave the little furred one behind." He was looking at Fen, who promptly bristled. "Only because, like that one"—he nodded at Lawrence—"we have had difficulties with similar creatures."

"'Similar'? Or the same?" Courtney asked, intrigued.

"Somewhat similar to them," Chiba said, pointing at Fen and the much bigger Sergeant Kaik. He frowned and nodded at Lawrence. "Exactly like that one."

"Color too?" Lawrence asked, clearly surprising Chiba that he could speak.

"Ah, yes."

"Is that so?" Silva murmured, looking at his friend.

Something thrashed in the grass nearby and Petey exploded up out of it, landing on Silva's shoulder. As usual, he'd hidden when the shooting started, but now he was back, acting as if nothing had ever happened. All the Japanese took a step back, startled by his abrupt appearance, and he looked around, big eyes wide with curiosity. Turning his little head, he nipped Silva's ear and cried, "Eat! Goddamn!"

Ignoring the display, Gunny Horn said, "I'll go with Pam—unless we're all going over there?"

"It might be best if we stay together," Courtney prodded. "And I do mean 'all,'" he pressed, clearly including Fen, Kaik, and Lawrence. "Our friends are no threat to you, and your people may as well get used to it."

"Very well," agreed Lieutenant Chiba, frowning and gesturing for them to join him as he turned.

Silva suddenly whistled while they all walked toward the trees. "A cruiser, huh? Where's she at? All by herself? How many crew?"

Lieutenant Chiba looked up at him, standing almost a foot taller. "And you are from USS *Walker*, yes?"

Silva hesitated. "Could be. You know her?"

"Yes," Chiba said shortly. "But more importantly, we have . . . monitored things since we arrived on this unpleasant world."

"Spyin'," Silva stated.

"Only passively and understandably, don't you think?" Chiba retorted with some heat.

"Sure. Which you'd need your cruiser's comm equipment for, I bet. Where's she at?" he repeated.

Chiba didn't say anything.

"Didja *lose* her?" Silva mockingly pushed.

"Really, Chief Silva," Courtney scolded. "As anxious as I am to learn, well, everything, even I can understand a little hesitancy. So should you."

"Okay. But we gotta sort one thing out right off." He looked back at Chiba as they stepped into the trees. "How many more Japs're we gonna run into out here? You said you was lookin' for us. I figure your scout plane or coast watchers seen us anchor, but there's lotsa trails through these woods, I bet. Mighty coincidental you just happened along the right one," he spat, and his expression darkened. "Where you set up ta bushwhack us."

Lieutenant Chiba finally nodded. "We positioned ourselves to meet you with as little risk to ourselves as we could," he confessed. "There was no hostile intent. And we may be joined by others," he conceded. "We weren't the only party searching for you and we did make a lot of noise, after all."

"Yeah. You just make sure nobody else shoots at poor Larry, hear? He's added enough extra holes for one day."

CHAPTER 15

Pam was able to stabilize one of the wounded Japanese sailors, probably hit by Horn's Springfield through the upper chest, under the collarbone, but there was nothing she could do for the other man, who was practically dead by the time she got started. He had a distinctively sharp half-inch hole in his left side, under his arm, and a fist-sized exit on the right. His right arm had nearly been blown off as well. That made it plain the wound was inflicted by a flat-nose, lead .50-80, fired by either Silva or Sergeant Kaik. His death made his comrades very unhappy and not a little hostile, but Lieutenant Chiba's low words dissuaded them from attempting any violence. That and the fact that Pam had clearly done her best and the rest of her party was obviously quite lethally armed and prepared. Silva in particular, though outwardly completely relaxed at a glance—rifle with his right hand gripping the wrist and the barrel resting on his shoulder, left hand negligently brushing the cutlass at his side from time to time—still radiated a strange sense of . . . amused malevolence to all around him while somehow seeming to preside over events. And though he remained physically among them, he was also apart, his single eye constantly in motion, never resting on anyone for more than an instant.

Fen whispered aside to Gunny Horn. "Is he always like thaat in situations like this?"

Horn flicked a glance at his friend and sighed before whispering back, "Son, I've known Dennis Silva longer than anyone on this world, from back on the China station before he even joined *Walker.* I'll tell you right now that he's 'always like this' even when he's *acting* like a happy, dopey teenager. He's just a little on edge right now—understandably—so it shows more, is all. I've never known *anybody* so ready for violence all the time, or who just flat *embraces* it when it happens." He grinned. "Good thing for us, huh?"

Fen blinked uncertainty. "It gives me the . . . creeps, I think you say."

Horn nodded and confessed, "Me too. But back in the old days, there was only a small handful of people in the world that he gave a fart in a typhoon—a 'strakka'—about. Then he came here and that number got bigger, mainly because Captain Reddy gave him a real 'father figure' for the first time. Somebody he'd rather die for than let down. There are others now, Pam's one, in ways he doesn't even understand, but Silva would charge up the Devil's asshole if Captain Reddy told him to." He shrugged. "And he cares a lot more about people in general now, whoever's on 'our side.'" He smiled at Fen. "Which means you too, kiddo."

Another dozen Japanese appeared and they went through the same series of accusations, emotions, and recriminations, despite the undisputed fact that the Japanese shot first, and part of the animosity seemed to stem from their reluctance to equate Lawrence, who they plainly considered a vicious beast, with one of their own people. Lawrence caught this as well, which replaced his ordinarily amiable nature with one of sullen resentment, equally obvious to the Japanese. Silva ultimately cheerfully suggested that if their new acquaintances wanted to "get back ta shootin'," he was happy to oblige. Otherwise, they could "simmer down or eat shit." It was all the same to him.

Courtney managed to smooth that out, though it didn't help when Petey proceeded to gleefully chant, "Eat Shit," all the way back to the beach where Bele, Jenks, and the launch awaited them. Another motor launch had arrived with a larger armed party, roughly split between veteran sailors and cadets. Ian Miles commanded the "troops," but Tabby had practically demanded to go and Ronson put her in overall charge. That was just as well. They'd come in response to the brief but spirited exchange of fire they heard, and there was no telling what might've happened if Tabby hadn't insisted they take the time to listen to cadets Bele and Jenks's full account. As soon as Miles heard Philan Bele quote the word "Japs," he'd been almost rabid for a fight. Like Gunny Horn, he'd once been a "guest" of some particularly sadistic Japanese and wasn't as philosophically flexible as the other former member of the 4th Marines. That clearly showed when the now outnumbered Japanese sailors accompanied Courtney's party into the open and there was another tense time while wounds and provocations were explained and reargued under the dwindling sunlight.

It was Pam Cross who finally got to the point. "We can sort out all this stuff later," she snapped, pointing at the wounded man that Sergeant Kaik was actually carrying on his back, quite effortlessly it seemed. "But I need to get *him* to the ship where I can try to save his life." She glared at Lawrence. "You too. You wanna get infected an' die?" She waved her hands. "The rest of you can stand here and shoot each other up, but I won't be here to care."

Lieutenant Chiba cleared his throat. "Actually, *none* of us want to be caught out on the beach after dark unprepared," he confessed. "There are . . . things to be wary of," he added cryptically, first throwing another skeptical glance at Lawrence, then waving at the trees, even the water. "Some are quite large. Our numbers and a big fire should keep them at bay while the rest of our searchers join us here, as was planned, and our own boats can come get us."

"Boats?" Tabby asked, even as Miles demanded, "There are even *more* of you?"

Now it was hard to tell what flustered, angered, perhaps even frightened Lieutenant Chiba the most; yet more hostility from Miles, the fact that Tabby was not only very feline, to his eyes, and quite obviously female in one of the most striking ways that stretched her khaki shirt with *officer's insignia* on the collar, or that roughly half the grim-faced sailors now confronting his own looked like children of various species. It was almost more than he could cope with, and he took a moment to direct his people to gather the firewood they needed.

"Sure," Silva said, deliberately needling Miles. "A whole *cruiser* full o' Japs! *Hundreds*, I bet." He looked at Tabby. "Which explains the boats. Scout planes too."

"I take it your cruiser is here, somewhere?" Abel asked Chiba. The man hesitated only a moment before nodding. "*Shonai* is . . . near, but not necessarily here. The boats will be closer. They dropped us off within walking distance of this anchorage."

Courtney blinked confusion in the Lemurian way. "Then why didn't you just come out to meet us in them, instead of on foot in the forest?"

Chiba looked at Tabby, then back at Courtney. "I told you 'our war' is over, and it is. The details are not mine to share," he quickly added, forestalling more immediate questions. "You will have them from my captain, Captain Okabe, in due course no doubt." He pursed his lips. "I will tell you this; we have been in a position, probably better than you, to monitor all sorts of transmissions from various sources. We know you have grown more careful with yours, even in waters you consider your own, but our equipment"—he paused, considering, then went on—"well, it is somewhat better than yours. When conditions are right, we still pick up a lot of unguarded 'short-range' traffic you have little reason to suspect that anyone can. That's how we know so much about you and your enemies," he explained, "but we also know that you—and they—have been on this world much longer than we have and could not be aware that 'our war,' as I called it, has ended." He attempted a smile, with a nod at Ian Miles. "So . . . considering how bitter our war had been"—he frowned—"and it got much worse after you left it, Captain Okabe was concerned that if you were approached by a boat full of Japanese sailors . . . you might simply open fire. We haven't the boats or people to spare," he added grimly. "As it was"—now he looked almost apologetically at Lawrence—"it almost ended just as badly."

"So," Tabby said. "Whaat now?"

His men having started a fire and begun heaping deadfall and dry driftwood on it, Chiba gestured at the swiftly gathering gloom beyond. That's when he finally managed a real smile. "That is actually what we were sent here to determine." There was a call in the darkness, and a Japanese sailor with what looked like a petty officer's markings shouted back. Another dozen or so men began to filter from the trees and approach.

"Shit," Miles growled.

"Easy, Ian," Silva said. "The way we're lit up, they could'a shot us ta ribbons if they wanted."

"I appreciate you taking our wounded man to your ship," Chiba said as if nothing were happening. "As I said, it would take considerably longer for us to get him the treatment he needs. The dead man will return in the boats with the others. If you have no objection, I will accompany you back aboard your"—he blinked—"amazingly resilient destroyer as well and lead a small party of your people back to *Shonai* in the morning."

"A 'small party'?" Courtney questioned curiously. "Why shouldn't we all just go there in *Walker*?"

Chiba pursed his lips again. "That . . . might be desirable at some point," he conceded, "but would not be . . . convenient at present."

Silva chuckled and said aside to Abel Cook, "That little Jap has fuzzy talk down to a art. I can appreciate that, bein' pretty good at it myself."

Abel sighed and whispered back. "Perhaps they are concerned about another violent misunderstanding, between our ships this time, which could be much more damaging, costly, and difficult to smooth over."

"That's what I was thinkin', Mr. Cook," Silva agreed.

Abel looked at him and said, still talking low, "Then under the circumstances, it might be helpful for you to 'think' about refraining from calling Lieutenant Chiba a 'little Jap.'"

Silva blinked his good eye. "What for? He *is* a Jap, an' he ain't tall . . ."

Gunny Horn seemed equally surprised. "'Jap' is just short for Japanese. It's not like he called him a—"

Abel held up a hand, shaking his head. "Just *try* to behave, if you please. Short or not, he's an officer, and you might respect the courage it takes for him to board *Walker*, essentially alone."

"Right," Silva seemed to agree, tone solemn. "*Mr.* Jap it is."

Tabby had been speaking with Courtney, who nodded. "Well . . . I guess thaat's whaat we'll do," she said at last.

"Good. Can we go now?" Pam grouched. She was kneeling by the wounded man, the back of her fingers gently resting against his throat. That seemed to spur everyone into motion.

"Take charge of our launch, Sergeant Miles," Tabby said. "I'll ride along with our guests in the first one. It isn't nearly as full."

"Aye, aye," Miles replied, then called to the second shore party, "Let's load up and shove off. Back to the ship."

"How long before your boats pick up the rest of your people?" Abel asked Chiba.

"Not long. Honestly, they are probably waiting to do so even now."

Tabby turned to look around. There was no moon yet and the only light now came from the stars. And the fire, of course, which hampered even her superior night vision. "Another layer of care, Lieutenaant Chiba?" she asked.

The young Japanese officer nodded. "We have learned a great deal about caution," he said. "The war we left behind on our old world taught us much, and if there is one thing that all we have endured on this one has reinforced with absolute certainty, it is that there is no such thing as being too careful."

Lawrence heard that and hissed as they began pushing their own boat back into the lapping surf. "'Too car'ul' got I shot. Again. They thought I is a Grik, I guess." He scowled at Silva. Like Lemurians, his furry but otherwise frighteningly reptilian face wasn't capable of displaying a wide range of expressions, but he was good at scowling. "Like you did, long ago."

Silva grunted, heaving against the friction of the sand with the others. "There ya go again. Always treasurin' grudges an' harpin' on the past," he grumped. "I didn't know there was anything looked like a Grik that wasn't one, back then. Leaves me sympathetic to the Jap that shot ya." The launch floated free, and he and Horn and Sergeant Kaik stopped it from going too far. "But 'too careful' also keeps you sittin' on yer ass when you *need* to be killin' what spooks ya."

"Sittin' On Yer Ass!" Petey cawed happily. "Eat!" he exclaimed, knowing they were heading back to the ship.

"That's our Dennis Silva." Horn chuckled. "Consistent to a fault in pushing his views that 'something, somewhere, always needs killing' and 'the best way to solve a problem is to shoot holes in it.'"

Silva nodded. "Damn right."

The first motor launch hooked on to port while the other went around to starboard, and Captain Rodriguez and the few other original American crew of the ship exchanged enough queries and had the time it took to hoist the injured man aboard to get used to the idea that they would be hosting a pair of Japanese sailors. It wasn't like that hadn't happened before, and the man who was now *General* Tomatsu Shinya was largely considered "one of them," but there was certainly a sense of Silva's offhand description of "wild Japanese" among those old veterans. The rest, particularly the cadets, were just curious and somewhat excited. And Lieutenant Chiba made a good impression on everyone when he climbed up the rungs on the side of the ship, turned to salute aft where the Stars and Stripes would've been gently stirring from the halyard on the mainmast if a muted evening colors ceremony hadn't already been performed, then saluted Ronson Rodriguez, solemnly introduced himself, and requested permission to come aboard.

Pam was brusquely supervising the transfer of the injured man forward and down the companionway to the wardroom, calling for Lawrence and Philan Bele to "get their asses down there too," when Ronson returned the salute of their visitor. Though somewhat taken aback, he managed, "Permission granted, Lieutenant. Welcome aboard." He gestured vaguely forward. "I'd invite you to the wardroom for coffee and something to eat, but Pam—I mean, Surgeon Cross—will likely be busy there for a while."

"What's Earl got on the spit, Skipper?" Silva asked as he and the rest climbed up on deck and Chief Bashear immediately started hoisting the launch with the davits, stopping it even with the deck as well. Cadets clambered into it, brushing out the sand and checking the engine.

Ronson gave Silva an odd look. "I'll show you." He grinned at Lieutenant Chiba. "Maybe you can tell us what it is," he added. The lights were on under the amidships deckhouse, illuminating a roughly 4′×8′ wooden table that had been erected next to the galley. Lying on top of it and drooping off each end onto the deck—it had to be more than twelve feet long—was another scaly nightmare from the deep, shaped as much like a giant fat eel as anything else. There was no distinctive tail, just a long iridescent dorsal and ventral fin with lethal-looking spikes protruding along the length of its body. The gaping mouth looked kind of like an eel's as well, the jaws a bit longer in proportion and filled with two rows of strikingly sharklike teeth. The weirdest thing was a spiraling horn about three feet long that protruded from the top of the skull, like a narwhal's, instead of being part of the upper jaw, like a swordfish's.

"What the hell, Earl?" Silva scoffed. "You didn't pull that in with your dinky little pole. What is it?"

"It's a fish, you idiot," Earl replied triumphantly, then conceded, "which I fought with my pole until me an' these fellas"—he gestured to his mess attendants—"latched on the line with the foremast hoist."

"So, *you* didn't catch it, the ship did," Gunny Horn observed. "How come it didn't break the line?"

"Braided steel," Earl confided, frowning, likely at the fact that Horn was right. He hadn't actually caught the thing, and at the very least, he had help.

"What are you doing to it?" Courtney demanded, pushing through the cluster of onlookers.

Earl blinked back at him, holding up a long, bloody knife and looking at it. "Well . . ." He hesitated. "I'm the cook," he said simply. "I like eatin' fish, as anybody knows, but this devil's big enough ta share." He shrugged. "I'm filletin' it. Cut the fillets into chunks, make a fine fish stew . . ."

"No!" Courtney shouted, voice almost shrill. "Has anyone here ever seen a fish like it? I haven't!" He turned accusingly to Captain Rodriguez. "And I have no doubt that no one even thought to record it, take measurements, draw pictures . . . And now that we've managed to make enough film beyond our strict need for reconnaissance, we even brought a *camera*, you know!" He pointed at the fish, one side of which was rather seriously demolished. "I understand that this voyage has taken on some . . . more pressing priorities, especially now, but surely there must remain the *slightest* inclination toward *discovery for its own sake*?" He gestured at the fish. "Especially when it just . . . drops in among us, as it were?"

Ronson was frowning, avoiding Courtney's gaze. "You're right, Mr. Bradford. I'm sorry. I didn't have a fella with your scientific tendencies around me that much for the last few years. On my other ships, we'd catch all sorts of things over the side wherever we anchored. 'Cats like fish at least as much as Earl. But 'what we've been doing' is no excuse. Earl," he said sternly, "get the mess attendants started making chow, and I don't care if it's just sandwiches. We're not waiting on you to cook that thing." His tone turned firmer. "But as soon as you're through cleaning your fish—and cleaning up the mess—you *will* catch another one just like it, only bigger! That's an order, Earl, and I don't care if it takes you all night."

It was clear that Ronson was perfectly serious, but Silva couldn't contain the short, snorting laugh that escaped. Ronson rounded on him. "What's so damn funny, Chief Silva?" he demanded.

"N-n-nuthin', Skipper," he barely managed before a full laugh exploded. Doubled over and holding his hands up, he tried to stop but couldn't. "It's just"—he gasped—"I've lived to see"—he seemed to gather himself for a fuller explanation—"you or any officer *order* Earl ta go fishin'!"

Now Ronson's severe expression cracked as well, and in moments it seemed like the entire ship was overcome with laughter. All the while, Lieutenant Chiba was looking almost nervously around him.

Abel caught his expression and pointed at him, laughing even harder himself. "He thinks he's boarded a ship full of lunatics!"

Courtney himself finally achieved a level of quiet by waving his arms and calling for silence, though he was red-faced and laughing as well. "It is I who owe you all an apology," he said at last. "I spent the whole war on this fascinating world utterly frustrated at my inability to study it. Now I have that chance after a fashion, at least as a tertiary concern." He turned his smile on Earl. "Perhaps in the future we might take better care to record and describe our specimens, but I believe, in this case, we can accomplish our purpose well enough by"—he smiled somewhat sheepishly—"simply flipping the thing over to the undamaged side."

More laughter erupted then, and even Lieutenant Chiba joined in. Catching Tabby's curious blinking, though he couldn't be sure what it meant of course, he cupped his hand and spoke into a furry ear that alone struck him as strangely as anything else he'd experienced that day. "We have heard, or surmised, quite a bit about your 'Grand Alliance' and what it has accomplished. All the foes it has faced. We have also learned something about the League," he confessed. "I may indeed be among 'lunatics,' as Mr. Cook suggested, but it is clear to me that . . . your combined peoples have been better suited in virtually every way to cope with those challenges than we have so far. Granted, we haven't been on this world as long as this ship has been." Tabby thought she caught a vague shudder in Chiba's tone at that, but he quickly recovered and continued, addressing Ronson. "In the morning, I will take you to my Captain and I think he will agree. I am sure it was your original intent to investigate the neighboring island tomorrow, and I apologize for any delay. There should still be ample time to travel there. But Captain Okabe can provide valuable . . . context to better prepare you for what you will find."

"Aactivity on the beach," came the cry of a Lemurian cadet lookout, and many turned to gaze at the bonfire. A ghost of a smile returned to Chiba's face as he watched silhouetted figures boarding boats of their own and shoving off from shore.

"We would have followed you there in any event, had we not become acquainted today, though we would have been forced to sail or row. What little gasoline we have has been reserved for our aircraft. There is none to spare for the boats."

"Why not steam over in your cruiser?" Ronson asked.

Courtney's eyebrows resembled leaping caterpillars. "Good heavens, Captain Rodriguez! Today's meeting still had a tragic outcome, regardless how carefully they attempted to avoid it, and Japanese cruisers of all classes have extraordinarily distinctive lines. What would you have done if one just suddenly popped up out of the blue?"

"*After* we all shit ourselves, Skipper," Silva urged, seeing where Courtney was going.

Ronson was already nodding. "Yeah. If it was close enough when we saw it, we would've had to start shooting—and hauling ass at the same time, while screaming our head off over the radio."

"And that last might have been the most damaging," Chiba said, "for the very same reason we did not simply contact *you* by radio."

"Because of who else would've heard," Tabby guessed.

"Correct," Chiba confirmed. "Do not think that your enemies are unaware that you are here," he warned. "We considered it . . . best, certainly safer for us, but possibly advantageous for you as well if they were not aware of *our* presence." He held his hands out to his sides. "And, in all honesty, *Shonai* hasn't got enough fuel to steam *anywhere*."

CHAPTER 16

High, wispy, salmon-colored clouds were smeared across the sky when the motor launch burbled away from the ship once more. The party was much the same as before, with the addition of Carl Bashear as coxswain, Lieutenant Chiba as guide, Fen-An-Raar, as the only one among *Walker*'s company who'd seen their objective, and Captain Rodriguez of course. Ronson had debated bringing Lemurians this time, not to mention Lawrence, but Lieutenant Chiba himself assured him it was probably best—with him along—to present themselves as they were: an equal alliance of "people" of every imaginable sort. He couldn't promise that *Shonai*'s crew would easily accept that, but it should convince Captain Okabe that his Japanese sailors wouldn't be their most unusual associates. He'd been told there were already Japanese in the United Homes, largely inhabiting the Shogunate of Yokohama, and General Tomatsu Shinya was the second-highest-ranking officer in the Combined Allied Army, but there weren't any Japanese in *Walker* at present, so that would be hard to prove.

Silva (now armed with a BAR) and Lawrence were in the bow with Ronson, Chiba, and the three cadets, who Chiba seemed extremely interested in, as the launch motored deeper into the lagoon. Large fins swirled the placid water and fish occasionally leaped clear to snatch gigantic dragonflies before crashing back in the water with splashes like small-caliber shellfire.

"That was a whopper," Silva observed. "Bigger than me, I bet."

"There are many things much bigger, and considerably more unpleasant, I assure you," Chiba told him.

"I doubt that," cracked Pam, back behind them. "Dennis Silva has never met a bigger, less pleasant butthole than him."

"Flatterer," Silva tossed back. "Ain't she sweet?" he seemed to ask Chiba, but the Japanese officer made no comment. "What's with these dragonflies?" he continued. "These're bigger than the lizardbirds. Some of 'em, anyway."

"Lizardbirds," Chiba echoed. "A good name." He pointed at one of the dragonflies pacing the boat. "You haven't seen these things?"

"I haven't. Not as big," Silva allowed, "though I heard o' some in the swamps o' West Jaava."

"Do they bite?" asked Fen, peering at them a little nervously.

"Sometimes," Chiba admitted, "but they are not poisonous. And they taste quite good."

"You *eat* 'em?" Pam asked incredulously. "Eww."

Chiba just shrugged.

The lagoon began to narrow, the forest rising steeply on the tightening flanks of rocky slopes rearing high up above them as the morning advanced. And even as the lagoon began to more closely resemble a river a couple of hundred yards wide, that wasn't right either, because there was no discernible current aside from the ebbing tide and the passage was clearly very deep. More like a bottomless crack in the island. Rocks occasionally tumbled down the slope to splash in the water, sometimes alone or among small avalanches, and they caught glimpses of large creatures high above that might be pacing their progress.

Silva occasionally raised the BAR, but ultimately lowered it with apparent reluctance. "Can't get a decent shot," he groused each time.

"Just as well," Chiba finally said a little ironically. "The insignificant wounds bullets cause tend to annoy them and pique their interest. There are few places they can reach the water along here and they will generally amuse themselves elsewhere unless provoked."

"That means 'don't shoot at 'em,' Dennis," Pam sniped.

They'd gone about four miles it seemed, rarely very straight for long, but deep into the interior, and Fen was surprised he hadn't seen such a glaring feature from the sky. Chiba was sympathetic, explaining their plane had "joined" the one he'd been in shortly before he would've noticed it. Fred's acrobatic reaction had been understandable, as was Fen's concentration on other things at that moment.

It was when the long lagoon opened up a bit more that they finally caught a glimpse of their destination and Chiba directed them to turn toward what at first glance looked like any other stretch of the densely wooded shoreline.

"There she is!" Silva suddenly exclaimed, pointing at a section of beach where there was no sand. Having focused there, everyone could see a long sweeping hull under a somewhat equally flowing superstructure, all amazingly well camouflaged with various grays, a bright green the same as the overhanging foliage, and a liberal coating of red-brown rust streaks.

"Damn," Ronson murmured, seeing the four large turrets on the relatively low-slung fo'c'sle that took up a third of the ship's length. "That's a Tone Class ship," he said, turning a somewhat accusing look at Chiba.

"Yes?" Chiba said, questioningly.

"When was she built?"

Chiba hesitated. "She entered service in 1940."

Ronson looked at others in the boat, then sighed and shook his head. "Not where we came from. In early 'forty-two there were only two of them, *Tone* herself and her sister, *Chikuma*. No *Shonai*." He exhaled. "Which means we *don't* come from the same world at all."

"But there *was* a USS *Walker* in ours," Chiba said quietly. "We, ah, hunted her ourselves, along with HMS *Exeter*, HMS *Encounter*, and USS *Pope*."

"What about USS *Mahan*?" Courtney immediately asked.

Chiba shook his head. "Only those. And we were in company with *Tone* and *Chikuma*."

"Fascinating!" Courtney exclaimed. "Very close 'frequencies' indeed!"

Abel Cook tried to explain. "Mr. Bradford believes there are . . . innumerable worlds, many different versions of . . . us, in fact, yet only those most similar to our own are capable of, well, coming here."

"Captain Okabe believes the same," Chiba said. "It makes no sense to me," he confessed. "Why would we have to be similar to come to someplace so wildly different?" He looked back at Ronson. "But we thought you *were* the same *Walker* we chased, because she escaped into a . . . weather phenomenon very much like the one that eventually brought us here."

"Amazing!" Courtney enthused. "This world is not the only . . . destination for those such as us. My mind boggles at the possibilities, the quite literally infinite potential numbers of," he blinked. "Well, *me*, for instance. I would quite enjoy meeting myself, I believe." He frowned. "Yet I suspect that may be one of the 'laws' that cannot be bent. But what makes the law? Who writes it? How is it enforced?" He reached out and surprised Chiba by taking his hand, shaking it vigorously. "When did you come to be here?"

"Ah, roughly a year ago," Chiba hedged.

Courtney didn't seem to notice. "You say your captain contemplates such matters? Wonderful. I'm sure he and I—and Mr. Cook, of course—will soon be fast friends!"

"Your new pal's ship is pointing a lot of guns at us, Mr. Bradford," Gunny Horn said, redirecting his attention. As they'd drawn closer to the cruiser, not only had she grown larger, a number of the secondaries had been manned by running figures. "Maybe you better give 'em the high sign, or whatever," he added to Lieutenant Chiba.

Only once they were aboard the ship and surrounded by a large number of armed sailors whose expressions ranged from curiously friendly to furiously hostile did they see a number of things. First, though undeniably impressive in size and design, *Shonai* suffered from severe dilapidation, quite a bit more than a single year divorced from proper maintenance would seem to account for. Second was a veritable settlement under the forest beyond her onshore. None of it would be seen from above, but there were a large number of huts erected along carefully laid dirt streets that only the trees interrupted. And close to shore was the beginning of a high, stout, defensive palisade that doubtless encircled the entire habitable area. What was immediately apparent was that none of the timber for the huts or palisade had been cut nearby and all had been dragged here with great effort from somewhere else. The only possible reason for this was so the local camouflage for the settlement and the ship wouldn't be compromised.

"Perhaps your people should surrender their weapons," Chiba suggested to Ronson when the hostile faces, voices, and gestures around them seemed to be increasing in number.

"No," Ronson said, tone turning angry as well. "Not ever. Maybe you better tell everybody that, and that we came here in peace at your invitation instead." There was shouting in Japanese nearby and some of the surrounding noise tapered off. Men began shifting, shuffling aside, making way for a pair of men dressed as officers to approach. "Larry, Gunny Horn, stand ready to knock Silva down if you have to. He's got that look on his face—and we might be about to get this settled."

Chiba started talking loud and fast in Japanese and many of the persistently hostile finally backed away, looking uncomfortably at Silva. He was just standing there, the heavy BAR on his right shoulder, but he wore an extremely disconcerting half grin.

"Dennis," said Pam, touching his upper arm. When that had no effect, she punched him in the same spot. "Dennis!" she snapped. "Down, boy!"

"Huh? What? Oh, hey, doll. Why'd you frog me, dammit?"

"You is going to kill all those Japhs," Lawrence confided.

Silva looked surprised. "Was not," he denied, then caught Chiba's look. "Not *all* of 'em, I don't think."

"You mustn't kill *anyone* today, Chief Silva," Courtney earnestly declared. "We have come to make friends, not more enemies."

"Would he have . . ?" Chiba softly asked Ronson. "*Could* he?"

"There's never much telling what that maniac can do—until he does it," Ronson gravely replied, then suddenly he was standing face-to-face with what he assumed was *Shonai*'s captain. Without hesitation, he saluted. "Commander Rolando Rodriguez," he said crisply. "You're Captain Okabe, I presume. We're already aboard," he added with a slight smile, "so I request permission to stay a short while."

Okabe was tall, almost as tall as Rodriguez, and his uniform was smarter than most, though obviously not new. Both officers wore pistol belts, but also had scabbarded katanas thrust into them. Okabe had black hair touched with silver and a lined, craggy face with a drawn, haunted air, but came very close to matching Rodriguez's expression when he returned the salute. "I *am* Captain Okabe," he said in only slightly accented English. "And this"—he tilted his head toward the other officer—"is Commander Ishida, my executive officer. I apologize for my tardiness in welcoming you aboard, but I was attending to issues ashore when you were sighted. I came as quickly as I could." He glanced around, eyes narrowing. "I also apologize for your treatment by men under my command." He paused. "We have been through a great deal, as I am sure you can imagine. Our story is not as lengthy as yours, but began with . . . particularly traumatic circumstances that may have adversely affected our very will to survive the extraordinary situation we found ourselves in." He glanced away. "The only thing that preserved me was my responsibility to my crew." He looked back at Ronson. "I think it is understandable that we have grown close, and though that might explain the behavior of some of them"—his tone turned harsh as he gazed around again—"it does not excuse it."

Many of the bystanding sailors looked down at the cracking linoleum deck.

Courtney pushed impatiently past Ronson, reaching to take the Japanese officer's hand. "I'm Courtney Bradford, Captain Okabe, and I'm fascinated, *fascinated* to hear your tale. And we have *much* else to discuss, not least of which what awaits us on the nearby island." He lowered his voice. "We have some small notion, but I understand you can enlighten us further? I'm also informed you have your own theories about the process or mechanism of transfer that snatches us from one world and deposits us on another. In any event, I'm so glad the . . . unfortunate first moments of our meeting yesterday can now be amended." He beamed.

"Yes. Well"—Okabe looked uncertainly at Courtney before refocusing on Ronson, then frowned and cleared his throat—"I look forward to our discussions as well, but first I must perform a final duty related to a part of the trauma that has lingered over us since even before we found ourselves so peculiarly stranded." He cleared his throat and sighed very deeply. "The first and last time any of us ever heard our Emperor's voice . . ." He cleared his throat again and straightened stiffly. "Am I correct to assume that you are the senior American naval officer present?"

Ronson frowned. "Ah, sure. I mean, you are. I am."

Okabe nodded briskly before removing the scabbarded katana from the belt around his waist. Commander Ishida followed suit. Both men hesitated only an instant before presenting the swords to Ronson. "Then, sir, it is my final duty to my Emperor to surrender myself, my crew, and my ship to you."

Ronson could only stand there stunned, hands actually going behind his back instead of reaching for the swords. "What the hell?" he finally managed. "Why would you do that?" He turned to glare at Lieutenant Chiba. "Why didn't you tell me?"

Chiba looked away. "I told you 'our war' was over. It was not my place to reveal more."

"Hot damn!" Silva grinned at Horn, poking him in the ribs with his elbow. "We must'a won."

"Shut up, Silva. Just this once, at least," Ronson growled back without looking. "I have to think." Nodding at the swords, he said, "And you guys hang on to those." He rubbed his face, glanced at Courtney, who seemed just as shocked as he was, then addressed Okabe again. "Look," he said, tone a little harassed, "we didn't come here to take anybody's surrender. Hell, the last we knew, we were *losing* the war back home and Japs were chasing us all over Java Sea, hunting us down like rats."

If a little resentment entered his voice, Okabe chose to ignore it, even solemnly confessing, "Yes. We were there."

"Yeah? That's what Lieutenant Chiba said. Told us you even chased us, specifically." He frowned. "Or *another* us."

Now Okabe looked confused, and Lieutenant Chiba quickly explained the discrepancies in their respective experiences that they'd noted earlier.

"Countless worlds," Courtney enthused, "but only those that are very similar, on quite close . . . frequencies," he said, as always, as if unhappy with the inadequacy of the description, "have ultimately wound up here. That explains why there are often differences, sometimes very slight, between our history and the histories of those we meet." He paused, thoughtful. "Though the farther back we go in the history of *this* world, the more divergent those other histories tend to be, if you know what I mean."

"I do not," Okabe confessed, glancing at Lawrence, then Fen and Sergeant Kaik, "though we haven't met nearly as many descendants of those . . . diverse histories as you." His expression turned grim. "Many things now make more sense than they did, however, when we got our first impression of the League and their Dominion associates."

"You've met them?" Courtney asked intently.

"Yes, in a sense," Okabe replied. Glancing around, he thrust his katana back in his belt. "Come to our wardroom," he said. "We have little to offer in terms of refreshment: boiled water sweetened with fruit and some local fare. Fish mostly."

"As long as it ain't bugs," Pam whispered aside to Cadet Bele.

"We only have electricity every third evening," Okabe went on. "We have no fuel oil at all and were forced to rebuild one of our boilers to burn wood so we can run our pumps and communications gear. Unfortunately, the boiler fills with ash rather quickly, so we only fire it up at night when the smoke can't be seen and for only long enough to keep the bilge relatively dry. In any event, there are no lights or fans at present, but the shade of the trees at this time of day makes the wardroom quite bearable."

Seeing their skipper and XO return their swords to their belts went a long way toward reducing the hostility of the sailors around them, though they still watched, distrustful or curious, as the party from *Walker* followed Okabe, Ishida, and Chiba forward, past the big shielded pairs of 5" guns alongside the single raked stack and then down a companionway under the forward superstructure. Entering a space not entirely unlike *Walker*'s wardroom, only three times as big in all dimensions, Captain Okabe politely gestured for them to join him around a big metal table with the same brownish linoleum on it that covered much of the deck, both inside and out on the ship. A pair of mess attendants hustled in, already carrying a tray of small, rolled . . . things, and a pair of polished silver pitchers. Cups were distributed from a cabinet.

"Thank you," Okabe told the sailors. "That will be all, though please pass the word for the department heads to join us directly." When the mess attendants departed, Okabe explained, "Our camp onshore was attacked last night"—his gaze turned to Lawrence—"by creatures remarkably like . . . that one."

"His name's Lawrence," Silva said. "He even talks!"

"Asshole," Lawrence muttered.

"See?" Silva exclaimed triumphantly.

Pam rolled her eyes and Courtney leaned forward. "Can you describe them?"

"He just did, almost exactly," said Commander Ishida, speaking for the first time. Unlike Okabe, his English had a strong accent and wasn't nearly as friendly. "The only difference between"—his lip curled at Lawrence—"that and the creatures infesting all the nearby islands we have explored is that your . . . domesticated specimen wears clothes." Now, even Pam's face flared with anger, but Ishida wasn't finished, pointing at Fen and Sergeant Kaik. "And *they* are much like other . . . savages we encountered on a much larger island before we came here. All of them killed some of our people and even the more feline variety wasn't above eating them." He glared at Lawrence. "But his kind will eat whatever they can catch."

Silva looked ready to jump across the table, but that made even Courtney mad. "It would seem that *your* 'savage' has slipped his leash, Captain Okabe," Courtney said, voice very clipped and precise. "We have fought and defeated some very bad Japanese on this world, yet we did not immediately treat you like them." He held up a finger. "And even their survivors have been allowed to willingly join us. I urge you to extend the same courtesy, the same benefit of the doubt, to members of our company, our firm alliance, who happen to resemble other cultures or races you have had difficulties with."

"Ishida!" Okabe snapped before trying to explain. "The commander has taken our losses very hard, particularly—and quite recently—the loss of a young ensign who was his sister's son."

Commander Ishida had lowered his gaze, but just for a moment. "I . . . apologize," he ground out. "And I shall extend that courtesy because my captain requires it. I must wait to see how ready I will be to do so willingly, however."

Ronson gazed into his eyes for a moment before simply shrugging. "Fair enough," he said. "But in the meantime, if you harm, direct harm, or even allow harm through indifference to any of my people, whatever they look like, I'll turn Chief Silva loose on you." He paused. "None of us wants that, but *you* really won't."

"Have we already degenerated to threats?" Courtney asked plaintively.

"No threat," Ronson replied. "Call it . . . a law-of-nature consequence, like an unequal but opposite—and disproportionate—reaction." He took a breath and frowned before regarding Okabe. "Now, why don't you tell me your story, including why you tried to surrender. When you're done, I'll tell you why I'll accept it—or not—what that means, and what your options are."

"Mightn't it be best to consult Captain Reddy?" Courtney asked aside, but Ronson shook his head.

"He's pretty busy right now and I expect, between you and me and the rest of us here, we know him well enough to do what he'd do. Maybe we should've brought Mr. Meek, but he'll go along with what we decide." Looking back at Okabe, he motioned him to begin, then took a first sip of the flavored water. "Gaah!" he exclaimed.

"You grow accustomed to it," Okabe assured.

"God, I hope not."

CHAPTER 17

As had been determined, *Shonai* was a Tone Class heavy cruiser, 620 feet long and roughly 63 feet wide, displacing about 15,000 tons. Her eight boilers, four turbines, and shafts could fairly easily drive her past thirty knots when in top shape, or as far as 8,000 miles at eighteen knots. Even farther if she went slower, which she had to for much of her final wartime mission. Her superstructure fairly bristled with secondaries and antiaircraft armaments, and her entire main battery of eight 8″ rifles were housed in four large turrets forward. Aft was entirely dedicated to air operations, hoists, crane, catapults, and workshops, and six Aichi E13A floatplanes, commonly called "Jakes" by her old-world enemies. Four were left and three were currently operational.

As was often the case throughout her career, *Shonai* had been operating with her sisters, *Tone* and *Chikuma*, on March 1, 1942, when they and another cruiser division pursued *Walker*, *Exeter*, *Encounter*, and *Pope*, dogging them with their aircraft, which harassed the fleeing ships and corrected fire for the cruisers chasing them. In another significant departure from the experience of those present, who'd now clearly been aboard a *different Walker*, this other fugitive destroyer hadn't been herded into the arms of the massive battlecruiser *Amagi*, which none of the Japanese officers telling their story knew to exist where they came from, but had "escaped" into a malevolent-looking green squall that the pursuing ships avoided. After the strange and unusually violent squall marched on, no sign of *Walker* was found and it was assumed at the time she'd somehow managed to evade them. *Shonai* and her sisters did catch another old destroyer later in the day, in company with a plodding oiler. The oiler was sunk by carrier aircraft, which damaged and slowed the destroyer.

Okabe appeared intensely distressed by what happened next, reporting in a monotone that he'd held his ship back when her sisters closed to point-blank range and demolished the helpless destroyer with gunfire. "It was not . . . honorable and I was shamed by what they did," he said. "I couldn't be a part of it." His expression darkened. "And that was before the war degenerated into the even more barbarous thing it would become." He spoke in vague terms of *Shonai*'s subsequent career, clearly proud of some of it, not so much about other times. He did confirm an attack had been launched by American carriers against Japan itself, shortly followed by a disaster at Midway, where four Japanese carriers were lost. This had been the latest "war news" any of the others received when Gunny Horn, Ian Miles, Henry Stokes, and quite a few others came to this world in the hellish transport *Mizuki Maru*, escorted by a rogue Kagero Class destroyer named *Hidoiame*.

"That's the ship that *fell* on me!" Silva blurted, apparently at random and prompting incredulous expressions.

Ronson only said, "She was destroyed."

Courtney added, "But many of the prisoners in *Mizuki Maru* were saved"—he bowed his head at Horn—"and much of *Hidoiame*'s crew and some people they'd enslaved ashore were . . . liberated from her officers, who'd gone quite insane."

Okabe rubbed his face and glanced at Ishida. "The whole world had gone mad," he said. "The war was going poorly and dreadful measures were employed." Looking away again, he said, "Eventually, we had more aircraft than experienced pilots, and young men were trained just barely well enough to crash their planes into American ships. They called them Tokkotai, or Kamikaze . . . And planes were not all they used. After the remaining bulk of our fleet was destroyed defending the Philippines, the mighty *Yamato* herself was sacrificed in April of 1945, given just enough fuel to reach Okinawa and beach herself to become an unsinkable battery." He shook his head. "She did not make it and was sunk on the way." He took a long breath. "Nor was she the only such sacrifice." He gestured vaguely around. "My own *Shonai* was sent on a one-way mission of her own."

The wardroom was utterly silent while Okabe sipped his flavored water. Ronson took a waxed paper packet of small cigars made from real "Nussie" tobacco from his shirt pocket, pulled one out, and offered it. Blinking with emotion and surprise, Okabe took it and stuck it in his mouth, waiting while Silva stood and flipped open his Zippo to light it. (Silva considered his treasured Zippo as important a part of his combat rig as anything else.) Drawing the smoke into his lungs, Okabe coughed lightly and said, "Ghastly," but it was clear he appreciated it. Shrugging, Ronson tossed the packet on the table, inviting anyone who wanted to take one. Ishida did, so did Horn and Sergeant Kaik. Silva fingered the pouch of tobacco in his own pocket but, seeing nothing to spit in, decided against taking a chew.

"Yes," Okabe finally continued. "*Shonai* was actually overfilled with fuel oil, using auxiliary bladders our submarines sometimes employed. Needless to say, just accumulating that much fuel was an extremely difficult project by then, but it still wasn't expected that we would have enough to actually return, since our objective was even more ambitious than *Yamato*'s. *Shonai* is orders of magnitude less massive than the great battleship, yet only relatively smaller, and steaming with stealth is no simple matter. Nevertheless, that is what we were sent to do: *sneak* past what was by then an unimaginably dense armada of American surface ships and their unknowably complex shipping lanes, countless scout aircraft and prowling submarines, and make our way all alone"—he paused, for effect, most likely—"to launch our aircraft bearing their maximum load of bombs against the Pacific locks of your Panama Canal." He snorted. "We were even ordered to move into range to *bombard* them, despite all the defenses."

He puffed the cigarillo for a moment before pronouncing, "Not so bad after all." He looked at Ronson. "It may be difficult for you to imagine, based on what was available to your navy in 1942, but the sheer scope of the force arrayed against us less than three years later . . . Suffice to say that we were all resigned to the fact that it was an impossible mission." He smiled a little wistfully. "Which may be precisely why we actually made it within range of our aircraft. No one else would have believed it possible either. Ultimately, we *could* have done it—for what little good it would have accomplished. A final, pathetically defiant, suicidal act," he ended grimly, then waved his hand in the smoke around his head. "We'd been monitoring the radio, of course, and there'd been an announcement that a single bomb dropped on Hiroshima had utterly destroyed the city and your president was demanding that Japan surrender before the 'rain of ruin' continued."

Courtney gasped and cast a significant look at Abel Cook, who nodded back.

"We dismissed it as propaganda, of course," Ishida bitterly commented. "But then there was word of a *second* bomb, dropped on Nagasaki." He looked even more morose when he added, "And finally, on August fifteenth, the very day before we would have been in position to launch our attack . . ." He paused and barely whispered, "The Emperor spoke."

"He *surrendered*," Okabe said louder, "though that wasn't immediately clear. The radio reception was poor and he delivered his address in extremely formal Japanese, which can be somewhat vague. Besides"—he blinked—"no one had ever heard the Emperor's voice before. Many who recognized the speech for what it was insisted it was a fake"—he glanced at Ishida—"or that we continue with our attack, regardless." He frowned. "It was the outpouring of jubilation over the airwaves, in the clear, that convinced me, along with the Emperor's mention of a 'most cruel bomb' that could lead to the 'extinction of human civilization.' Finally, it was my interpretation of his admonition against engaging in 'outbursts of emotion' that might cause 'needless complications' resulting in Japan losing 'the confidence of the world' that persuaded me that our attack, so soon after the Emperor's declaration, might itself result in another of those weapons being used."

"Captain Okabe persuaded all of us of this," Lieutenant Chiba said quietly, "and he was right to do so. Within days, we received orders in our own current codes, not directed specifically at us, but all naval forces still at sea, to surrender to the first enemy vessel or installation we encountered."

"Those bombs—atom bombs, we suspect—must have been quite 'cruel' indeed," Courtney said quietly as well. "Their effects, ah, leaked over to this world in the vicinity of where Hiroshima and Nagasaki would be. Fortunately, those areas are heavily forested on this world and only sparsely populated. We know of no one who was injured by them here, though I suppose it's possible they were. Perhaps a woodsman or hunter." He cleared his throat. "The Shogunate is a member of the United Homes and is not only populated by many Japanese, but also a large number of Lemurians." He paused. "Mi-Anakka, they call themselves," he said, gesturing at Fen and Sergeant Kaik. "You can all go live there as well, if you like."

"That is . . . possible," Okabe said, "but first let me finish my account. Then we all may better decide whether we should surrender to you or join you, and on what terms we may do the latter."

Ronson arched a bushy eyebrow, intrigued, but indicated Okabe should continue.

"Obviously, we did not surrender to the nearest ship or outpost," Okabe said, smiling slightly. "Perhaps it would have been better for us if we had. All that would have been required was to steam straight to the forts near the end of the long breakwater and strike our flag." Okabe's jaw muscles tightened. "Tempting as that was—just imagine the embarrassment of the defenses there!—we were not prepared to do so. There was concern over how we would be treated and how long we would be detained, and most of us just wanted to go home." He shrugged. "We didn't have enough fuel for that, but we could have gotten closer. My plan was to steer for Australia, though somewhat south of the most direct route for a time, hoping to avoid detection and get closer to our destination before we were apprehended. Again, this was solely an attempt to get home," he stressed, "thinking it possible we would simply be escorted there, or at least nearer than we were, instead of being interned for an indefinite time thousands of miles away." He straightened in his chair. "Another dreadful mistake, I fear. The weather deteriorated as we approached the French islands and the sea state rendered our surface radar useless—"

"Wait," Abel interrupted. "You have radar?"

"We do," Ishida replied guardedly. "Surface and air search. The latest thing, though not as good as the Americans'."

"That's . . . interesting," Ronson said, trying to hide his excitement. "Is it operational?"

Ishida shook his head. "The surface set has been inoperable for a while. No spare parts," he added dismally. "The air search apparatus may still function, but we can't even test it down in this crack."

"How long have you been here?" Courtney asked.

"I will get to that," Okabe said, possibly a little annoyed by the distraction from his narrative. "Where was I? Yes. The weather continued to worsen and with diminishing certainty about our position, we steered farther south. I knew the sea would mount even higher in the lower latitudes, but the risk of striking a shoal or island in the storm-lashed daylight or darkness was reduced. Still"—he drew on his cigar again—"I have rarely encountered higher wind or rougher seas. Particularly for so long a time. Perhaps that is what caused it . . ."

"By 'it,' do you mean . . . ?" Courtney began tentatively.

"Yes. We barely saw it, of course. It was dark already and the spray-lashed bridge windows were opaque for all practical purposes, but miserably cold and wet lookouts on the air defense command post above the bridge reported a greenish *glow* to the lightning shortly before a disconcerting number of . . . frightening and uncomfortable events and sensations occurred."

"A terrible screeching noise inside your head?" Ronson asked.

"A dreadful nausea and terrifying falling sensation?" Courtney pressed.

Okabe, Ishida, and Chiba all exchanged looks. "Those things and more," Okabe confirmed softly. "It seems we did indeed experience a similar event. But the aftermath was even more awful. The ship seemed to *slap* back down on what was suddenly a comparatively calm sea—which opened a few seams, by the way, as if she actually *fell* a short distance. And the storm was gone entirely, the sky clear, the stars and moon precisely where they belonged. We found our position then and, unsettled as we were, determined to steam northwest, repairing our damage as we went, and present ourselves to the first American ship we met." Stubbing out his cigar, Okabe clasped his hands on the table in front of him. "That turned out to be yours."

"When was your first indication that you were . . . no longer where you were?" Courtney asked.

"That is quite simply answered," Okabe replied. "As I said, we made our position with excellent accuracy, but the very next day—it is fortunate that it was day—we made landfall on the southeast coast of what turned out to be a very large island, perhaps larger than Japan itself, where no such island should exist. And the creatures and"—he looked at Fen and Kaik again—"beings we observed upon it as we followed the coastline were unlike anything we ever knew on our world. In retrospect, I believe I already suspected the scope of our predicament, though I had not yet begun to even contemplate the how and why and where of it all."

"I'm sure you and Mr. Bradford will enjoy comparing theories about that at length," Ronson redirected, "but for the moment, if you please, how did you wind up here? And what do you know of our objective?"

"Yes, of course," Okabe agreed. "Haste is required and there may be less time than you think." He raised his gaze and seemed to contemplate the far bulkhead as he resumed his tale. "As you might imagine, my very first concern was our dwindling fuel state. We were catching snippets of your communications from the start, much in code or an entirely alien tongue"—he glanced at Fen and Kaik once more—"and therefore somewhat difficult to unravel, particularly in the aftermath of your own dreadful war. I was strongly inclined to make contact then, but our communications gear had suffered a casualty due to the rough handling during the event that brought us here. We could monitor transmissions but couldn't send our own. Even now, our ability to do so is limited. Without more information, I couldn't risk just steering north and putting ourselves at your mercy, yet we couldn't just continue steaming about, wasting the fuel we had left."

There was a knock on the door to the passageway aft, and after a look at his captain, Ishida said "Enter" in Japanese. A mess attendant opened the door and two more officers came in. Both paused, reacting much like others upon seeing Lawrence and the two Lemurians, but Okabe motioned them toward chairs beside the long table. "May I present my gunnery officer, Lieutenant Mihara, and engineering officer, Lieutenant Nakao. Both have been coping with repairs to our perimeter after the recent attack by the creatures so similar to your, ah, Mr. Lawrence. He has behaved himself quite admirably, by the way, which is enough to convince me that, though he looks just like the savages that plague us, he is perhaps not one of them after all." This was clearly said for the benefit of the newcomers.

"Thank you, Ca'tain Aka'e," Lawrence said in a tone Silva knew was sarcastic.

"Refresh yourselves, gentlemen," Okabe told his officers as they sat. "I was just describing our adventures." He looked back at Ronson and Courtney. "We found an inviting anchorage on what I will refer to as the 'mainland' and went ashore." He frowned. "We were attacked almost at once by monsters that . . . defy description, both in size and appearance. Ferocity as well," he added grimly, "promptly slaughtering seven of my men. This first attack was only driven off by the ship's secondary batteries, but we have since identified various vulnerabilities that can be exploited."

"We've encountered numerous similarly dangerous beasts," Courtney consoled.

"I do not doubt it. We amassed renderings of some that we've seen. It may amuse you to compare them to those you are familiar with."

"I'll be most pleased to do so, when appropriate." Courtney graciously accepted the offer, demonstrating what everyone later agreed was admirable restraint.

"We made a camp onshore, somewhat similar to the one you saw here, and began exploring in search of things we needed." He shrugged. "Fuel oil, of course, though the best we knew to do was look for surface deposits: tar pits or petroleum seeps, I suppose. We were not optimistic. We needed food and water as well." He sighed. "And there we stayed for months, listening to the radio and learning what we could, but putting off the inevitable as much as anything. And it wasn't as if we ever became comfortable there, since the giant monsters weren't the only ones. There were those like Mr. Lawrence"—he pointed at Fen and Kaik—"and them. Though these others weren't as close a match. I understand you are a 'cadet,' Mr. Fen? Perhaps not fully grown?"

Fen blinked embarrassment, tail twitching behind him, but said, "Thaat is correct, sir."

"And I am sure that Sergeant Kaik is an adult. I see that in his large expressive eyes as much as his size." He looked to Ishida as if for confirmation. "The somewhat similar beings we encountered were generally taller, less well developed in the chest, shoulders, and arms—more like a human in that respect—with shorter tails and lighter-hued fur. Almost uniformly a tannish color."

Courtney gasped again. "That sounds amazingly like the Gentaa!" he exclaimed.

"It does, don't it?" Silva agreed.

"Are these 'Gentaa' you know also not murderous, barbarous savages?"

"No!" Courtney exclaimed. "They're thoughtful, civilized people who live in peace with many races in the Republic of Real People." He paused. "Though they do remain somewhat . . . enigmatic."

"The beings we met were certainly intelligent," Okabe granted, "enough to be cunning, perfidious, conniving, and above all, treacherous. We thought we had an amicable understanding with them and even cooperated with them against our mutual enemies"—he flicked his gaze at Lawrence—"but they abused our trust and turned on us most viciously, costing us over a hundred lives."

"Perhaps a primitive offshoot of the Gentaa we know," Abel mused, "or that land was the ancestral home of them all." He shook his head at Okabe. "No one, not even the Gentaa, know their earliest origins."

"Well, there was no way we could remain there, not with such a large land full of them. The ones like Mr. Lawrence, we called them *hachurui*—reptiles—because despite their fur, they look so much like them . . ."

"We call 'em lizards too," Silva blurted. "Sometimes," he amended.

"Yes," Okabe murmured impatiently, "but though they were openly hostile, they could be coped with." He looked almost apologetically at Lawrence. "Once we killed enough of them, they left us alone." His expression hardened. "The others only seemed more determined to exterminate us, no matter the cost.

"We no longer had the fuel for a lengthy voyage, having kept a boiler lit to power and maintain the ship, as well as continue monitoring communications. It was probably about then, in fact, that we began to suspect a League presence somewhere in our vicinity, and what little we had learned of them"—he nodded at Ronson—"even secondhand by the way your people spoke of them, left us disinclined for them to find us. That is largely why, even after we restored our ability to make limited transmissions, we did not. We steamed away from our temporary home, about four hundred nautical miles, and were virtually out of fuel. Stopping at the island that is your destination, we found yet more of the savage reptiles. More than we wanted to live with, at least until we investigated *this* island, which we could see from there."

"That is undoubtedly what saved us," Lieutenant Nakao said.

"True," Okabe agreed. "We were anchored in the very lagoon where your ship now rides when we witnessed the most impossibly bright light from the island we had departed. I imagine we would all have been blinded by it if we'd been able to see the source directly, but it apparently originated below the crest of the mountain surrounding a great volcanic bay. Then came the most titanic roar and a stunning gust of wind. Having heard of the atom bombs dropped on Japan, we immediately suspected such a weapon, but why would anyone use one here, on what was essentially nothing? Our first inkling they had not, at least not directly, came when the highest lookouts reported that a towering stalk of smoke was pushing up from within . . . a roiling greenish squall that had enveloped the distant island."

"My God," Courtney murmured. "It *must* be energy! I've thought so all along. Whatever it is that . . . well, happens, requires a massive discharge of energy. The question is . . ."

Okabe was nodding along as if he agreed entirely, but Ronson impatiently asked, "What then, Captain?"

"We went to investigate, of course." Okabe hesitated a moment. "Not at once. I know little about the theory of atomic weapons other than that they would be very powerful—and every party to the war we left behind had been actively seeking to develop one. Obviously, some were more successful than others. I do believe, however, that there has been some agreement that the . . . residue left in the aftermath of a detonation might have unhealthy properties."

"Mr. Bradford has a gizmo that checks for that," Silva piped up.

"Indeed?" Okabe inquired. "Well, we waited a bit more than a week . . ."

"Did it rain?" Abel interrupted.

Again looking somewhat annoyed, Okabe nodded slowly. "Yes, twice I believe. Once rather vigorously. And it has often rained again since then." He spread the fingers on his hands. "It is a common occurrence here."

"Excellent," Courtney said guardedly. "I think your people should be all right. None of them have been sick?"

"Only from the water some drink, too idle to boil it." He frowned. "There has been a general apathy, but that began before. I think it has to do with a sense of purposelessness."

"I'm sure it does, and perhaps we can help with that." Courtney's expression turned intent. "What did you see? It was ships, wasn't it? Ships that weren't there the first time you visited."

Okabe looked surprised. "How did you know? We thought that would come as a huge surprise to you."

Ronson leaned his head toward Fen. "He was aboard a ship searching for others that disappeared, and got captured by League pirates. He saw the missing ships there, and a 'ghost fleet' of steel ships. He later escaped and reported what he witnessed."

"The League," Ishida almost growled. "We . . . met them there as well."

Now everyone truly was surprised. "When?" Abel asked.

"As I said, roughly a week after the blast." Okabe paused, considering. "Some months ago now. I could consult the log for the exact date."

Ronson held up a hand. "Sure, later, but tell us what happened. How did you know they were Leaguers? What did you do? What did *they* do? How did they get there?"

Okabe and Ishida exchanged another glance. Finally, Okabe sighed. "They sailed into the . . . I suppose 'lagoon' would be the proper term, but it is *much* larger than the one where you are anchored. It more closely resembles a bay in size, though I am nearly certain it is yet another immense crater, almost surrounded by the high remains of an ancient volcano that constitutes a considerable percentage of the island." He looked thoughtful. "Have any of you ever seen Santorini? No?" He shook his head. "It would be an imperfect analogy in any event. But their vessel was a small wooden sailing ship, no threat in itself, and I have no doubt its crew believed we were just another empty derelict at first. That they so boldly entered the anchorage without hesitation in spite of the"—he finally smiled very slightly—"the quite intimidating sight within, made me confident they had already been there."

Courtney looked at Fen. "Did you ever have the impression your captors had any notion something like *Shonai* was nearby?"

Fen blinked and shook his head. "No sir."

"Good," Okabe said. "Our . . . precaution seems to have worked."

"What did you do?" Abel asked.

"They did eventually notice us and sailed over closer, within hailing distance." Okabe rubbed his chin. "We hadn't been *hiding*, after all, and I am sure they were surprised to see men on the deck of one of the ships." His eyes narrowed and his frown returned. "They shouted at us in several languages. Spanish was one, I think. When they tried Italian, Commander Ishida understood them. He was a member of a naval delegation to Rome in the thirties," he explained, then his eyes narrowed even further. "This ridiculous man on that little boat was demanding, no, *commanding* that *Shonai* and her crew declare their 'rightful' allegiance to the League of Tripoli or leave the anchorage and ships the League had claimed and 'suffer the consequences!'" Even now, Okabe's voice rose in disbelief and fury.

"Damn. What did you do?" asked Gunny Horn.

Ishida cleared his throat and actually grinned, the first example of such an expression they'd seen on his face. "Captain Okabe instructed me to invite that man and any others he chose—there were three altogether—to come aboard and 'consult' about the subject. As soon as they came up the side, they were disarmed"—he shrugged—"and their ship was destroyed."

Silva barked a laugh that was credibly mimicked by Petey.

Okabe spread his hands on the table. "Thus we learned a great deal about the League—certainly enough that we wanted no part of it—and their dispositions in the region. Most important at that moment was that the little expedition we disrupted was merely sent in preparation for a major salvage effort."

"How 'major'?" Ronson asked.

Okabe looked at him. "They are determined to salvage what they can, particularly in terms of technology, and may even attempt to take some of the ships away. Ultimately, they will scuttle the rest."

Courtney blinked. "Young Fen declared that some of the ships are quite large indeed. That would imply they have something big enough to *tow* a large vessel . . ."

"They do, or will," Okabe quickly said, then sighed. "Perhaps already *did*, by now. We were able to learn that from our guests. I think you have already discovered the League has had assets in regions you consider 'yours' for some time, in several cases longer than you even knew the League existed?"

"Yes, that's true. We believed we'd rooted them all out," Courtney grumbled.

"You have not," Okabe stated simply. "We are sure they have operated a base of some sort on the big main island we first discovered for some time"—he frowned—"and may even have a firmer understanding with the . . . 'Gentaa'-like folk than we did." He paused. "They certainly have a pair of destroyers and either have or are awaiting the arrival of something bigger. A cruiser perhaps."

"I don't know how they'd get anything here now," Ronson said absently, twisting the ends of his bushy mustache. "We've got all the known approaches sewn up pretty tight."

"Yet *Shonai* got through a far more formidable net than you can possibly match," Okabe reminded.

"It would be difficult, but they might come around Africa," Courtney pointed out. Glancing at Okabe, he resumed, "The Pass of Fire, our own

'Panama Canal' of sorts, if you will, is firmly under our control, and it's doubtful they can approach around the horn of South America. Too much ice, you see."

"Nevertheless."

"Can *we* talk to these Leaguers?" Abel asked, and for the first time Okabe looked a little embarrassed. "Unfortunately, we kept them ashore when we returned here."

"Don't tell me they escaped," Ronson said with a groan.

"Not by themselves," Ishida said dryly. "Just a few days after we established our position ashore in this place, before the stockade was complete, the reptiles attacked in large numbers." He shrugged. "Our prisoners were not armed, of course, and were dragged into the forest. I am afraid that they were eaten."

"Woops," Silva said, earning him a glare from nearly everyone. "I'm not blamin' the Japs!" he defended. "I mean, who'd care? And I bet everybody else ashore was most int'rested in savin' their own asses at the time."

"Silva, . . ." Ronson grunted.

"Sure, Skipper. Shuttin' up."

"Shuttin' Up!" squawked Petey.

"Why come back here in the first place, though?" Pam suddenly asked. "I mean, you were so low on fuel, why burn it comin' back? Sounds like there's just as many 'lizards' here as there."

"And more of them come all the time," said Lieutenant Chiba. "They are not entirely mindless"—he glanced apologetically at Lawrence—"and not only can they communicate with each other, they make crude boats. We suspect they summon allied tribes from other islands, including the one we left."

"We didn't know that then," Ishida chided.

"Nor did we know if we could ever contact you," Okabe explained to Ronson and the others. "We feared we would be all alone in the face of whatever the League has out here. It was deemed best to remain uninvolved if we could, until we had an arrangement with you. And only recently, when we got the strong impression you were coming—via nearby *League* radio chatter," he warned, "were we fairly confident of your approach. It was your own low-power communications that prompted us to launch an aircraft to search for you."

"That's kind of thin," Ronson complained.

"But true," Okabe persisted. He sighed. "You have worked wonders since you came to this world. Even our League prisoners conceded that. Perhaps it has been too long since you were in our position: all alone with no friends, no support of any kind. Such an existence can foster a timidity that is otherwise not in your nature."

"I get that," Ronson said, and he did. "So, what do you want to do? You already know this world's like an opium dream and a big enough threat by itself, even without having enemies. The Grand Alliance, United Homes, and American Navy Clan can use all the help we can get. Or, we've already told you we'll see to it you're taken care of, in the Shogunate or wherever." He'd picked up a cigar for himself but hadn't lit it. Now he pointed it at Okabe. "It's up to you."

Okabe didn't even look at the other Japanese officers. Most likely, they'd already discussed this. Instead, he said slowly, "If we *surrender* to you, you will have *Shonai* of course, but we become your problem that you must feed and arrange transport for, all while you have greater concerns to deal with here. If we *join* you, your alliance still has the ship, but she comes with a crew that knows her and can fight her. That sounds like the simpler choice on the surface, but *Shonai* has no fuel and needs significant maintenance before she can fight again, or even put to sea with confidence. With fuel and some time, we could assist your efforts here. These things we shall do without further conditions."

"That's . . . reasonable," Ronson said, looking at Courtney and Abel, who nodded.

"But we must attach other conditions to actually *joining* your American Navy Clan," Okabe warned, frowning. "Does that sound as strange to you as it does me?"

"You have no idea," Horn said. Silva was still minding his manners. Horn took a deep breath. "But we've fought with enough Japs on *our side* here that nerves aren't as raw as they were. What's your catch?"

Okabe straightened again. "We will fly the flag of your clan, your alliance, but we will also fly our own. If my men must fight, they will do so under their own flag, the Hinomaru."

Silva clenched his teeth, then actually covered his mouth with his hand.

Pam rolled her eyes at him but suggested, "That'll probably have to go higher than us, and it ain't just *because* of us. See, some *really bad* stuff happened on this world under that flag o' yours. It wasn't you that did it, but a whole lot of people won't know it." She looked thoughtful. "'Course, I doubt anybody'll care what you fly in a fight."

Ronson was nodding and looked at Okabe, who said, "I suppose we will have to learn more about what has happened here. If we fight, we will fly it. Otherwise, we will see. There is another thing, though—which might certainly benefit the Alliance, but has great meaning for myself and my crew."

"What's that?" Ronson asked suspiciously.

Now Okabe's face slowly cracked into a genuine smile. "Lieutenant Chiba will accompany you to your destination. He will show you and explain." He paused, then added cryptically, "Perhaps we will all soon be better equipped to defend our people on this world."

CHAPTER 18

Despite it still being fairly early in the day when most of the members of Ronson's party, including Lieutenant Chiba, returned to *Walker* (Courtney Bradford and Abel Cook remained behind on *Shonai*), the old destroyer / school ship didn't make for the nearby island until the following morning. Instead, with Chiba serving as her pilot, she raised anchor and crept up the somewhat chillingly confining passage the launch traversed at dawn, finally coming alongside the big Japanese cruiser and rigging out the equipment, hoses and pumps, necessary to transfer enough fuel oil to *Shonai* for her to steam back to the lagoon where *Walker* anchored the night before. So that when the expected oiler arrived, it could replenish *Shonai*'s bunkers enough for her to cross to the other island herself.

Captain Okabe understood Ronson's refusal to transfuse more fuel from *Walker*. The last anyone knew, there'd already been a League presence where she was going, and they didn't know what they'd run into. *Walker* had to have enough fuel to maneuver, run away, or fight if she had to. Okabe was less understanding why the oiler wouldn't top his ship off when it got there—until Ronson figured out the problem was one of expectation and explained that the whole ship that was coming wasn't big enough to fill his bunkers. "My fault," he'd said. "I should've described her better. Our newest 'fleet oilers' are bigger steel-hulled tubs, but they're all off in the east with the fleet or on their way back and forth. The one coming here is an auxiliary, these days. She was a big advancement during the war—a dedicated oiler, for sure, with steam power and copper holding tanks and pumping equipment of her own—but she's got the same wooden hull as our mid-war steam/sailing frigates. She's pretty small. Don't worry; there'll be more."

Further controversy came aboard *Walker* herself when old hands like Isak Reuben and Carl Bashear had to supervise the transfer of *their* fuel to "wild" Japs. (Silva's throwaway crack had spread and caught on.) Both had stood on the hot deck (only the Japanese had shade) throughout the operation, hands on hips, scandalized expressions on their faces.

"You keep one o' your big buggy eyes on that flow rate," Isak had snarled in his reedy voice at the Lemurian cadet supervising the task on the fo'c'sle. "An' shut that valve the *instant* we've passed them devils what the skipper said we would. Not a drop more!" He'd looked at Bashear. "They'll suck us dry like a spider if we let 'em, an' toss our dry husk aside. That's *my* oil, Goddammit! For *my boilers*!"

Bashear looked at Isak. "You know, this might be the first time I ever agreed with a single word you said." He nodded up at *Shonai*, and it was a *long* way up. The Japanese cruiser was more than twice *Walker*'s size and displaced ten times as much. "Doesn't seem right. Not natural—and it's hard to even say why."

"They're Japs!" Isak almost screeched incredulously.

"Sure," Bashear agreed. "And I hated 'em for what they did to us. Pearl, the Philippines—especially when they bombed Cavite. Then there was the Java Sea and what happened after . . ." He rubbed his nose with a knuckle. "I always kind of admired them, though. Not what they were doing in China before they jumped on us," he quickly clarified, "but they were good sailors in handsome new ships."

"Their ships look weird to me," Isak scoffed.

"Maybe," Bashear hedged, "but way more modern than this one." He tapped the deck with his shoe. "That made 'em scary. And I was scared of the Japs too, the way they were kicking hell out of us all over the place. Another reason I hated 'em, I guess. But that was a long time ago now. Seems like it, anyway." He pointed at *Shonai* again. "Not as long for them, though. I wonder how *they* feel about having to take fuel from us."

"I hope they gag on it," Isak grumbled. "Hurry up," he called at the detail as if they had any control over how fast the pump worked.

"Ay, ay," called the 'Cat cadet in a patient tone.

"I'm going to get some chow when we're through," Bashear said. "Nothing but sandwiches again today."

"Just as well," said Isak. "Sammitches is the only thing Earl can cook that's fit to eat."

Walker steamed back down the passage at dawn, through the long lagoon and into the open sea, immediately beginning to heave and pitch on long, high ocean swells. Lizardbirds followed in her wake, snatching at morsels churned up by her screws, but even though they kept shitting on the deck, cadets were called to swab the ship down, fore and aft, to scour away the astonishing accumulation her short period of relative motionlessness allowed. The day was humid and hazy, the sun a dull orange orb behind a gray featureless sky. The waves were gray as well, as was the island they steamed for, just a darker somewhat jagged shape looming high on the horizon.

"Kinda creepy, huh?" Pam asked, coming up behind Silva, Lawrence, and Petey where they stood behind the number one gun on the fo'c'sle.

Expecting an abusive response by the diminutive woman from Brooklyn to whatever he said, Silva merely replied with a noncommittal "Hmm." That didn't save him.

Poking him in the ribs, Pam said, "I'm serious, you big jerk. What do you think about . . . well, everything?" she demanded.

Silva gawked at her and blinked his good eye. "You ain't gave a damn what I think about *nothin'* for so long—"

"I do now," Pam harshly interrupted. "This is your sort o' thing, after all. Crazy situations. Figgered you'd have an opinion."

Silva looked at Lawrence, then shrugged. "Fine. We're all gonna die."

"Right," Pam responded, rolling her eyes. "I've lost count of how many times we were all gonna die *for sure* an' everybody thought so but you. Not you," she added almost angrily. "*Nothin'* can kill the great Dennis Silva," she added sarcastically.

"It ain't yet."

"So you just keep lookin' to find what will," she accused. "An' the hell with ever'body else's feelins. Even poor Lawrence."

"Don't get I in this," Lawrence said, taking a step to the side.

Silva exhaled a long breath. "Look, doll," he began patiently, but Pam flared with fury.

"Don't you 'doll' me! You ain't got that right anymore."

"Fine. Swell," Silva said, tone a mix of anger and hurt. "I said I was sorry. 'Bout ever'thing! I just can't miracle myself into somethin' I ain't never been—like a fat pooch on the floor ta prop yer feet on. I been around me longer than you have, an' I know me pretty good by now. I'm a destroyerman through an' through, always will be, but more than that, I'm a . . . destroyer o' what needs destroyin', see? That's what I do, it's what I am. I'll never be fit ta settle down behind a white picket fence, trimmin' rosebushes. Hell, I ain't even *seen* any rosebushes here." His eye narrowed. "I thought you knew *that* about me by now. At least that much. I tried to taper off on some o' my ways. Might've even held the line." He shook his head. "But I can't *ever* be a house pet, not for anybody." He looked away. "Not even you."

"I . . . never asked that," Pam said, voice uncharacteristically soft. "Did I?"

"As close to as not," Silva said, still gazing across the water. "But as for what's gonna happen . . . This has been as weird o' trip as I've been on. A shipload o' snot goblins—which're actually comin' along," he allowed, "but another whole cruiser load o' wild Japs that was fightin *us* the last time they fought anybody." He nodded ahead. "Now a mystery island of dead ships, man-eatin' lizards, an' prob'ly Leaguers as well . . ." He looked down at Pam with his signature gap-toothed grin. "See, that sounds like a *hoot* to me. It may not've ever drawn you like it does me, but you didn't used to shy off from stuff like that." His grin faded to a gentler smile. "Now, was that just to catch me or did you miracle *yourself* into somethin' you never used to be?"

"Those two . . ." Susan Raj chuckled aside to Aalak-Maraan. Both, along with Philan Bele, were standing behind the splinter shield protecting the number one gun. "Anybody can see they are in love."

"I don't see it," Bele said, leaning down to speak lowly where the much shorter cadets could hear.

Aalak blinked skeptically and swished his tail. "I do not think so either," he said guardedly. "I think they hate each other."

"Males," Susan sniffed.

Approaching slowly, carefully, it was still less than two hours before Fen and Lieutenant Chiba, both in the pilothouse because they'd been here before, advised a wide approach from the west of the island.

"There are shoals thaat extend a distance out to sea," Fen said.

"A large portion of that island *is* a volcano," called Courtney through the breeze on the port bridgewing, confirming all speculation. He was gazing through his binoculars and his tone was one of certainty. "Well, the whole thing's volcanic, no doubt. A very large one indeed. The western cone is quite high as well, perhaps three or four thousand feet above sea level. Quite impressive. It may have been higher still before the eruption that blew a quarter or more of the mountain off, out to the west it would seem."

"Maybe thaat's what it was?" Tabby speculated. "The flaash that waas seen waas an eruption, not a bomb."

Courtney was shaking his head. "No, no, my dear. Such an eruption would be a thing of *legend*. And it likely is—to any sentient beings within a thousand miles. No," he repeated, pointing, "that island hasn't endured a major eruption for hundreds, perhaps thousands of years. The forest on the outer slope is old, thick, and quite robust." He paused. "Except at the peak, along the jagged ridge at the top. Trees up there do seem to have suffered some trauma. Many are denuded or have fallen outward from what I must assume is the center of the crater. Yet even there I can see what looks like the result of long ages of natural erosion."

"I wish the sun was brighter so the lookout could see deeper in the water," Ronson said aside to Tabby, nodding at Fen. "His shoals," he added unnecessarily.

"They do not extend out this far," said Chiba. "But he is right; swing slightly farther to the west."

"Helm, make your course two, four, zero. All ahead slow," Ronson said as the ship eased to starboard to parallel the long, sloping flank of the mountain where it eventually plunged down into a tumultuous sea. Everyone on the bridge was aware of a building tension as they left the headland behind, catching their first glimpse of the broad bay beyond. And this really was a bay: miles across and almost entirely encircled with the ancient shell of a mighty mountain. "Sound general quarters," Ronson said abruptly. "All hands to battle stations; this is no drill, and we'll have live ammunition in the ready lockers." Even as the bugler took his place by the microphone to sound the call to battle, Ronson was turning to Tabby. "And your place is aft, at the auxiliary conn."

"Surely—" she began, but Ronson shook his head.

"The last time Lieutenant Chiba was here, they met Leaguers. And Fen saw even more activity. We have to assume they're here and won't be happy to see us." He caught Chiba's attention. "Put on a helmet."

Once Chiba was sure they'd cleared the shoals—composed of rock expelled from the mountain's ancient explosion, Courtney thought—*Walker* turned east once more, ready for anything. Or so her people thought. Waves crashed and swirled among the breakers to port, but after *Walker* passed around them, the sea turned almost calm. Lizardbirds swooped and capered among the signal halyards, their raucous cries overwhelming the muted rumble of the forced-draft blower behind the bridge as the ship crept through the wide, jagged gateway to the heart of the island, dead slow now.

"It's like sailing into a big steaming busted bowl of soup," Ronson complained uncomfortably, and it wasn't a bad analogy. The haze within the irregular embracing confines of the gigantic crater, combined with the dreary light of the overcast day, made for poor visibility. There were numerous indistinct shapes, however, practically immediately, and almost everywhere, it seemed. Dark ghostly outlines of what were obviously ships of every shape and size loomed out of the vapor. The closest was right in what was basically the mouth of what, as Fen had described, really would make a wonderful natural harbor. If it weren't for the spooky ships.

"What's that thing?" asked Abel Cook, referring to the smallish strange-looking vessel they approached, off the starboard bow.

Ronson was gazing at it, absently fussing with his mustache. "No idea, Mr. Cook."

"A landing craft of some sort," Courtney speculated. "It looks large enough to land vehicles."

"It is," said Lieutenant Chida. "One of yours," he added to Ronson before explaining, "We were taught to recognize the silhouettes of enemy vessels." He nodded beyond it. "Those larger ones that look like merchantmen"—some had a single stack, others two, but all appeared equipped to handle heavy cargoes—"they are transports," Chida said.

"None of them look terribly battered," Courtney observed, sounding almost disappointed. "I would have expected more damage from the weapon we've speculated about." He paused. "Oh, look! That one has a crumpled funnel!"

"I do not know why some of the ships you shall see are more badly damaged than others, and some in unusual ways that Captain Okabe believed was the result of an explosion in the sky. We couldn't see that from where we were, of course, but only a few of the ships appear to have damage to their sides and those may have been farther from the strongest *downward* force." He looked perplexed.

"That's consistent with what Mr. Cook and I noted when we investigated the sites in the Shogunate," Courtney mused.

It was then that a bright beam of sunlight broke through the late-morning cloud cover as if a giant arc light was glaring down on the unnerving anchorage ahead.

"Look! They're red!" called one of the cadet lookouts on the bridgewing, raising alarmed, even superstitious shouts from around the ship.

"Stow that crap!" came Chief Bashear's voice, drifting up from the fo'c'sle, but even he sounded disconcerted. Most of the ships, more than two dozen at a glance, were indeed a dark bloody red color with streaks of pink and grayish white, and all the obvious warships deeper in were arrayed in an apparently haphazard fashion, like the bodies of blood-drenched armored knights after a battle with one another. And now, of course, the damage they'd sustained was easier to discern as well. Railings, masts, and aerials were bent and warped, some having fallen completely, and the thinner steel of lighter ships and the upperworks on heavier ones was badly wrinkled and washboarded.

"I should haave waarned you," Fen confessed. "Everything is rusted up, even worse now than when I waas here, but they were already rusting then."

"The blast must've scorched the paint," Courtney guessed, "all the way down to the steel underneath. Then, between the salt air and all the rains since"—he gestured forward through the pilothouse windows—"a rust-red fleet. I think it is now clear what happened, however. There was no battle here, no attack on an anchored armada." He looked at Ronson, gesturing with his binoculars.

"What then?"

"They were the targets of a test," answered Lieutenant Chiba. "A test of the weapon used on my country to see what it would do to ships."

"What makes you so sure?"

Chiba motioned at the binoculars as well, and Ronson raised his own to gaze out at the amazing sight. Aside from the transports, there were cruisers, battleships, destroyers, and submarines. He thought he even recognized a few. "One of those 'wagons' near the far shore looks like *New York* or *Texas*. That one, straight ahead past that beat-up-looking cruiser, looks like *Arkansas*! She's listing and low in the water," he added, "but the cruisers—there's two of 'em—are fairly new, and that tin can on the starboard bow is a gold plater!" "Gold plater" was a term four-stacker destroyermen used for anything bigger and more modern than their own primitive ships. "If these are all targets, why waste the new stuff?"

Courtney cleared his throat. "'New' is a relative term," he said dryly. "And with the war over, as Lieutenant Chiba assures us it was—is—whatever, the oldest of the new is still old. Those battleships are certainly not new."

"But I still don't see why you can be so certain," Ronson objected, glassing slowly to starboard. "Oh," he suddenly said, "a lot of the ragged shapes I took for debris on the decks . . . It *is* debris, but it's from trucks and tanks, airplanes . . . all sorts of things, really busted up." He lowered the binoculars. "Stuff they put there to see what a big-ass bomb would do."

"Indeed," Courtney agreed. "But why only our—I mean *American* ships?" he asked, looking at Chiba.

"That . . . is not all that is here, you shall see, but the answer is really quite simple." Chiba sighed. "There was very little left of our navy and quite enough beyond the requirements of yours that they could easily sacrifice"—he waved almost bitterly ahead—"all this."

"Wow," Ronson said a little bitterly as well. "Throwing away stuff, just blowing it up, that we'd absolutely *love* to have."

Chiba stood straighter. "Well, Captain Rodriguez, because of what they did, you *do* have it now. Perhaps a little worse for wear, but I imagine most of what has floated this long can be returned to service. *If* we can keep it. Which brings me to the final request Captain Okabe asked me to convey." He nodded beyond the listing shape of what might have been *Arkansas*, and Ronson lifted his binoculars again.

"Oh," he said, "I see what you meant earlier." He hissed. "Looks a little more 'worse for wear' than the others, though," he added skeptically.

"The only guarantee my captain requires is that you *try* to save her, if you can. She means a great deal to all of my people."

"What is she?"

Chiba almost bowed in the direction of the distant, scarred derelict. "That is *Nagato*, Captain Rodriguez."

"She looks pretty rough," Ronson said doubtfully. "What's the big deal about her?" he asked, but he wouldn't get an answer yet.

"Submerged wreck, port bow!" called the portside lookout beside the torpedo director, and Ronson paced out there to look.

"Yeah," he grumbled, spotting the twisted tip of a mast rising up from the gloom below. "No reason to think the water's as deep as it was in the lagoon on the other island. And as many ships as apparently survived the bomb they set off here, we have to assume a bunch of 'em sank."

"Or saank even since I was here," Fen piped up. "There don't seem to be as many."

"Really?" Courtney asked, but another call, this one from the crow's nest lookout, diverted their attention.

"Staarboard side on the slope aashore!"

Moving over to the opposite bridgewing, Ronson gazed through his binoculars and gasped. "Jesus. That's . . . the *stern*, maybe *half*, of a whole damn *aircraft carrier* laying up on land. And look just a little above it. Is that the *rest* of the carrier buried in the mountain sticking out of the ground?!"

The inner slope of the crater all around them had been wooded as thickly as the outside before the effect of the blast accompanying the rusty fleet to this world blew the forest down. Again, like the blasts in the Shogunate. That left countless thousands of trees sprawled with their tapered tops and denuded branches pointing downward or even lying in the water until about a quarter of the way up the slope, where they were scattered and shattered in a haphazard fashion. Beyond that, all the trees, regardless how steep the grade had become, were lying in an upward orientation. "More evidence of an airburst, I think," Abel Cook observed.

"And that the water level is lower here than it was where these ships came from," Courtney agreed. "Which we already knew, of course—if that place is more *like* where we came from." He sighed. "Sometimes I even confuse myself. But I wonder if the rest of that ship is buried in the side of the mountain . . ."

"A mountain that wasn't where it came from," Abel suggested. "*Can* something from there and here exist in the same place at the same time?"

Courtney chuckled gleefully. "I'm *soo* excited to find out! We shall dig it out if we must!"

"Gentlemen," Ronson called, glancing through his binoculars between paces as he moved to the other side of the pilothouse. "Keep looking," he said. "That's not the only one."

Now they knew what to expect, they saw what looked like the partial remains of various other ships and possibly as many as two submarines either embedded to some degree in the mountain at about the same elevation as the carrier or lying smashed on the slope between there and the beach. And other ships, mostly partially collapsed and half sunk, trailed out from the beach into the water.

"Wow," Ronson said again, a mixture of wonder and horror in his tone. "No way to know *at all* how many ships they wasted here!"

"Or how many are gone," said Fen, who'd stepped out on the port bridgewing, looking a little behind them now. "And why," he warned.

"What?" asked Chief Carl Bashear, who'd stepped up onto the bridge from aft.

"I think I know what he is referring to," Chiba said, moving over beside Fen and gazing beyond the port quarter. "There was another large warship, possibly a cruiser, over near the northwest shore inside the crater. It is no longer there."

"Maybe it sank?" suggested Ronson.

"Perhaps. But it appeared in much better condition than most of the other vessels we see. Other than those transports we already passed. Like them, it may have been farther from the blast."

"Well . . . We'll sort it out," said Ronson. "We're getting close to those battlewagons. There's another one," he said, pointing a little northeast, "that isn't all just rusty red. Somebody painted it *orange*." He shook his head, mystified. "Anyway, we're getting close to the most valuable iron in the water here and we'll anchor soon. Start looking around." He paused. "Uh, Mr. Bradford? Maybe you ought to break out your 'gizmo' and fire it up? Make sure it's safe to even *be* here, huh?"

Courtney looked horrified. "Oh dear. Yes, of course! I entirely forgot."

"I'll bring it up, Mr. Bradford," Abel Cook volunteered.

"Thank you, my boy." Courtney glanced at Ronson. "Perhaps you might pass the word for Mr., I mean, Lieutenant Meek?"

Easing up closer to the nearest large warship, the badly listing cruiser they'd seen from a distance, all eyes in the pilothouse were on her. "*She* sure took a beating," said Bashear. "Looks like a Northampton or Pensacola Class. One of ours, though, for sure. Masts're knocked down, superstructure's crumpled up, stacks are smashed down to the deck." He frowned. "I bet a stiff breeze would push her on over and sink her. Probably not the highest priority for salvage," he added dryly.

"Too bad, but agreed," Ronson replied. "Steady as you go," he instructed the cadet at the wheel. A couple more transports lay to the north, their upperworks just as chaotically smashed, but afloat. "You know," Ronson murmured as much to himself as those around him, "we can't write anything off. It's been quite a while since these ships got bombed, and these survivors've floated all this time. And judging by the 'test junk' on their decks, the transports might be full of stuff we can use." They were still headed generally toward what they thought was *Arkansas*, and there wasn't a whole lot directly to the south other than a submarine with a flattened conn tower and what looked like a wrinkled high-sided freighter.

"Skipper?" said Bashear, a little hesitant it seemed. "Look at that thing. I think it's another *carrier* . . . sort of. Not much bigger than the old *Langley*, though."

"You may be right, Boats," Ronson said doubtfully, "but whatever it is, it's the biggest piece of junk I ever saw floating."

Turning their attention back to *Arkansas*, they confirmed she was listing as well, with all her top hamper smashed and funnel knocked flat. There were more wrecked vehicles on her charred wooden decks, and more tanks too. They at least, aside from being rusty, looked amazingly well preserved. Shortly after Jack Meek reported, Abel reappeared carrying a wooden packing crate with the help of a human cadet. Setting it on the deck strakes, he unclamped the top and opened it. Packed inside was what looked like a simple sheet-brass box, longer and taller than it was wide, with a tapering cylinder protruding from one end that looked like a gun barrel. Retrieving another cylinder, a leather strap, and what looked like a phonograph crank from the crate, he handed those to Meek. Then, with the help of the cadet, he lifted the brass box out of the crate, kicked the lid shut, and set the contraption on top.

"Careful, Mr. Cook," Courtney admonished. "We only have two of those, you know."

"Yes, Mr. Bradford," Abel said patiently.

"You helped Mr. Riggs assemble the gizmos, didn't you?" Ronson asked Meek.

"Yes sir," replied the Republic snoop with the gruesome scar on his face. "This one and the other one like it, anyway. I still don't understand it, but I know how it works."

"It's a GM meter," Courtney said proudly. "Essentially a Geiger-Mueller device, though the tuning eye is my own contribution," he added with false modesty.

Ronson looked at Chief Bashear, who shrugged. "So, how does it work?"

"Mr. Meek, Mr. Cook, will you do the honors?"

Meek leaned over and inserted the cylinder he held into a socket on top of the box, then threaded the crank into the side. Taking the strap off his shoulder, he hooked both ends equipped with snaps to a pair of rings secured to the box. Hoisting the whole thing with some effort, he slung the strap over his neck and shoulder.

"It's still rather cumbersome," Courtney apologized, "but the best we could do for a portable unit. Better than the one Mr. Cook and I took to the Shogunate. It really was an ion chamber, but required a great deal more voltage than our current battery-making capacity can conveniently supply. We had to carry the batteries for it in a cart!"

"Well . . . how does this gadget work?" Bashear asked impatiently. "I mean, if we're getting poisoned as we speak, maybe we ought to get on with it?"

"I doubt that's the case," Courtney said, condescendingly. "All the evidence points to an airburst, as I said." He frowned. "I suspect it would be different if the bomb exploded directly on or under the water. I don't really know that for certain, of course." He smiled again. "But this device should warn us if dangerous radiation is present. The operators, ideally two people as we're demonstrating, will . . . point the, ah, detector at the suspect source. It shouldn't much matter where it's pointed just now. The air around us will be sufficient." Ronson and Bashear shared another look. "The other operator will vigorously crank the handle to generate a charge"—Abel started doing so, and a rumbling, whining noise began to rise—"while peering into the observation tube at a tuning eye, the intensity of which—measured by concentric circles—should give us a good approximation of how dangerous the radiation we encounter might be." Courtney beamed.

"Swell," said Chief Bashear, "but like with any instrument you use to measure stuff, you'd have to calibrate it somehow. You *did* calibrate it?" he asked.

"Of course!" Courtney exclaimed, then he looked a little uncomfortable. "We did it with the X-ray machine in Baalkpan, subjecting shaved skuggiks to progressively more intense exposures. The maximum safe display on the tuning eye was marked at much below the intensity that resulted in skin irritation, I assure you!"

"It'll measure higher exposures, though?" Ronson asked.

"Yes!" Courtney said. "Quite a lot higher. Mr. Riggs and I struggled to agree on a term reflecting the intensity based on potential lethality. He jokingly suggested calling these measurements 'Silvas,' since the chief gunner's mate is the most lethal thing he knows." He tilted his head back and looked down his nose. "I was not amused. Besides, Chief Silva has named countless things he had no right to, or at least it has been his own irreverent appellation that stuck." He shook his head. "Not this time. I won't allow it!"

"Good for you," said Bashear. "Silva's head is big enough as it is. What name did you come up with?"

Courtney looked embarrassed. "We could never agree. Just now, the levels are simply indicated by numbers from one to ten 'rings' on the tuning eye, how far the blue light expands with the intensity it measures, you see. One through three should be perfectly safe—'one' being present at all times in the sunlight, representing normal ambient radiation levels. If that, at least, isn't seen, then the machine is malfunctioning and mustn't be trusted," he cautioned. 'Five' is quite likely to cause discomfort, even something like a sunburn if one is exposed to it for long. It might even cause long-term harm. I won't countenance anyone remaining where a 'five' is indicated any longer than it takes to get away from it."

"I take it you tested the skuggiks past that? What happened?"

Courtney pursed his lips. "They died, poor things. Skuggiks may be carrion eaters, land vultures if you will, but I don't enjoy cruelty of any sort for any reason, and what happened to them made me *feel* quite cruel."

Ronson cleared his throat. "So . . . don't go above 'four.' Got it." Turning to Abel, he asked, "What's it show?"

"Just 'one,'" Abel said, "as expected."

Bashear wasn't the only one in the pilothouse who let out a long breath.

"Fine," Ronson said, now gauging the distance to *Nagato*. *Walker* was barely moving at dead slow. "We'll anchor just astern of her." He pointed. "That'll leave us equally close to about everything in the bay. We'll form two boarding parties, one for each launch"—he nodded at Courtney's device—"and each gizmo. Nobody goes anywhere without one until we're sure it's safe."

"'Safe' is another 'relative' term, Skipper," reminded Carl Bashear. "We still haven't seen any Leaguers." He looked at Fen. "You think they're gone?"

"I caan't see where the ships were anchored from here. They were generally where thaat big orange ship now is, close to shore. It is blocking my view." He blinked and swished his tail. "I think it haas moved."

Ronson was looking at the odd-colored ship again. "Is that so? Maybe it came unmoored," he speculated, frowning. "I wouldn't bet that anything that made it through the bomb that hit them, then . . . dropped in here, is still arrayed exactly as it was originally placed." He was studying the orange ship more intently. "I don't even know what *she* is. The hull looks like *Nevada*, but everything up from there is more modern, like a North Carolina Class. Shorter, though." He adjusted the binoculars. "Could be grounded too." He shrugged and called out, "Anybody see any sign of the sailing ships Fen described?"

"No sir," replied the lookouts on both bridgewings, and the little 'Cat bridge talker spoke to the crow's nest and other stations around the ship.

"Nothing is seen, Caap-i-taan," she reported.

"Well," Ronson said somewhat reluctantly, looking at Courtney, "I'm just as anxious as you to start exploring, but we better take a look where Fen last saw the enemy." He nodded toward the rusty orange shape. "I guess they could've cut her anchor chain and towed her over there to hide behind. Helm, steer zero, four, zero. Keep her dead slow," he advised the cadet by the EOT. "Lookouts, skin your eyes for ships' masts past that funny-colored battlewagon, but especially for wrecks in the water."

Bashear already had a detail casting a lead on the fo'c'sle, calling out depths. The last loud Lemurian shout reported a comfortable twenty fathoms, but some of the derelicts they could see might stick up that far from the bottom if they sank.

"Why don't we put the scout plane up?" asked Lieutenant Daanis. He didn't make suggestions very often, but when he did, they were good ones.

Ronson considered it but shook his head. "I guess we should've already done it, huh? Now there isn't enough wind and we aren't moving fast enough for me to feel good relying on the catapult. And frankly, I don't want to take time to set the plane in the water to take off on its own." He nodded forward. "We'll do this the old-fashioned way."

CHAPTER 19

The sky had brightened as the overcast burned off, and the sun was standing almost overhead, now brilliantly illuminating every part of the gigantic traumatized crater and its contents. With the ship moving so slow, there was barely a breeze and it was getting hot, the gun's crews sweating at their stations. They were getting nervous too. The suspicion that an enemy might be concealed behind the ship they were approaching had spread very quickly, and the idea that they might be facing action of some sort was suddenly very real.

"Easy, fellas," Silva told Philan Bele's crew on the number one gun. He and Lawrence had stepped up alongside the cadets when general quarters sounded and Pam went below to the wardroom, both somewhat surprised by her sudden change in demeanor. She'd always had a whiplash personality though, as changeable as the wind and capable of similar extremes. It was never wise to expect such shifts to endure, though her stormy side seemed to be her standard setting, at least where Dennis Silva was concerned. "Just relax, damn it," he said to Maarik-Fas, the little female 'Cat from the Filpin Lands, surprised to see her practically hopping from foot to foot. She was usually the least excitable of them all.

"I gotta pee!" she exclaimed, voice strained.

Silva blinked at her. "Wow. No shit?"

"*Pee*, Chief Silva!" she stressed.

"Oh. Yeah." The little 'Cat was a good pointer or trainer (when she had something to sit on), but others were already in those positions and she'd donned the heavy leather gloves of a "hot shell man." "Well"—he nodded at the raised hatch forward—"haul yer fluffy tail down there, use the chief's head, then scamper back as quick as you can. We won't hold up the fight for ya, though," he warned. "An' if you hear shootin', don't come back up that way, whatever you do. Go aft first, hear?"

"Ay, ay, Chief Silva," she called, already sprinting forward. There were a few nervous chuckles.

"That's a new excuse," Lawrence said, tone amused.

"Naw, Earl used to hit the head every time we went in action. 'Course, that was because his mess attendants doctored his food to give him the screamers. He ain't a chicken an' neither is Maarik," he added loud enough that her crewmates would hear.

"Range, seven hundred," called Bele, repeating the estimate Gunny Horn made on the fire control platform over the bridge and relayed through the earphones under Bele's helmet.

"Range, seven hundred, aye," repeated Haan-Ara, or "Hanna," as she turned the wheel to adjust the gun's elevation. She continued to do so as the range estimates kept coming. At roughly four hundred yards, Silva could see a lot more detail of the big orange ship. As with all the other close vessels, the aerials and cranes were tangled junk and the deck was covered with irregular shapes that might've been vehicles or other things. It was difficult to tell how much was actual damage to the ship.

"We're easing a bit to port," Silva said. "Should be able to see if anything's behind it pretty quick."

Bele suddenly shouted, "Chief Silva, Gunny Horn says there *are* masts back there! We are turning farther to port. Keep casting the lead," he yelled at the detail up forward, relaying another command, "but be ready to get out of the way!"

Daniel Baker was training the gun out to starboard, keeping it vaguely on target as the ship's aspect changed. Suddenly, there were bright flashes, blooming out from amidships on the big battleship amid gray-brown gouts of smoke. Smaller flashes flickered dully along the rail among the debris on deck.

"Somebody's shootin'!" Silva roared unnecessarily, just as a big splash erupted about a hundred yards short. Much smaller splashes started spurting up, initially short as well, about the time the crackle of fire and the boom of the bigger gun reached them. "Machine guns an' at least one o' them twin gun mounts, second from forward, higher than the first," he shouted at young Baker.

"I saw. I'm tracking it," Baker called back.

Bele must've reported this to Horn because he quickly relayed the response. "Commence firing in local control!" he cried.

"On target!" Baker shouted. The .50 and .30 caliber machine guns opened up on the fire control platform and amidships deckhouse, sending arcing red tracers to probe and scatter among the debris on the orange ship.

"Firing!" Haan-Ara almost squeaked. The gun spat fire and jumped back with a roar, twin hydraulic cylinders swiftly slamming it back into battery. The *shoosh* of the projectile was short, but they watched the bright tracer smash into the superstructure with a satisfying smoky flash just above the boxy gunhouse shielding twin weapons that shot at them.

"Too high!" Baker snapped at Haan-Ara.

"Really?" the female 'Cat spat back.

The breech of the gun was already open and Kaan-Dis-Ar, who'd noticeably grown on this trip, pushed one of the heavy shells in. The number three gun on the starboard side of the amidships deckhouse barked, somehow *feeling* louder than their own gun. Samuel Jenks was that gun's captain, and the shell smashed a gunhouse on the big ship, sending twisted orange plates spiraling away, but it was the wrong one. Its guns might've been manned as well, there was no telling, but now the first one flashed again, both guns shooting this time, sending a pair of tall stalks of spray jetting up less than a dozen yards off the starboard bow. Maarik-Fas was inundated by the spray as she ran back from the forward hatch. With the gun training ever farther to starboard, she must've thought she was safe.

"Still wet yerself, didn't ya?" quipped Silva as she trotted to a stop beside him, water dripping from her furry face.

"So did you," she retorted, then grinned. "And I got a better reason!"

Some of the spray had indeed landed on Silva and Lawrence, provoking an indignant shriek from Petey. Silva grinned back. “Fair enough. Grab that loose shell before somebody trips on it—or it drops over the side.” There wasn’t much chance of the latter. *Walker* was still barely moving, and the loose shell had come to rest against a stanchion. That they were just creeping along while being shot at bothered Silva a lot, though he guessed Ronson was risking holes in their topside in preference to maybe hitting something and causing underwater damage.

“On target!” Baker cried.

“Firing!” shouted Haan.

Boom! Shoosh! Bam!

This was a direct hit, right on the face of the gunhouse between the protruding tubes. Flames jetted out through the slots around them before the whole structure seemed to bulge and fly apart in an unexpectedly large explosion. The number one gun’s crew was too astonished to even cheer.

“No steen,” Lawrence observed.

“Right,” Silva agreed. “No *steam*,” he translated for the others, “so they didn’t have power for the ammunition hoists an’ prob’ly collected a buncha ammo in there with ’em.” He shrugged. “Too bad for them. Sneaky, though. Never thought to take fire from one o’ these rust buckets.”

None of the big ship’s other secondary battery guns were shooting at them and of course the great main battery weapons had never moved, but a clattering sound of bullets hitting the ship reminded them they were still under machine-gun fire.

“Do we keep shooting?” Maarik asked.

“Sure,” Silva said. “Why not? They’re still shootin’ at *us*. An’ nobody’s told you to stop. Pretty fun, ain’t it?”

Walker’s machine-gun crews continued hosing the areas the incoming tracers seemed to originate from, and the number one and three guns fired twice more each before the call to cease firing came. By then, all enemy weapons were silent, but a cluster of wooden sailing ships were visible anchored in shallower water between the orange battleship and the shore. The closest one looked familiar, and that’s the one that opened fire, indicated by another dart of flame and bloom of smoke. An instant later, *Walker* shook with an impact and explosion forward that smashed the starboard billboard and launched the anchor over the port side—along with two cadets who'd been crouching there during the fight, still casting the lead. Two other cadets were sprawled on the buckled fo'c'sle deck.

"Son of a *goat*!" Silva seethed. "Pound that bastard!" he shouted at Bele before turning and cupping his hands to shout back at the bridge. "We got casualties out here!" Looking back at the gun's crew, he saw, despite his command, every member staring numbly at the wounded—maybe dead—cadets to their left. "Shake it off, dammit! You're gonna take punches in a fight. What matters is you keep punchin' back so the enemy can't land another one!" The number three gun fired, throwing up a geyser of spume just short, but red machine-gun tracers arced onto the target.

"On target!" shouted Cadet Baker, voice a little shaky but determined.

"Ah . . ." said Haan-Ar, turning her elevation wheel as she peered through the telescope in front of her. They were only about three hundred yards away. "Firing," she barked, stomping the trigger pedal.

The bow of the "enemy" ship that Silva now realized was USS *Scott*, shooting at them with its own gun identical to theirs, flew apart in a kaleidoscope of shattered timbers. Another hit came from the number two gun, blasting more debris farther back and toppling the ship's mainmast. The complex of rigging pulled the foretop down with it when it fell. The number four gun on the aft deckhouse would finally bear and sent a round of its own into the maelstrom that looked like it impacted a different ship behind the first. For a moment then, all three guns that would bear to starboard kept up a brisk fire in local control until *Scott* was a sinking, burning wreck and everything behind her had taken damage of some sort.

"Cease firing, Cadet Bele!" shouted Lieutenant Daanis, who'd stopped behind Silva as Chief Bashear and a detail of mixed regulars and cadets scrambled forward to retrieve the wounded and begin performing damage assessment and control. Bele didn't seem to hear even though his earphones had dropped down around his neck. "Chief Silva!" Daanis said. "Cease firing this crew at once!"

"There's still somethin' floatin' over there," Silva replied in what would've sounded like a reasonable tone to someone who didn't know him.

"Which haas struck its colors!" Daanis said sharply, blinking with fury, tail whipping behind him. "It haas surrendered!"

"Do they get to do that after what they done?" Silva asked.

"Of course!"

Silva sighed, then said, "Cease firin', Cadet Bele. Somebody's told us to now."

The gun was already up, but Haan-Ara leaned back in her seat. So did Cadet Baker, taking his hand off his own adjusting wheel.

"Eight faathoms!" called a 'Cat who'd retrieved the lead and tossed it.

"It gets shallo'er," Lawrence said, trying to redirect everyone's attention to practical matters.

Bele blinked as if coming out of a trance. "Yes," he said. "The ship that shot at us has sunk but it still burns."

"Grounded then," Silva said, nodding, and Daanis looked at him curiously. "That big orange piece o' junk is aground," he explained, gesturing at the still smoldering battleship. They'd come around astern of it now and could see the raised letters there. "*Nevada*," Silva murmured. "Imagine that." He looked back at Daanis. "We're goin' aboard, right? An' sendin' fellas over to what's left o' them ships?"

"Yes, but *you* are not going. We waant prisoners to question."

"I can take pris'ners," Silva objected, narrowing his eye. "We'll see what the skipper says."

"He is the one who told me to send Gunny Horn and Iaan Miles."

Silva grunted. "We'll see," he repeated.

"No," Ronson said. "Not now," he qualified before Silva's good eye could go as wide as it likely would and his argument just got . . . weird. Nobody could rationalize like Dennis Silva when he got a running start, and Ronson didn't have time for that. "I'm sending Miles to clear the ship and Gunny Horn to take the surrender of the League pirates. I guess that's who they are. And whether they are or not, *Marine* or not, the gunny's less likely to just kill everybody we need to get answers from."

"I can get answers just fine," Silva defended.

Ronson actually rolled his eyes, getting annoyed. "Sure, you'll get an answer or two out of whoever lives long enough to spit 'em out, but that may not be who we *need* 'em from by then!" He waved a hand. "I promise you can menace folks to your heart's content if we can't get 'em to blow."

"But . . ." Silva tilted his head at Courtney. "Who's gonna pertect Mr. Bradford?"

"Gunny Horn—and the whole rest of his boarding party."

"But *Fen* gets to go." Silva sounded almost pouty now.

"Fen can identify the pirates who took *Scott*, if any are still alive." Ronson's tone hardened. "*You* and Lawrence will stay aboard here with the gun's crews you trained in case somebody else opens up on us."

"You figger that's likely?"

Ronson snorted and waved out at the anchorage full of battered ships. "What do you think? They could be anywhere, and we have to clear all those ships. Do you have any idea how many *hundreds* of miles of passageways and compartments are out there to hide in?"

Silva was scratching the beard on his chin. "No," he confessed.

"Me either." Ronson sighed. "We don't have enough people here."

"There's the Japs," Silva suggested, "an' I bet there's plenty of fuel oil out there, just in the hulks we don't want."

Ronson dipped his head at Chiba. "We already discussed that. We have to get them here first. In the meantime, I'm sending the Nancy up to look around, then go tell Captain Okabe what's up."

"Have you sent a message to Cap'n Reddy yet?"

"Not yet," Ronson said, pursing his lips. "Mr. Meek is coding a message detailing what we know so far, but I hope to know more soon. Pass the 'well done' to the gun's crews." He looked down. "Condolences on the kids we lost as well. The two wounded are in pretty bad shape, by the way."

"I know," Silva said. He'd stopped in to see Pam on the way up to the bridge. "Poor scudders had no business bein' here from the start," he murmured.

"Maybe not," Ronson agreed, "but they are."

Walker inched in closer to shore, finally anchoring in about six fathoms barely a hundred yards from the port quarter of *Nevada* and the same distance from the chaotic shore littered with fallen trees and the burning hulk of USS *Scott*. The former Navy Clan auxiliary was resting on the bottom, even shallower, and all her masts and rigging had withered and crashed down into the flames still leaping from her deck. There were two smaller vessels beyond her, both of which had suffered serious damage but didn't appear to be in danger of sinking. It was one of these, rigged like a topsail schooner with wildly tangled yards, that had what looked like a white sheet streaming from her foretop mast in a growing breeze.

The party under the command of Ian Miles was almost entirely composed of veteran *Walker* sailors, with just a smattering of the most promising Marine cadets, their launch motoring swiftly to the side of the beached battleship. The other launch, technically under Abel Cook's command but with Gunny Horn, Sergeant Kaik, and another handful of Marine cadets, was taking Courtney Bradford and young Fen-An-Raar to "reason" with the enemy, as Courtney put it. They hadn't taken one of the "gizmos" with them, but Ian Miles had, a pair of his cadets having been instructed in its use. Courtney had no intention of going ashore just yet, and none of the sailing ships had been here when the bomb went off. They should have negligible contamination.

Shouting for everyone to stay back from the rail, Horn and Kaik scrambled up the side of the schooner. Horn led with a Thompson SMG instead of his Springfield, and Kaik had left his Allin-Silva rifle behind in favor of a Blitzerbug. Both could effectively spew a stream of .45 ACP, the same caliber as a 1911 Colt, at close range with devastating effect.

"Stay back, damn you! Let me see your hands! Get 'em up!" Courtney heard the shout from above as Abel Cook and the Marine cadets, also armed with Blitzers, practically ran up the side of the ship. Only when Abel finally poked his head back over the side and told them it was clear did Courtney and Fen go up, leaving just the coxswain and a single armed guard below. Upon gaining the deck, the first thing Courtney noted was how few people seemed to be manning the ship. Right at a dozen, he suspected without counting.

"Goodness gracious!" Courtney exclaimed. "Is this all there are?"

Horn jabbed in the direction of a young black-haired man with a double pencil mustache in the rather threadbare remnant of a uniform of some sort. "That one speaks English. Says this is all of 'em, on this ship at least. About the same number on the other one."

"Two dozen men," Abel said doubtfully. "Perhaps enough to sail these ships, but just barely."

"There were more on the one you destroyed," the man said resentfully. "I don't think any escaped."

"Tough," grunted Horn. "They shot at us. How many were on the battleship?"

The man only straightened before saying, "I will not say."

"He *will* say," Sergeant Kaik said with certainty aside to Gunny Horn.

"Who are you?" Courtney asked, stepping forward, closer to the man.

The prisoner seemed to hesitate, then shrugged. "I am Tenente di Vascello Gavino Barbieri of the Marina Populare Italiana, in association with the Lega di Tripol." He gestured at the other sailors. "I speak for these men of various nationalities, but all are Lega sailors."

"You're League *pirates*," Courtney said simply, remorselessly, "who *took* the vessel we were forced to destroy and then fired on us without cause or warning." He paused. "Unless you claim to have done so officially, perpetrating acts of war under orders of your League superiors . . ."

Tenente Barbieri hesitated again before firmly stating, "It is the policy of the combined powers of the Lega to maintain peaceful relations with your unnatural alliance." He spoke the last words with a curling lip.

"Pirates then, Gunnery Sergeant," Courtney said to Horn. "Do you recognize any of them, Cadet Fen?"

"No sir," said Fen. "I do not think so. Certainly not the most murderous and treacherous one I knew, who caalled himself 'Ames.' Perhaaps they were aboard *Scott*," he worried aloud. "I hope their prisoners were not," he added anxiously."

"I pray that's the case," Courtney agreed, then appeared to ask his companions in a questioning tone, "What do we do with pirates again? What is the *only* consequence for their behavior?"

Horn looked thoughtful. "Actually, there's two possibilities, Mr. Bradford." He gazed steadily at Barbieri. "We usually just hang 'em, if they don't hurt anybody, but we have two dead and at least two wounded. No choice," he said, shrugging. "We have to feed 'em to the fish. I wonder what they're like around here?"

Barbieri's face went white, and three other sailors immediately went on their knees, begging loudly. That proved that they, at least, understood English as well.

"Interesting," said Abel Cook, glancing at Courtney. "I suppose we *might* be inclined to be merciful to the first two or three fellows who tell us what we want to know."

Tenente Barbieri was the first to step forward.

Ian Miles wasn't very happy. Not only was he running around on an orange-painted battleship that might or might not be poisoning him (the "gizmo" said no, but how would some screwy brass box know that?), he was also in charge of a bunch of kids with deadly weapons, two of whom had been responsible for operating the gizmo he had no faith in. Most of all was how far he felt he'd fallen. He'd been a colonel, albeit self-proclaimed, in command of the human-Lemurian resistance against the Grik invasion of Madagascar, and he'd done some good work there. It was probably what he'd been made for, he figured—free to lead his enthusiastic force however he saw fit in frequent, desperate skirmishes against implacable foes. He'd felt useful, even indispensable to his task, and that was a heady sensation. But now he was just a sergeant, doing what he was told. He was in charge of this boarding party, though, clearing the ship however he thought best, and his troops were actually pretty good, regardless of some of their ages. In fact, it wasn't too long before he quit feeling sorry for himself when they started taking fire.

Bullets *spang*ed off the mangled wreckage of a truck scattered across the scorched deck, and he and his squad jumped back under cover.

"Two guys with rifles," said one of the human cadets. "Up on the level above us, past the number three turret barbette."

"Good eye," Ian said, a little surprised. He hadn't seen where the shooting came from. "You three, with me," he told a trio of 'Cat veterans. "Give us some covering fire," he told the rest. "Now!" he cried. Blitzers opened up, spewing .45 caliber bullets in the direction the cadet suggested, while Ian and the older 'Cats sprinted forward, past the barbette and under the overhanging deck. All three pulled pins on grenades and tossed them up on the level above. *B-b-boom!*

"You two that way," Ian shouted, pointing forward. "Bound to be another way up!" He looked at the remaining 'Cat sailor. "Let's go!" Running back out in the open, Ian made for the closest ladder. A bullet spattered on the superstructure steel beyond, but Ian kept going, the clatter of Blitzers reminding him the cadets were still giving cover. Peeking over the next deck level while trying to control his breathing, he saw a leg and a rifle sticking out from behind a heavy piece of equipment he couldn't identify. Taking aim, he squeezed off three rounds, shredding the leg. The rifleman dropped his weapon and shrieked in agony, leaning forward to clutch his wound. Ian stitched another three rounds across the man's torso, sending him sprawling. Easing slowly upward, eyes all around, Ian finally stood and trotted over to the body. Another man was still writhing just beyond him, countless grenade fragments in his lower body. A clatter came from forward, sounding like a Blitzer, and Ian saw one of the 'Cats he sent that way step over and look down at something, probably another enemy.

"Half of you kids, locate and watch as many companionways going below as you can find. The rest get up here." He looked at the 'Cat who'd followed him. "We'll clear the topsides first, then go below." He sighed. "It could be a pretty long day."

CHAPTER 20

It was a very long day indeed: hot, sweaty, and bloody as well. Only four ships were ultimately boarded, each testing "safe" with Courtney's gizmo, but only two were thoroughly searched. *Nevada* was the only one where they met resistance, but it got fierce in the dark labyrinthine passageways below, where Ian's party lost one veteran 'Cat dead and two more cadets wounded. It was ultimately determined that, in addition to the nearly thirty initial defenders slain by *Walker*'s guns, twenty-two more had to be killed or convinced to give themselves up. The last three Leaguers had holed up in a magazine, prepared to blow up the ship—they claimed—but surrendered quick enough when they were promised their lives. And it was all a wasted effort, in a sense. *Nevada* was clearly the most heavily modernized battleship in the anchorage, but not only was she hard aground, she'd worked too long against undersea rocks and was too badly damaged to pump out and float off. No doubt she remained valuable, possibly even salvageable, but not with what they had on this trip.

Nagato was quickly checked with the gizmo and for general condition—which was bad—but Miles meticulously explored a Sims Class destroyer, USS *Hughes*, which was pretty beat-up but surprisingly dry. His boarding party spent more time in her than intended on their way to examine the New York Class BB, which turned out to be USS *Texas*. She was "clean" as well, but also in remarkably good condition at a glance. Just as rusty as everything else, the big windows in the foretop and aft fire control towers smashed out and her unarmored structures wrinkled, the wooden decks were only lightly scorched. She had a list due to leaks in a washboarded torpedo blister on the port side, but a quick excursion below revealed her main hull bilge had only filled with ordinary seepage, which was to be expected after months of neglect. In any event, Ian Miles's first brief surveys were encouraging, and it looked like they could save some of the ships, at least. More disappointing was his report that, aside from all the extra equipment arrayed on the ships he inspected, quite a bit seemed to have been removed. He didn't even know what to look for when it came to possible advanced technological wonders that Steve Riggs longed for, but particularly noticeable aboard *Texas*, there were a lot of empty protective gun tubs, especially aft, where 20mm and 40mm antiaircraft weapons had been. He knew this because not all of them were gone, only most. The question was, had they been taken off to preserve them before the test that sent everything here, or had the League already swiped them?

According to what Courtney's boarding party saw for themselves and what the prisoners revealed, the League had been quite busy here in ways that were immediately troubling for USS *Walker* and her crew, and the Grand Alliance in general.

"So they definitely took stuff?" Ronson asked Courtney in the wardroom that evening during a crowded open meeting of all officers and chiefs, even such cadets as young Fen, Philan Bele, and Samuel Jenks. Those three had emerged as leaders and de facto representatives of the cadet cadre, and there were essentially no secrets anymore, at least in regard to what they were doing, if not the dual status of some. There was no point in revealing that.

Courtney nodded, stuffing his pipe. "Two old destroyers and a small oiler arrived just days after *Shonai* destroyed the small vessel that fired on her. This was seen from shore," he reported in a significant tone, glancing at Lieutenant Chiba. "But it is perhaps fortunate for her that she was believed to be one of ours that simply left to report her discovery."

"How could they think that?" Chiba asked.

"Because you made no transmissions and"—he pursed his lips—"the 'witnesses' had no reference from which to make the distinction. They were locals, you see." He nodded at Lawrence. "Very much like him in appearance, as you said." He leaned forward, and his tone grew more enthusiastic. "But here's the really fascinating bit! We all thought the battleship *Savoie*—which is now ours, of course—was sent to intimidate the Republic of Real People in southern Africa all alone. She was not. She had, in fact, originally been accompanied by a larger support group and escort. Only sensible, in hindsight. The rest of these ships went on to supply preexisting League outposts—very few at the time—and establish new ones. Most of those we have happily found. The one on the . . . pseudo-continent to the east we have not."

"They been there alone all this long time?" Silva shook his head and spit tobacco juice in a mug. Pam shuddered, but even she didn't gripe at him. Nearly everyone else was smoking. "Talk about a 'dame famine'!"

Courtney was shaking his head. "Apparently knowing how open-ended their deployment might be, they brought women with them. Slaves," he added starkly, "taken during their conquest of the Mediterranean. They may have found other humans here and there," he speculated, "but I only caught a vague reference and forgot to pursue it." He smiled a little. "Uncharacteristic of me, I know, not getting sidetracked, but I was quite distracted by more pressing revelations." He looked at Chiba again. "Long before you came to this world and touched on that initial land mass, the League already had its own 'understanding' with the beings you encountered. Some tribes of them, at least. That was certainly why the apparent cousins of the Gentaa suddenly became violent; they were told to."

There were a few gasps at this revelation, and a number of people spoke at once, but they all went silent when Courtney resumed. "It gets rather ironically more involved," he promised. "Though the League does not consider Gentaa to be people, precisely, the Grik-like tribes, possibly related to dear Lawrence here, are considered little better than savage animals. Useful but unreliable and unpredictable. They do love the things the League trades them, however, particularly iron weapons they can use against enemy tribes. This makes them happy to spy for the Leaguers, and they have a fairly sophisticated communication network"—he dipped his head at Chiba again—"as you already surmised. It was them who not only saw but quite tragically experienced the transferred effects of the bomb that exploded"—he shook his head—"in a different 'here.' This broad oceanic caldera has been a sacred place for them, almost a capital, with a surprisingly large population. They lived in timber dwellings among the trees, so it may be difficult to discover their remains, but I'm afraid they suffered rather terribly from it"—he paused and arched a brow—"and have been encouraged to blame us."

There was an incredulous outburst at that, but Silva, Gunny Horn, and Lawrence sat silent, nodding understanding.

"Purty damn clever," was all Silva said.

"Has anyone seen any of these natives since we got here?" Ronson asked loudly over the tumult, but no one seemed to hear him.

"Silence!" roared Chief Bashear, and it was as if someone yanked the needle off a phonograph.

"Has anybody seen any of 'em?" Ronson asked again.

"Lookouts might haave," Tabby said. "A couple reported possible movement high up on the crest of the crater, but couldn't identify it." She shrugged. "Most were more focused on looking at the mouth of the bay or other ships."

Ronson turned to Fred and Kari. Kari had taken the Nancy up with another cadet for a look around. Kari shook her head. "The whole daamn islaand's covered with trees. There's clearings here an' there, like on the other islaand, but we didn't see nothin' but some canoe-like boats on a couple o' beaches. I tole you thaat, an' we'd been expectin' 'em. Didn't see any at sea between the islaands, though."

"Well, they're here," Courtney confirmed. "Our prisoners were using them for much of their labor force."

"Doing what?" asked Miles, and Courtney looked at him.

"Why, taking things off of some of the ships and loading them aboard those two destroyers and the oiler I mentioned earlier. I did mention them, didn't I?"

"Yes, Mr. Bradford," Ronson assured. "Did you find out what happened to the crews of the ships they took, like the *Scott*?"

Gunny Horn stiffened, and Courtney glanced at Fen, who was suddenly blinking almost too fast to see, and he stared down at the table for a moment, his voice quite different when he replied. "Some of them seem to have been taken away to the primary League outpost. The surviving prisoners *will* show us where, I assure you."

"Surviving prisoners?" Tabby asked quietly, noting the sudden tension.

"I shot some of 'em," Gunny Horn said with a complete lack of emotion. "Seems that, of all they did tell us, they were most . . . reluctant to spill that."

Silva arched the brow over his eye patch at his friend in appraisal.

"Shot Some Of 'Em," Petey somberly confided.

Ronson cleared his throat. "What for?" he asked guardedly.

"Because they *fed* some of their prisoners—*our people*—to their friends who look like *him*," Fen erupted, pointing at Lawrence, but his fury wasn't aimed at him.

"Yes," Courtney murmured. "They were some of the ones 'responsible' for the outrage against their god, after all, and there was apparently a most unpleasant ritual involved." He looked over at Fen. "I was most surprised and grateful that young Fen didn't shoot the rest of them. They all deserve to hang," he said forcefully, "but we still had much to learn." Finally lighting the pipe he'd prepared, he coughed and resumed.

"Yes, well, it seems this is the part where a great many things begin to make more sense. The ever-benevolent Leaguers, the source of such largesse to the natives, have quite graciously offered to restore these sacred waters to their original state by removing the dreadful remnants of the cataclysmic event that may anger their god into blowing up the whole island. That's what they think caused the great crater in the first place, by the way. A Noah's flood sort of 'cleansing' event, if you will. In any event, not only have they already taken things away, they'll doubtless attempt to chase us off and claim the rest when they complete some essential maintenance to their ships that have been allowed to languish to some extent. I know this has been a common theme with League naval assets, but I suppose there's more justification in this instance. Regardless, they'll have the locals to help them and we won't have long before they try."

Ronson twisted his mustache, thinking. "Well, that's a worry, sure," he allowed. "Even if all they have is a couple of old DDs, we'd be outnumbered and"—he glanced at Fen and the other cadets standing by the coffee counter—"there's other things to consider."

"Quite a bit else, I'm afraid." Abel Cook spoke up, apparently growing impatient with Courtney's rambling explanation. "First, there's the timing. Think about it. All the 'rising tension' around the Azores kicked off about the time this happened." He waved at a porthole, indicating the scatter of derelicts outside. "The League in the Med clearly got word what was here and determined to 'distract' us from it while they took their time recovering what they could. It's worked too. *Walker* is, quite literally, the only potential 'combat asset' of note we have anywhere near this vicinity. They're probably most puzzled, thinking we know about it too, why their demonstration has worked so well."

Ronson nodded at Chiba. "We'll have *Shonai* with us soon. No two destroyers would willingly tangle with her and us together," he said confidently.

Abel glared at Courtney, exasperated. "But that isn't all they have!"

"Did I miss . . ." Ronson began, but Abel shook his head.

"I'm sure Mr. Bradford was 'getting to it,' but our main problems are these: *Savoie*'s escort and supply cohorts weren't just composed of two destroyers and a small oiler. There was another oiler, a transport, and a heavy German cruiser, one of *Hessen*'s sisters in fact!" Abel waved a hand as if it were almost immaterial before he added, "There was also a very old French battleship, even older than *Savoie*, that was more another transport for personnel than anything, but still has all her guns. What's actually worse than all that combined, I think, is that the League outpost on the big island didn't just send people to take things off the ships; they sent some of their German sailors to seize a *modern German cruiser, with all the latest advancements*! That's the ship Fen noticed was missing right off." He looked at Lieutenant Chiba. "Like *Nagato*, she was apparently a war prize sent to be expended as a target for American atomic tests. Some stuff had been taken off of her too, for study most likely, but she was largely intact, and the scratch German crew was happy to *steam* her out of here!" He turned back to address them all. "Which brings up our biggest imperative and most important duty to the American Navy Clan and Grand Alliance: Not only can we *not* allow the enemy to 'chase us off,' we can't let *them* get away! Not with all the technology they've already acquired."

"That's askin' a hell of a lot," Pam stated grimly, but to everyone's surprise, her tone was more despondent than outraged. "What?" she demanded more hotly when she saw the surprised expressions directed at her. "I hate it, but he's right," she snapped. "But it *is* askin' a lot of former enemies we just met." She gestured at Chiba with a respectful nod. "An' it would be expectin' too much—again—of this poor old ship even if she still had a full veteran crew"—she waved a hand and glanced apologetically at Fen, Bele, and Jenks—"which she doesn't have." She took a long breath. "But like I said, Abel's right. It's *that* important. If we're all that's here, we gotta do what we can."

Dennis Silva broke the ensuing thoughtful silence by spitting loudly in his mug. "Sounds like we got our work cut out." Looking up at the many staring faces, he just grinned. "What? We need more ships, right? Well, if them damn Leaguers can raise steam on one o' them rust buckets out there, why can't we?"

"Rust Buckets!" Petey cawed triumphantly, before tentatively adding, "Eat?"

Everyone present except Lieutenant Chiba, who may have had other reasons yet seemed almost offended by Petey's very presence during such a momentous discussion, burst into nervous laughter.

Ronson briskly rubbed his scarred scalp with his fingertips and managed a vague smile. "Okay," he said. "We're going to need to keep up our air patrol," he told Fred and Kari. "Can't afford to be taken by surprise." He made a gesture encompassing everyone else. "We'll start clearing and surveying any ships that look fit to fight in the morning. Don't even worry about those that're bashed all to hell or half sunk. We might even want to start preparing those hulks for scuttling," he added with a frown, then sent a glance at Tabby and Isak Reuben. "You two will be the final authorities on whether something can steam. That's the very first thing we have to determine before we spend any time on it, clear? I don't care how good it looks otherwise. If it can't steam, it damn sure can't fight and it's no use to us." An idea seemed to strike him. "That said, don't neglect the transports. Who knows what's in 'em, and we might use 'em to tow ships away." He looked at Gunny Horn then. "You and Silva and Mr. Meek will get busy evaluating the combat usefulness of what we can get moving—functionality of weaponry, directors, and comm status between them. We also have to know if there's ammo. That's another reason to explore the transports. But that's the second criterion: if it can't steam or shoot, it gets towed or scuttled."

"How the hell're we gonna do all this stuff with just us?" Isak asked, his reedy voice as belligerent as usual.

"You'll start," Ronson said. "We'll have more help soon." He held out his hands. "I don't know how much, but some. You'll also have to start figuring how to steam and shoot with the fewest people possible, of course, not to mention designing a crash training program." He finally looked at Lieutenant Chiba. "What do you think about all this? What will your people and Captain Okabe think?"

Chiba blinked. "I would certainly appreciate an opportunity to ask him. I understand you won't want to leave this anchorage with your people scattered all over it." He looked at Fred Reynolds. "But perhaps I might be flown over to him?"

"Of course," Ronson said. "But what do *you* think, Lieutenant?" he pressed. "The oiler should be here in a matter of days"—he shrugged—"and I guess *Shonai* could take all the fuel and just sail away from all this."

If Chiba was offended by the implication, he didn't show it. "My . . . sense of it is that Captain Okabe made a deal with you, Captain Rodriguez, and he will 'stick to it,' as you say. Besides, what good would it do us to leave you? We will have missed our chance to be your friends, and I personally cannot stomach the notion of allying myself with the fiends we now know not only caused the death of my shipmates through their surrogates, but fed helpless prisoners to monsters. I will make that plain to Captain Okabe as well, and believe that *Shonai* will be here beside *Walker* as soon as she has the fuel to move."

"One good thing in that respect," Ian Miles contributed. "I checked on that, and *Nevada* by herself has enough fuel in her bunkers to fill up a cruiser more than once. I doubt she's the only ship out there with fuel left over from the trip to get"—he shook his head and looked at Courtney—"wherever they went to get bombed."

Ronson popped a cigar in his mouth, lit it, and leaned back. "I think we've got enough to make a report to Captain Reddy now. I just wanted a plan of some sort to go with it, and I guess we'll see what he has to say."

CHAPTER 21

EASTERN ATLANTIC
THE AZORES

Captain Matthew Reddy's voyage to the Azores in the refloated USS *Impero* had been lengthier and more eventful than he'd hoped, marred by breakdowns, malfunctions, near catastrophic failures of critical repairs made during her time in the pit, and numerous issues stemming from her crew's unfamiliarity with her systems and their operation. There was also the fact that she was just so damn big, the largest steel ship anyone in the Grand Alliance—aside from Matt Reddy and some of his "old hands" who'd seen the old-world carriers *Lexington* or *Saratoga*—ever touched. The earliest Allied carriers like *Big Sal* were bigger, converted from monumental wooden seagoing Homes, but weren't anywhere nearly as complicated. None of these things could be helped, of course, and the only option was to cope with—or bull through—each of these situations as they arose.

Then there had been the weather. Not only was this the greatest distance, by a lot, that Matt had personally ventured into the Atlantic on any world, it was the farthest north as well. It had become increasingly dreary with heavy seas like he would've expected in the North Atlantic—of course this *was* the North Atlantic on this world—and in a word, it was cold. He'd forgotten how uncomfortable cold could be, and despite many of them having fur, none of *Impero*'s crew liked it either. With the exception of some from the Republic or Shogunate, most had never felt cold in their lives. Yet even then, Matt and those aboard *Impero* had been spared the worst of it since, regardless of the many issues complicating her operation and preparation, requiring constant maintenance and training, the ship's very size let her ride considerably easier and dryer. That wasn't so for the poor souls aboard *Impero*'s escorts, many of which were practically copies of USS *Walker.* Her Wickes Class and the similar Clemsons had always been wet ships, and her "daughters" had pitched just as horribly in the heavy seas they'd met, streaming spray as they precariously climbed the towering swells only to plunge down in the bottomless troughs, their flush decks swept from bow to stern by the frigid, foaming torrent. It was fortunate that the weather had moderated, the sea turning more tranquil by the time *Impero*'s battle group finally neared the Azores.

Matt was standing out on the narrow starboard-side walkway outside Impero's flag bridge about halfway up the towering forward superstructure, leaning on the rail and gazing out at the distant Azore Islands—as they were manifested on this world. Like so many other land masses, they were somewhat different—quite a bit higher, due to a generally lower sea level Courtney attributed to an ice age of sorts, but there were also fewer of them, more connected and with about twice the square mileage they should have. For example, Flores and Corvo Islands to the north were just one bigger island, confirmed by aerial observation, and Faial, Pico, and Sao Jorge Islands, where Matt's attention currently lay, were combined into a single larger forested and mountainous land as well. Graciosa, Terceira, Sao Miguel, and Santa Maria hadn't been inspected before League and Allied aircraft started shooting at each other, so it wasn't yet known what they looked like.

Interestingly, these latest aerial confrontations had been surprisingly even. It was believed the League had expended about half its modern aircraft during its Caribbean adventure. They'd tragically savaged the more primitive (with a very few exceptions) Allied aircraft, but the Allies had many more of them and their pilots had more experience. The latter made greater difference than the former, Matt thought, but the League had apparently learned the lesson and finally started building "new" planes of their own and conserving their more advanced aircraft. It had been inevitable of course, but it reminded him that their one current advantage over the League, their industrial capacity, might be fleeting.

That diverted his thoughts back to what they'd heard from Ronson Rodriguez about the situation Matt's old ship had run into in the Pacific, and a terrible suspicion he'd harbored in the dark depths of his heart began rising up closer to the light. He knew there was such a thing as coincidence, but he'd learned never to count on one and to always exhaust the possibility that some larger plan was at work before accepting events as unrelated. He now knew what Ronson and his new friends thought, and that was a *possible* explanation for everything currently going on. If true, he'd been played—they all had—but they'd acted without knowledge of the "coincidence" and their world was just too big for them to know everything, be everywhere, all at once. Their meager forces were spread too thin. If he could avoid a full-scale war with the League at present, the enemy might find that their clever machinations—if that was indeed the case here—had backfired, serving to reawaken the Grand Alliance to the threat they posed, as well as the urgency of preparing more quickly for the inevitable showdown. *Meanwhile, however,* he sadly mused, *aside from what pitiful resources I've scraped up to send her way, USS* Walker *is practically all alone. Again.*

"Cap-tan Reddy," came the voice of Juan Marcos behind him, almost shouting over the stiff cold breeze. "Admi-ral Lelaa-Tal-Cleraan's respects, an' will you quit bein' stupid an' come in out'a this damn cold so she can tell you somethin'? Ever'body's waitin', anyway."

Matt chuckled, looking back at his Filipino friend, eyes sweeping forward as he did and passing over the two massive gunhouses just ahead with six 15" rifles protruding from them. He was even more amused to see the red-and-white "barber pole" paint scheme on the forward deck. Much to Spanky's annoyance, there'd never seemed to be time to paint over it. Matt secretly believed time would've been found to *change* it instead of simply covering it up. A lot of their Lemurian crew would decorate anything if nobody stopped them and seemed rather fond of the colorful fo'c'sle. That apparently never occurred to Spanky. "I doubt Admiral Lelaa put it like that," Matt said, turning to follow his peg-legged keeper back inside the flag bridge.

"That's what she *meant*," Juan defended.

"I expect so," Matt agreed.

"We've been contaacted by the enemy," Lelaa abruptly told him when he stepped through the hatch and joined her, Spanky, Henry Stokes, and Chack-Sab-At, whose entire Raider regiment was aboard as the ship's Marine contingent. Others were there, including Captain Toryu Miyata of *Fitzhugh Gray* and Kapitan "Willie" Dietrich from *Hessen*. They'd linked up with *Savoie* and her battle group the day before, and Captain Russ Chappelle would be over later.

Matt gestured at the plush, ornately decorated chairs, a legacy of *Impero*'s former owners. "Let's have a seat—and some coffee, if you please?" He asked the latter of a pair of stewards standing out of the way. Looking back at the brindle-furred Lelaa in her spotless whites, he inquired, "What did they have to say?"

Comfortably situated with her own cup of good, real coffee all the way from Madagascar, Admiral Lelaa leaned forward, freeing her tail from the confines of the chair. Lemurians generally preferred cushions or stools, and there were stools present, but these chairs were fine if they lounged against the puffy armrest. Lelaa produced a folded message form from her tunic pocket and passed it across to Matt. He didn't open it, but waited for her to report the contents for the benefit of them all. She blinked her understanding and proceeded to do so.

"It's from Ahmmiraaglio Gherzi himself," she said, blinking a combination of irony and surprise. Everyone else was surprised as well. Gherzi had commanded the League naval effort that culminated in defeat at the Battle of St. Vincent Island, and it was generally assumed he would be . . . removed for what no one could argue was not a costly disaster. The thing was, the Italian Ammiraglio Gherzi was a consummate professional, utterly nonpolitical—a vanishingly rare specimen available to the factional League Triumvirate indeed—and had probably done as well as anyone could under the constraints of the schizophrenic strategy imposed by Capitaine De Fregate Victor Gravois in his position as Gouverneur Militaire du Protectorat des Antilles. Gravois had been maniacally ambitious and probably insane and was last reported wandering the wilderness of South America in the company of the Blood Cardinal Don Hernan, the deposed Supreme Holiness of the Dominion. No one knew where they were now, or if they even still lived. Apparently, however, the ruling League Triumvirate, composed of bickering French, Italians, and Spaniards, had recognized what Matt almost feared they would (having come to grudgingly respect Gherzi himself): that the unassuming Italian officer's defeat at St. Vincent wasn't altogether *his* failure, and he remained their best and most experienced choice for a fleet commander.

"Well," Spanky said, "I kinda wish they'd shot him, but I guess I'm glad they didn't. What did he say?"

Lelaa indicated the folded page in Matt's hand. "His laanguage waas most polite, full of plaatitudes and pleasantries, but it comes down to thaat he waants to meet," she informed them.

"Where?" asked Colonel Chack-Sab-At. "Not on the big islaand of Pico, surely?" That's what they called the apparent conglomeration of islands just to the east, which they'd found to have the best anchorages and most advanced infrastructure, not to mention the majority of naval assets, airstrips, and antiaircraft protection. There could be just as much on the islands beyond, because observation of them from the air had been the most contested.

"No," said Lelaa, "nor aboard one of their ships." She blinked. "He proposes to come aboard here. Says thaat we 'let him go once and he trusts we will do so again.'" She looked at Captain Reddy. "He seems to haave a high regaard for your honor, and your word he will be released is all he requires."

"He's a gutsy little goombah, I'll give him that," Spanky grumbled. "If he *really is* in charge," he warned.

"How does he want to do it?" asked Captain Miyata.

Lelaa blinked unhappiness. "This is the paart I don't like. He will come out in a single ship—I would bet their very biggest one," she added cynically, "to meet this one all by itself."

Kapitan Dietrich stood. "Unacceptable!" he barked, then looked pleadingly at Matt. "It is a ruse, a chance to meet our"—he gestured around—"rusty rapier with a pistol in a duel."

Matt looked at him thoughtfully. "That may be," he conceded, "but this 'rapier' will be deadlier close up, where we can bring her main and secondary batteries to bear in local control." *Impero*'s sophisticated fire control was proving difficult to master. "And *Big Sal*'s battle group will be in range to whistle up an airstrike by tomorrow."

"Which they caan do just as easy to us from the islaand," Lelaa reminded.

Matt nodded agreement but gazed straight ahead at nothing, lips pursed in thought. Finally, he spoke. "Good point," he said, "but the funny thing is, I trust Gherzi too." He waved a hand. "Don't get me wrong. If it comes to a fight, he'll do what he has to, to win. He may not like the Triumvirate, but he's as 'old-school' as they come and he'll follow orders." He shrugged. "But like he said, we let him go. I suspect he'll tell us first if he means to fight." He paused. "Which may be what he's coming to do, I guess." He looked back over at Lelaa. "Send back to Ammiraglio Gherzi, as flowery as you like, but the essence of our response will be 'Come ahead.' Whatever he wants to talk about, I've got some questions of my own."

Impero was cruising all alone as the sky turned pink, then gold, bathing the black sea with its brilliance. The ship was at general quarters, and the lookouts immediately alerted them to the approach of an enormous shape from the direction of Pico. Matt was on the navigation bridge with Spanky and Lelaa, and they stepped out onto the bridgewing to see.

"Holy shit," Spanky said. "What the hell is that?"

"It's big," Lelaa noted unnecessarily. "As big as us. *Impero*, I mean."

Matt was looking through his own battered binoculars. "I'll be . . . She's still nose on, a few miles out, but looks like a French Richelieu Class. Two forward turrets both have four big guns each. Fifteen inchers, I'll bet."

"Jeez," Spanky objected, "if she *is Richelieu* . . ." He looked at Lelaa. "The French didn't even finish her until 1940 where we came from, a year *after* the Leaguers're supposed to have got here."

"And if I recall, her design was intended to compete with the Littorios." Matt lowered his binoculars and put a hand on the rail. "Like *Impero*."

"So she is a maatch for us?" Lelaa asked.

"*Meant* to be," Spanky said, "though I guess they wound up complementing each other." He snorted. "Till now."

It turned out that the enemy battleship wasn't *Richelieu* after all, but a different lead ship—*Suffren*—of what was essentially the same class. That weird answer came when Spanky later asked Capitano Campioni, who came aboard what was actually his old ship, along with Ammiraglio Gherzi. His purpose was probably to evaluate the functionality and combat readiness of his former command, but Spanky and Lelaa carefully guided his movements and "entertained" the increasingly bitter officer who seemed more intent on finding fault with the different decor in the wardroom and other superficial things, sniffing with disdain at rust streaks and issuing scandalized protests over the tarnished silver service.

Matt and Gherzi met alone, except for Juan Marcos, who served them coffee and something approximating dried fruit cookies, in the admiral's quarters.

"You look good, Admiral," Matt complimented with a smile. Gherzi was short and immaculately dressed in a blue officer's uniform, but his face was fuller and he was certainly rounder than Matt remembered.

Gherzi chuckled. "Compared to the moldering corpse you thought I would be?"

Matt tilted his head to the side in a kind of nod.

Gherzi coughed lightly and sipped his coffee. "Yes, well. I would be lying if I said I hadn't expected that myself. But you were right when we last spoke. Our people, like yours, are our greatest resource, and the Triumvirate has finally recognized that experience and competence—though possibly dangerous—can be as important as political reliability. I am perhaps more 'politically reliable' than anyone since I am not political at all."

"I hope I won't regret turning you loose," Matt said dryly, his smile fading a little.

"You said much the same when you did it," Gherzi acknowledged, "and I still pray you will not." He sighed. "If I was not here, it would be someone else, perhaps more comfortable with their apparent material advantages and without my respect for the capacity for competence among your, ahem, nonhuman personnel. Most of my peers remain arrogantly convinced that the other . . . races in your Alliance are mere savages, capable only of mimicry. Useful for menial tasks perhaps, but nothing more. I know differently, of course, and have managed to convince at least two of our three principal rulers. Field Marshal Messe remains . . . skeptical." Gherzi brightened slightly. "And at least you and I can meet and converse like civilized beings. I fear that if I was not here to meet you, our forces would already be engaged in open, wasteful conflict once more."

"You've shot down two of our scout planes," Matt abruptly accused. "That's a breach of our armistice."

"And you have destroyed one of ours," Gherzi countered. "Yours were flying over the Azores, territory we agreed you would not encroach upon—or go beyond."

Matt shrugged. "We had to see what forces you were assembling." His tone hardened. "A lot more than you need to guard the approach to the Med."

Gherzi was nodding. "Which we *allowed* you to observe before we engaged subsequent flights," he agreed reasonably. "But you shot ours down over open water."

"Beyond the Azores," Matt pointed out.

"Of course," Gherzi agreed, then leaned forward in his chair, expression earnest. "But we did not both assemble our fleets in this ridiculous place to shoot down a handful of each other's planes."

Matt sipped his coffee and nodded. "No, and I think I've figured that out. You gathered a large force, bigger than you thought we could match, to threaten a breakout and resumption of hostilities. That might still be your plan if you think you can give better than you take, but then why would you wait until we gather all our strength? I'm sure you know we've got more still on the way, and if we can't already stop you, we can hurt you bad enough that we can hunt down what gets past us."

Gherzi was nodding slightly. "That may well be, and I have already reported that assessment to the Triumvirate."

Matt frowned. "So this"—he gestured in the general direction of the big island—"*all* this really has been a distraction from what you've got going in the South Pacific."

If Gherzi was surprised that Matt had guessed the League's overall strategy in this, he didn't show it, but he had the grace to look somewhat uncomfortable. "I do so dislike such underhanded maneuvers, and as one man to another, I apologize. The initial operation was not my plan." He snorted. "I wasn't even aware we still *had* any assets remaining in 'your' waters and *hope* I would have had the integrity to inform you before I ever signed my name to the armistice agreement between us." He cleared his throat and looked Matt in the eye. "Be that as it may, as you have clearly surmised by now, we have had . . . resources on a large island in your southern Pacific for some time, and they made the Triumvirate aware that some . . . phenomenon similar to that which brought us all to this world deposited a number of powerful ships in the vicinity, all abandoned. Naturally, as your people are no doubt also attempting to do at the moment, ours have been trying their best to salvage whatever advanced technology they might discover." He held up a hand and urgently added, "There need not be any conflict! I'm told the only actual *ships* they will attempt to take away are a few that belonged to members of the League where we came from. Our *own* ships, if you will."

"A certain modern German cruiser and massive Japanese battleship?" Matt appeared to guess.

Gherzi was nodding again. "Yes! Just those."

"But it seems that where *they* came from, they'd been surrendered to *my* navy after their countries were defeated," Matt countered. "That makes them *mine* on this world."

Gherzi pursed his lips before sipping his coffee again. "We had guessed that much as well, based on reports of the . . . context of the site. And I told the Triumvirate you would see it that way in terms of ownership if the operation was revealed: your property in your waters. I argued for the opportunity to negotiate a compromise."

"But the overall operation . . . we're lured all the way here with less than we'd like to confront you, leaving . . . less to send there. Don't try to tell me you didn't cook that part up."

"As you have guessed," Gherzi confessed.

Matt rubbed his nose. "The 'compromise'?"

Gherzi managed a tentative smile. "Our people salvage the site together!" He hesitated and added, "Well, separately, of course, but at the same time, each side claiming what they want and the other respecting their ongoing efforts to do so. With luck, all involved will acquire enough technological treasures that we can maintain a mutual deterrent to future conflict. You must believe me when I say that I never want to fight you again," he ended earnestly.

"Oh, I *do* believe *you*, Ammiraglio Gherzi," Matt said, "but I assume your Triumvirate has instructed you to demand assurances that we allow the unmolested passage of your assets out of the region with whatever they've managed to steal?"

Gherzi tried to smile again but failed. "Reclaim," he countered, before pausing and glancing away. "Ah . . . your people on-site, your own gallant old *Walker* and her crew of young students, I believe, would necessarily be required to disarm and place themselves into the loose custody of our representatives for the duration of the voyage home. Naturally, none of her people would be harmed and you would be allowed to refuel her as necessary."

"Surrender themselves as hostages," Matt ground out through clenched teeth. "That's not gonna happen," he said flatly.

Gherzi sighed. "I know," he said simply. "That was the best I could do."

"And there have already been hostilities," Matt told him.

"Oh dear. I hadn't heard."

"There'll be more," Matt added.

Gherzi leaned back, frowning. "Most unfortunate," he breathed, shaking his head. "I pray that calm heads on both sides will prevail. There is nothing more that you or I can do to alleviate tensions there. For my part," he continued unhappily, "my orders are to detain you here, however I must, to prevent you from sending significant forces to aid your isolated mission. Even if you divert some of what is already coming, I will know." He shrugged. "Nothing of consequence that we are aware of could arrive in time to provide substantial assistance in any case."

Matt gestured around him at the ship. "What if I just steam away?"

Gherzi frowned deeply. "Then I must follow and fight you. You cannot escape battle. As much work as you have done to this ship and *Savoie*, I still have more capital ships, and mine are faster. We will get hurt, especially if your Republic friends arrive in time to help you," he conceded, "but we have finally begun to plan for the future and are starting to build our own new ships. Some would say it might even be a good thing for us to lose more of our old ones, to make us less dependent on them. At best, for you, I fear we would have a terrible battle of mutual annihilation, resulting in a renewal of general hostilities between us. If I 'win' our battle and destroy you, my orders are to break out and carry renewed hostilities to all of your allies touching the Atlantic." He seemed to consider adding more, but ended by shaking his head.

Matt spoke slowly, rubbing his chin. "Your people must've found something really important, some serious edge, for the Triumvirate to be willing to go all in on this."

"I suspect that is probably the case," Gherzi agreed. "Perhaps even something fairly innocuous, yet which, once combined with our—or your—new construction, would render all we had obsolete." He frowned. "Or perhaps it is something that *none* of us should have." He looked intently at Matt. "My most sincere advice to you as a friend—I do have the highest regard for you—is to order your *Walker* to accomplish what she can in the next, oh, say ten days or so, and then simply leave the island of derelicts behind. If my understanding of our assets' schedule there is correct, it will take about that much time—" Gherzi caught himself with a snort and a cough. "I beg your pardon. Once again I find it difficult to guard my words around you, yet I must. I do urge you not to let them stay longer than eight or ten days, however, unless you reconsider my earlier proposal. Just seeing what is important to each other might have some value, don't you agree?"

"*Walker* won't surrender, 'loosely' or otherwise," Matt said, "which makes me wonder how your people and whatever they've stolen and are trying to get operational will manage to escape without hostages."

"There are . . . ways," Gherzi said, then actually scowled. "And I'm told there are other hostages as well."

"Yeah," Matt said darkly, "though *we've* had reports that some of those have been *fed* to the locals to ensure the continued cooperation of the rest."

Gherzi's eyes narrowed and his lip curled in disgust. "I . . . know nothing of that, I assure—"

Matt stopped him. "I didn't think you did. It's true, though." He took a long breath. "I guess I could just as well attack you at anchor. Wait for the rest of my forces, steam over, and hammer away. We both just wreck each other."

Gherzi was nodding seriously. "That's probably what I would do in your place—if I did not care about maintaining our fragile peace. You might even inflict a defeat upon me. I know you will have attack aircraft"—he held up a finger—"but I do as well, not to mention an impressive array of air defenses and pursuit aircraft that will not be caught by surprise."

Matt sat silent awhile, finishing his cup. "Listening to us discussing these things so dispassionately, it all sounds like some goddamn game, doesn't it?" he asked in a bitter tone. "Just a damn war game."

"It does," Gherzi solemnly agreed. "If I may make yet another suggestion?" Matt gestured for him to do so. "Let's keep it that way, shall we? Let's sit here in a face-off for a few more weeks, perhaps visiting again now and then, while things beyond either of our control play out. However that ends up, there's little we can do about it, and it isn't worth restarting our war over—is it?"

Matt nodded slowly, disgusted with himself. Orders from the Triumvirate or not, he knew the strategy behind all this, at least insofar as the best way to mousetrap and immobilize the bulk of the Allied fleet, had to have been Gherzi's. Matt had beaten him at St. Vincent, essentially with unexpectedly raw aggression, and now—in this first real strategic battle of what many were calling the "phony war" between the League and Grand Alliance—Gherzi had counted on that aggression and lured him into confronting a perceived threat head-on. Whether he would really chase and attack them if Matt turned his fleet and steamed away was almost immaterial. Neither of them wanted a battle, and Matt wouldn't risk one over what, as Gherzi rightfully reminded him, he couldn't really do anything about. Oh, there might be a *few little things* he could do to help his friends and his old ship out, but he wouldn't even let those thoughts touch his face.

"Okay, we'll keep it a game," he finally agreed. "For now."

CHAPTER 22

"So that's it, we're on our own," Ronson told the detail working aboard the battleship *Texas* after he and Isak Reuben climbed the accommodation ladder, saluted the flag someone had found aboard and run up aft, and called everyone together. There were almost fifty aboard at present: a mix of cadets and some Navy 'Cats from a couple of auxiliaries that showed up and, ironically, some Japanese sailors from *Shonai*. The big former enemy cruiser had been fueled as promised, and Captain Okabe brought her over as agreed. He was even happier to top off his bunkers, pumping oil from the grounded *Nevada*, which was serving as a kind of fortified headquarters for the expanding endeavors in the ancient caldera. Leaving *Shonai* moored to the grounded battleship, Okabe's people focused their efforts on *Nagato*, like Chiba said they would, but at least a quarter of her crew helped *Walker*'s with other projects, initially actually raising steam in a couple of the transports that must've been farthest from the blast.

Ian Miles had led the only foray ashore, to a stockade built by League personnel where a few hostage sailors were said to be kept, but he'd found the stockade empty of Leaguers or anyone else. He did make first contact with a dozen or so naked Grik-like natives, however, who'd apparently been scavenging the abandoned stockade and savagely attacked his shore party on sight, armed with obsidian-tipped spears propelled by long throwing devices, like atlatls, or attempted to close with short, crude swords. Several of Miles's party, including him, were lightly wounded, and one was killed. The lavish expenditure of Blitzerbug ammo broke the murderous charge, and a couple of the creatures escaped, leaping the palisade and vanishing in the maze of rotting deadfall. More were seen from the water after that, seemingly appearing at random from within the dead forest, possibly moving about by means of hidden pathways or tunnels cut through the scorched, fallen trees. They made no further attacks, but it was clear they were always watching.

A great deal more had been learned and accomplished in the roughly two weeks since *Walker* entered and sort of captured the anchorage. First had been Abel Cook's discovery of papers in a briefcase left in *Nevada*'s wardroom. These contained a map of an atoll—*not* a mountainous island—where the test was supposed to occur and included a representation of how the target ships had been arrayed. This confirmed there'd been a *lot* more ships involved than were still present in the huge lagoon. Some had surely sunk and others were clearly . . . buried somehow, in the slope of the crater wall surrounding those that remained. Courtney had gone white while examining the papers and stiffly informed them *another* test had been planned relatively swiftly following the first. Reading on, he was somewhat relieved to see that it *should* have already happened. Contemplating that over the next few days, he and Abel Cook formed the opinion that either the "frequency" connecting this place with another on a different world had been disrupted by the energy discharge that created the link in the first place, or whoever decided such things there had deemed it inadvisable to explode *another* weapon like the one that just . . . disappeared a whole fleet without leaving any wrecks or debris. "*I* certainly wouldn't've done *that* again!" Courtney had said, then happily resumed boarding ships with his gizmo, making notes of what he observed, but also pragmatically listing useful items he found.

The destroyer *Hughes* and an almost pristine-looking submarine (aside from rust, of course) named *Parche* had been towed closer to *Nevada* through the maze of hulks where they could be worked on more easily. And as far as warships went, a couple more destroyers, a cruiser, and another submarine looked rather attractive as well. The most shattered-looking thing still afloat was the weird, smallish aircraft carrier they finally identified as USS *Independence.* Despite how mangled her flight deck and unarmored upperworks were, she simply refused to sink and didn't seem inclined to. Ronson permitted a salvage crew to go aboard and cut up what appeared to be a ridiculously wasteful number of smashed aircraft and throw the aluminum down into a pair of the large landing craft they found bobbing somewhat randomly around the bay. They'd actually got several of those running fairly easily. Special care was taken transferring a number of the big radial engines, and it was a crying shame there weren't any intact aircraft found. Hope remained there'd be some modern aircraft in crates aboard one or more of the best-preserved attack transports.

As far as the capital ships present were concerned, USS *Texas* appeared to be the simplest to put into operation. The list Abel found had included the *Pennsylvania* and *Texas*'s sister ship, *New York*, but neither were there. They'd either sunk, been embedded in the mountain around them, or somehow hadn't made the trip. But *Texas*, so far, was a prize to preserve. As was discovered earlier, a lot of her antiaircraft weaponry had been removed (which seemed schizophrenic since many other ships still had theirs), but some of her major wartime upgrades remained semi-intact, most notably her amazingly sophisticated fire control suite and what Jack Meek and Lieutenant Chiba were both certain was at least part of a more advanced radar apparatus than *Shonai* had. *Hughes* definitely had radar, but the set hadn't been as well protected.

Additionally, despite the venerable superdreadnought's age, she'd weathered the terrible power of the atom bomb better than just about anything else within what Courtney believed was the closest proximity to the blast. *Arkansas*, *Nagato*, both the "new" cruisers, and at least one submarine had apparently been even closer, and everyone had already written all but *Nagato* off. Only the determination of the Japanese kept her on the list to be saved. The smashed, heavily listing cruiser they'd passed close aboard when they arrived had finally lain down on her side and gone down a few nights before as if passing away in her sleep. Quite a few had heard the long dying gasp and gone on deck for the somber vigil. Ronson had been affected for a number of reasons beyond those naturally felt by any mariner watching a fine ship die. He'd determined then that they wouldn't waste time or risk any lives boarding anything that didn't look like they could at least tow it home as it was. That meant there'd been only one lengthy visit to USS *Arkansas* and that only to salvage more aluminum from several mangled aircraft.

Now, however, going on three weeks since their arrival, word had come straight from Matt Reddy describing his meeting with Gherzi and the very strong hint that they only had a week or so left to do what they could.

"So, what's the plan, then?" Silva asked, words a little garbled before he could step to the rail and spit a stream of tobacco juice over the side.

Ronson frowned at him, then shifted his gaze to the woman who was Isak's sweetheart, whether he knew it or not, Boilermaker First Class Sureen. She'd been in charge of bringing *Texas*'s machinery back to life. "You said she'd steam?"

"Aye, Cap'n," the former Impie gal confirmed. "She's tired," she conceded, "and we figure she had a long, tough war before she wound up here. But we could've lit off at least two of her boilers the day we found her if there wasn't so much salt water in her fuel lines." Like most of the ships they'd found, *Texas* hadn't only been festooned with smashed aircraft and vehicles of all sorts, clearly to gauge the destructiveness of the atom bomb on things besides ships, but she'd carried an almost full load of fuel and ammunition. The latter might've simply been a case of those testing the bomb having no more use for it than they did the old battlewagon anymore, or maybe they'd wanted to know if the bomb would cook it all off. Either way, though the ammunition in the magazines had been spared that, and even any water damage from flooding, the crumpling damage to her portside torpedo blister had been sufficiently communicated to the inner hull to allow contamination of the fuel oil in the nearest bunkers. Worse, it appeared that, unlike most of the ships they'd inspected, four of *Texas*'s six Dyson boilers had been lit and steaming when the test took place. The increasingly contaminated fuel resulted in a godawful mess, clogging filters and sludging up burners until the fires went out. Unfortunately, they didn't all go out at once, and two boilers—and the space they were in—had been pumped calf deep full of unburned (though not unburnable) black goo. Sureen had been supervising testing the fuel in other bunkers and pumping out the bad stuff—which helped correct the ship's list, somewhat—and isolating the contaminated lines to make sure only good fuel went to the undamaged boilers. This had gone slowly and with monumental difficulty without any power in the ship until one of the amazingly intact attack transports, USS *Banner*, was brought over to provide it.

"I think we can light off two boilers today," said Sureen.

"What about engines?" asked Isak.

"And guns?" Ronson added. "Can she fight?"

"She'll steam," Sureen repeated, "and probably move. We haven't found anything wrong with her engines besides." She shrugged. "Just age. They ain't turbines, you know. And once she has power, her guns ought to move, even fire, but who's gonna shoot 'em?"

"Gunny Horn'll be aboard to start sorting that out," Ronson said. "He had experience of that sort in the old *New York*, once upon a time, and he trained up the gun's crews in *Savoie*, which has a similar layout."

"But who's actually gonna *shoot* 'em?" Silva pressed. "An' does all this mean you wanna stick around an' fight when the damn Leaguers come?"

Ronson pursed his lips and gestured for Courtney Bradford, still fiddling with his gizmo, to move closer. "You and Mr. Cook have inspected the ships we'd like to save in the time we have, if we can. Are you ready to give a definitive answer whether all are entirely safe to be on?"

Despite the cursory assurance his radiation detector had given them, a number of troubling discoveries had been made of animals (mostly goats and pigs) that had been left exposed to the effects of the blast. Those left chained out on deck had quite obviously been killed, their carcasses subsequently fed on and scattered by lizardbirds, most likely. What raised new concerns were the reeking carcasses discovered *inside* the heavily armored gunhouses of *Nevada* and some other ships. Courtney's expression turned serious. "I expect it's more than possible those poor creatures died of starvation or thirst, but I'm afraid they would've fallen victim to the blast radiation in any event." He waved his hands while the cadet supported his gizmo. "The, ah, *pulse* of radiation attendant upon the blast itself"—he nodded at his machine—"that swiftly diminished. I think that even aboard many of the least damaged ships, that radiation could've been extreme enough to eventually sicken and kill anyone exposed, no matter how deep in the ship or well protected they were. A quite dreadful weapon indeed." He frowned. "That said, I simply don't know enough to be positive, but I'm morally certain my machine would detect it if there was enough of that particular radiation left to be harmful. I wouldn't risk people aboard any of these ships if I wasn't quite sure of that." He paused. "Had their second underwater test proceeded as scheduled, showering the ships with radiant"—he seemed to ponder that term and nodded as if to himself—"radiant water or even material blasted up from the seafloor, I doubt it would be safe for us to stand here even now. But the little persistent lingering radiation from what actually occurred has been washed off by rains. I can confirm this to a degree, having detected slightly higher levels—still barely registering a 'two'—in places such runoff might've accumulated and lingered."

"So . . . whatever we can snatch and escape with is safe?" Ronson pressed.

Courtney straightened and looked down his nose. "I'm confident enough that I've repeatedly and near continuously exposed *myself* and all the young cadets assisting me," he said, tone somewhat annoyed.

"Swell," Ronson said with a sigh. Looking at Silva, he continued, "So here's what we're gonna do over the next week or so Cap'n Reddy thinks we have: First, we'll use the three transports Isak's got powered"—he nodded at *Banner* lying alongside—"that one, as well as *Fillmore* and *Niagara*, to tow a couple more ships that can't move out of this crater and anchor them outside." He quirked his lips. "All of 'em have stuff stowed below, but we haven't even checked what a lot of it is. I expect we'll find much of it useful. Anyway, *Walker* and that weird big-mouth bastard marked 'LST-661' that's loaded with tanks"—he grinned—"that Isak also got running will tow the two best submarines we've looked at—*Parche* and *Dentuda* are their names—out past the entrance as well, along with the two best 'gold platers,' *Hughes* and *Mayrant*, and that one old cruiser it looks like we might save, *Salt Lake City*. Once they're out, *Walker*, the transports, and the LST will commence towing the others for Respite. None of the auxiliaries that've joined us can pull anything. Maybe a sub in a pinch, but they'd be too slow and might make easy targets if the League gets here quicker than we think." He gestured around. "This thing'll stay until last as a rear guard. Pretty intimidating, I'd say." He looked at Silva. "Hopefully, she won't have to shoot."

"What about the Japs?" Silva asked, looking at Chiba. "What about *Shonai*?"

"We'll use some of their people to help operate the tow ships. *Shonai* will tow *Nagato*. Defend her if she has to." Ronson grunted. "Word is that she's almost as big a piece of junk as she looks. No chance of getting her underway." He hesitated. "But if she *can* be saved, maybe reboilered and re-engined, she'll be the toughest, most powerful thing we have on the water. *Sixteen-inch* guns," he stressed. "On the one hand, I wish they'd just scuttle her—which we'll do to everything we have to leave for the Leaguers," he added, "but I get why they want her. We can sure use her." He shrugged. "And we promised to help 'em try. They're giving us more of their people to help us too, maybe up to half. Between them and the draft we've taken off the auxiliaries, we should have enough crews to do what we want." He looked around. "Finally, that leaves *this* old tub. Last to head out, like I said, with most of *Walker*'s veterans aboard. And if anything we move there gets left outside the bay, she'll take it in tow as she goes."

"Can't hardly fight an' tow at the same time," Silva pointed out. "Against maybe two Kraut cruisers, a couple tin cans, an' a French battlewagon for Chrissakes. That we know of."

"All those ships except the cruisers are very old," Ronson pointed out, "and the cruiser that was here is likely . . . somewhat diminished."

"So? I say we lure 'em in an' sink 'em. Oh, I'm all for a wide-open sea in a fight," he conceded, "but we won't have a battle line, just a buncha straggly-assed derelicts."

"Sink 'Em!" Petey shrieked. Even Lawrence was nodding at that.

"And why detach *Walker* as a tug?" asked young Bele, who, along with some other gun's crews in *Walker*'s deck division, had come over to help Silva inspect the big guns on *Texas*. "She is our fastest, most maneuverable ship. She should be unencumbered to screen the other vessels."

Ronson looked at the lad. "Because, cadet"—he deliberately stressed the word—"*Walker* is more than just a ship to the Alliance. More than just another tin can. On top of that, she has more than just another crew on board her."

If Bele's face wasn't so dark already, it would've reddened deeply. "You don't think we're ready to fight *Walker* if we must," he accused. "But

I assure you that we are. Readier than many other crews she has had," he added forcefully.

Ronson rolled his eyes. "You know what I mean, damn it."

"I do not," Bele insisted. "And I know I speak for the vast majority of the other cadets when I say, what difference does the number of years we have lived make if we can do the job? What makes our few, *less experienced* lives more valuable than those who will remain aboard here?" he asked more harshly, gesturing around. "Protecting those lives at the expense of others is a *political* decision, Captain Rodriguez. Not a sound tactical one," he accused.

Ronson looked ready to explode but finally chuckled instead. "You're right, son," he finally confessed. "But politics can be just as important to Allied strategy as tactics are." He waved it away. "I'll think about what you said, but chances are we'll be long gone before the League comes back and it won't make any difference."

"Are us going to still send out scouts?" Lawrence asked. Kari or Fred flew every day, having repaired their "own" personal Nancy, and now that Okabe had replenished aviation gasoline from *Nevada*, he sent *Shonai*'s own scouts even farther toward where the enemy base had been described. They didn't go all the way because the League might have air assets of their own, but they'd flown over a part of the massive isle to the east, observing chilling new wonders from the sky. Like on any land widely separated from others on this world, the animals were vastly different from those they knew. The Impies had named the place "Ogygia," after the isolated island in Homer's *Odyssey*, but Courtney had begun insisting they call it "Caprona" in honor of Edgar Rice Burroughs's mythical land. Nobody really objected or cared at this point. Let him argue it out with Governor/Empress Rebecca McDonald. Regardless, they should have warning when the enemy moved.

"I hope to have something in the air almost constantly on watch, during daylight at least, until we're out of here," Ronson replied.

That wasn't entirely what Lawrence meant. Silva was thinking the same as he pointed at the mass of wreckage strewn on the inside of the gigantic volcanic cone in the distance, almost on the opposite side of the bay: what was clearly the stern of a very large ship they were all pretty sure was an aircraft carrier. "I still wanna go over there," he announced. "Courtney's list of target ships says that's *Saratoga*." He shook his head. "Why would anybody ever wanna blow *her* up? Even Chiba"—he nodded at the Japanese officer overseeing some of his own sailors aboard—"says the very newest US carriers weren't any bigger. I wanna have a look. Nobody's seen any Grikly sorts wanderin' around on that side o' the bay," he urged. "Why would they? The only things that seemed useful over there, we already towed over here or alongside *Nevada*. More an' more of 'em is hangin' out ashore o' *her*." He was right about that. It was difficult to tell, considering how easily the island Grik—or whatever they were—seemed to move through the deadfall and tall grass shooting up around the great trunks, but lookouts had estimated there might be three or four hundred of them now. They'd even caught glimpses of what might be humans, Leaguers no doubt, moving among the locals. "If they try ta catch an' eat us, we oughta have half a day's warnin' they're comin' before they get there," Silva argued.

Ronson frowned at him. "This is a Navy expedition. You won't get any prize money for aluminum you find," he pointed out.

Silva waved that away. "I'm richer than I'll ever need ta be off that wrecked Jap bomber we found on Borno." He was too. Aluminum still couldn't be made in large quantities and was worth more than its weight in gold. This whole trip would "pay" for itself many times over just in the aluminum they'd already salvaged. "I don't give a shit about that," Silva went on. "I just figger if there's anyplace we'll find a whole modern airplane, it'll be in the ass half of the hangar deck on that thing. An' the way it's slid down close to the water, we might get it out'a there too. Load it on that ship with the big doors in the bow."

Ronson twisted his mustache, staring at the distant wreck. "Makes sense, I guess. Not that it won't be bashed up," he qualified, but then nodded slightly. "But you might find something that looks less like confetti than the ones left on *Independence*." They'd salvaged as many airplane fragments from her as they could, but the flight deck on the light carrier—which they now knew had been built on a cruiser hull—had trapped many more when it largely collapsed, smashing anything under it. "Are you caught up with the gunnery-related projects you described?"

Silva shrugged. "Hell, my *cadets* can take over deck gun trainin' at this point. We have a mess of different sizes on the different ships, from three-inch fifties to five-inch thirty-eights and five-inch fifty-one secondaries, like they got aboard here." He tilted his head toward the amidships casemates at the base of the ship's forward superstructure. "Them're bag guns, o' course, but otherwise they all load, point, an' train the same an' follow the same central fire control procedures—if Gunny Horn an' Jack Meek ever get that sorted out." He gazed at the nearest armored gunhouse with its pair of the ten 14"-45s that made up *Texas*'s main battery. "They're workin' on them beauties too, tryin' ta sort out the fire control for 'em. Way too complicated for me," he admitted, shaking his head. "Besides"—he grinned—"if, from time ta time, you don't let ol' Dennis go make some smoke, he's liable ta break somethin' ya don't want broke." A delighted expression crossed his face. "Hey! I made a po-eem! Point is, I know me pretty well, an' all work an' no play makes it hard ta keep me pointed in the right direction, if ya know what I mean."

That was true enough as well, unfortunately, and Ronson yearned to take a whole airplane back, banged up or not, almost as much as the ships. "Okay," Ronson finally agreed, but warned, "Don't think I'm giving in to your poetic blackmail, though. And it won't be just you and Lawrence running around on the loose, see? You'll take enough people for security and to actually accomplish something other than tromping around on dry land, looking for something to kill." He assumed a stern expression, tilting his head at Bele. "You can take some cadets if you like. We won't be here much longer, and they've earned a trip ashore. But one of 'em *will* be a radio operator, and you'll maintain line of sight contact with *Walker* at all times. Finally, if you see a *single one* of those local lizards, you'll scamper back to *Walker* at once. Got it?"

"Sure thing, Skipper." Silva grinned. "C'mon, Larry. You too, Cadet Bele. We'll see if we can scrape up some o' your pals. How's that?"

"I shall accompany you as well," Courtney proclaimed, clamping his big straw hat tight on his head against a sudden strong gust of wind. Looking at Ronson with a bushy brow raised, he challenged, "I've behaved quite well enough to earn my own trip ashore, and I simply *must* solve the puzzle of what remains of the ships, or parts of them, that materialized within the very rock itself. I shall bring tools!" he declared.

CHAPTER 23

The landing party set out for shore early that afternoon and included Lawrence, Courtney, Sergeant Kaik, and the fat cook Earl Lanier (who'd served aboard *Saratoga*'s sister ship, *Lexington*, and a couple other Pacific Fleet ships before being banished to the Asiatic Fleet). The rest of the detail was otherwise fairly heavy with cadets, including Fen, Bele, Susan Raj, Daniel Baker, Maarik-Fas, and Haan-Ara. Samuel Jenks, Kaan-Dis-Ar, and Aalak-Maraan wanted to participate, but the first two were drilling auxiliaries on the guns aboard other ships and Aalak was scheduled to fly with Fred. The only other adult to show up at the last minute, somewhat unsurprisingly, was Pam Cross. She slid down the falls into the motor whaleboat without a word, once again wagging her medical bag and a Blitzerbug. No one objected, not even Silva, who knew it would be pointless. Tabby insisted they take more "Marines," even if they were still cadets, and they added another three, filling the seats in the boat. *Walker* had carried them close to shore, and they motored the remaining distance to the beach before dropping over the side in the sand and spreading out while the boat was secured. Already fairly close to the stern of the gigantic ship (it really was *Saratoga*, and even with her basically broken in half and lying on her port side, it was easy to see she'd been the biggest thing involved in the test by far), they couldn't help feeling rather insignificant in comparison, while equally disconcerted by the sheer . . . wrongness of the scene.

"Jeez," Silva gasped, looking up—and up—at the pointed, rumpled fantail. It started at the bottom with a gigantic rectangular rudder now wrenched radically askew, and flared past the raised letters that spelled the ship's name and directly into the squared-off bottom of the flight deck, the port side of which looked from a distance like it was almost touching the ground. Here in its shadow, they could see it was in fact at least thirty to fifty feet up, depending on how much of the shattered forest the sliding wreck scooped into chaotic piles. At the angle she lay, a little more than forty-five degrees, all but her outboard port propeller, deeply buried in the rocky earth and timber she'd displaced on her way down the slope, had been protected. The other four-bladed bronze giants were tarnished greenish-brown but otherwise pristine. Even from *Walker* they'd observed that a fair percentage of the superstructure, the part encasing the mighty ship's exhaust funnels, had been folded down in ravaged ruin atop the flight deck. Whether it was flattened by the bomb or collapsed when the ship broke, there was no telling. Beyond that, there was nothing but the disturbance in the side of the crater that had drawn Courtney's specific attention. "Jeez," Silva repeated. "Just *this half* of the ol' gal is as big as *Texas*!"

"Nearly," Earl agreed. "I was on *Lex*—her sister," he added for the benefit of the others, "almost a year. Never did see the whole damn thing."

"How do we get in it?" Pam asked.

"Let's go see," Silva said, tilting the front of his helmet up. "Almost has to be to port, I guess." He tugged on the grapnel and coil of heavy rope slung over his shoulder, weighing him down along with all his usual weapons and ammunition. Nearly everyone else was similarly burdened.

"I ain't climbin' no damn rope," Earl stated flatly.

"Then you ain't no good to us, are ya?" Silva sneered back. "May as well wait at the whaleboat. We ain't haulin' yer fat ass up."

"Gentlemen," Courtney interceded. "Perhaps it might be simpler to work our way forward and attempt to enter through the broken open end?"

Silva glared at Earl but shrugged. "I hope he at least brought somethin' ta eat," he grumbled.

"You wait here, five minutes," said Sergeant Kaik, motioning two of the cadet Marines to follow him. Checking his weapon once more, a Blitzer like most were carrying, he grinned at Silva, tail whipping. "We will . . . sulk it out."

Silva rolled his eye. "*Skulk*, you fuzzy, simple-minded jarhead. Yeah, you do that. Me an' Larry'll herd the rest o' these sprouts, Mr. Bradford"—he glared at Earl again—"an' our pet dinosaur along."

"I'm coming too," Pam said defiantly.

Silva just blinked at her. "'Course you are, doll. I knew that before we even got in the boat."

Giving Kaik the time he asked for, Silva and Lawrence led the rest of the party forward. It was hard going, climbing over and through the maze of fallen trees, nearly losing their bearings in the unnaturally deep grass shooting up from the occasional patch of bare earth. They did make a concerning discovery in those places: many seemed to contain log canoes hollowed out of the very trees surrounding them. That meant many were scorched to some degree, but when Silva and Bele turned one over, the wood looked freshly chopped out.

"I find it rather too coincidental that we are only finding these in the clearer spaces," Courtney observed, gesturing around at the carpet of wood chips all around. "No scorching on the waste," he pointed out, looking at Silva. "These quaint vessels are newly made."

"But where's the snaggletooth little monsters who made 'em?" Silva questioned, peering intently around. Visibility in the clearings was nerve-rackingly limited. "Let's get on along," he urged. Progress remained slow, and throughout it all, the massive hull and overhanging flight deck loomed above them like an unstable cliff edge.

"I cannot banish my sense that this great heap of iron wreckage will roll all the way over on us," Philan Bele murmured between gasps of humid air as they scrambled atop another hill of splintered deadfall, perhaps a little more than halfway to their goal.

"Nonsense," Courtney puffed, wiping his sweaty face with a rag. "No doubt it's as secure as the mountain it clings to, by now."

"But how *tightly* does it cling?" pressed Susan Raj. "To the *steep grade* it lies upon?" she pointedly added.

"It is too like a tunnel," Lawrence agreed with her. "I don't like tunnels . . ."

"Poor Larry has hydrophobia," Silva explained, shaking his head.

"*Claustro*phobia, you big dope," Pam scolded.

"Whatever," Silva conceded airily.

"Looks . . . unnatural," Lawrence sulked.

"Kinda like Earl," Silva cheerfully acknowledged, "an' he was just as *dead* for a while too. I *seen* it. An' even bein' dead didn't keep him from shiftin' around on his own from time to time."

"Shut up, you maniac," Earl snapped. "I wasn't all the way dead."

"Shut up, both of you," Pam groused. "Sound like a couple o' gooses honkin' away . . ."

Pam's own fair imitation of a grumbling goose was interrupted by the breeze-muffled *pop-pop-pop* of a three-round burst of .45ACP from a Blitzer.

"Ever'body shut it an' listen. Stand ready," Silva snapped, suddenly entirely serious. He'd been carrying his BAR at roughly port arms and swiftly brought the butt to his shoulder. He wasn't aiming it, just pointing in the general direction they heard the shots. Several minutes passed before they heard the call of one of the Lemurian Marine cadets from beyond another heap of jumbled deadfall. "All is well! You maay proceed!"

"Hoo shot?" Lawrence challenged.

"Sergeant Kaik. A . . . thing attaacked, in the taall grass! It nearly get me!" Like nearly all 'Cats, this one's English was affected by excitement. "Sergeant Kaik get it first."

"Okay, we're comin'," Silva said.

"Can you describe the creature?" Courtney asked.

"Give the kid a break, Mr. Bradford," Pam said. "You'll see it yourself in a few minutes."

"Hmm. Quite right." He raised his voice. "Never mind, young fellow, but please do leave it where I can see it."

"No problem" came a voice that seemed to shudder just a bit.

"All right, kiddies," Silva said, moving forward. "Quiet, an' eyes peeled."

They had no difficulty finding the beast that looked something like a stunted me-naak, the famously ferocious cavalry mounts from the Filpin Lands. Those resembled furry crocodiles with much longer legs and were armored by a thick case over their vitals like rhino pigs or old-world wild boars. This looked like a cheetah version of that, much smaller, but even more swift and agile. Two bullets from Kaik's short burst had caught the thing in the head (one in the eye), and it had apparently thrashed about a bit. Blood festooned the long grass for quite a distance in every direction.

Silva was kneeling to inspect it while Courtney practically caressed the thing, making appreciative cooing noises and wondering aloud how they'd get it back to the ship. "That Sergeant Kaik's either mighty lucky or mighty good," Silva conceded, standing. "But you don't want that one, Mr. Bradford."

"Of course I do! Why would you say such a thing?"

Silva pointed with the muzzle of his BAR. "He busted the head bone. Ain't you always tellin' me not to bust the head bone?"

"Hmm. Yes. I suppose," Courtney reluctantly conceded. "You'll get me another? *Without* destroying the cranium?"

"I'll sure try," Silva waved at their companions. "Should be a snap if it goes for one o' them instead o' me." The others exchanged nervous looks.

"A Snap," Petey almost whispered, staring at the carcass with naked hunger. "Eat?"

"Not now, you greedy little shit," Silva hissed back at him. Pam arched an eyebrow at the pair, noting how sometimes when Dennis spoke to Petey, it was like he was talking to himself. In more ways than one. "Let's get moving," Silva said. "Easy does it."

They finally reached the break in the big carrier, and the devastation was as shocking as they'd expected. Most of the deadfall had been smashed flat or pushed away by the impact of what was evidently a little more than half the huge ship slamming down and sliding on the slope, leaving a debris-strewn area almost void of the interlocking tree trunks that might've extended a hundred paces farther up the grade. There they could see what looked like a jagged, rusty cross section of the rest of the ship protruding a short distance from the wall of the crater.

"My word!" Courtney exclaimed, rushing forward. He'd been carrying his trusty Krag but now slung it and retrieved a short-handled shovel from the basketlike pack on his back. "Come along! All of you. We need to start digging!"

"I ain't diggin' nothin'," Earl Lanier gasped, looking for something to sit on.

"Useless bastard." Silva scowled at him, but he didn't reach for his own shovel either, moving forward to post himself with Sergeant Kaik and his band waiting for them there. Turning to look back at the bulk of the visible wreck, Silva whistled again. The flight deck had crumpled down as it sheared off, smashing the hangar deck and numerous unidentifiable lower compartments until the ship's boilers were exposed. He'd never seen anything like the twisted nightmare of pipes, conduits, and other shredded internals. "Looks like her guts are hangin' out," he muttered aside to Pam, who'd joined him and Lawrence.

"It does, in a way," Pam agreed softly. The only other sound at the moment was the clank and scrunch of Courtney's excited digging. It grew louder as others joined his efforts.

"It's hard to believe one bomb did all this," Pam murmured, almost shivering.

"No bomb did *that*." Silva pointed.

"It could have if it hit," Pam argued. "And it did in the sense that it"—she waved at the whole of the ghost fleet beyond gathered in the flooded caldera—"that it put everything here for all this to happen."

Silva sighed. "Always lookin' on the gloomy side o' things." He grinned. "Gave us a new adventure ta play in, didn't it?"

"I'm not sure it wouldn't be 'adventure' enough for me, just the two of us at peace for a while."

"We tried that, doll," he reminded as gently as he could.

"I know."

"Eureka!" Courtney shouted gleefully and they all turned to see what he'd found. "Look here!" he cried, now on his knees, scooping at volcanic soil with his hands. "This is hull plating," he insisted, "but the steel underground is . . . merged with the earth as if they were somehow melted into each other! Feel this!" he directed Daniel Baker, who'd crouched closest to him, swiping the exposed steel with his hand.

"Feels rough," the Cadet reported.

"Which it would, bein' the outside of the hull underwater," Silva suggested.

Courtney shook his head, sloshing some water from his canteen on the shattered edge of the ruptured hull plate. Wiping it with his hand, he pointed. "The very steel itself has been invaded by the dirt! I was right! The only way the forward part of this ship, or the fractions of those others we see around the inner slope of the mountain, could inhabit the same space as the rock at the same time is to *mix* with it. Become *part* of each other! I *must* view a sample with a microscope!" He nodded back at the rest of the wreck. "And that's why the aft portion snapped off entirely rather than just sagging down, still attached." He used both hands to indicate the admittedly strange-looking steel he'd uncovered. "The . . . amalgamation ruined the structural integrity of the buried metal. All its elongational properties were lost and it became ridiculously brittle. I shouldn't wonder if you could shatter this part I've revealed with a hammer, like glass."

"Well, I'm happy you're so happy with yer discovery, Mr. Bradford," Silva drawled. "Fascinatin' as hell to us all, I bet. Downright amazin'. But now you've figgered that out so quick, why don't we get on with explorin' the rest o' the wreck, maybe find something we can actually use?"

Courtney frowned up at the big man. "Really, Chief Silva, I must protest your dismissive, arguably sarcastic tone. This is the first practical revelation we've found that relates to the peripheral effects of the phenomenon that brought us all here!" He glanced at Sergeant Kaik and the Lemurian cadets. "Some of us, at any rate. Perhaps *all*, at some point! No one knows!"

"An' they'll likely throw you a parade or somethin' when we get back. Name a new school—or bug—after ya. But I bet we'll get the most thanks for the things we bring back that'll help the most when it comes ta defendin' us from our enemies."

"The big jerk has a point," Pam conceded. "This"—she pointed at the weird wreckage that had practically become part of the planet—"ain't goin' anywhere, an' you can come back to it. Our biggest job is savin' what we can before the damn League comes an' takes it."

Still frowning, Courtney stood and dusted off his trousers. "You're right, my dear, as usual. That's one of the reasons I wanted you with me on this expedition. And Mr. Cook as well, of course. My various . . . enthusiasms sometimes require practical constraints, and you're both quite accomplished at pointing those out."

"Ain't that what I did too?" Silva asked.

Pam looked up at him, hands on hips. "Why should he listen to you?"

"But . . ." Silva shook his head, then tilted his helmet toward the five or six hundred feet of wreckage stretching away downslope of them. "Let's go see if we can get in that."

After about an hour of investigation, it ultimately proved impossible to enter the wreck from the "broken end." Even when they were initially successful at squirming some distance inside through the maze of wrenched and twisted machinery and unnaturally warped high-pressure steam lines—lines of all sorts, in fact—they were thwarted by impossibly wedged or sprung hatches that couldn't be pried open. Finally, it was decided they'd have to climb up to one of the overhanging platforms arranged alongside the hangar deck that were most devoted to antiaircraft defenses.

"I *told* you I ain't climbin' no ropes," Earl declared. "I'm too fat," he reluctantly admitted. "An' even if I got up there, how am I supposed to get around? Hell, I'd roll right off the ship."

"That'd be a comic sight," Silva agreed. "But the only option is walkin' back to the boat."

Lawrence suddenly stiffened, raising his head, snout upward.

"What is it, Larry?" Silva asked. "You smellin' somethin'?"

"Listening," Lawrence corrected, before looking at Earl. "You can't go the 'ay us go here," he said flatly. "None o' us can."

"Whatcha got?" Silva asked his friend, all seriousness once again.

"I hear . . . sounds, *location* sounds that critchers like La'rence use . . . us hunting."

"Whoa, shit," Silva hissed, looking quickly around.

Courtney sounded extremely concerned when he explained, "You have all heard the low-frequency Grik horns, the ones they used to control their armies in battle?" Everyone nodded, even those who'd never fought Grik. "Wild" Grik still existed in more parts of the world than they'd ever known, and those horns had been demonstrated to the cadets. "Well, it seems that most, if not all, Grik-like races can keep track of each other over quite a distance by vocalizing even lower-pitch sounds that humans can't hear."

"We hear it," Fen said, nodding at the other Lemurian cadets. "We didn't know what it was. It sounds like a moaning wind."

"There you are!" Courtney acknowledged happily. "I thought you might hear it too. In fact—"

"Mr. Bradford," Pam pressed urgently.

A worried expression clouded the Australian's face. "Yes, of course. In any event, as has been noted, our Lawrence seems remarkably closely related to the natives here. Can you understand them?" he asked.

Lawrence snorted. "Not talking, just noise."

"How close?" Silva asked.

Lawrence hesitated. "Not close. Getting close, though." He lifted his snout to the gun platform above. "Us could get there afore they get here." He shook his head. "Not to 'oat."

"The boat's out, Earl," Silva said, nodding at the Thompson SMG the cook toted. "You stay here an' keep 'em off us . . ."

"The hell you say! You'll just leave me to get eaten?"

"*Until*," Silva continued, "there's enough of us up there to lift your fat ass."

"Oh," Earl grumped. "Fine, I guess. Ain't very dignified."

"Since when has there been *any* damn thing 'dignified' about you?" Silva laughed. "You couldn't even stay respectably dead. You prob'ly would'a had a statue by now if you had."

"Us *go*," Lawrence urged.

"Go!" Petey chirped. It was possible he heard the sound too, or maybe just sensed the growing tension.

The platform above them was only about forty feet up, but it took a couple of the cadets several tries to snag the rail, dodging the hooks as they fell.

"Waatch it!" snapped Haan-Ara at Fen. "You nearly baash my brains out!"

"Aapologies," Fen murmured, blinking rapidly. Nearly everyone else except Earl was already pulling themselves up their lines, and Pam was the only one having trouble. That was mainly because of the weight of her medical bag, weapon, and ammunition—which she wouldn't let anyone else carry. Fen tried again and missed once more. He was strong but so short he couldn't get the hook to swing enough to throw any distance.

"Just use mine," Haan told him. "I don't waant you to hit me while I'm climbing."

Fen probably would've blushed if his face weren't covered with fur.

"Hurry up, damn it," Earl called up. "I see that tall grass movin'. I think the lizards're here!"

"Oh, shut up, fatso," Silva scolded. "Prob'ly just the wind."

A long, light-shafted spear suddenly lofted out of the grass, revealing little more than the arm and some sort of spoon-headed staff that threw it. Despite seeming to wobble in flight, the spear barely missed Earl and smashed hard into the side of the ship with a boom like a gunshot, the black-bladed head shattering in a cloud of shards.

"That weren't no wind!" Earl bellowed, firing a short burst at the grass.

Silva had already hauled a pair of dangling lines up and was busy whipping the ends into crude harnesses. Tossing them down, he shouted, "Put those on!"

"Like hell! Look at those things. You'll pinch off whatever I stick in 'em!"

"You waant to get eaten?" shouted Sergeant Kaik. More spears were flying now. "Suppressing fire in the graass, short bursts, whether you haave a taarget or not. Miss Cross," he said to Pam, "pull up the other ropes, if you please."

Silva had targets, dozens of them climbing over a mound of deadfall before they dove into the grass. They *did* look like Lawrence, without clothes of course, even down to the orange-and-black tiger stripes. All were carrying a sheaf of spears and some kind of thrower, like an atlatl, but some had a sort of blade thrust in leather sashes tied around their waists. The dozens were becoming a swarm, and he fired a full twenty-round magazine from his BAR into their midst. "Time to fly, fatty," he called down to Earl, who was shooting more himself. So was everyone else, even Pam, who'd already pulled the other lines up. The rapid fire of Blitzerbugs was almost continuous, and the screams of their enemies were mixed with roars of rage. Leaning his BAR against the rail, Silva shouted at Kaik. "C'mon, Sergeant, let's pull." Kaik nodded, slinging his weapon and grabbing the closest rope. They heaved.

"Wait, goddammit! I'm barely in!" Earl bellowed. Spears were slashing past those on the platform now.

"It's now or not at all. You better be in good enough to hang on, 'cause we ain't waitin'!" Silva pulled with Kaik. "Jee-hossafat. How much do you weigh?" he expelled when he and Kaik together could barely lift the man below. Both were very strong, but considering the slope they were on, the rail offered the only leverage. Unfortunately, it also created considerable friction for them to pull against.

"Not that—" Earl interrupted himself by firing the rest of his first thirty-round magazine. "Got *that* bastard, but I'm empty. An' the way I'm hangin' like a goddamn string puppet, I can't reload!"

"Then shut yer face an' pertend yer a feather!" Silva barked back, straining.

"Bele! Baker! Maarik! Haan! Lend a haand!" Kaik shouted at the cadets. "The rest of you, keep shooting!" The extra muscle made all the difference, and Earl was swiftly pulled tight against the rail.

"How am I s'posed to grab on facin' *out*!" Earl ranted.

"Should haave thought of thaat before you hooked on," Kaik shouted back.

Silva grinned at the veteran Lemurian Marine. "I like you."

Lots of spears were flying now, with astonishing range and power. They didn't seem terribly accurate, fortunately, not at the fifty or so yards most were coming from, but sheer numbers were eventually enough. Baker swore and clapped a hand to the top of his left shoulder near his neck when the blade of a spear (Courtney had called out that they were tipped with volcanic glass—black obsidian) skated across it, cutting his combat smock and the flesh beneath as cleanly as a scalpel. Pam's medical bag caught one, and since she was holding it, it nearly spun her off the sloping platform. Bele grabbed her and kept her from sliding off under the rail.

"Get her through that open hatch, back behind you," Silva bellowed, helping haul Earl over the top of the rail. "C'mon, you," he told the cook. "Off yer ass an' let's move!"

One of the Marine cadets—Silva didn't even remember the 'Cat's name, only that he'd been an enthusiastic student on the guns—took one of the wicked spears square in the chest. Dropping his weapon, he clutched the spear with both hands before pitching over the rail without a sound.

"Shit!" Silva roared, raising his BAR and hammering away at the growing nightmare mob below. He'd fought Grik more times than he could remember and thought he'd never have to again. The horror of watching their slashing jaws and claws tearing the cadet's body into gobbets of meat brought back too many memories. "I'll *get* you, you bastards!" he seethed, oblivious to the spears raining around him.

"Let's *go*!" Kaik shouted, grabbing his arm. Silva shook the hand off as he dumped his magazine and inserted another. "Comin'," he growled, finally realizing he and Kaik were the only ones left on the platform. Leaning hard against the angle of the deck, he worked his way up to the hatch. Kaik went through, but Silva paused once more to look back. Only a couple of the creatures were still throwing spears. The rest were already doing something else. "Shit," he said again before taking his first steps into USS *Saratoga*'s gloomy hangar deck.

It was almost quiet inside the cavernous rusty steel space, the only sounds the muffled roaring of their enemies and the quick panting of his companions. Easing past Pam, he squeezed her to his side without thinking before making his way into the light. There wasn't any from the break up forward, the deck having pinched it off quite thoroughly (Silva could hardly imagine how momentous *twice* as much room would seem), but one of the ship's two massive elevators, big enough to lift whole airplanes to the flight deck above, had apparently been blown down by the bomb or collapsed when the ship sheared in half and fell. Either way, he was now bathed in a big rectangle of light from above. The elevator had come off its tracks and slid and crashed hard against the port side of the hangar bay, smashing a whole treasure trove of toys underneath. They knew at once this was the case because even more dusty aircraft stood at their unnatural angle beyond the devastation, wings folded but securely lashed to the deck.

"It's Christmas," Pam murmured, a tone of awe in her voice. She didn't mention Silva's thoughtless, protective hug.

"One might certainly think so," Courtney happily agreed, gazing about. "Such a treasure of modern aircraft! And look!" He pointed upward. "Even more are suspended from the rafters of the flight deck! What are they?"

Silva shrugged. "I ain't no Airedale."

"Some look like Wildcats. F4Fs," Earl clarified. "I remember a little somethin' about my time in carriers. Didn't ever *have* Wildcats then, but"—he shrugged defensively as if about to confess a major character flaw—"planes are interestin'. I kept up." He squinted. "These ones look like they have taller tails, though. The others?" He shook his head. "No idea. Maybe some sort of bomber. They're bigger than Devastators or Vindicators."

"Many look at least somewhat damaged," Courtney conceded with a moue, his vision growing more accustomed to the shadows past the fallen elevator, "but I'm sure some of those can be repaired. Others appear to have no damage at all. We simply *must* have them!"

"Too bad," Silva said firmly, his tone still . . . different from usual. Pam recognized it. So did Lawrence, and he shifted uneasily. Most of the times he'd nearly been killed doing something stupid, Silva sounded like that: focused but somehow detached as well. He gestured toward the hatch. "Them devils'll be here pretty quick."

"What? How?" Courtney demanded.

"They're already buildin' a ladder out'a dead trees. Maybe more of a pile than a ladder, but there's hundreds, maybe thousands of 'em now. Won't take long."

"Raadio," Kaik said, snapping his fingers at one of his remaining Marine cadets whose only real burden, besides his weapon, had been one of the heavy devices in a pack on his back.

"Good luck crammin' a message out past all this steel," Silva said, gesturing around. "I bet they already know we're in trouble, anyway."

"But perhaps not where we are."

Silva shrugged. "Either way, there ain't time to set it up. We need to get movin'." Allied storage battery technology was most hampered by an appropriate material to encase the lead-acid. Bakelite was being made, but it was too fragile unless built just as heavy as what it contained. Field radios were therefore still powered by a bulky hand-crank generator actually lighter and more reliable than a battery. That didn't help them at the moment.

"So, what do we do?" Pam asked, tone neutral.

Silva was looking at each of them. "I see two o' you kept hold of your ropes." Actually, only Susan Raj had retrieved hers. Fen had rolled his back up and carried it along. "That's good," Silva said. "But keep yer eyes peeled for somethin' longer as we work our way aft."

Several of the cadets, even the human ones, blinked questioningly at each other, but no one seemed to know what he intended and he decided it was best to explain.

"First chance, after we're past about where that big hunk o' junk fell on the flight deck, we'll go up top. Fight them boogers in the open when they find us. *You* will, anyway," he added cryptically. He slapped Earl Lanier on the shoulder. "We got other plans."

Earl goggled at him. "We do?"

Silva grinned. "Sure. Me an' Larry'll need somebody who knows their way around a tub like this, an' you're it. Besides, you may be a disgustin' slob that can't cook a pickle, but I know you can fight. I seen you do that before too." He looked at Kaik. "Your job's to get Pam, Mr. Bradford, an' all these kiddies back to the ship. Slide 'em down off the flight deck over the fantail, then haul ass." He held up a finger. "Leave the rope, though."

All the cadets surged toward him. "We want to go with you, help you," said Susan Raj.

Silva's expression changed, hardened. "No way," he barked, then his tone, at least, softened a little. "You gotta help Sergeant Kaik pertect Mr. Bradford and . . ." He sent an almost pleading glance at Pam. "An' her."

"You have to take at least one of us," Philan Bele insisted. "At this moment, we stand in the stead of every cadet on this mission. If something happens to you and none of them were even represented, how could we ever face them? Why are we even here?" he pressed, then took a deep breath. "What is the purpose of teaching us to flee when we need to learn when to fight?"

Lawrence made a throat-clearing noise. When Silva looked at his friend, he saw him flick his eyes at Earl. "Us could use a extra hand. Just in case."

Silva frowned. "Fine." He looked at Bele and poked him in the chest with a finger. "You'll do. You're . . . the tallest." He looked at the others. "Now, no more shit, you hear? You do like Sergeant Kaik says."

Just getting over the elevator was difficult. Not only was it canted because of all the crushed aircraft underneath, more wreckage had piled atop its sliding leading edge, creating a maze in what had become a kind of valley where it met the hangar deck bulkhead. That meant they had to creep along the steep slope above it. The 'Cats had little trouble, their innate sense of balance and peculiarly shaped feet giving them an advantage, but the humans were reduced to scooting along on their butts. "I'd recommend we take off our shoes," Courtney said, "but the grain of the wooden decking, though scorched, has been rather alarmingly raised."

"It's full of splinters, he means," Pam translated. "Doesn't matter. We'll be over it in a minute an' would just have to put 'em back on. Too much sharp junk everywhere, an' the last thing we need is cut feet slowin' us down." They actually used the underside of the wing of one of the bigger planes, flipped upside down, to slide off the elevator and onto the sharply leaning deck. The steel was coated with something like what had been done to improve traction on *Walker*'s decks, and they moved more swiftly in the darkening space among largely intact planes that had been firmly secured. Surprising and somewhat disconcerting were the numerous bombs and torpedoes strapped on pallets and secured among the aircraft. Courtney was fascinated by this.

"Clearly, they were equally interested in discovering whether the heat or pressure generated by an atom bomb would result in sympathetic detonations. Apparently not."

"Seems not," Silva said, looking at all the ordnance mingled with the aircraft as they wove their way through. "Damn shame, an' not just the planes. I'd love ta take one o' them fish apart," he added.

"What?" Pam asked. "Why's that a shame?"

Silva just looked at her and shook his head before nodding farther aft in the gloom, where an intact companionway obviously went all the way up to the flight deck or perhaps one of the antiaircraft gun positions alongside it, since there was no other reason for it. "I think that's where you get off, doll."

"What're you gonna do?" she asked lowly, not to be heard, but Silva caught the real worry in her voice.

He blinked with surprise, then shrugged. "What I do," he replied simply. "Just get yer fine ass the hell off this ship as fast as you can." He paused and gave her his signature lopsided gap-tooth grin, peeling Petey from around his neck and holding him out.

"No! No!" Petey shrieked, gaping at Pam in abject terror, digging his claws into Silva's arm.

"Ow! Dammit! Belay that shit!" Silva gave Pam a sheepish look and said, "I know you hate his guts, but you won't let the little bastard get killed on purpose. Take him with ya, will ya?" Pam's eyes filled with tears as she took the little monster and put him on her shoulder, where he settled in with a suspicious sidelong gaze. Then she moved to embrace the big man, but he'd already turned and started striding farther aft. The dull roar of the terrifying natives took on a new intensity and a different, more resonant quality. Silva shouted at Kaik, "Them boogers're fixin' ta get in, if they ain't already. Take our people out, Sergeant."

Kaik blinked agreement and started herding his charges toward the companionway.

Courtney called back, "Whatever it is you mean to do, Chief Silva, try not to make too much of a mess."

"No sweat, Mr. Bradford," he replied. "I'll do my best." Lowering his voice, he caught Earl by the arm. "Now," he almost hissed, "best you remember, if a fella was to set a hellacious big fire in this dump, what's the best way ta do it . . . an' maybe still get out?"

"Shit Dennis! What the hell? How should I know? I'm a *cook*!"

"Keep yer voice down! Yer a shitty cook, but you ain't stupid. Yer bound to've had a thought er two over the years besides fishin' an' ruinin' food. Why, *I* ain't never been on a ship—'cept maybe *Walker*—I didn't ponder on blowin' up."

"That's 'cause he's crazy," Lawrence commented, matter-of-fact.

"But all these planes? All the things here . . . we can't *destroy* it all," Philan Bele objected.

Silva looked at the tall cadet. "We'll never save any o' this stuff. We're pullin' out, right? Maybe there's more on the transports. We been more worried about gettin' 'em goin' than doin' a inventory. Don't matter. I'd rather burn everything up than let the goddamn Leaguers get it." He nodded in the direction of the Grik-like swarm; some were obviously inside now, hooting and snarling nervously like they were hesitant to continue. They were probably wondering where their prey had gone as well. That wouldn't last. "Besides," Silva said, upper lip curled, "we never done a thing to them bastards an' they killed one o' ours. I wanna get even."

"Even?" Earl snorted. "Shit."

Bele was confused. "But . . . we've already killed a lot more of them—"

"'E'en' is . . . di'rent to Dennis," said Lawrence as Earl reluctantly led them aft into what were evidently the aviation workshops. "E'en is . . . 'equal' to us, right?" Bele gave a hesitant nod and Lawrence shook his toothy snout from side to side. "Not to Dennis. He likes . . . *extra* equal."

"Whaat the hell is going on over there?" Tabby murmured to the lookout who'd summoned her to the port bridgewing, taking the offered binoculars.

"A fight," the young Impie told her. "I thought I heard shooting earlier, but the wind is picking up and it was indistinct. I couldn't really *see* anything either."

Tabby was gazing through the binoculars now and saw a *lot* of the

Grik-like natives swirling around the port side of what had become the forward part of the huge wreck. Even despite the bright orange between the black stripes on their feathery fur, they still somehow blended well enough she wasn't sure she'd see them even now if there weren't so many moving so swiftly. Still . . . "In the future, when on lookout duty or not, you'll report whaatever you *think* you see or hear whether you caan identify it or not, understood?" Turning, Tabby called out to the bridge talker. "Sound 'general quaarters.'" Jack Meek, Gunny Horn, and the rest of the detail helping train new gunners had reported back aboard shortly before. Horn and Meek had both been bound back for *Texas*, and it was only luck that either was present. "Messenger, go down to the comm shaack and raadio Caap-tain Rodriguez on *Texas*: 'Shore paarty is under attaack by a laarge force of locals and I believe they haave taken refuge inside the wreck they went to investigate. I am preparing to open fire on the maassing locals now.' Send it at once and get a reply."

The messenger finished scribbling and bolted for the ladder aft, and Tabby strode over to speak into the shipwide circuit just as the alarm began sounding. She much preferred the bugler, but *Walker* only had one and he was over on *Texas* too. "Generaal quaarters, generaal quaarters. This is the XO." She paused, realizing this was the first time she'd ever given the following order other than at drill. She'd never given it when she was in charge. "All haands, maan your battle stations. This is not a drill. Our people ashore seem to haave pissed someone off. Staand by for surfaace action, port."

The thunder of running feet sounded from all over the ship, the loudest from behind as the fire control team raced up the ladder alongside the chart house to the fire control platform above. Gunny Horn paused and looked at her, standing aside as a pair of cadets rushed past him with belts of ammunition for the .30 caliber guns up top. "When do we shoot?" Horn asked.

"As soon as I get word from the skipper," Tabby told him, "or we see for *sure* thaat our people are in trouble. Honestly, I bet they are and I won't wait long for the word. Even so, you might haave to do some careful shooting." She took a breath. "Are the gun's crews ready for thaat?"

Horn pursed his lips. "Yeah. I mean, I sure hope so."

Tabby stepped back out on the bridgewing. "Whaat's haappening?"

"They—the enemy—are definitely trying to board the big wreck and seem very insistent on doing so."

"XO!" cried the talker, another Impie but female. "Foremast lookout in the crow's nest says . . ." Her eyes went wide. "Says *canoes* are putting off from every beach he can see, all around the anchorage! Hundreds of them, with eight or ten locals in each. They"—the girl caught her breath—"all appear armed and act as if they're rowing out to attack us!"

For an instant, Tabby could only stare. Then she shook her head and called for another messenger. "Tell Mr. Meek to add this for Caap-tain Rodriguez, if he hasn't already seen for himself: 'The natives appear to be launching a large-scale attaack against all of us.' Must've been getting it ready for days, creepin' down through the deadfaall and we never haad a clue. I doubt they intended to do it now, though. They were probably waiting for daark." She looked back at shore. "Whaat are the chaances Chief Silva kicked over a grimmil hive? Pretty fair, I guess."

"Grimmils" were very much like hornets, only bigger. They didn't sting, but their big vicious mandibles could take a bloody plug out of a victim and an annoyed, determined swarm could be lethal.

The wind carried sounds of sudden heavy firing from the big Japanese cruiser. They clearly had no doubt about the intentions of the locals in canoes. They'd fought them before. *Shonai*'s fire at the closest ones would be masked by *Nevada*, but the grounded battleship had some machine guns mounted shoreward. "All stations report 'manned and ready,'" the talker said, then responded to a signal from the comm shack and switched the circuit to her earphones. "Comm says Captain Rodriguez replies that we are weapons free."

"Very well," Tabby said. Horn hadn't waited for word, but it was just as easy for her to step out on the bridgewing and call up to him. "We're weapons free, Mr. Horn," she told the man leaning over the rail to look at her. "You maay commence firing!"

"Already targeted, XO," Horn called back, motioning at the cadets on the gun director. The complicated machine could calculate a wide array of variables based on the input estimations of course—range, speed, etc.—and communicate the solution to all guns. With *Walker* and her primary target both essentially stationary, her range finder—notoriously unstable at speed—would offer fairly precise information for once, and all the gun director had to provide was range and target-center solutions. Few of the sudden swarm of canoes were in range of the ship's machine guns yet. "Match pointers," Horn instructed his own talker, who repeated the command to the ship's three 4″-50s that would bear.

"On target!" chorused both the pointer and trainer on Samuel Jenks's number two gun on the port side of the amidships deckhouse. Unlike when they were firing in local control, they weren't gazing through telescopic sights, but at the dials near the cranks they used to adjust the weapon's windage and elevation. The salvo buzzer rang and young Jenks shouted, "Fire!" The pointer, Maarik-Fas (sitting on a life jacket), stomped her foot on the trigger. There was just the slightest hesitation before the ship's gyro decided *Walker* was on a perfectly even keel and allowed the circuits to all guns to close. *Wham!* Three 4″ naval rifles spat flame, gray smoke, and a trio of bright red, converging, and only slightly arcing tracers at the milling Grik-like mob attempting to swarm aboard the shattered *Saratoga*. Gouts of dark smoke, earth, and shattered tree trunks erupted among them, barely a mile and a half away, blended with mangled weapons and body parts.

"No change, no change. Commence rapid fire!" cried Jenks as the breech slammed open and the empty brass shell arced back to clang on the deck.

Another young female 'Cat with thick gloves, the "hot shell man," scooped up the shell and threw it in a big basket. (Not only did the empties need to be saved for reuse, they had to be kept out from underfoot.) A burly male Lemurian, new on the guns, slammed a fresh shell in the breech.

"On target!" confirmed the pointer and trainer, having checked to make sure their setting hadn't been changed by the gun's recoil.

"Fire!" yelled Jenks.

Tabby was watching through binoculars on the bridgewing as salvos slammed out every seven or eight seconds, buffeting her with the overpressure and churning the ground to port of the wreck with high explosive "common" shells. A single massive cloud of smoke, dust, and splinters was suspended all over and around the target. After two minutes and more than forty rounds, she shouted up at Gunny Horn to cease firing and *Walker*'s guns abruptly fell silent.

"We're not securing," Horn called down. It wasn't a question.

"Neg-aative. I'm trying to see whaat we've done!" Tabby replied. "Staand by." The dust and smoke was drifting away from the wreck, and a charnel field of shattered timber and steaming gore was gradually revealed. Tabby felt the gorge rise in her throat and gulped. They hadn't hit the wreck that she could see, and a lot of the natives closest to it looked wounded or confused, but many were still trying to clamber aboard. Whether still chasing her people or trying to find cover from the bombardment, she didn't know. That's when she saw shapes, human and 'Cat, sliding down a pair of lines from within a gun tub on an antiaircraft platform alongside the very aft end of the flight deck. Her breath caught. Even with her superior vision, enhanced by binoculars, it was difficult to identify anyone, but Courtney Bradford was distinctive in his ridiculously wide-brimmed hat. "They're getting out!" she called triumphantly. "I don't know how maany, but some at least are escaping from within the wreck." She frowned, noting a growing stream of black smoke starting to pour up out of the front of the wreck and the gaping rectangular hole where one of the ship's elevators had been. She also saw a growing number of the Grik-like locals boiling up on the flight deck as well, scurrying aft as fast as they could. "Maybe we hit the thing after all," she mused. "There seems to be an internal fire . . ." Movement drew her attention back to the smashed and cratered area by the wreck, and her blood chilled at the sight of it filling back up with countless sprinting natives. It was as if they just materialized out of the deadfall and tall grass. "Resume firing, same target!" she shouted up at Gunny Horn. "How maany of those daamn critters haave sneaked up on us?" she asked herself.

"Aye, aye, XO," Horn replied but pointed. "A bunch of those log boats're getting close enough that we might want to put fire on them."

Tabby nodded. She couldn't really imagine the Grik-like creatures in canoes doing much to threaten them, especially since they weren't making much effort to mass. *They seem pretty confident with those spears, though*, she conceded. Those could hurt her people if they got close enough. "Very well. Have the machine guns open fire at convenient targets. Resume firing the main battery," she repeated.

The salvo buzzer rang.

With a bellowed obscenity, Earl Lanier fired a sustained burst from his Thompson through an open hatch forward into what he'd remembered as the "dope shop," though he didn't know why they called it that. It was full of machines and jigs with some re-covered aircraft control surfaces scattered around. He and Lawrence were in what he was sure was the engine testing shop, the very last compartment in the ship, one level up from the hangar deck. Stepping back, Lawrence replaced him for an instant and fired his Allin/Silva rifle. A shriek pierced the growing smoke in the dope shop.

"Where the hell are those two idiots!" Earl shouted, replacing his magazine and firing again. "I bet they run off an' left us!"

"They did not," Lawrence scolded him harshly. "Dennis is an asshole," he conceded. "He's a *good* asshole, though, and no co'ard. 'Hat kind o' asshole are you?"

"Smart-ass lizard," Earl grumped, then spun to look behind them at a noise.

Smoke was gushing up from a companionway behind them, and Philan Bele clanked and coughed up the steel steps, just a greasy, dusty rag wrapped around his face.

Silva pushed up behind him. "We gotta scram," he barked hoarsely.

"What did you do?" Earl demanded, firing back through the hatch. A pair of spears flew through and crashed against more machinery.

"I set a fire, dumbass. Like I said."

"We're gonna choke on the smoke," Earl growled, nodding back at the swelling stream rising from where they came from.

"Nah," Silva denied and coughed. "Most of it'll go forward. Forward's up, right?" He shook his head. "We'll get blown to hell *long* before we choke."

"Shit," Earl hissed. "How'd I get roped into this detail? You didn't even take my advice about what to do!"

"I *sorta* did," Silva denied, "but mainly I didn't want yer fat ass slowin' everybody else down. Now shut that hatch an' dog it. We've drawn enough attention an' they think we're trapped. Let's go."

"Where?"

Silva pointed at the overhead. "Up."

Earl slammed the hatch and spun the wheel while Lawence wrenched the latch levers in place, leaving the space in near total darkness. The only reason it wasn't complete was the growing red glow from below. Young Bele was coughing constantly now, and Silva was glad they didn't have a 'Cat with them. For some reason, Lemurians were extra susceptible to oxygen deprivation. So was Lawrence, for that matter, but he seemed okay at the moment.

"C'mon," Silva said, groping his way aft. "This ladder goes up to a hatch, right on the bulkhead. Hope I can open it," he said with a lurid grin. "There ain't gonna be much air up there, even if I do. It'll suck all this smoke out the hole. So don't start up until I get through, got it?"

Even Lawrence was coughing now, eyes streaming, but they all nodded. Silva bolted up the ladder to a little rounded hatch barely bigger than a porthole and started wrenching on a wheel in the center. The thing wouldn't turn and he redoubled his efforts, teeth clenched, eye closed, hot smoke burning his nose. With a roaring curse, he gave it every last ounce of his strength, and the wheel finally spun with a crackle of breaking paint. That's when it dawned on him the hatch probably hadn't been opened since the ship was built. Turning the wheel more easily, lungs bursting from holding his breath, the hatch finally popped open. He'd been right. As soon as he did, the smoke in the compartment practically hosed out past him, and the glow down below got brighter. *Uh-oh*, he thought, squirming out and onto an antiaircraft platform. Gasping in relatively clean air, he stuck his head back in the hatch. "Let's go! Earl's last."

"Why am I last?" came the indignant shout.

Silva hesitated, then decided to tell the truth. "It's a *little* hole, Earl. Can't risk you stoppin' it up, an' it might need all of us ta pull you through."

Silva was right. He and Lawrence and Bele did ultimately manage to jerk Earl past the lip of the hatch, but he'd have bruises all over his torso and might've even cracked some ribs. As they sat gasping and coughing together in the bottom of a gun tub, their short rest and refreshment was rudely interrupted when a pair of tiger-striped locals, naked versions of Lawrence, jumped down at them, stabbing with spears. Only the weird angle of the deck probably saved them, making their attackers misjudge their targets and stumble when they landed. Bele shot one of them almost instantly and the creature toppled over the rail with a scream. Silva kicked savagely at the other's ankle, creating a sickening *pop-snap!* sound, and the thing dropped down on its side. That's when it finally appeared to notice Lawrence, and its eyes and jaws went wide, but Lawrence stabbed it in the chest without hesitation with the cutlass he'd swiftly drawn. It made a keening sound as the blade sank deep, then raspingly jabbered something in its own tongue before blood surged out of its mouth and it lay still.

"Huh," said Lawrence, blinking his wide yellow eyes. "Did you hear that?" he asked Silva.

"Sure did," Silva said, shrugging, as he popped up over the edge of the flight deck. "Next!" he shouted, then glanced at Lawrence. "Some kinda Grikish gibberish. Greek to me." He chuckled. A spear skated off the flight deck and bounced over his head. "Woops. Guess they thought I was serious. More of 'em comin'!" He paused. "There's a *shitload* o' lizards up here."

Shells whistled in and started exploding where it was obvious many others already had. "That's the style, *Walker*!" Silva cried gleefully. "Them skunks're hunkerin' down. Let's git!"

"This must be the same place the others went down," Bele said. "Two lines are secured to the rail over there."

"Right." Silva waved. "Take off, cadet, but look before you leap," he warned. "Slide on down if it's clear. Can you manage that, Earl? You go next."

"I can do it!" Earl snapped irritably, yelling over the falling shells and explosions.

"Swap guns with him, Larry," Silva told his friend. "We'll need that Tommy gun."

"Perhaps I should—" Bele began, but Silva shook his head.

"I'm fixin' ta *throw* you off. No time for jawin'."

Bele jerked a wide-eyed nod, grasped the line, and dropped out of view. Earl went next, with a lot of grunting and wincing. Finally, it was down to just Silva and Lawrence, and both opened fire, though they barely heard their own weapons over the roar of the bombardment from the ship. Grik-like natives fell and slid or tumbled off the steeply sloping flight deck. Their claws gave them better traction than Silva's party had enjoyed, however, and many kept coming.

"Dennis!" Lawrence shouted in Silva's ear and gestured with his snout at the creature he'd killed. "Greek to you, 'ut *I* understood he."

"No shit?" Silva called back before firing another burst from his BAR. A handful of monsters crashed to the deck.

"I understood *exactly*," Lawrence stressed, "like they're *Tagranesi*. I think I could *talk* to they!" Originally hailing from the tsunami-drowned island of Tagran, Lawrence and his few hundred surviving tribal relatives called themselves Sa'aarans now, having been given a place to live on the Filpin Lands island of Samar.

"Fascinatin'," Silva replied irritably, "but kinfolk er not, they're tryin' ta murder us. Another minute an' you can yarn all ya want with 'em. We've bowled 'em over for a second, so we gotta go *now*!"

"Okay." Lawrence nodded and inserted another magazine in the Thompson. "You go, then I go."

Silva hesitated an instant, then nodded. "Sure, pal. Don't fool around." Giving Lawrence a pat on the back, he slung the BAR and crab-walked to the dangling lines, avoiding a couple more spears. With a last shout at Lawrence to hurry, he practically jumped the rail, snagged the line with his hands, and locked it between his shoes, braking his slide as he descended. Hitting the ground about fifty feet below, he found Philan Bele alertly guarding the line. "Where's Earl?"

"I suggested he start for the boat." Bele gave a tentative smile. "He *is* rather slow."

"Good thinkin'." Silva looked up to see Lawrence peering down at them, smoke from the hatch billowing out beyond him, but to Silva's absolute shock, his friend simply waved as if shooing him away—or saying farewell—and dropped the Thompson. He was gone before the weapon hit the ground butt-first and fell over in the grass. "What the . . . ? *Larry!* What the hell? *Get your stripey ass down here!*"

"What's happening, Chief Silva?" Philan Bele anxiously asked.

"No clue," Silva snarled back. "Larry! Goddammit!" he bellowed. "You're gonna *burn*, you stupid shit!" To his horror and anguish, the rail above was suddenly lined with local lizards, which immediately started launching spears down at them. One barely missed Bele, and Silva sent a burst from his BAR at the rail. The assailants fell back, and slinging the heavy weapon, Silva reached for the nearest dangling line.

"What are you doing?" Bele demanded.

"I'm goin' ta *get* his crazy ass! Cover me while I climb back up!"

"No!" Bele cried, grabbing his arm. "If they're already past him, you can't help!" Silva effortlessly flicked the tall cadet off him and the youngster fell heavily against a fallen tree trunk. He quickly jumped back up, however. "Fine!" Bele shouted. "I'll cover your climb, but you'll just die for nothing when you get there." He pointed at where the shells were still falling with tight dispersion but close enough to rain dust and splinters around them. Grik-like warriors on this side of the impacts were starting to flood their direction as well, scampering over the deadfall. "Then I and all the others still waiting at the boat will likely be killed before we can escape," he went on relentlessly.

Face twisted with a mix of fury and grief, his one eye streaming, Silva saw that Bele was right. A spear slashed down close enough to cut the side of one of his boondockers. "Shit!" he thundered, emptying his BAR at the rail again. "Let's git," he added ferociously, but with a hint of helpless resignation. "Get his weapon." Bele scooped up the Thompson and they ran, pursued by more throwing spears.

"I never doubted Larry'd get killed someday," Silva panted as they scampered swiftly over the tops of dead trees. "Both of us," he added. "I just never figgered he'd go so *stupid*," he seethed. Climbing over another heap of deadfall, they finally saw the boat, and both were surprised to see their comrades, even Pam, shooting at a large cluster of natives racing at them along the beach. Silva had reloaded his BAR as they ran, and he planted his feet in the sand and fired a hammering burst into the attackers, bowling many down. Bele fired as well, short bursts at survivors that appeared startled by their sudden isolation. The rest of the enemy paused momentarily and Silva barked, "Run!"

The tide was coming in and the whaleboat was already floating, some of the defenders standing in water up to their knees. Silva felt an unaccustomed thrill of terror for them and himself since the lapping waves were already deep enough for the voracious fish. "Get in the boat!" he shouted, firing another burst at the natives. A couple of the cadets were already aboard and one, at least, looked wounded. The rest splashed over and hurled themselves in, resuming their fire when they could. Pam and Sergeant Kaik leaped into the bow and held out their hands as Silva and Bele splashed up to them, tossing their weapons over the gunwale and leaping aboard themselves. Silva fell hard, hurting his shoulder, but then swiftly stood, retrieved the BAR, and worked his way aft. One of the cadets had already started the motor and it was burbling contentedly as Silva engaged the drive. Empty magazines and a rain of brass shell casings were dropping in the water and the whaleboat as it arced away from the beach before Silva threw the shaft into neutral and engaged the forward drive, slamming the throttle to the stop. A handful of spears pursued them from the surviving attackers, but only one came particularly close, plunging down in the boat and punching through the bottom, standing like a short spindly mast with a thin stream of water jetting past it. For the first time, Silva looked up at the stern half of USS *Saratoga* from a distance, where he could see the whole thing once more.

Dark smoke was gushing from every orifice now, particularly from the gaping elevator void and up forward where, pinched off or not, the hangar deck was still technically open. It was coming from other places too, like countless sprung plates along the length of the hull that made the whole thing look like a split smoldering log. Pam gasped when roiling orange flames belched out where the elevator had been and a stream of fire seemed to squirt through the tiny hatch the late arrivals left open on the port quarter. Some of the dugout canoes on the water were making for them now, but *Walker* had ceased firing her main battery and was engaging them with machine guns, white geysers leaping up all around them.

"Where's Lawrence?" Pam suddenly demanded, looking around the boat. Silva said nothing, watching one of the canoes get smothered by lead and spray. Bele pursed his lips and shook his head at Pam.

Courtney stepped unsteadily aft and plopped next to Silva. He'd lost his hat, and his wispy gray hair was sweat-plastered to his skull. "Lawrence is gone?" he asked gently.

That's when far more violent things began happening inside *Saratoga*. A great internal blast bulged the starboard side of the hull, throwing heavy steel plates in the sky. Moments later, the explosions redoubled, wracking the great hulk until the side of the hangar deck blew out and a large portion of the deck itself flipped up in the air and smashed down on itself.

"My God, Chief Silva. What did you do?" Courtney asked quietly.

Silva grunted and replied, voice flat. "Tell a fella where to find aviation gasoline, fuel oil, bombs, torpedoes, freakin' *rockets* . . . it's amazin' what he can do with a Zippo." A momentous blast erupted then, blowing the whole wreck wide open under a towering column of smoke, scattering flaming debris for a shocking distance and setting fire to the deadfall all around. Silva looked at Courtney, his eye red and full. "What did I *do*, Mr. Bradford?" He turned back to the destruction he'd wrought. "I blew up my best friend, that's what."

CHAPTER 24

The uncoordinated broad-daylight dugout attack didn't last much longer, obviously doomed from the start to even the most fanatical participants. Most started turning back after *Saratoga* began blasting herself apart, the thundering explosions reverberating around the broad bowl-like anchorage, and those that did were allowed to retreat. Fighting around *Shonai* and *Nevada* lasted longer, both ships being stationary and close to shore. And the Japanese on the cruiser, having fought these creatures wherever they went, were somewhat less forgiving or willing to let their tormentors retire in peace. Even they stopped shooting when their enemy reached shore. They only had so much ammunition, after all, and the creatures that made it to shore swiftly vanished more easily than anyone thought possible.

"How do they *do* that?" Captain Ronson Rodriguez asked himself out loud. He'd stayed aboard *Texas* throughout the weird fight, prepared to direct her defense, but despite how close she was to shore as well, she hadn't drawn much attention.

"I bet they got tunnels. Not just through them dead trees, but creepy holes down in the dirt," Isak Reuben wheezed through the stream of cigarette smoke he spewed. He'd been chain-smoking the things filled with his own reeking brand of tobacco from Aryaal. He and his half brother Gilbert and the 'Cat they called "Pepper" were the first to figure out how to smoke the waxy leaves that grew there. Their initial brisk business was undermined by the discovery of how they did it, however (they used "brontosarry" piss as a solvent for the wax), and the recent availability of better tobacco had hammered the demand for PIGcigs even harder. Isak probably didn't like them himself, but still used them out of sheer mulishness and maybe in remembrance of Gilbert. "Boogers prob'ly grub around underground like moles," he speculated.

Ronson gave him a thoughtful glance. No matter how strange he was, Isak wasn't stupid, and that was actually possible. Some Grik along the Zambezi River lived in holes burrowed in the bank. "Well, they're gone or going now, wherever it is. We need to keep on our toes, especially tonight. That's when Tabby thinks they were preparing to hit us, but"—he waved southeast at the roaring wreck in the distance, heavy detonations still torturing the increasingly shapeless hulk—"whatever happened with Silva's and Mr. Bradford's landing party set 'em off early." He frowned. "Word from *Walker* is that *most* of the landing party is on its way back. Looks like they had casualties."

"'Course they did, with that damn Silva along!" Isak exclaimed, shaking his head. "Not even sayin' he's to blame, but he's *gonna* find trouble if any's there. Fact o' nature."

Ronson didn't comment. Isak was being simplistic, but wasn't necessarily wrong. "I'm going back to *Walker*. See what's what. You stay here and keep working. I'll send Gunny Horn back to stay, most likely, with some of the auxiliary sailors who've been training on secondaries, but Sureen's going back to *Walker* with me. You're the engineering officer aboard here now. I want those clean boilers lit off. If you manage that, how soon before we can get this fat tub underway?"

Isak was obviously disappointed that Sureen was leaving but screwed his weaselly face into his usual "thinking expression." "*If* we get steam, I guess we can test her engines with the people we got aboard. Might get another boiler by tomorrow too. She'll need a bigger crew to move her, though. *Way* bigger to try to fight her at all."

"I know," Ronson agreed. "Like I said, the auxiliaries will give us twenty people each for the transports and leave about a hundred more for *Texas*." He held up a hand. "And that's leaving the auxiliary *ships* here, which hasn't made me popular." He waved around. "I know, still not enough to fight her. Not properly."

"Not even close," Isak griped.

"No. I'm taking *Walker* over to *Shonai* to talk to Captain Okabe. See how many more of her people we can count on."

"More Japs," Isak grumbled unhappily.

"I hope so—and so do you," Ronson said. "You know what the Leaguers may have coming at us and how much time we have to get gone or be ready for them. Days at best, but maybe only hours."

Isak nodded with a scowl.

"Anyway, we'll start the transfer of ships outside the bay immediately. It's time, and some won't even wait, like the LST pulling the pigboats and the transports hauling the tin cans and that poor cruiser. I want them *gone* right now." He looked around at the shore and saw nothing moving at present. "But today . . . that weird attack has only made me even more anxious to get the hell out of this spooky damn place." He seemed to shake himself. "It might feel less like a ghost fleet now, with some of the ships coming back to life. Especially when you raise steam in this tub. But it'll always feel like a graveyard because of the ones we have to leave. Graveyards always gave me the creeps—and this one has real monsters in it. I'm not looking forward to dark."

Dennis Silva stood on *Walker*'s fo'c'sle, just to starboard of her number one gun, watching the resurrected assault transport USS *Fillmore* steam slowly west into a red setting sun beyond the gaping mouth of the flooded crater. Trailing along behind her like a baby duck was the slightly battered silhouette of a Benton Class destroyer, USS *Rhind* (DD-404). Both were following in the wake of USS *Niagara*, which had taken the Sims Class USS *Hughes* (DD-410) in tow. Silva was personally amazed that the new skippers of those transports—a pair of 'Cats from Baalkpan who'd gently grounded their former commands before taking over the operation of such massive and unfamiliar vessels—hadn't run them into anything on the way out. Even more concerning, neither had ever towed anything either. Ronson had plotted their courses to Respite Island to be as unchallenging as possible, and each destroyer had a skeleton crew aboard to manually adjust the steering if necessary. It was still a risk, and all had standing orders to abandon the destroyers and cut them loose if the weather turned bad.

Silva moodily spit a stream of tobacco juice over the side, figuring it was only proper they should focus on saving destroyers first. The battered cruiser *Salt Lake City* would depart behind the transport USS *Banner* in the morning, and the two pigboats they'd selected for salvage, USS *Parche* and USS *Dentuda*, were supposed to be towed in tandem by the already heavily laden LST-661. "That's gonna be a goose pull," he muttered to himself. A fourth transport, USS *Dawson*, which they'd determined was barely a couple years old and almost untouched by the blast, had been made operational and would be retained to tow *Nagato*. That would leave both *Walker* and *Shonai* unfettered. "Ronson must'a listened to young Bele about tyin' *Walker* off to some giant sea anchor target," he mused lowly.

Philan Bele heard and wondered if that was true. He was sitting on the deck by the gun with Fen and Maarik-Fas, having surreptitiously shadowed the big destroyerman almost since they came back aboard. The only time he hadn't been under their observation was when he and Courtney and Sergeant Kaik went to speak with Captain Rodriguez when he returned. Since then, a lot had happened. Isak raised steam in USS *Texas* and, after testing her engines and mooring gear, called to report. They'd all seen the smoke rising from the rusty battleship's funnel and there'd been some muted cheering. Ronson went back aboard her and, perhaps encouraged by how her pilothouse was virtually identical to tiny *Walker*'s, even in size, decided to move her closer to the rest of their labors. With just those aboard, he raised her anchors and conned her very slowly over in the vicinity of *Nagato*. There, he triumphantly dropped a massive anchor once more and then stepped out on her bridgewing with rubbery legs and shakily shook out a smoke.

Already alongside *Shonai* by then, *Walker* hadn't done much else that day, and Silva just stood there and watched—while Bele, Fen, and Maarik watched him, excused from other duties by the XO, who saw what they were doing and said, "Just keep an eye on him." She'd paused and added cryptically, "But stay out of reach. He'd never hurt a kid, not in his right mind, but the Maker only knows whaat he's capable of when he isn't."

But that's where they were when Pam stepped out on the fo'c'sle under the sunset and walked over to stand beside Silva. Reaching out, she gently put her hand on his arm by his elbow. He didn't react, but he didn't pull away. "I'm sorry, Dennis," she said very softly. After a long moment, he seemed to sag slightly, all the tension that kept him standing so stiffly flowing out.

"Yeah," he rumbled as if the word came from deep in his throat, part grunt. Slowly, he looked at her. "Where's Petey?" he asked. "You didn't murder 'eem, didja?"

Pam chuckled lowly. "No. Earl fed him half to death, though. He's asleep on that disgusting apron Earl shouldn't be allowed to wear when he's cooking."

"Nearly lost Earl today too." Silva snorted. "Again."

"I know."

Silva nodded out at *Texas*, now riding at anchor with a few surviving lights lit. A blower was rumbling, sucking air for a boiler like she was alive and breathing. "Larry would'a been tickled ta see that. He's always wondered how we think o' *things* as bein' alive. Watchin' her come ta life today . . . why, it gave me a chill. I think he would'a finally been convinced. Maybe understood, at least."

Pam nodded, cocking her head to the side near his arm. "She *is* kinda beautiful," she conceded. "I mean, not like a destroyer, of course"—she gave a tentative smile—"but in a no-nonsense, bash her way through whatever it takes to beat the hell out of ya sort of way." She gave his big arm a squeeze. "Like you, Dennis. That ship ain't really pretty, but she's beautiful for what she can do—what she's capable of doin' for the people we care for. *That's* how she reminds me most of you."

Silva snorted. "I couldn't even—"

Pam slapped his arm hard. "Lay off that crap, that self-pityin' *bullshit*. That ain't you. Lawrence was a great friend. He would'a died for you . . ." She paused. "Maybe he did, who knows? But he did what he did *on purpose*, an' you couldn't stop him. One thing, though, if you didn't do what *you* did, an' then show up at the beach *right when we needed you most*, me an' the whole rest of the shore party would be dead. Period." She turned and looked at Bele and his friends and spoke to them. "I won't forget who was with you—an' us—either. Go on along, you guys, an' thanks. I got 'the duty' now. Get some chow."

Everyone remained on edge, expecting another attack by the locals, but with all the ongoing salvage efforts and preparations consolidated roughly on the northeast side of the anchorage, nighttime security was easier to maintain, especially with *Walker*'s and *Shonai*'s searchlights scanning the water and shore all around. Even *Texas* added a searchlight, and once warped over closer alongside *Nagato*, one of her massive boat cranes was able to help clear debris from the deck of the much bigger Japanese battleship. *Nagato* really was a "piece of junk" in the sense that she had a lot of damage that apparently predated the bomb test, and it was doubtful she'd managed to position herself for it under her own power. She'd never leave that way either, the Japanese engineers themselves having pronounced her boilers beyond realistic repair. But her armor and massive 16" guns were intact, and a dry dock could fix all the leaks that portable pumps were coping with now. She'd be another useful addition to the Allied fleet someday—and just the fact that the League wanted her was sufficient motivation to save her themselves.

Silva stayed on the fo'c'sle all night, sitting on deck and leaning back against the front of the bridge structure, BAR in his lap. Pam remained with him until called away to help tend to the inevitable injuries caused by cutting and moving heavy jagged steel or welding necessary reinforcement for sagging structures. Philan Bele, Susan Raj, Sam Jenks, Dan Baker, Haan-Ara, Fen, even Courtney, Horn, and Abel Cook, drifted by alone or in pairs to sit with Silva awhile. Earl Lanier brought him a stack of sandwiches and dropped a sleepy Petey on his shoulder, calling him a "maniac freak." They didn't come out of pity or worry anymore once Pam declared he'd be "fine," but just to show him he still had friends and people who admired and cared about him. That's what he needed. Silva never had many real friends, never cared to until he came to this world. He hadn't "cared" about much of anything, in fact. Now he did, and despite how he acted, some thought it possible he cared almost *too much* about certain people, things, even ideas. His devotion to the Navy Clan, the Grand Alliance in general, and Matt Reddy in particular, ruled his life like a religion. Pam might still accuse him of "romping through life like a giant lethal wolf puppy," and that probably wasn't far off the mark, but he was a crazy loyal puppy to his master and his pack. He finally slept for a while, his and Petey's sated snores blending strangely.

He woke to the roar of a Nancy engine at full throttle and opened his eye to see Fred and Kari's plane skimming across the water and taking to the sky. Rising swiftly, it burst from the shadows cast by the eastern slope of the mountain and flashed into the sunlight of dawn. Waggling its wings in a lighthearted farewell, it kept climbing as it banked slowly around to the east. Looking to the side, Silva saw Pam had rejoined him at some point, tired enough to sleep through the takeoff. Stretching, he stood, then reached down to put a hand on her shoulder. She looked so peaceful, almost childlike in sleep, no tension in her pretty face. "Wake up, doll," he said gently.

Pam's eyes opened and she smiled up at him, bringing bittersweet memories of better times between them. "It's mornin'?" she murmured muzzily.

Gesturing at the brightening day, he grinned. "As you can see. C'mon, let's get you fed."

"They never sounded morning GQ," she objected, as if that meant morning was impossible.

"We been at condition three all night. Ever'body's so tired, I guess they decided to let them that could sleep get what they could. Fred took off a minute ago, prob'ly had Aalak in the back seat."

"How do you know it wasn't Kari?" Pam asked.

Silva chuckled. "She's always too busy flyin' ta wave so long."

"Yeah." Pam raised her hand and Silva pulled her to her feet. Just then, the general quarters alarm aboard *Shonai* sounded and she sent *Walker* a shriek on her horn to get her attention.

Silva blinked. "I wonder what that's about?"

"No tellin'," Pam replied, "but the way she's situated, with her high superstructure, she can see past *Nevada* better than us. I bet it's somethin' over there, onshore."

"Say, I bet you're right. C'mon." Silva led Pam through the forward superstructure hatch on the starboard side and through the open space beyond alongside the comm shack. Mounting the ladder, he climbed up past the signal flag locker and strode into the pilothouse across the wooden deck strakes. "Permission ta come on the bridge?" he asked Tabby, who noted his and Pam's arrival.

"Sure," she said, then grinned. "Since when did you ever aask?"

Silva shrugged. "What's up?"

Captain Rodriguez came up behind them, eyes bleary, coffee in hand. He nodded at Silva and Pam and then looked at Tabby expectantly. Tabby said, "Good morning, Skipper. Sorry you got woke up. We're waitin' for *Shonai*'s report on the TBS." She indicated Jack Meek, standing in the talker's usual place, wearing the headset.

He held up a hand, listening, then said, "Something . . . screwy, as you say. Seems a large number of locals have assembled onshore in the vicinity of the League stockade." He blinked. "They're flying a white flag," he said as if he didn't believe it. "How the devil . . . ?"

"Only two possibilities I can think of," Ronson said. "Either the Leaguers onshore suggested it, though I can't imagine why, or . . ." He looked at Silva while trying to smooth out his pillow-disordered mustache. "Did you actually *see* Lawrence get killed?"

"No, but . . ." Silva clamped his mouth shut.

Ronson turned to Meek. "Ask our Japanese . . . friends"—he blinked and grinned—"not to fire on the lizards ashore unless they begin hostile behavior. We have reason to believe their apparent desire for a parley is real." He looked at Tabby. "Pass the word for Mr. Bradford. Is Mr. Cook on board? Good. Him too. We'll go aboard *Nevada*, where there's a decent security detail, and invite the locals to meet us there."

CHAPTER 25

This is so weird," Silva said aside to Abel Cook. "Us an' them critters was doin' our best, all out, ta kill every one o' each other just yesterday. Now there they are, maybe *two thousand* of 'em, peaceable as can be, not a weapon in sight." Captain Rodriguez, Silva, Abel, Courtney, Sergeant Kaik, and young Fen had gathered on *Nevada*'s port quarter by the accommodation ladder with Captain Okabe and Lieutenants Chiba, Mihara, and Nakao, as well as a handful of armed enlisted personnel. They were fairly well protected, however. More gunners had clambered aboard *Nevada* to man her portside secondaries, and *Walker* and *Shonai* had repositioned themselves to better cover the throng ashore. Still, the only reason Fen was there was in case he recognized any Leaguers that might come aboard. They didn't.

Only two canoes set out from shore with eight or so locals apiece. All were naked in the usual fashion, but most wore some sort of feathery headdress accentuating their natural dark crests. Some had strange jewelry composed largely of bones: necklaces, armbands, or even woven into the dark plumage on their short tails. One was vigorously waving what looked like a dingy (and possibly bloody) undershirt.

Silva was straining his eye, but if Lawrence was among them, he couldn't tell. "They all look the *same*," he complained to Abel.

They managed to secure their canoes efficiently enough (no one waited to help them below on the confining platform) and filed out of their vessels and up the ladder, spreading out slightly on deck. A couple were carrying fairly large furry leather bags. Only then did Silva realize one of the tiger-striped "locals" without any headdress or jewelry was also bound around the abdomen with what looked like very soft leather. This creature took a step forward, rendered an awkward salute to Captain Rodriguez, then opened its mouth and spoke: "Gunner's 'ate La'rence, sir, and delegates o' the Rarorani ruler, Sashakara, request your okay to co' a'oard."

Ronson returned the salute and smiled. "You gave us quite a scare, sailor." His eyes flicked at Silva. "Some more than most. I assume you're here of your own free will and vouch for these . . . other visitors?"

"I do, sir."

Ronson nodded. "Permission granted."

When Lawrence dropped his salute and nothing violent happened, there seemed to be a general relaxation among the creatures accompanying him.

"I swear, Larry," Silva growled, "I don't know whether ta beat ya to death or hug ya—you squeaky little skink."

"Sorry I scared you," Lawrence said seriously. "I scared *I* a *lot*. I think it's a good thing, though. You'll see."

"I'm sure of it!" Courtney exclaimed. "You've clearly negotiated a truce of sorts with these savage monsters."

Lawrence nodded briskly. "These"—he gestured at the collection of "monsters" that looked just like him—"these are so like Tagranesi—like closer than cousins to La'rence—us understand each other exactly. Their attacks on us"—he dipped his snout at the Japanese officers—"and you, in all the islands, is due to a rotten, cruel . . . un-understanding, caused using lies told to they . . . through the League."

"Why am I not surprised?" Ronson breathed.

Lawrence proceeded to relate a strange tale in his somewhat disjointed English that essentially confirmed all they knew and much they suspected. The only real surprise was how thoroughly the League had suborned the Rarorani and, to a lesser extent, the Gintarra—which truly did seem to be the same race the Allies knew as Gentaa. Courtney immediately got sidetracked, however, wondering if Lawrence's Tagranesi were descended from Rarorani or the other way around, and then gleefully speculated the same about the Gentaa and Gintarra, but Ronson got impatient and Captain Okabe firmly redirected the questioning to more pertinent issues.

"If we survive long enough, you may satisfy your curiosity about everything else at your leisure, Mr. Bradford," Okabe gently scolded.

Courtney's face reddened. "Of course," he conceded.

Lawrence went on, occasionally consulting one of the Rarorani he called Chee ("Chief") Houk, who was wearing an extra-large headdress.

As he told it, the League first arrived on the "big island" of Raror (which Courtney still wanted to call Caprona) about eighty crescent moons before—or forty months, according to Lawrence. He'd once reckoned time the same way when he was a Tagranesi. The first to come was a small ship they said looked a lot like *Walker*, with four "smoking pipes." The humans in her, the first the Rarorani or Gintarra had seen in tens of hundreds of crescent moons, were armed with magic weapons like those used against the Rarorani the day before, so they could not be easily eaten. (Lawrence was asked to confirm this description, which he did.) Unable to destroy them, the Rarorani determined to befriend the invaders, who were soon joined by a "fat stinking ship with one smoke pipe"—an oiler, it seemed—that aided the humans in establishing a modest facility in a fine harbor. The locals commenced trading labor, protection, food, timber, and "rocks," they said, for metal, "smart words" (which probably meant technology), and "magic weapon" assistance dealing with large marauding monsters. Soon, they were all great friends.

The League presence got bigger over time, the harbor and settlement more extensive, and then came the biggest ships any locals ever saw until the calamity that occurred here. Before that, however, it seems that *Shonai* made her appearance. The locals initially thought they were the same folk they'd been dealing with. They obviously looked and talked different, but they were humans and controlled a huge iron ship. The Gintarra and some tribes of Rarorani greeted them as friends, at first. It was only after their League benefactors told them these new visitors were evil enemies who engaged in terrible and unnatural practices (Lawrence wouldn't describe those) and had to be driven away that all the Rarorani and Gintarra made war on them. The League would only trade metal with and promise not to "eat" real friends who shared their enemies.

Courtney spoke up at this point in the narrative, expressing doubt that Leaguers actually ate their enemies, but Lawrence explained that was a near universal practice in these islands, perhaps even the very definition of war to its various races. One's enemies were those that they ate. In any event, all that tracked with Okabe's account of their relations with the locals from the start.

It was after the cataclysm on this island, one of the holiest to the Rarorani, if not the Gintarra, that the League personnel on Raror told their clients that their enemies on *Shonai*—and elsewhere—were responsible for all the death and destruction accompanying the dreadful event and any strangers who came to take away the evil ships that desecrated the sacred isle had to be stopped. The Leaguers themselves benevolently swore to cleanse the isle of its intruding monstrosities, showering their friends and allies with "much metal" and possibly even magic weapons with which they could fight each other. (This seemed to confirm the Rarorani and Gintarra, possibly other races, were prone to "eating" one another as well.) Thus was the prevailing situation when *Walker* steamed into the anchorage and drove off the League "cleansers" working here. Confusing at a glance, but actually fairly straightforward.

"An' you told yer pals different?" Silva asked Lawrence.

"Yes," he concurred. "They nearly kill I"—he gestured at the supple wrap around his abdomen—"so I talked *really* hurry!"

"I bet." Ronson nodded.

"They thought all Tagranesi cousins are dead. I told they, 'Not all,' and those that didn't die are now 'Sa'aarans,' sheltered and cared and li'ing in the lands o' those the Rarorani are trying to kill." He gave his version of an amused snort. "Rarorani not . . . delighted to hear they are lied to. *Not* delighted they side along Leaguers that lie to get they to kill guardians o' last Tagranesi."

"So . . . we lost some people, that kid with us—a couple others hurt—and more when Miles went ashore," Silva growled. "An' they can't be tickled about how many of 'em *we* killed." He arched the brow over his good eye. "I expect we got a heap of 'em—though maybe not as many as I figgered at first if they got you clear before the ol' *Sara* blew."

Lawrence shook his head. "I told they it is going to . . . do that and got a lot a'ay. That actually aided I to get their trust. They are sad, 'ut know the deaths are not our doing. Is their error and they are sorry they attacked us. All that died—us, they—is due to League lies. All Rarorani on our side to 'eat' Leaguers 'ith us."

"Eat?" Petey tentatively chirped. He lived in a constant vague state of fear of Lawrence, and with so many creatures like him so close, he'd remained very still, avoiding their attention. Mere terror wasn't enough to prevent a reaction to his favorite word, however. Silva negligently thumped him on the head and ignored him.

"Obviously, we won't be 'eating' anyone," Courtney scoffed, "but that begs the question of what they've done with the rest of the Leaguers that were here. Have they told you that?"

Lawrence spoke to Chief Houk and then gestured at the furry sacks some of the Rarorani were holding. Jabbering among themselves, they unceremoniously dumped out eleven severed heads that thumped and rolled on the deck. There were a few gasps of surprise and disgust, but no one embarrassed themselves. "They ate they," Lawrence said matter-of-factly. "*I* didn't," he swiftly, piously assured everyone.

"Shit," Silva grumped, lightly kicking one of the heads, "I would'a asked 'em some hard questions."

"I did that," Lawrence assured. "I tell all I know." He hesitated. "Good news, not-good news."

"Cadet Fen," Ronson said, slightly surprised the young Lemurian hadn't recoiled from the grisly sight. "Do you recognize any of these . . . ?"

Tail whipping, Fen stepped forward and peered at each head, reorienting a couple with his shoe. "Perhaaps one or two were mutineers on USS *Scott*, but the worst, Mr. Ames, isn't here. He's still out there somewhere." He looked up at Lawrence, blinking angrily. "But whaat of *their* prisoners? We understaand your . . . friends also ate some of them." He waved at *Scott*'s charred wreck in the shallows. "Whaat haappened to the prisoners off thaat ship?"

Lawrence spoke with Chief Houk at some length, both gesturing quite a bit. Finally, Lawrence turned to report. "Us already knew they didn't eat *all* the hostages. Leaguers took *Allied Na'y* sailors to their anchorage on Raror."

"But who did they *count* as 'Navy sailors'?" Abel mused aloud.

"Quite," Courtney agreed. "*Scott* was the only Navy ship here, a reserve auxiliary at that." He glanced at Fen. "Most of her crew were civilians. Let's hope the enemy didn't make such distinctions."

"Chee Houk is sorry he can't tell us all us 'ant to know. He trusts it console us that *all* hostages they ate are . . . tastier than Leaguers."

Fen snarled and stepped forward. So did Silva and even two of the Japanese lieutenants.

"Hold! Hold!" Lawrence insisted. "Is another un-understanding. To they, it's an *honor* to taste good."

"Damn, Larry! You think like that too? You never told me that," Silva grumbled, pulling Fen back.

"Not I," Lawrence denied. "Tagranesi didn't eat ene'ies." He cocked his head to the side. "O' course, Tagranesi didn't ha' ene'ies. Didn't e'en know Rarorani any'ore. I think the only reason Rarorani still know Tagranesi is 'cause there's a *lot* o' they."

"Enough to keep histories, it seems," mused Abel Cook.

Lawrence pointed at him and nodded vigorously. "Right," he said. "Not e'er lots o' Tagranesi."

"Well, *I* damn sure don't wanna taste good," Silva declared. "Anybody eats me, I hope they choke an' die in agony."

"I'm sure they will, Chief Silva," Ronson said wryly.

"The point is," Courtney interjected, "if they *did* eat our people, they're sorry. More importantly, at least while we're preparing to depart, we no longer need fear them and might even enlist their aid in various pursuits." He seemed to be thinking, tapping his lip. "They might be quite useful indeed," he finally said, tone firming.

"For what?" Silva grumped, but Courtney ignored him.

"My dear Lawrence, would you kindly inquire whether your kinsman Chief Houk might be willing to help us *get rid* of the League in these lands?"

"I'll ask," Lawrence said.

Ronson questioned Courtney. "What're you thinking? Turn them loose against the League base? That's swell, but it'll sure get a lot of them killed."

"That, certainly, but perhaps more as well—doing something only slightly less risky, but which might be infinitely more useful." He smiled and blinked before adding, "Like helping to man our ships."

"What?" Silva barked. "What a load . . ." He stopped himself, then looked at Ronson. "Shorthanded as we are, what do we need more than anything to help fight our ships? Like *Texas*, most of all?"

"People," Ronson carefully replied.

"Yeah! An' mostly nontechnical people, right? Shell handlers, hoist operators, lotsa hands to move powder bags. Snipes too, but mostly doin' stuff anybody can under supervision. Ain't that so?"

"I see where you're going," Ronson acknowledged, "but just a bunch more bodies running around and getting in the way won't help."

"If we're in a runnin' fight, haulin' ass—which is what we been expectin'. But what if we do somethin' *they* ain't expectin'?"

Abel Cook cleared his throat. "Between the League prisoners we took and likely direct observations by the locals, we should be able to put together a fairly complete picture of the League anchorage and facilities on the big island."

"That an' other stuff," Silva agreed, looking at Fen. "Like where they're keepin' our people." He grinned. "Let's go *get* 'em!"

There was a stunned silence, and Silva pressed on. "Goddammit, I'm tired o' creepin' around, takin' whatever the League throws at us. I *guarantee* Cap'n Reddy is too, stuck in the Azores while the League throws its weight around out here. In *our* backyard! Let's shake things up. These Ro-ro-annies know right where they are, they can throw powder bags around, an' we know they ain't scared of a fight. Let's quit scurryin' around gettin' ready to run, waitin' for what the Leaguers do to us. Let's go do somethin' to *them*!"

Okabe had looked surprised, skeptical, then increasingly intrigued.

Ronson slowly began to nod as well, eyes casting about the grounded battleship they stood on. A ship, like many others still in the anchorage, that he *really* didn't want to leave for the Leaguers—or destroy. "A lot of potential for Keystone Kops chaos," Ronson said, seeming to object, "and there's no way to teach Lawrence's new lizard pals to be real battleship sailors in a day or two—to cope with engineering issues or properly deal with damage control . . . but we *can* teach 'em things like you said, I bet." He nodded at Courtney. "Especially if we have them doing it on all three of our ships: *Walker*, *Shonai*, and *Texas*, while trained personnel supervise and do what they can't." He looked around and confessed, "I've been a timid idiot, thrown back on my heels from the start. Ever since my school ship mission turned into something . . ." He shook his head and patted Fen on the shoulder. "Way beyond me, is what. But Cadet Bele was right. These kids know what they're doin' now, at least as well as others their age had to during the war. Better." He dipped his head at Captain Okabe. "It goes without saying for your crew. If we've got the time and catch a break for once, we can do this!" He grinned at Silva. "Y'know, this might not wind up the stupidest idea you've ever come up with."

Silva chuckled. "Thanks, Skipper." He nodded around, even at the Rarorani. "But it seems to me it just sorta oozed out of ever'body all at once. Maybe because it's what we all been naturally wantin' ta do from the start."

"We need a plan," suggested Lieutenant Mihara.

Silva rolled his eyes. "Plans're for shit an' drop in the pot faster than it takes to make 'em."

"That is quite often true," agreed Captain Okabe, "and is certainly the case the more complicated the plan starts out," he added bitterly, as if remembering a specific example. He looked at Ronson Rodriguez. "But we must agree on our overall objectives at least, and who and which of our ships will be responsible for what—and where—so we are at least best prepared to act appropriately when"—he nodded solemnly at Silva—"the *details* 'fall in the pot.'"

Ronson took a deep breath and released it. "This might all be moot, depending on the results of Fred and Aalak's morning scout. Nothing we can do if the League squadron's already on the way. Even if it isn't, we have to act quick." Twisting his mustache, he looked at Lawrence. "No point in getting ahead of ourselves either. Lawrence? Can you ask your new friends if they're willing for some of their number to . . . join the American Navy Clan?"

"We'll need some for the Marines as well," Abel Cook proposed, making Sergeant Kaik blink rapidly in horror. "Landing some of them will be the quickest way to alert the natives around the enemy facilities to the new . . . arrangement between our peoples," he explained to the Lemurian Marine, "and I believe Chief Silva's part of the plan, to rescue our people in captivity, will require a substantial force onshore."

Silva huffed. "If the landin' party's gonna be my rice bowl, best let me decide how 'substantial' it is." He looked at Kaik. "But Mr. Cook's right. We're gonna need some of 'em, at least, if we don't wanna be fightin' lizards an' Leaguers both."

Lawrence had been talking with Chief Houk and a couple of the others with ornamental headdresses. Now he got Ronson's attention. "The Rarorani cannot consult their ruler Sashakara on such short notice, yet are certain she'll enthusiastically endorse this undertaking. She doesn't like Leaguers any'ay. These"—he gestured at his companions—"are honored to join us. Use all their 'arriors us need."

CHAPTER 26

Fred and Aalak returned and landed on the water later that day, reporting no enemy movement, at least for as far as they went. They did confirm an interesting feature of the "main" island that *Shonai* had missed on her initial, perhaps understandably less than comprehensive coastal survey and that might be of use to their new ambitions. Raror itself wasn't a single huge island after all, not anymore at least, and was split by a generally north-south deep-water fissure or channel, the southern opening of which had been concealed from *Shonai*'s passing observation by a long, imposing clutter of rather strange islands that Fred described as "big, mossy, turtlebacks" from the air. They didn't follow the "Slot" all the way to its northern entrance/exit—"whichever you want to call it," Fred told them. It was a *big* island, he reminded, and too far out of the way for the flight he'd been tasked to take. He was confident a complete passage existed however, since the 'Slot' had clearly been scoured by a significant current over the ages. This was easily confirmed by the "locals" now, once they thought to ask them, of course. Captain Okabe promptly dispatched one of his own planes to examine the feature more closely and he, Ronson, and Courtney Bradford put it in their pocket, for now.

Fred and Aalak had flown almost as far as the enemy outpost. It *was* barely in range for the little Nancy, but they couldn't risk the Leaguers knowing their position had been identified. And now that they had the support of the locals, they could rely on Lawrence translating their description of the layout. (This process was an eye-opener. Not only did the Rarorani have an understanding of maps, they proceeded to confidently draw the islands and coastlines, reinforcing their status as competent mariners.) Courtney had said they had to be if they were willing to venture to sea in their tiny canoes. The very idea of that gave Silva and others the creeps—paddling along in a vessel just the right size for a top-water lure to tempt many of the local aquatic denizens. A couple of the Rarorani "chiefs" had actually been to the League station itself and described its orientation and defenses quite well. Silva, Kaik, Ian Miles, and Abel Cook were building a rough plan for their part of the operation based on that.

Meanwhile, even as the last operational transport, USS *Dawson*, took the battered *Nagato* in tow, heaving its dark bloodred carcass around, and began plodding westward under the scorching afternoon sun, USS *Walker*, USS *Texas*, and IJN *Shonai* were frantically making preparations to get underway themselves. It turned out that a handful of cadets and auxiliary sailors understood a smattering of "Grikish," which was similar enough to the local tongue to share a few terms and concepts. Along with the liberal use of sign language, they could sometimes make themselves understood. Lawrence was still run ragged, doing his best to be everywhere while gaggles of Rarorani were turned over to various chiefs and divisions on the ships, struggling to swiftly instruct the recruits in their new duties.

"I bet you would'a just let 'em eat ya if you knew what a pain in the ass this'd be," Silva hooted at Lawrence when he brought another score of locals aboard *Texas*, where Silva had come over to help Gunny Horn figure out the final touches on what they could do about the ship's fire control set up.

"No, I not," an agitated, harried Lawrence denied, missing Silva's humor.

"Where're you takin' 'em?"

"Handling roo's"

"Rooms? Okay, scram. I hope you have better luck than me an' Arnie." Lawrence jerked a nod and herded his new charges below. Silva gestured upward, and he and Arnold Horn and some cadets they'd chosen to assist them mounted the first of many ladders they'd take to reach the dizzying foremast "fighting top" high above the forward superstructure. The primary gun directors for the main and secondary batteries were there, the mighty 14"-45s and 5"-51s, but with the windows smashed out, they'd been exposed to the weather for quite a while. Most of the effort so far had been devoted to shooing out hordes of savage and combative lizardbirds and cleaning out their nests, then tenderly resuscitating wildly complicated director machinery. Left until now, a lot of the wiring insulation had been cooked by the heat of the blast and turned into what looked like brittle woven char-cloth, and many of the terminals were corroded.

And once they succeeded in bringing the directors to life (if they did), the whole marvelous apparatus available would be little better than the primitive fire control arrangement on USS *Walker* because they had no idea how the ship's more modern refinements operated, or if they were even entirely *present*. They'd determined *Texas* had indeed been equipped with radar-guided fire control, but not only did they have no clue how it worked, there were a number of suspicious places on the deck and bulkheads of the fighting top where it looked like important-sized gizmos had been unbolted and removed. Twisted, corroded, forlorn-looking wires dangled like probing roots. That made them hesitant to even try to power some of the stuff up before someone—Steve Riggs in particular—had a look at it, fearing they'd screw up whatever was left.

Then there was the "plot room" deep in the hull, in what had once been a fireroom when the old battleship had more boilers and burned coal. There was a dead reckoning tracer (DRT), table, stable element mechanism, some ancient rangekeepers—fire control computers—and electrical panels for all the guns, even secondaries. These should work with the available gun directors in the foretop if the wiring remained intact. More modern rangekeepers and gun directors might've once been in there as well, but were even more obviously gone. The nagging question that remained was whether the older, apparently "backup" equipment was still in the circuit and capable of communicating with the five big gunhouses.

Huffing from their climb, they passed the flag bridge, pilothouse, and fire control platform (where directors for the ship's largely missing antiaircraft weaponry would've been) and kept going up the center ladder into the lower level of the structure itself.

"Whew," Silva gasped, breathing hard and looking around, out the big broken windows. "Helluva view." It was. Horn had visited here frequently, but this was the highest Silva had been. The different angle gave him a new appreciation of the scope of the massive flooded crater, its surrounding walls, and of course the number of vessels still floating within its confines. He took a long breath. "Our scheme better work," he said. "Too much stuff here just to leave or sink. It'd go a long way to evenin' the odds with those fascist League bastards."

They became aware of a roaring noise aft, like a blower winding up, and then felt as well as heard a loud hollow *bong*. A dense plume of black smoke gushed up from the funnel and the wind carried it directly at them. In seconds, they were coughing and sputtering in thick dark soot streaming through the windowless structure.

"Goddamn mousy little snipe!" Silva ranted. "That Isak just blew tubes all over us. Must'a known we were up here an' did it on purpose too!"

One of the 'Cat cadets was shaking his head. "Not just blowed tubes," he said, *kakking* a Republic Lemurian laugh. "I bet Chief Isak 'haard lit' the third boiler. Cleaned it out as best he could, then lit it off. Burnable gaas not all clear from uptake . . ." He grinned. "Big boom. But I bet we got another boiler!"

"Dumbass," Silva coughed. "Like as not, he ruptured the uptake an' *none* o' the boilers'll draw worth a damn."

Due to his inability to make certain sounds, it was hard for Lawrence to speak English without coming off as just a little dopey, but he was much better spoken in his own language, even "Grikish," and didn't have to think as far ahead to phrase things understandably. His native Tagranesi was slightly different from Rarorani, but not as much as one might expect. That's why the recruits he was roaring at down in the powder handling room of USS *Texas*'s number two turret understood him perfectly.

"Which one of you just *took a shit* down here?" he demanded incredulously. The smell was quite distinct. A young Rarorani with a short crest hesitantly pushed himself forward. "I looked for a better place," he defended, "but there is no grass, no dirt. I found a corner . . . Where are we *supposed* to go? Do humans not shit?"

"Of course they do, in specific places!"

"Where? You didn't show us."

"I *did*!" Lawrence insisted. "Those seats over the metal trench with water flowing in it."

"We can't sit on those!" a different Rarorani objected.

"I thought they drink there," said another.

"You move the board seats and crouch," Lawrence snapped, "like I showed you."

"I couldn't hold it anymore," complained the original miscreant.

"You will now! You'll go *get* that turd and *carry* it to the place I showed you and throw it in." They all waited a moment while the perpetrator grimly retrieved a pair of hard dark objects and, crest lying flat in humiliation, disappeared the way they came. "Now pay attention!" Lawrence commanded, opening a hatch and stepping into a space filled with large metal cylinders. "This is a ''owder' room in this ''agazine' and each of those 'canisters' holds two ''owder' bags." Since there weren't equivalent Rarorani words for some of the things he described, he was forced to name them in English as best he could.

"What is 'canisters'?" asked one recruit.

"All those things in here!" Lawrence snapped shortly.

"What is ''owder'?" asked another.

Lawrence considered that, frankly still a little unsure himself. He knew his people, now Sa'aarans, made various types of gunpowder in the Filpin Lands, but he'd never watched them do it. "It's the . . . food for the magic fire that throws the great . . . spears out of the mighty 'guns' above us," he ad-libbed. "You will be in here, removing the bags—there are two in each canister—and carrying them to this device, this 'scuttle' in the wall." He wasn't going to call it a 'bulkhead' since he couldn't even say it right himself. Of course, he couldn't say 'powder' or 'magazine' right either . . . This was going to be hard.

"Lots of new words. That's a 'scuttle,'" one recruit whispered to the others as if he'd named it himself.

Lawrence activated a lever and the thing produced a heavy clank before he raised a lid up above it. "A loud noise will sound, and you each put a 'owder bag in here, one at a time," he said. "They are quite heavy," he added. "The noise tells you those on the other side are ready for the bag." He shut the lid and rotated the scuttle before stepping back through the hatch. Waiting until the students joined him, he lifted a lever opening another heavy lid, exposing where the bag would now be. "You or someone else in here then take the 'owder bag"—he took a few steps and indicated a platform at the bottom of a long, semi-enclosed cylinder leading up—"to this hoist, which lifts it up to the gunhouse for you."

"Hoist," murmured a recruit, his tone almost reverential.

Lawrence closed his eyes for a moment and took a deep breath before gesturing around. "All this . . . big iron will move around as the guns are aimed from side to side, so this hoist might be elsewhere when you reach it, and it takes *four* bags to load each of the two great guns . . ." He paused, gazing at all the wide eyes. "You will see a demonstration and others will correct your mistakes, but it's not as complicated as you seem to think—or as I may have described it."

"All this iron . . . *moves*?" one of the Rarorani almost whispered.

"I have a question," another said, pointing back at the hatch. "If the bags are so heavy and we must move so many, why not just bring them through there instead of pushing them through that thing in the wall?"

"No, no," Lawrence said. "That 'hatch' in the wall must remain shut at all times during action." He thought for a moment, then asked, "How many of you saw the great ship on the shore explode?"

All indicated they had.

"Good. If you're in there"—Lawrence tilted his snout back into the magazine—"and open that hatch during battle, without orders, the same thing will happen to this ship and all of you in it."

Wide-eyed expressions were exchanged all around. "It will be hot in there," one said softly.

"Yes," Lawrence agreed. "Learn your duties obediently and well, *do not* shit on the deck, and pray the magic 'owder doesn't get loose and make it hotter still." He sighed. "A detail will be down to work with you soon. Touch *nothing*. I have another group like you waiting in the 'shell.'" He caught the confused expressions that he alone of any of his friends would notice. "The gigantic . . . ah, spearpoints the magic powder spits from the great guns. Each is heavier than one of your largest canoes, so be thankful you are here and not there," he added by way of farewell.

"It sounds like this kind of fighting is more about moving heavy things than facing our enemies," a Rarorani warrior complained.

Lawrence paused, nodding. "It often is, for some. And when giant *enemy* spearpoints you can't even see are coming back, hitting your ship, it can take *far more courage* to keep moving heavy things than it does to watch them come. Don't make me a liar. Prove that you have it."

It was dusk by the time Silva and Horn clomped down from the fighting top, having repaired all the bad connections they could find, replaced a number of wires from spools brought up, and confirmed restored communication and firing circuits from the gun directors in the top to and through the rangekeepers down in the plot room, and all five 14"-45 gunhouses. With power restored, they even tested the ability of the main battery to match the directions they sent, the great gunhouses traversing from side to side, their massive rifles elevating and depressing to match their input. Stuff *seemed* to be operating better than they'd nervously expected. They—Gunny Horn in particular, who once again found himself acting gunnery officer of a battleship—would have to rely on primitive range finders and his own estimates of target distance, course, and speed for initial salvos, but he hoped the remaining fire control apparatus in the ship was sufficient to rapidly compensate and correct fire based on his observations and subsequent input.

"It's all held together with baling wire, gum, and hopeful thoughts, and a whole bunch of wires dangling down independent of the conduits before they're tied back in." Horn sighed. "But it's still a helluva lot better than what I had to work with in *Savoie*. Farther and better visibility too." He shook his head. "I need beer."

"Me too, but there ain't none aboard here," Silva commiserated as the two waved the helpful cadets along and paused beside a lonely dual-purpose 3″-50 antiaircraft gun on the main deck over the ship's casemate, where her big 5″-51 secondaries lurked. Humans, 'Cats, and a few Rarorani shell and powder handlers were drilling on those, and shouted commands rose up to them. "I hate ta leave ya, ol' buddy," Silva finally confessed. "Seems like, the last few years, we always get split up in a scrap."

Horn was nodding. "Seems like. And I'm a *Marine*, dammit. I'd much rather be toting a weapon ashore with you."

Silva chuckled. "It *is* kinda ironical. I'm always doin' *your* job, off wadin' in amongst 'em on dry land, while yer fightin' a ship on the water—all on account o' you spendin' a hitch on this ol' tub's sister, *New York* . . . what? A decade ago now?"

"A bit more than that," Horn conceded. I didn't like it much then either." He frowned. "I wish we could keep Lawrence. We're gonna have more of his weird, scary friends roaming around *Texas* than anywhere else—and no way to talk to them."

"After thinkin' the dumb shit was dead, I wish he was stayin' here too, but we're liable ta need him even more ashore."

"Dumb Shit Lawrence," Petey abruptly awoke to proclaim. The little tree-gliding reptile had worn himself out, gleefully launching himself out of the smashed windows of the fighting top, soaring around snapping at lizardbirds before using the exhaust gasses rising from the funnel to loft himself back into the rumpled structure. Twice, he'd been chased by things bigger than he was and had to dive down and take cover before climbing back up high enough to jump in the hot exhaust once more. That left him sleepy—and hungry—and Silva only got him to quit shrieking "Eat!" by promising to feed him as soon as they got back to *Walker*, and threatening to pitch him in the water if he didn't shut up.

"They decide who's gonna skipper this tub?" Silva asked Abel Cook as the young man strode up to join them.

"They didn't tell you?" Abel asked innocently.

"No, dammit," Horn said. "We didn't go into that kind of detail while we were cooking up our cockeyed scheme." He gestured at Silva, then upward. "We've been sorta busy since."

Abel grinned. "Then you'll be pleased to know that *Mr. Bradford* has consented to take command of this ship."

"Oh God," Silva moaned.

"You forget that Mr. Bradford was briefly an *admiral* in the Navy of the Republic of Real People," Abel scolded lightly, "commanding a *squadron* of their 'battlecruisers,' which were each"—he paused, looking thoughtfully around—"almost half as big as this thing."

"He prob'ly conned a toy duck in a tub once too," Silva snorted.

Abel laughed. "Never fear. Lieutenant Daanis will actually command. He has some experience with larger ships and I'm told one of the Japanese officers will be his XO, ready to assist him in that respect, as well as advising him on maneuvers in battle. But Mr. Bradford has authority over any . . . strategic aspects of this mission and he does have experience with that." He pointed at Silva. "And giving him that responsibility was the only way to keep him from going ashore with you."

"Oh." Silva chewed on that a moment. "So why're you here?"

"I brought the whaleboat to get you, Lawrence, and a few of the cadets we're going to need aboard *Walker*." He hauled his Impie-made watch out of his pocket and glanced at the hands, which were barely visible in the failing light. "For better or worse, we get underway in about forty minutes."

CHAPTER 27

USS *Walker* was first to steam out of the strange anchorage in which she'd resided for weeks, moving slowly and as gently as possible past a host of bobbing Rarorani canoes festooned with torches, marking the deepest channel. No one had asked them to do that, but it was certainly appreciated. Once in open water, Ronson commenced a leisurely search pattern, not because he expected to find anything, but in order to wait for the other ships in their bizarre task force. *Shonai* cleared the anchorage next, steaming in a wide circle to the south, then east. Her distinctive silhouette with four gunhouses forward, ahead of her flowing pagoda-like superstructure, was just visible under the bright stars and waning crescent sliver of a moon. USS *Texas* came out last, her war and atomic test scars invisible in the darkness and her blockier, bulkier silhouette equally distinctive in an entirely different way. She was noticeably shorter than *Shonai*, but just as obviously more massive, churning instead of slicing up a growing phosphorescent bow wave as her two big screws pounded the sea to increase her speed to twelve knots—about the best she could do on only three boilers.

They steamed like this generally southeast for a while, swinging wide around the south coast of the island while monitoring the bigger ships' machinery for any undiscovered issues related to their long sedentary existence to manifest themselves. No doubt there were a number of these, but nothing incapacitating arose and *Walker* was finally released to sprint ahead, due east, all four boilers lit and surging through the mild, warm sea at thirty-one knots.

Silva, Pam, Lawrence, Ian Miles, Fen, Abel, Lieutenant Chiba, and Sergeant Kaik were on the aft deckhouse gazing astern while the crew of the number four gun put their weapon through its paces, responding to Carl Bashear's commands from the gun director on the fire control platform.

"I wonder if we'll ever see them again," Pam said, nodding aft. Only the utter darkness where their shapes blocked the stars and the phosphorescent wakes betrayed the presence of the mighty ships quickly dropping back behind them now.

"Sure, doll," Silva said. Then he chuckled. "Hope so, anyway. *If* our act is a hit, an' *if* the charts Chiba and Larry put together with the help of our Raro-ranni pals are close ta right, an' *if*—"

"No more 'ifs,' if you please, Chief Silva," Abel urged a little impatiently.

"Sure, Mr. Cook," Silva amiably agreed. He looked back at Pam. "They'll be right where we want 'em when we need 'em," he piously declared, "an' we'll see 'em right before the enemy does." He grinned. "Last thing the Leaguers'll ever see, though."

"If," Abel conceded himself.

"That's right, Mr. Cook." Silva nodded. "That's the trouble with plans. Ever' single thing you prepare for in advance has a whole raft o' 'ifs' smeared all over it—an' that's before the enemy starts pitchin' more of 'em at it by the double handful."

"You would prefer to just make everything up as you go?" Lieutenant Chiba challenged.

Silva seemed to consider that. "For my part, yeah. Our part," he revised. "Always seems ta work just as well. An' since we don't really know shit about this League settlement aside from roughly where some o' the buildins are, we *have* to adjust what we do based on what we find. Can't even send Fred an' Kari flyin' over for a look before we go." He held up his hand, looking at Fen, who was blinking worriedly at him. "That said, me an' Larry an' even Pam've done this sorta thing before. So has Miles, for that matter. I know Sergeant Kaik's more used to big stand-up fights, but he didn't last as long as he did in the First Marines out'a luck." Silva arched a brow. "You neither, Mr. Cook." He patted Fen on the head. "An' this little guy, well . . ." He grinned. "We'll be fine."

In spite of the charts being largely confirmed by landmarks as they steamed east through the night and following day, the Rarorani didn't have a good grasp of "miles," so they had to extrapolate distances based on what the Japanese had marked on the chart. Using that as a baseline, the League base was estimated to be about a hundred miles farther up the coast from where *Shonai* made her first attempt at a settlement, and that was fairly well established at roughly five hundred miles from the ghost fleet at Fen's Island. Lieutenant Chiba identified the place with a high degree of certainty during the midafternoon. It was almost entirely overgrown and reclaimed by the surrounding forest, but the cluster of small islands offshore from the mainland confirmed it. These were unusually desolate rocky monoliths jutting straight up out of the sea and surrounded by clouds of lizardbirds.

There'd been quite a few of these little islands all along the coast, and increasingly more of the weird "mossy turtleback" sort Fred and Aalak reported toward evening, which posed a serious hazard to high-speed nighttime navigation. It was easier to understand how *Shonai* had missed the entrance to the Slot, forced to steam farther from the mainland. Those aboard *Walker* never saw it either, passing wide around it to the south in the dark. But Chiba's calculations tracked well enough with native descriptions to make him fairly certain of their position, and Captain Rodriguez slowed their advance to arrive near the League outpost as near to midnight as possible.

That's when the Rarorani members of their expedition who'd been here before had to take over. Even in near perfect darkness, stars hidden by pregnant clouds and what little was left of the moon already below the horizon, they excitedly and confidently guided them, through Lawrence, to a beach just a couple miles short of the enemy anchorage. Dark as a tomb, *Walker* hove to and lowered both her motor launches into the water about two hundred yards from where the phosphorescent surf rolled up on the shore. She'd pull away a couple more miles before launching both her aircraft at the appropriate time.

"Be careful, Mr. Cook," Ronson told Abel, who was theoretically in overall command of the landing party, as he shook the young officer's hand. There was no doubt his admonishment was directed at all of them and undoubtedly Silva in particular, though he probably accepted that Silva and Pam would both likely do pretty much as they pleased. Lawrence was in charge of the dozen Rarorani, of course, and Miles was responsible for the "Marines," made up of Sergeant Kaik, six of *Walker*'s "old hands" and ten of the most promising cadets. The inclusion of the latter had required Philan Bele to repeat his earlier argument, and Ronson was rather lamely reduced to complaining that too many members of the ship's gun's crews were going on the raid.

"That's why we train everybody on every position, Skipper," Silva said reasonably. "Backups can handle what you'll need 'em to do, an' we'll have these other kiddies back on the ship before the job gets complicated enough for the first string." Now, with a nod at Ronson and the other dark shapes gathered around, he slung his "happy sack" full of hand grenades and the Thompson he'd "borrowed back" from Earl when he dropped Petey off with the cook again and slid down the falls into the starboard-side launch. Pam came down last, as usual, and cadets made space for her and her medical bag. "So long," Silva called up. "We'll be back for mornin' chow, so don't let Earl sweat or spit in the akka eggs."

With the engine burbling, Silva steered the launch around the rolling destroyer to join the boat waiting to port. Together, they made their way through the light rollers, and it wasn't long before they scrunched ashore in the sand. Silva and the cox'n of the other launch, a black-and-gray-furred Lemurian called "Hazy," cut their motors and urged their cargoes out. Feet splashed in the surf and willing hands heaved both lightened boats up on the beach, someone from each rushing to nearby trees with lines to secure them.

"Okay," Abel said to Lawrence, voice likely lower than necessary, given the shooshing waves and distance to their objective. "You and your . . . fellows are up. Lead the way, if you please."

"I wonder what maanner of monster we'll find roaming around out here in the daark?" Fen whispered nervously aside to Philan Bele.

Tiny little Maarik-Fas jumped in to answer with a grin splitting her furry face. "Scary ones!"

"I mean it," Fen objected, discomfited as usual by Maarik's somewhat . . . brazen gaze. He had little experience with females, but rather fearfully suspected she was "sweet" on him. She was certainly attractive—and just a little "scary" herself.

"I is told they *are* scary," Lawrence informed them all as he moved to follow one of the chiefs—or whatever he was—and some of his warriors, who took the lead on a well-worn trail. "That's one reason the Rarorani lead. They use s'ear throwers, us see any. No shooting."

"I can't see a thing," Sam Jenks objected as Lawrence, Silva, and Pam vanished ahead.

"Us 'Caats caan," said Haan-Ara. "Almost as good as in the daay."

"What about them?" Bele asked as one of the Rarorani filtered into the trees alongside the trail to screen their passage.

"Not as good as us," Maarik said disdainfully. "Better thaan you, I bet."

"Pipe down," growled Ian Miles. He, Sergeant Kaik, Abel Cook, and the "old" hands were bringing up the rear.

"You think they'll hear us?" asked Sam Jenks.

Miles shook his head. "I don't know, son. Something might, and I don't want *anything* to even know we're here, so shut your traps."

Bele felt something touch the back of his hand and raised his face to the sky, feeling gentle but accelerating impacts. "Swell," he said, using the strange but increasingly universal term brought to this world by the "original" destroyermen. "Rain," he grumbled.

Rain there was, falling harder by the minute until it settled into what was likely to be a prolonged deluge, the sound of it on the "doughboy" helmets all the 'Cats and humans wore drowning all other noise. Aside from the soaking they were getting, this made everyone more uncomfortable than anything, but at least it seemed to suppress the mosquitos. And as it turned out, the land approach to the League base was uneventful and the only injuries were bumps and bruises from falls (mostly humans tripping over roots and rocks) or cuts and scrapes inflicted by thorny branches and leaves that everyone endured. Such things bothered the Rarorani least of all, and they seemed generally better formed in all respects to move through this environment.

Almost like they were made for it, Abel thought just as Lawrence might as well have used magic to silently materialize out of the damp darkness and gesture back behind him. "League ahead," he hissed. "Lots o' lights."

Creeping forward, the whole party gathered at the edge of the forest overlooking a vast clearing around a sprawling lagoon. "Clearing" was an imprecise description because, though the trees and brush had been cut back and used in the construction of an expansive stockade and numerous structures, huge jagged rocks jutted up out of the ground almost as thickly as the graying tree stumps. They could tell they were gray because, like Lawrence reported, the whole place was lit up by hissing, steaming arc lights in several towers at the corners of the stockade, likely powered by a noisy steam generator near the largest structures along the shore where extensive docks had been constructed. Others lanced out from the old French battleship tied up to the pier near an impressive battery of fuel storage tanks. The result of this security measure, obviously aimed at local threats, was somewhat mixed because the rain glare was intense enough to make the whole settlement seem to glow—except for the long shadows cast by the stockade and standing stones that left numerous avenues of approach for creatures or beings that knew how to use them.

"Not much worried about the locals, are they?" Abel commented.

"Nope. Just boogers, I guess," Silva agreed.

"That's going to change," Lawrence promised, before he began speaking lowly to the Rarorani. Pairs of them started darting away, sticking to the shadows, but clearly intent on specific approaches. As had been earlier agreed, their first objective was to locate any sentries and make contact if they were "kin." If they could be persuaded to reveal where the prisoners were and join the rescue, they'd be welcomed to do so. If not, they'd be killed. The "inner garrison" within the stockade might be a different matter. Whether because they were slightly easier for Leaguers to communicate with or just looked vaguely more like "people" to them, Gintarra were responsible for securing more sensitive structures, facilities, and access to the docks and onshore League accommodations. They were directly supervised by League personnel.

"What are we supposed to do now?" Bele asked Sergeant Kaik.

Lieutenant Chiba gestured at Silva. Despite how well they were hidden from view, the diffused light revealed an intently thoughtful expression on his face. "I believe Chief Silva is in the process of making something up," he whispered dryly.

Kaik blinked unhappily. He'd already voiced skepticism that the Rarorani would do what they had to, if necessary. "We wait for Laarry's lizaards to get baack an' report, right?" He tilted his head at Silva. "Even *he's* waitin' on thaat. I hope."

They crouched in the rain and observed the complex and anchorage over the next half hour or so, doing their best to identify the various things they'd expected to see and speculate about others. All the enemy ships they'd been told to expect, information coughed up by the League prisoners they took early on, were preset, either lying at anchor or, in the case of the old French battleship and one of the oilers, tied up at the dock. The battleship was the Courbet Class *France*, one of the very first French dreadnoughts. Completed in 1914 and armed with six twin turrets for a total of twelve 12″ rifles and more than twenty 5.5″ secondaries, she'd been heavily modernized in the late twenties to somewhat resemble *Savoie*. Their prisoners had resentfully implied that she'd been deemed even more expendable, however, being a glutton for fuel even after her conversion to oil-burning boilers. Her range was quite limited, and after all the effort of getting her here, it had never been contemplated that she'd return.

Much the same was expected for the old four-stacker French destroyer *Enseigne Gabolde* and the Italian Sella Class destroyer *Bettino Ricasoli*. Both had limitations that made them disposable as well, thus their original inclusion as escorts for *Savoie* and their ultimate virtual abandonment here. That said, they'd been as well maintained as possible and were each, on paper, a match for USS *Walker*.

The one ship present that nobody in the League wanted to lose was a relatively recent arrival, the German heavy cruiser or "panzershiffe" *Elsass.* She'd been sent here during the war as much to weaken German influence in the League (she was one of only two German capital ships) as to add her firepower to this remote outpost. Especially after the loss of her sister, *Hessen*, to the Grand Alliance—or maybe because of it?—Courtney suspected her people, if not the ship, had essentially been permanently banished here. Too bad they didn't have any of "their" Germans along to try to suborn her crew.

Other than these four ships and the docked oiler, there was another even older oiler that was clearly a mere derelict now, being stripped for her steel. A pair of tugboats that looked locally built were chugging around out beyond the anchored ships as if acting as pickets, or just getting ready to move what was, of course, potentially the most dangerous prize the League had collected at Fen's Island so far: the German heavy cruiser *Prinz Eugen.* Even bigger than *Shonai* and just as powerfully armed, she was also just as handsome—in an entirely different, perhaps more conventional way. She dominated everything else in the big lagoon, even the old French battleship. Like *Texas* and many of the other ships that survived the atomic test in good shape, there'd been some superficial damage, and a lot had been taken off her beforehand, including for some reason a pair of 8″ rifles from her forward turret. Unfortunately, it seemed her radar-assisted fire control, while likely not currently operational or understood, was apparently fully intact. The "new mission" that Courtney, Ronson, and Captain Okabe had all agreed upon, aside from rescuing the hostages, must focus on preventing the enemy from seizing any more technology from the ghost fleet in general, and specifically the capture or destruction of *Prinz Eugen.*

"Ships're just sittin' out there," Silva observed. "All of 'em look like they got steam up too"—he arched his brow at Abel—"like they're fixin' ta get underway. An' there's work bein' done on that big cruiser they swiped, weldin' thick plates over the holes in the front o' that empty gunhouse. Like they're gettin' her ready ta fight," he added significantly. "I guess we might'a got here just in time."

"So it would seem," Abel grimly agreed.

That plainly amused Dennis Silva—that they were here to attack the

League while they were getting ready to return the favor. He appeared to have no doubt about the outcome, or hesitation regarding the cost. "This is *just* the sorta stunt Cap'n Reddy would pull," he practically chortled.

The Rarorani began to return, reporting through Lawrence the results of their efforts. There'd been no problem approaching their cousins, whether they belonged to the same tribe or not. Even if their chiefs were at war, Sashakara was the ruler, the "mother" of them all, and they could always fraternize to a degree in her name. They couldn't truthfully say that she had, herself, yet sanctioned the Rarorani realignment, this new . . . adjustment they'd agreed upon with the very folk their League friends had told them were their worst enemy. The word of whatever chief or his representative that approached them was good enough for some but not all, and those individuals, sentries mostly, had to be slain. A few made some noise, and some of the Gintarra that came to investigate had to be killed with throwing spears as well. Most unfortunate, really, and some of the Gintarra corpses couldn't be easily dragged into shadow and would soon be discovered. The rest of the Rarorani guards, about thirty warriors, were waiting to join them.

"Shit. See?" Silva accused. "*Why not* make shit up as we go?"

"We must hurry," Chiba agreed. Abel Cook and Ian Miles both nodded.

Lawrence gave the word to his friends and they led off at a trot, sticking to the shadows, the rest of them following while he related what they confirmed or told him about the layout of the camp. "The long houses are 'arracks, like us thought. Gintarra in the outside houses, Leaguers in the inside. 'Orkers, Gintarra and hu'an, stay in long houses close to docks, there they use . . . 'achines? Heal sick things on shi's." He shook his head in furious frustration.

"S'okay, Larry," Silva consoled. "He means there's workshops to repair stuff, an' both Gintarra and humans're there." He looked back at his friend while holding his "happy sack" tight so it wouldn't make noise while he ran. "Where're they keepin' our people?"

"In a shack alone all around it." Lawrence paused. "Exce't close to the oil tanks near distantest dock and oiler." He gestured off beyond where the *France* was tied up and they could just make out a small tanker. All the other ships were lying at anchor, but even *France* had steam up, the smoke and rain haze above two of her three stacks illuminated by her own lights.

"I'll get 'em," Silva said. "You with me, Fen?" he asked the little Lemurian.

"You bet," Fen earnestly replied, hefting his Blitzerbug.

"Us too," Bele insisted, waving at the other cadets.

Silva grunted as he kept jogging behind their guides. "This ain't gonna be a romp on the monkey bars," he objected. "I gotta get as far as fast as I can, all while I do my thing—which means raisin' enough hell to confuse the shit out'a ever'body as I go. Make 'em easy pickins for ever'body else." His expression turned hard. "I ain't takin' no pris'ners, neither."

"We understaand," Maarik assured.

"It's usually just us . . ." Lawrence began to object, but Silva shook his head.

"Sorry, pal. *You* gotta stay with Mr. Cook an' Miles an' keep hold o' yer' relations." He grinned. "You might detail a handful ta go with *us*, though. Keep *their* relations from thinkin' we're Leaguers." He looked back at the cadets. "I'll take half of you. Y'all sort it out."

CHAPTER 28

They reached the deep, soggy shadow beyond the palisade where their fresh Rarorani allies were waiting, then worked their way along to the east gate (there was one in each wall of the rectangular stockade, away from the water). This gate was propped closed with the bodies of two Rarorani and a Gintarra. Philan Bele and Abel Cook leaned down to look at the creature, the first they'd seen.

"The same as Gentaa in every way, like we suspected," Abel whispered.

"I . . . Do you suppose we'll have to *shoot* some of them?" Bele asked nervously. "They truly are just like some of my people in the Republic. It doesn't seem right . . ."

"*Guaranteed* ta kill some, Cadet Bele, just like we'll kill every armed human we see," warned Ian Miles. "Or they'll kill you. And it sounds like Gintarra are the main guards inside. Get ready for that or stay here."

Bele took a long breath and nodded. "I'm ready."

"Well, I ain't," Silva said. He looked at Abel, water sluicing off the rim of his helmet. "Gimme five minutes if ya can, ta get to the north gate, right? I'll go in there an' we'll all hit 'em together when you pop the signal—unless you gotta go early, o' course."

"I'm coming with you," announced Lieutenant Chiba, and Silva only shrugged like he'd expected it.

"Me too . . ." Pam began, but Silva shook his head.

"Not this time, doll. You're the only doc we got, an' *somebody's* gonna get hurt." He gave Abel a significant look. "She needs to stay here, or wherever gets safest soonest—for the wounded—an' she's gonna need help." By "help" it was clear he meant "protectors" as well.

Abel nodded, and Lawrence reluctantly counted off six of the Rarorani who'd come with them from the ship, instructing them to fight with and protect his friends.

One of the Rarorani with a big crest thumped his chest and said, "Ragag!"

"Swell ta meet ya, Raggy," Silva said, nodding pleasantly. "Let's get stuck in!"

The rain-muffled sound of clunking weapons and canteens, as well as the rattle of throwing spears in the big quivers Rarorani carried on their backs, accompanied Silva, Chiba, Philan Bele, Sam Jenks, Fen, Daniel Baker, Maarik-Ar, "Raggy," and five other Rarorani as they hustled away in the shadow of the palisade. Lawrence was standing with just his head poking through the gate, surveying the brightly lit settlement beyond. Now he saw an example of one of the Rarorani's "goofs," a Gintarra warrior in a kilt lying on his back in plain view, a throwing spear standing straight up from his chest. "Shit," he murmured to himself, amazed that no one had spotted it yet. A little less than five minutes later, they did. Shouts arose inside the outpost, and running figures sent long, weird shadows stretching across the standing water and muddy sheen on the normally hard dirt ground.

"Us go," Lawrence urgently hissed behind him. Abel nodded. He was already holding the brass frame copy of a Remington Mk III flare pistol and he simply pointed it in the air, cocked it, and pulled the trigger.

Silva, Chiba, and the cadets were breathing hard, almost sprinting, feet sometimes splashing loudly right behind a pair of the borrowed "lizard warriors," the rest bringing up the rear. The north gate just now loomed from the gloom. Silva was about to try to slow the leaders, unsure how he'd do that, when they pulled up on their own, staring intently ahead. There were more bodies on the ground, but the only motion was the slanting rain. Silva took a gulp from his canteen, motioning for the others to do the same, then hauled out his pouch of tobacco and stuffed a huge chaw in his mouth. Noting "Raggy's" interest, he offered him some. An instant after the Rarorani chief experimentally dropped a few leaves on his tongue, he spat them out with a wide-jawed "Ghaawk!"

"Yep," Silva consoled, chewing vigorously. "Sorry, Raggy. Don't always agree with ever'body." A dull *pop* sounded above and they all looked up in the sky to see a bright red flare slash at the heavy wet darkness. "Flare didn't go as high as I expected. Hope *all* our friends seen it," Silva said. He shrugged as if it didn't matter, then nodded forward. "Game time."

Like the previous gate, this one was currently only guarded by the dead. Shoving them aside with surprising care, the foremost warriors cleared the way, and Silva and Chiba peered through. "Shadow from the closest barracks stretches all the way over here," Silva assured those behind. "Stick to it—an' stick to me like malaria," he warned. "C'mon!" He bolted through the gate, and everyone else swiftly followed, shoes and clawed Rarorani feet splatting and sloshing all the way up to the elevated barracks wall. There was plenty of other noise to cover theirs. A hand-cranked siren's wail was beginning to mount, feet were pounding inside the barracks, and a few shots were heard to the west where they'd left the rest of their party. Silva opened his "happy sack" and retrieved a big handful of grenades. Passing one each to Chiba, Bele, Jenks, and Dan Baker (the only ones tall enough), he hissed, "We're goin' that way." He nodded to the east. "Pitch 'em in the windows as we go. There ain't no covers over 'em an' they're mostly for fresh air, I bet . . . Now!" Taking off at a squishy lope, he pulled the pin and tossed his own grenade through the head-high window, a light just now springing to life inside, and kept running. Chiba understood immediately and lobbed his grenade in the next one. Bele, Jenks, and Baker each had to slow a bit and fumble a little, but managed to pitch their grenades in the last three openings just as the first ones began to explode. The detonations were muffled inside the timber building but the screams didn't sound like they were. Silva stopped at the corner, still in shadow, his grin lit by the flashes of the last three grenades. "Pretty fun, huh? Here's some more. We'll do the same at the next barracks." The rattle of Blitzerbugs, crack of rifles, and stutter of another type of SMG, possibly a smaller caliber than .45ACP, were rising from the direction of Abel and Miles's attack.

For the first time, they had to cross the rain-lashed light, but they made it through, only drawing a couple of hurried shots. Fen and Maarik both replied with short bursts of fire and took up positions to cover their rear as the rest slung more grenades. *Whump! Whump! Whwhumpmp!*

"Fen! Maarik! Let's go!" Silva shouted and the two little Lemurians scampered after them. Someone had redirected the light back at the shooting, and they rounded the corner in darkness.

That was good because Fen slipped, fell hard on his ass with an "urk!" sound, and slid right out in the open. Maarik grabbed his arm and dragged him back, even as growing fire was directed at where they'd been shooting.

"You *owe* me," Maarik archly told Fen, who could only meekly blink acceptance.

Silva racked the bolt back on his Thompson. "We'll all jump out in a line at the front corner, hose off a magazine, then run for the shadow behind that next barracks in." He got Raggy's attention, pointed at his eye, and then waved around. Raggy jerked a diagonal nod.

"What are we going to shoot at?" Bele asked Jenks. The other cadet only shrugged. "I suppose we'll find out." They did.

Breaking cover around the corner of the building, they saw Gintarra boiling out a couple of doors. Some were clearly wounded from grenade fragments, but all had bolt-action rifles. They were looking the other way, back where humans from between two inner barracks were still shooting at where Fen and Maarik had fired.

"Smoke 'em!" Silva barked, and seven SMGs opened up on the clustered enemy, who staggered and jerked like spastic marionettes. Raggy's Rarorani launched a couple of throwing spears in other directions at different targets they saw. As soon as a shooter's smoking, steaming bolt locked back, they ran where Silva had told them. The west-side arc lights had been shot out and the ones to the north and east still glared out at the forest, their Rarorani operators having defected or been killed. For the most part, that left only those high up on the battleship to go crazy, scanning back and forth for the cause of the growing chaos. This actually contributed to it, creating wild whipping shadows that drew bursts of fire from confused, panicking Gintarra and humans, sometimes into each other. Silva's party was completely hidden by shadow again, however, no matter what the lights did, and took a moment to pass around more grenades and catch their breath, even while listening to concerned and angry humans shouting in the barracks they crouched beside. An occasional muzzle poked out a window above them, but didn't fire. The shooting was growing to the west again.

"Them Catmonkeymen," Silva whispered, then paused and looked at Fen and Maarik, "Gintarra, I mean, look armed with Mausers, seven-fifty-seven Spanish ones, I bet." He spat a big stream of tobacco juice and glanced up at the closest window, apparently confident no one would hear them over the noise inside. "Leaguers got some kinda subgun with wood stocks an' vented barrels. Don't know what they are. Sound like nine-millimeter."

"What difference does that make?" asked Lieutenant Chiba, hissing tone perplexed.

"None, I guess," Silva admitted lowly. "Just thought these kiddies'd like to know what they're gettin' shot at with. An' it's weird the Leaguers trust Gintarra with rifles at all, seein' how they don't even think 'Cats're people."

"They may not have any choice," Chiba mused. "Manpower issues, like us."

"But that's the thing," Silva pressed, spitting again before nodding at Raggy. "We even count Rarorani an' *Grik* as 'people' now, thanks to Larry—an' gettin' ta know 'em, o' course. Leaguers, the real nasty bastards in charge, don't count *nobody* else as people, not hardly even other humans on this world that didn't come here with 'em. I just wonder if some o' these ones out here for so long has started to." He scratched his chin under his soggy beard. "But that don't matter either," he added philosophically. "They're still *servin'* the League an' wanna run us off or kill us, so we gotta kill them first. C'mon, same drill. Enough lollygaggin'." Standing, he pulled the pin on the grenade he'd been rolling in his hand and lobbed it in the window.

There were a couple of terrified cries within, but everyone had already followed him, throwing their own grenades before a man actually leaped out the first window just ahead of the blast. Splashing down in standing water hard on his back, his breath driven from him, he looked entirely helpless, and Fen and Maarik, turning toward the sound, hesitated. Both were knocked nearly silly by the muzzle blast of a Thompson's three-round burst right between their heads, the bullets stitching across the man on the ground.

"What the hell's the *matter* with you two?" Silva roared as he and Chiba grabbed them and dragged them along while more blasts and screams shook the inside of the barracks. "You *ain't* gettin' killed, not with me."

"He waas helpless!" Maarik protested.

"An' you knew that *how*?" Silva demanded.

More grenades went off and bullets started striking the timbers around them, enemies around other barracks shooting at the shadows.

"He is right," scolded Lieutenant Chiba. "I could barely see him. He might have been pointing a pistol at you even as you stood there. Never hesitate in a fight."

"Thanks, Mr. Chiba," Silva said. "You're okay, for a Jap."

"And you, for an ignorant American savage," Chiba solemnly replied.

Silva grinned at him. "C'mon. They'll be boilin' out the front, like last time."

He was right, but they weren't as oblivious as the more surprised Gintarra had been. Some were already covering their comrades' escape, firing bursts from their strange SMGs as soon as one of Raggy's warriors peered around the corner. He was struck in the eye and snatched out in the open, where he convulsed as more bullets struck him.

"Dammit," Silva snarled. Palming a pair of grenades in his big hand, he pulled both pins and slung them, exposing only his left arm for an instant. That was enough for him to catch a scorching graze below his elbow. "Shee-it!" he hissed. *Cra-crack!* went the grenades, and Silva fired around the corner until his bolt locked back again, rain flashing to steam on the hot barrel of his weapon. An arc light on the battleship barely a hundred and fifty yards away lit them up. "Get that damn light!" he shouted. "Shoot high!"

Three Blitzers opened up, and just as bright red tracers from the ship started probing for them, the big light blinked and died with a glaring flash. The tracers kept coming, blasting away the corner of the building.

"Left!" Chiba shouted. "Run left!" A larger structure, one of the suspected workshops, cast a shadow for them there. Even as they sprinted for it, replacing magazines as they ran, they saw many of the people from the barracks and elsewhere streaming toward the dock beside the old French battleship.

"They're *fleeing*!" Jenks exclaimed, surprised.

"Some," Silva agreed as they kept running themselves. "Headin' for the safety o' the ship. Must think we're hittin' 'em harder than we are."

"That was the idea, was it not?" Chiba asked, breathing hard.

Silva grinned again. "That's *always* the idea when you ain't got the numbers." They were all starting to realize there were a lot more people here, of all sorts, than they'd expected.

More rounds cracked past them as they dodged into the shadows once again. "Hold fire," Bele cried. "They'll see our muzzle flashes."

"Good thinkin'," Silva complimented. "I wonder what's in here?" he said, gesturing at the big building they approached. It was taller than he'd thought from a distance and one end appeared to open right onto the dock. "Looks almost like a hangar." A door opened, and armed men were silhouetted by a light inside. One must've seen them and started to bring up a weapon, only to be met by a clattering fusillade that cleared the doorway. Silva charged straight through, over the blood-drenched twitching bodies. The first thing he noticed—he couldn't help it—was this was indeed a hangar, at least part of it, protecting a big gray biplane with an in-line engine on twin floats, a German bar-cross insignia on the side of the fuselage. He was distracted less than a second before a bullet caromed off the top of his helmet and he swung to stitch a man with a pistol wearing an officer's uniform. The man fell back into the wooden chair he must've just stood from and dropped the pistol. Spinning around, Silva noted the others following him in, shooting at other men emerging from behind the plane, but he caught movement in the gloom beyond a line of steel drums next to a big milling machine, probably off the battleship. Firing at the movement, he heard a cry and a clatter, but then came a chorus of strained shouts from behind the drums.

"USS *Scott*! USS *Scott*!"

CHAPTER 29

Whoa there, hold fire this way!" Silva bellowed. There were a few more seconds of shooting past the aircraft before a semi-silence descended in the smoke-hazed space. "Who's there?" Silva demanded, covering the drums.

"USS *Scott*!" came a single voice, a shadowy figure rising up.

"An' I'm the goddamn *Merry-mac*," Silva snorted. "Gimme more than that, chop-chop, or I'll chop *you*, see?"

Fen was rushing toward the drums, a couple more figures struggling to rise. "It's Chief Handy! Handy Allen, off the *Scott*!" Fen cried.

"Wull . . . who'd I shoot then?" Silva asked a little tentatively.

"Don't worry, Chief Silva," replied the only human standing. Two others were clearly Lemurians. "Ye got the one of 'em set tae watch us. Well done, that."

"Lucky as well, it would seem," rasped one of the 'Cats as both of them moved into the light, but Allen bent down to lift another smaller form.

"You said my name. Do I know you?" Silva asked suspiciously.

"Aye, we met a time 'er two," Allen replied as Fen joined him, recoiling slightly from what he saw. "Sorry lad, didnae mean tae frighten ye," Allen told the young 'Cat. "We've all looked better." The two strange Lemurians looked like walking skeletons with bulging eyes, their fur horribly matted and filthy. The tall man appeared just as emaciated with a scruffy beard hanging from a narrow, bony face. The unconscious form in his arms looked even worse. All were dressed only in rags.

"Is . . . is that Waldo?" Fen asked, voice cracking at the sight of his best friend. He knew it was him at once but didn't want to believe it.

"Aye," Allen said gently. "'Tis he—an' he's alive, enow. Don't ye fret." He looked up at the gathered youngsters, Chiba, and the Rarorani. He recovered quite quickly from his surprise. "They didnae feed us well, tae keep us weak," he explained. "Seems we tried tae escape too often." He looked fondly at Fen. "Yet clearly our faith in ye was well placed!"

"I am Lieutenaant Jun-Soraat, XO of USS *Scott*," said one of the 'Cats before gesturing at another. "And this is Chief Saan-Min, her engineering officer." He nodded at the unconscious youngster. "Along with young Waaldo Dhaar, we are the ship's sole survivors, 'saved' only due to our status as reserve naval officers." He paused. "Waldo was . . . a special case. Other hostages . . ." He couldn't continue.

"We know," said Lieutenant Chiba, who quickly identified himself and the others.

"We were just fixin' ta rescue you fellas," Silva said expansively. "One o' the main reasons we're here. But you ain't where we thought. Hadn't got there yet."

"Then it is fortunate for us that you approached our place of confinement by this route," said Jun-Soraat.

"Aye." Allen nodded at the scruffy-bearded officer in the chair, who, surprisingly, was still alive, gasping and watching them from his narrow-spaced eyes. "That's Mr. Ames—at least, that's the name we know him by. He came fer us when your attack began, tryin' tae get us on a ship. He's kept us alive all this time, but fer nae other reason than his own."

Firing was growing closer, more intense outside, and Ames turned his head to listen. Clearing his throat, he spoke, voice strained with pain. "Ah," he said, "it sounds as if your little raid is meeting increased resistance." He gestured at himself as Fen stepped over, stony-faced, tail whipping, and picked up the little Beretta automatic the man dropped. "I'm not too badly wounded, just two holes, I believe," Ames went on, gently exploring himself. "Painful, certainly, but nothing vital hit." He seemed to be mocking Silva's marksmanship. "My name is indeed 'Ames,' and I hail from the Empire of the New Britain Isles, but I joined and rose quickly within the Italian OVRA, which has become the most efficient intelligence-gathering organization for the League of Tripoli." The OVRA, or Organization for Vigilance and Repression of Anti-fascism, had been Benito Mussolini's secret police and initially served the same purpose here as it had on the world it came from. That role had expanded dramatically. Ames smiled. "I see by your expressions you've heard of it. Good. Then you know I'm sincere when I say that, like them"—he tilted his head toward his former prisoners—"you all have value to me." He chuckled harshly. "None of you will be eaten."

Silva flicked his gaze at Raggy. "Why don't we let 'em eat *you*?"

Ames gently coughed and then cleared his throat again. "Because you are trapped here and will soon be killed. But if you throw your weapons away, tend my wounds, and peacefully await the arrival of the men I sent for just moments ago, I give you my word you'll be treated well as my prisoners."

Bele was looking outside. "There really *are* men running this way," he called in alarm.

"How many?" Silva barked.

"Maybe . . . twenty? All human." No doubt he said the last so they'd know for sure it wasn't their own people coming for them.

"Hmm. Cover that piece o' shit, Fen. You others, can you fight?" Silva asked the former *Scott* sailors.

"We will," said the 'Cat named Saan-Min. Shuffling back behind the drums, he retrieved their dead guard's weapon while Baker and Jenks went to retrieve others from the men they'd killed by the plane.

"They're stopping," Bele announced. "I think they saw me and got suspicious. Now they're splitting up."

"Good," said Chiba, then he shrugged at Silva. "We cannot all shoot at them through that door, but if they come around and try to enter through that open hangar entrance . . ." He nodded at the rain-lashed darkness beyond, where a ramp sloped down through the dock to the water.

"Hmm," Silva said again, looking around, taking in the drums and a large quantity of coiled rope that was most likely used to haul the plane up the ramp. He grinned. "Hey! I *think* I just made up a plan! Bele, you an' Maarik open up on them devils outside, make 'em head for the hangar mouth. Two o' you others, tie off that dopey-lookin' plane, but give it about thirty yards slack, see? An' make sure *this* end o' the line's secure," he warned. Bele and Maarik opened fire, using the thick timber walls around the doorjamb for cover. "The rest of us gotta hurry. Start rollin' them drums down the ramp."

Chiba had looked skeptical until then, but now he grinned as well. One of Silva's bullets must've gone astray, knocking a hole in a drum, and the smell of leaking aviation gasoline was strong. "What is your idea for the plane?" he asked, tipping the first leaking drum on its side and giving it a shove.

"You'll see. I kinda hate to do it, but it's about the ugliest damn plane I ever seen."

"I wonder where they got it?" Chiba shouted, raising his voice over the rumbling drums—several more had been started, even the Rarorani pitching in—the gunfire and the pounding rain.

"Who knows?" Silva shrugged, shoving a drum of his own. "Prob'ly that big Kraut cruiser out there. Not the one they swiped, the one that came with the League."

That made as much sense as anything. In minutes, all the nearby drums were bumping against each other, low in the water at the bottom of the ramp, the lapping waves keeping them pushed up against it. "Now the plane!" Silva shouted. "Take hold an' heave!"

"Look out!" shouted Chief Allen. He'd set Waldo down by the door close to its defenders, since—if nothing else was perfectly clear about Silva's "plan"—that would be their only exit. Now he saw shapes peering in around the hangar entrance. He fired one of the curious SMGs he appropriated from their enemies.

"Keep pushin'," Silva roared. "It's over the hump. Downhill from here!"

Muzzle flashes flared at them from the darkness, bullets whipping past, some striking the plane. In seconds it seemed like all the attackers had assembled to shoot in at them. Lieutenant Jun cried out and fell, as did another one of Raggy's warriors. Danny Baker fell to a knee without a sound.

"Give it a shove an' haul ass to the door," Silva shouted. "Grab up whoever needs it!"

With its floats resting on wheeled trucks, the big biplane accelerated toward the water and the Leaguers briefly checked their fire, possibly afraid it would hit them or they'd damage it too much, or perhaps that someone was in it, attempting to escape. Either way, there was a moment of confusion that the landing party and hostages used to retreat, dragging their fallen. Almost as an afterthought, Silva grabbed the OVRA officer by the collar and dragged him to the doorway just as the plane hit the water fast, the floats digging in and scattering the barrels. The line had been secured a little too high on the big milling machine, and the weight of the plane pulled it over with a crash, but there was no way it could move it farther. Like a goose hitting water, the plane bobbed violently up, splashing seawater (and probably a fair amount of aviation fuel) over their League assailants.

"Who's left outside?" Silva demanded.

"We don't think anyone," Maarik replied. "They all went around where we weren't shooting at them."

Silva grunted. "Don't count on it, but y'all gotta get out. Get our hurt people out," he stressed. The enemy was shooting blindly in at them again and Silva fired back, aiming at the barrels. His bolt locked back and he inserted another magazine before hosing a long burst at the plane itself. He'd suppressed the incoming fire for an instant but snarled, "Git, goddammit!" when he saw none of his companions had moved.

"We won't leave you!" Bele insisted.

"You ain't!" Silva practically screamed at him. "But how the hell am *I* s'posed ta get out with *you* all gaggled up in the way? Scram!" That's what it took to get them moving, and Silva was relieved when he heard only distant shooting outside. It picked up again inside, though, and he returned it, supporting the heavy Thompson one-handed while he fished a grenade from his sack. "Don't forget this little buzzard turd," he said, kicking Ames. He must've struck the man near one of his wounds because he shrieked very loud. "I've heard *bunnies* make manlier sounds than that," Silva sneered as Chiba lifted the OVRA operative. The Japanese officer was the last one out, and he and Silva exchanged a significant look. "Get 'em back," Silva said. "Maybe a pretty good distance. Fumes," he added with a shrug that said, "Who knows?" Chiba nodded and started shouting.

Silva reloaded his Thompson once more, suspecting he'd just inserted his last magazine. A couple of the enemy were now venturing inside and he carefully shot the dark shapes. "Fumes may not be that bad yet," he murmured to himself in the wake of his bright muzzle flashes. "Might live through this yet." Still holding the Thompson by the pistol grip, he hooked his trigger finger through the ring pin of a grenade, pulled it out, and flung the little bomb. He knew he should've ducked through the door, but it just wasn't in him not to watch the destruction he wreaked. He barely saw the splash next to the plane, but the bright spume it threw up with a *poomp!* sound was obvious. And that's all it did.

"Sonovabitch!" he growled. He'd started to grab another grenade when more enemies ducked into the hangar, shooting and splintering wood all around him. Something punched him high up in the muscle between his neck and left shoulder, and the pain was instantaneous and fierce. "Ack!" he hissed, firing back with his right hand again, knowing he was through throwing things with his left. That's when the meager light in the space revealed the erratic trail of gasoline the drum he'd punctured left. "Well, hell," he muttered, emptying the Thompson before flinging it out the door and reaching for the 1911 Colt holstered at his side. He winced as his other hand fished in his pocket for his trusty Zippo.

Most of the barracks buildings were burning now, doubtless set alight by Abel and Miles's "main force" after Silva's detachment emptied some and the ensuing ruckus sent the rest of the inhabitants toward the dock, where fixed defenses and the big battleship could protect them from this ferocious, unknown assailant. Chiba, Bele, Raggy, and Chief Allen had fought their way while everyone else was busy helping or being helped back around to the north side of the last barracks they attacked. Tiny Maarik cried out and dropped face down in the mud, her helmet sent spinning from her bloody head. Fen just froze for an instant, then went nearly berserk with fury, snatching her up in his arms and spitting vile curses at Ames in his native tongue as he ran. The building they sought refuge by was only just starting to burn and was having trouble doing so. As wet as everything was, all the fires would've had to be spread from inside, and with no other members of their force in evidence nearby, this one might've got its fitful start from the grenades they tossed in. They had only just taken cover, gasping in the sodden air, when the hangar/workshop they'd escaped blew up.

"Did Chief Silva get out? Did you see him?" Philan Bele demanded, stepping out to see the rising ball of flames and shattered roof debris spreading out in the sky. The heavy timber walls had bulged outward but remained relatively intact. Still, no one could've survived inside.

"Get back, you fool! Get down," snapped Lieutenant Chiba, tight against the corner, peering around it. "Stay under the eaves. Crawl under the foundation, if you can." There was probably just enough gap under the floor for them to do so. Heavy beams and timbers started falling all around, crashing down on the roof above them and probably even on the nearby battleship. Cringing a little, Chiba waited until he thought the worst was over, but before he could look again, he heard Fen's voice rising behind him.

"You vile, revolting piece of filth!" he was snarling at Ames, who was standing with the assistance of one of the Rarorani. More concerning than his words and state of mind, Fen was pointing the little Beretta up at Ames's pale face. "This is all your fault!" the little 'Cat roared.

"Hardly . . ." Ames began, holding up a placating hand.

"It *is*," Fen insisted. "You took my ship, murdered Captain Morsey, tortured and killed my friends—and the Maker only knows who else. You *made me swim in the ocean*!" he practically screeched, the repressed trauma of that clearly still raw. "You fed our people to the Rarorani and set them against us, getting more of both of us killed. All while you were starving my last living friends and getting ready to kill us all—"

"My dear fellow," Ames objected, "I am *not* in charge here—"

"But you're importaant enough to do whaat you waant!" Fen seethed.

"And if it waasn't for you, none of us would even *be* here, not them"—he flicked his blazing eyes at Allen, Jun, and Saan-Min—"and not us. Then Daanny, Waaldo, *three* of Raaggy's warriors, Maarik"—his voice broke, then firmed—"and now Chief Silva wouldn't be dead. All because of *you*!"

"I'm *not* dead, you silly creature," Maarik objected groggily, carefully touching her head, "but your rage at the possibility is very sweet." She paused, blinking bleakly at the boy in the mud beside her. "Poor Daanny is dead, though, so if you're going to shoot him, I waant to watch."

"I . . . I have done my best to *care* for your friends," Ames objected, genuinely fearful now. "I gave young Waldo enough food to survive *against* my orders, all as a favor to your officers!"

"That's a lie," Allen snarled. "We *know* it was you who chose tae set us aside from all the others you fed tae . . ." He looked at Raggy and shook his head bitterly.

"But look!" Ames declared, pointing. "Waldo still lives! He just moved!"

It was true, for the moment at least. The boy's head was shaking back and forth, lips moving. He seemed lost in a fever.

"That's swell," groaned a voice from the rain, and Dennis Silva limped up to them, beard and clothing singed and muddy, helmet askew. The Thompson was secured by its sling diagonally across his back, and he had his pistol in his left hand, battered Navy cutlass in the right. He nodded at the relieved smiles and blinking. "An' I ain't dead neither," he growled, "but like the girlie, I'm grateful for the kind thoughts." He nodded at Fen, then looked at Ames. "Other than them little details, the kiddo's pretty much right, but *I'm* glad we're here ta put a stop to yer doin's, which we never would'a known about if you hadn't taken *Scott*."

"You *still* have no chance," Ames began, but Silva held up a hand and grinned.

"It's nearly dawn, ain't it? Can't hardly tell, cuzz'a how dark the sky is"—he seemed to reflect, then paused and grinned—"but this joint's lit pretty bright." He grinned even bigger. "You hear that? Airplane engines—an' they ain't yours, dumbass," he scoffed at Ames. "I reckon we trashed the only plane you got in this dump." His gap-toothed grin turned beatific. "I don't hear as good as I did anymore—kinda goes with the trade—but I can tell when I hear Nancy engines, even when they're two different kinds." He looked around. "Sounds like Fred an' Kari are here." He poked Ames hard in the chest with his Colt. "An' you, *Mr.* Ames, are gonna miss the pretty show they put on."

"What—" That was as far as he got before Silva pulled the trigger twice, blowing two big holes through the OVRA officer's heart. The Rarorani warrior who'd been supporting him jumped back in surprise, dropping the dead man in the mud.

"Why did you do that?" Chiba demanded. "We could have learned—"

"Nothin'," Silva stated flatly. "Not a thing we won't get from bigger fish later." He looked at the Japanese officer. "When this is all over, we'll either have a whole mess of 'em or we'll be dead. Two better reasons, though." He looked at Fen. "First, we gotta get the hell out'a here, an' it looks like ever'body's gonna hafta carry somebody else." He shook his head. "I ain't sure I can carry my own sore ass right now. Damned if I was carryin' *him.* Second"—he scratched his temple with the hot muzzle of his pistol—"prob'ly the *real* first reason is that Fen was gonna kill 'eem anyway." He holstered the pistol and put his hand on Fen's shaking shoulder. "The kid's fed up. I seen it. Hell, I *been* there before. Sometimes the only thing left in the world is ta kill the thing eatin' ya under yer skin. *Smush* that ol' wolf worm a'wigglin' away!" He shook his head. "Thing is, he ain't the sort to get over killin' a helpless enemy. Not yet. I wasn't either, once, an' I turned that way too young." His hard-eyed glare swept across Chiba, Allen, then Jun and Saan-Min, only the adults. "Let's spare Fen that t'day. Don't make no difference ta me anymore." He took a deep breath. "Besides, like I said, no pris'ners. Now let's git. If I know Fred an' Kari—which I do—we're too damn close to what they'll hit as soon as they flutter around an' find it."

They located Abel Cook and the remains of his command near the first gate they'd approached. Miles, Lawrence, and Pam were fine, but Sergeant Kaik and two cadets were seriously wounded, Kaik sitting on a narrow native cart and grousing with a hole in his thigh. They'd lost two "old" *Walker* hands and a cadet killed as well, one of the Marines. Miles had taken it hard and seemed even more bitter than usual. Ten of their

Rarorani had also been killed, which left them with over sixty, since they'd "enlisted" more as they went along. The Rarorani had actually been most responsible for setting the fires.

"We never even seen any Roo-roonies besides the ones we brung," Silva objected while Pam brusquely tended his bullet wound,

"Us had *I* along," Lawrence said with what could only be a smug expression on his lizardy face. "I and others call they."

"How come *you* didn't call any o' your pals?" Silva asked Raggy accusingly.

Raggy, of course, just shook his head, baffled.

CHAPTER 30

Making their way up the gentle but muddy slope in a slightly less urgent deluge, now pulling carts provided by their Rarorani allies for all their wounded and dead, they'd just about reached the forest surrounding the League outpost they'd mauled when booming thunder drew their attention back.

"Woo! Look at that!" Silva hooted when the League's carefully conserved fuel oil reserve, hopefully for the entire region, burst from ruptured tank batteries and went up in glorious flames, the result of a direct hit by one of the Nancys. The other had set the oiler afire. It didn't seem badly damaged, but the flames would be hell to extinguish, maybe impossible, considering Abel's team had wrecked the shoreside power plant that would be responsible for any firefighting pumps. The Nancys weren't alone either. Veteran pilots or not, it had apparently been agreed that Fred and Kari's little floatplanes with their limited payloads would only go after less well-protected targets. As they watched, the faster, heavier, more capable Aichi E13A "Jakes" off *Shonai*—all three that remained airworthy—bored in out of the dreary morning half-light straight at *Prinz Eugen*.

She wasn't really well protected either, since the aerial attack had come as a complete surprise. A few tracers rose against the big floatplanes from both nearby destroyers and even the big cruiser herself as men scrambled to defend them, but all three aircraft managed to release their single big Type 99, Number 25, Model 1, "Ordinary" 551-pound bombs. Two exploded close alongside, possibly near enough to open seams, throwing up towering stalks of spume. The third bomb struck the fo'c'sle directly in front of the disarmed forward turret, blowing a large section of armored deck up and forward to collapse on itself like a sardine can. There was no secondary blast, not even a fire, and that seemed to be about it since all the planes now climbing out, apparently undamaged, had expended all their ordnance.

Alarms were finally blaring on the ships, however, calling their crews to battle stations. Only *France* had sounded hers earlier, to man what few weapons she had that could contribute to the defense ashore without destroying everything there. Abel Cook was looking at his Impie watch, the hands becoming visible in the growing gray light, when Silva suddenly hooted louder, with unsuppressed glee. Looking up, Abel saw two more even larger geysers erupt alongside the recovered German cruiser. Moments later came the rain-muffled knocking booms of torpedo strikes.

"Yes!" shouted Bele and Jenks together as Silva capered in a circle in the mud like an insane ape. Pam's cursing attempt to catch him and hold him still caused an explosion of tension-releasing laughter. Miles was pointing at the distant mouth of the lagoon, only now becoming visible for the first time. "It's *Walker*!" Abel said, catching the swift movement of a slightly lighter shape racing against the dark trees beyond, an oversize Stars and Stripes streaming from the foremast the only hint of color. She was already turning, sharp bow aiming right at them for a moment as she presented her starboard broadside battery, which spat rapid-fire flashes from her numbers one, three, and four guns, firing in local control. At less than a thousand yards, even her "second-string" gunners could hardly miss, and blast after blast shook the burning oiler, accelerating her destruction, and at least one of the anchored destroyers. Before anything could even fire in response, she'd already turned her tail to streak away, laying a dense, impenetrable cloud of smoke. Both enemy destroyers fired into it, as did the secondaries on *Elsass* and *France*, but they simply didn't have a target.

"That's the style, *Walker*!" Silva bellowed while Fen and Maarik hugged and danced in a circle as well. All the surviving cadets and even weakened hostages cheered. Catching the mood, Raggy and his Rarorani made satisfied howling sounds.

"Captain Rodriguez *told* us he'd be offshore watching for the flare so he'd know our attack had started," Abel said with a look at Miles. "Said he'd do what he could if he saw the chance . . ."

"Which all the commotion ashore and the airstrike gave him," Miles agreed, glaring at Silva. "*You* knew."

"*Sure*, I did," said the big man. "I've known Ronson an' Tabby, Fred, an' Kari—all the rest—a long damn time. Makin' an' takin' chances is what we *do*. Didn't know *exactly* what would happen, but I knew Fred an' Kari were flyin', *Walker* was offshore"—he grinned at Chiba, who was smiling back—"an' I got the feelin' yer Cap'n Okabe weren't above 'makin' shit up as he went,' neither."

Another rumbling blast rocked the lagoon, drawing their attention to *Prinz Eugen*. Flames were climbing amidships of the handsome cruiser and she was already leaning rather sharply toward them. Men were climbing down onto barges that had been arranged around her and others were snaking down lines into boats.

"Working on her like they were, I suspect all her internal hatches are open. It seems kind of a shame to see her go like that," Abel commented and even Silva sobered.

"Yeah. Fine-lookin' ship. Came all this way after whatever she went through where she's from. Nothin' for it, though."

They watched in silence as the big cruiser kept rolling over, lingering awhile on her side before turning turtle entirely, beginning to slip lower by the head.

Pam coughed and rubbed her nose on her sleeve. "Well, even if we don't accomplish anything else, we've won a big fight for the Alliance." She dipped her chin to the hostages and all their new allies. "Aside from gettin' them, we've wrecked this League base and sunk what they came for."

Abel was shaking his head. "This fight isn't over, not at all."

Silva was nodding. "All we did here was kick a anthill. They *still* got more guns than us floatin' out there, an' all them angry ants're gonna come fer us, grumpy as a Grik with a toothache."

"But . . ." Pam waved at the devastation.

"We've left them no choice," Miles put in as if finally realizing this for himself. "The only way for them to accomplish *their* mission is to knock us off and retake the ghost fleet at Fen's Island." He shrugged. "We sank their prize and burned up all their fuel. That's the only place they can get more of either."

"An' they'll come a'runnin'," Silva agreed. "Prob'ly pullin' their hooks right now. We gotta get back to the beach where *Walker* dropped us off. She can't wait for long."

The loud shriek of an incoming projectile bashing through the thick air and an explosion of dark earth barely seventy-five yards short of the woods added emphasis to his words.

"They see us. Thaat came from *Fraance*," Fen called. "One of her secondaaries!"

"Grumpy as a Grik," Silva repeated. "Let's git."

The rain tapered off, and the trail they stumbled down the night before was much easier in daylight. It seemed to have been deliberately blazed just wide enough for the narrow Rarorani carts as well. Of course, their initial burst of speed was encouraged by a spiteful, if ineffective barrage from the old French battleship, including an astonishing salvo from at least part of her massive main battery. It missed them by a significant distance, but the power and sheer fury of it was quite clear as the shells splintered and uprooted swathes of massive trees. Exhausted as they were, it was the memory of that and what it boded for their strange little task force that spurred them on all the way to the beach where the grounded motor launches awaited. To their immense relief, *Walker* was already there, standing offshore, and Tabby had landed in the whaleboat with a handful of Marine cadets and a couple of Pam's sick berth attendants.

Tabby blinked her eyes in surprise at the size of their party, augmented by the Rarorani. Fists on her hips like she'd seen her mentor,

Spanky McFarlane, do so often, she flicked her tail and asked, "Whaat haave you dragged home *this* time, Dennis?"

"New pals. I figger ol' Raggy's settin' up for king of a new tribe, er somethin'."

"He not do that," Lawrence put in seriously. "He's already a . . ." He pulled off his helmet and gestured at the flattened crest on his own head, then held the helmet above it.

"Already a chief?" Miles asked.

Lawrence nodded. "An' they're not going 'ith us. They're going to see Sashakara, get her . . . okay to all they has already done."

Abel blinked. "Is there any chance she'll object?"

Lawrence shook his head. "No. I already told you. She hates Leaguers. Us trade they iron, stay nice to they, they'll stay good allies."

"What about the Gintarra?"

Lawrence shook his head. "I don't know. *Rarorani* don't know. Gintarra are . . . di'rent." He paused. "And no care to the side they is on, us did kill a lot o' they."

Abel rubbed his face with his hand. "Yes. I'm afraid we did."

Everyone else had been piling the weak and wounded in one of the launches before pushing it out in the surf, then shoving the other one out.

"I hate to rush you," Tabby said, "but you might've seen us make a number of big, powerful ships very angry at our very smaall one."

"Seen it firsthand," Silva laughed. "You *sank* that Kraut cruiser, by the way. Rolled plumb over on her back, wavin' her screws in the air."

Tabby grinned wide enough to bare her sharp canines. "Thaat's *swell*," she said. "We couldn't haang around to see."

"We seen it for ya. It was great." Heading for the launch, Silva looked back at the gathering of Rarorani onshore. He waved. "So long, Raggy! Fellas! We'll be back an' throw a proper party. Lotsa booze an' broads. Don't get ate!"

Pam snorted, still trying to catch Silva again and put a sling around his neck for his left arm, but he was too tall and wouldn't bend over. She was muttering something about "idiots who collect bullet holes like stamps" and "broads."

"Glaad *somebody* saw it," Tabby groused, waving the whaleboat off and making for the same launch as Silva, Abel, and Pam.

"The view weren't free," Silva said, sobering, and finally dipping his head for Pam as he gestured at the other launch, pulling away with their wounded and dead.

"We never thought it would be," Tabby agreed, tone matching his, "an' it'll break Ronson's heart. There was always the chaance we'd lose a few caadets, just in training. They knew they were striking for a dangerous job. We're liaable to lose more of 'em too," she went on relentlessly, then shrugged. "But I gotta think they'd raather go doin' their jobs than training."

"Maybe so," Silva agreed, hopping in the boat. "Move away from there, dammit," he called to one of the "old" Lemurian hands, preparing to serve as coxswain. "I still got one good flipper an' I could steer this little tub with my toes."

The sky was still smeared with a gray blanket of clouds, but it was beginning to thin. The sun was a blurry purple-orange ball as the boats bashed through bigger rollers than when they'd come in, packets of spray whipping back on them. The launch with the wounded approached the closest falls, and Silva took his around to the other side once more, careful not to interfere with the recovery of the second Nancy. The first was already aboard.

"I'm glaad to see thaat," Tabby shouted. "They may be the best pilots in the Graand Alliance, but they've lost so maany planes, I always worry when they fly."

"Hmm," Silva said noncommittally as he brought the launch alongside the wallowing destroyer, jockeying carefully while young Bele and Jenks hooked on to the falls. Stuffed canvas bumpers had been dropped over the side to prevent damage to the boat while it was hoisted up level with the deck and the passengers started climbing out. Petey launched himself from the top of the quadruple-tube torpedo mount and lit in his usual place. "Ow! Dammit. Watch yer step, you useless little turd! I got a new hole up there." Petey had already noticed, sniffing the bloody bandage. There must've been something distinct about the smell of Silva's blood because Petey didn't start chewing the bandage. He even seemed to avoid tromping on it once he knew it was there.

Pam noticed the behavior and shook her head. "Little shit may not be as stupid as I thought."

Petey's big eyes peered at her from around Silva's neck. "Little Shit Not As Stupid As You Thought," he righteously proclaimed.

Pam narrowed her eyes at him, then shook her head and sighed. "And out of the blue, he says somthin' like that, that makes you start wonderin' all over again."

Lawrence heard what she said and sniffed.

"He never has been as stupid as you think," Silva bragged, helping her out of the boat and onto the deck. "'Least not quite," he qualified. "Ain't sayin' he's *smart*, exactly. Maybe sharper than a goat—but not a crow."

"Crow!" Petey squawked derisively.

"What do you know?" Silva scolded his pet. "You never seen one." He scratched the blond tobacco-stained whiskers on his chin. "There's critters *like* 'em here... But I once watched a pair o' crows cookin' grasshoppers on hot asphalt before eatin' 'em." He thumped Petey on the head. "Never seen *you* cook nothin'." He seemed to think about that. "Earl neither, for that matter, even before he got killed the last time. Guess that means he ain't as smart as a crow neither."

"Yuk it up," Earl Lanier groused, following Captain Rodriguez as he approached. "Next time you eat one o' my sammitches, you should wonder if I been carryin' the bread in my drawers all day."

"Oh my God!" Pam objected. "What *are* all you men, about six?" She hustled over to starboard, where the wounded were being lifted aboard. "Get 'em down to the wardroom," she said.

Ronson watched her, then went straight to Abel Cook, who saluted. "Report, Mr. Cook."

Abel proceeded to describe the raid, the damage done, and the approximate casualties inflicted. Ronson was watching the emaciated hostages being assisted forward and then saw the bodies. "We lost two cadets killed, a couple more wounded," Abel explained. "Total *Walker* killed was four, and about twice that many hurt." He nodded at Silva's sling. "Most can still perform duties."

Ronson nodded grimly. With as little as they'd known about the layout of the raid's objective, he'd frankly steeled himself for worse losses.

They were still bad enough. "Fred Reynolds kept an eye on the anchorage as long as he could and reported that *Prinz Eugen* was sunk," he waved aft, where the second Nancy was being lifted aboard. "Called it in just before he landed. So, we've accomplished our most important mission. I wonder if the rest of what we planned is still worth the risk."

"I have to say yes, sir," Abel asserted strongly. "We destroyed their fuel reserves and they'll *have* to take Fen's Island, now. And we must assume they'll salvage at least as much technology there as they've lost. I know you and Mr. Meek have made arrangements to scuttle much of what's left, but other things, like *Nevada*, can't really be sunk. Not entirely." He paused. "After all the enemy has done—you really need to speak to the few hostages we found alive—if we leave now, they'll still win. I'm . . . not comfortable with that, sir."

"Me neither," Silva growled. "Ask anybody else, they'll say the same."

Ronson rolled his eyes. "This isn't a democracy, Chief Silva."

"No sir, it ain't," Silva agreed, "but ever'body knows a big chunk o' the job ain't done. I . . . respectfully suggest that ain't a lesson we want our cadets learnin' ta live with, is it?"

Ronson sighed deeply. "No." He continued brusquely. "Very well. Mr. Reynolds also reported that the remaining ships in the anchorage were preparing to get underway. The destroyers'll come out first, no doubt, and they might be faster than us. We need them to chase us, so they have to see us, but we can't let them get too close. Time to get moving."

"All right, you heard the man!" shouted Chief Bosun's Mate Carl Bashear. "Let's get these boats secured and make ready to get underway!"

CHAPTER 31

Steaming west across moderate, windblown seas at fifteen knots, USS *Walker* stayed within a few miles of the south coast of Raror. And once the cloud cover finally burned off, everyone was struck by the almost surrealistic beauty of the scene: the huge heavily forested main island's sharp colors only slightly muted by a lingering humid haze, the monolithic islets jutting from the sea like gigantic black teeth, eroded into fantastic shapes. Bright lizardbirds swooped and capered among the monoliths, some with their very own ecosystems high on top or clinging stubbornly to their sides. These seemed to serve as roosts or breeding grounds for the numberless fliers, flitting in tight formations between there and the main island shore, sometimes slashing down into the tumultuous surf to pounce, en masse, on schooling baitfish. Rainbow-colored back fins rose from the sea in huge numbers as pods of spiny plesiosaurs swept along, probably feeding as well.

"You writing all this down, Mr. Cook?" Ronson asked, gesturing around.

"Trying to, Captain," Abel said, writing swiftly in his journal and making the occasional sketch.

"Mr. Braadford'll be green with envy," chuckled Tabby.

"He'll be seeing some of it," said Jack Meek, "though if he and *Texas* have reached the place Captain Okabe suggested they linger, that was before the great monoliths."

"Plenty of little islaands poking up, though," Tabby mused, "and he'll haave longer to glaass whaat he sees thaan we do."

"I thought we brought a couple of cameras?" Ronson asked. "Haven't used them much." There were plenty of cameras around—nearly every original destroyerman had a little "Brownie," for example—but making film for them was still a low-output industry, focused more on providing 35mm for better-quality, higher-resolution surviving equipment used in photo reconnaissance.

Abel shrugged. "We took some pictures of the ghost fleet, but I guess I'm more used to drawing things now." He waved out to starboard at the island. "Black-and-white photos wouldn't do it justice anyway."

"Crow's nest lookout reports aircraaft ahead," said the little female 'Cat bridge talker. Ronson stepped out on the bridgewing and focused his binoculars on two of *Shonai*'s "Jakes." They were soon overhead, winging east. "Well, we ought to know if we're being followed soon enough," he called back in. With the enemy potentially closer to *Walker*, she wouldn't launch her own seaplanes again until action seemed imminent. She needed the planes off the ship in a fight, but couldn't stop to recover them either. Almost immediately, the talker spoke again; "Com shaack receiving from Jaapanese planes. They see enemy destroyers just over the horizon from us. We barely not see them ourselves, they think. Both remaining caapital ships're not faar behind."

Ronson looked at Tabby. "I doubt *France* can make much more than twenty knots, max. *Elsass*'ll be faster, but hanging back with her. The DDs are probably just now casting ahead." He looked at the cadet who had the deck and conn. He'd take both himself when things started happening. "Make turns for twenty knots. When the DDs get closer and spot us, we'll speed up some more, try to keep the same interval."

"Turns for twenty knots, aye," repeated the cadet loudly for the benefit of the 'Cat on the EOT.

"Whaat if we caan't?" Tabby asked. "Whaat if they're faaster thaan us?"

Ronson shrugged. "I hope we've got some help by then. If not, I guess we start shooting."

Quit mopin', Miles," Silva scolded the Marine. "With Arnie off playin' battleship sailor an' Carl Bashear pretendin' ta be our gunnery officer, I want you up on the 'midships deckhouse watchin' both crews in the fight. There ain't but one o' me, an' I might be runnin' my ass off, fore an' aft."

"Shut up," said Ian Miles.

Silva frowned. Both were on the aft deckhouse staring at the wake, wondering when they'd catch sight of the pursuing destroyers. General quarters hadn't been sounded but the number four gun's crew was already gathered, checking their weapon over. Lawrence had gone to the head. Fen, who'd otherwise glued himself to Silva, was checking to see if Pam was going to release Maarik for duty. At the moment, Silva and Miles were alone as far as anyone who might hear them speaking lowly was concerned. Silva had done his best to put Danny's loss aside, for now, but Miles seemed determined to blame himself for the loss of his young Marine.

"Since when did you start givin' a shit about anybody but yourself?" Silva asked brutally, and Miles glared at him before finally giving a slight nod.

"That's fair, I guess. A good question for the asshole I used to be. But that was a couple of years ago."

"Nobody just quits bein' a asshole," Silva scoffed.

"Maybe not," Miles agreed. "You'd know. But I also hear that you learned to give a shit—same as me."

Silva waved that aside. "I always did . . . a little. For some folks. I guess I've expanded my horizons a touch when it comes to them I consider 'under my protection,' as it were. You sayin' that's what happened to you, rompin' around Madagascar?"

Miles frowned. "Yeah, I guess. First time anybody ever really counted on me, needed me to be my best, see? Now these kids . . ."

"You've done a good job trainin' 'em to fight." Silva paused. "An' they're *gonna* fight an' maybe get killed. T'day or five years from now.

That's what happens in fights." He fished out his pouch of tobacco. "I liked that Danny Baker. He was a good boy an' had the makins of a fine destroyerman. It's crummy as hell that he's gone. Bad luck."

"Bad luck?" Miles snorted.

"Sure," Silva said. "He wasn't shootin' or thowin' grenades—he did all that right—he was just helpin' push a airplane down a ramp. Long story," he added. "Point is, a hardly aimed bullet just found 'eem. If he wasn't there, I might'a been. Somebody else *would'a* been, an' they'd'a been the one dead. You think on it an' tell me it was somehow your fault yer Marine was right where he was, doin' what he was doin', the instant he got shot."

"He might've been," Miles said. "I ordered him . . ."

"Ta stand there an' catch the bullet that got 'eem? Ta march straight into a machine gun? I doubt it. I don't even know what happened, but how many times did you give the same order ta somebody else? If it always got somebody killed, then you're a idiot an' a menace to the Navy Clan an' the whole Grand Alliance. Might be anyway if you get like this every time you lose somebody."

Silva saw his words sting the man, but then watched as his expression slowly changed. "*You're* an idiot," Miles finally blurted, "but . . . thanks."

"Anytime. Like we agreed, we'll watch each other's backs. I ain't a philosopher like Mr. Bradford—who's actually pretty wise about stuff like this—but I seen enough crazy shit happen in a fight . . . I mean, why the hell am *I* still standin' here? I ain't a little target, y'know."

Lawrence and Fen both returned together. "Maarik's been released for duty, if we need her," Fen reported.

"Good."

Just then, the shipwide comm system crackled and Tabby's voice came over the circuit. "This is the XO. There is not yet any need to go to generaal quaarters, but the enemy is in sight astern. Do not be alaarmed. It is our intention thaat they see us." Her tone slightly changed to one of calm amusement. "That said, if any instructors haave projects underway, disassembling things we might need in a fight, now is the time to put them baack together. Thaat is all."

Silva gazed aft again, shading his eyes. He couldn't see a ship, but the lookout probably could from the crow's nest. There might've been a slight haze of smoke too. "Well, I guess we're gonna need her," he remarked, finally stuffing a wad of leaves in his mouth.

"There's a plane!" Fen exclaimed, pointing. Silva and Miles exchanged glances and shrugged. Neither could possibly compete with young Lemurian eyesight. It wasn't long before they saw it, though, just one of the two Jakes that flew over earlier. They'd been higher then, and nobody knew if they'd carried bombs. This one didn't, so if they'd had them, they dropped them. Miles pointed this out.

"So, either one of 'em hung back to keep an eye on things or it got shot down," Silva guessed. "You hear that, Fred?" he asked louder as Fred and Kari climbed up the ladder to join them on the aft deckhouse.

"Hear whaat?" Kari asked.

"Just . . . I expect we'll kick y'all off the ship before the big bullets fly," he speculated, and Fred nodded.

It was SOP to launch planes before a surface action. If for some reason they couldn't fly, they had to be thrown over the side. The fire hazard they represented was just too great. "That's the plan. We'll spot for the guns."

"Good." Silva nodded. "Just don't get too close to theirs." He tilted his head up at the lone floatplane now roaring over. "I bet the other one o' them did."

Their pursuers, the two League destroyers for certain, gradually grew closer as late morning passed into afternoon, inexorably creeping up within ten thousand yards. "When're we going to baattle stations, Chief Silvaa?" asked Haan-Ara, serving at the number four gun captain.

Silva turned and looked around. "Appears to me you already are."

Haan blinked rapidly. "Yaa, but they haaven't sounded it yet and the enemy's in range *now.* Why don't we staart shooting?"

"That's pretty *long* range, sailor," Silva reminded skeptically. "You really think you can hit 'em that far?"

"Sure!" Haan said confidently, swishing her tail in anticipation. "They're just coming right at us, no zaag-zigging."

"Proper technical term's zig-zaggin'," he replied. "But Skipper's got his reasons. We'll go to Gee-Kyoo quick enough when they start shootin' at us. Thing is," he elaborated, "best I understand, it ain't our job ta sink them bastards, not yet, but drag 'em along with a ring in their nose."

"We caan do that with one as well as two," Haan said slyly. "An' if they think they're caatching us when maybe they shouldn't be, won't they expect us to try to slow them down? Wouldn't they staart wondering why we aren't?"

Silva blinked back at her, contemplating her excellent point. The DDs were getting closer, but he doubted they were making thirty knots. More like twenty-six. It was possible that, conserving fuel, they were just going as fast as they had to, but they were gaining on a ship they probably thought could do thirty. "Say, you may have somethin' there. Pass it along to the skipper with my backin'."

Haan blinked back in horror but did as he said, and whether Ronson had already figured it out himself or Silva's endorsement convinced him, the speaker crackled and the general quarters alarm finally sounded.

"All hands, this is the captain. Man your battle stations. I repeat, man your battle stations. Surface action, aft."

Silva winked his good eye at Haan and her crew. "I'll stick here for now, see if you were braggin'," he grinned. "You better get up on the 'midships deckhouse, Miles. Skipper's liable to shake our tail a little so one 'er the other o' those guns up there'll bear."

Miles nodded and grinned back. "You bet."

A helmet already on her head, Tabby hauled herself up the ladder and led her navigation crew to the auxiliary conn, positioned at the forward end of the aft deckhouse, just behind the mainmast. Like every fighting position on the ship, with the exception of the meager splinter shield mounted on the number one gun, it was entirely open and unprotected. There was nothing they could do about that. Enough armor just to stop small arms fire in the most crucial places would probably capsize the ship.

Silva waved at Tabby. "Hidy, XO."

"Get your helmet on," she scolded back, all business.

"Hmm. C'mere, Lawrence. Put your helmet on your pointy head—an' get out from in front o' that gun. They're fixin' ta shoot it, y'know."

"I know that!" Lawrence snapped back.

The loud roar of a Nancy engine running up to full throttle swept back over them just before the *boom* of the impulse charge hurled the little plane off the ship, foul-smelling white smoke gushing past as well.

Silva glanced forward for the first time in a while, noting that they were heading closer to the coast and that seemingly countless larger, high, rounded, "knob" islets were growing in the distance ahead. He had no doubt they'd be steering in among them and wondered how they could possibly do so at speed without proper charts of the bottom.

"Ain't my rice bowl," he muttered unhappily, eye drawn to the rushed effort to lift the second plane—he saw Kari-Faask haranguing the crew—up on the catapult. Fred's plane was swiftly gaining altitude and Silva wondered what he saw.

Perhaps the commanders of the League destroyers had the same thought Haan did, that they were close enough to try it, or maybe they were getting suspicious and decided to poke *Walker* in the ass to see what she'd do. Either way, at about nine thousand yards, they both opened up, the dull boom of their guns muffled by the churning wake, rumbling shafts, and the three big splashes a couple of hundred yards astern.

"Well," enthused Silva, forgetting his worries and clapping his hands together, "here we go!" He nudged Lawrence with his elbow when he joined him. "Won't be a big fleet action like St. Vincent, but I bet it'll be pretty fun."

Haan-Arą hadn't been bragging, and her crew managed a hit on one of the distant destroyers on her third shot. Granted, Carl Bashear was doing a creditable job calling directions from the gun control platform and his range estimation had been dead-on from the start. Still, the thirty-three-pound projectile was in the air for more than fifteen seconds and had to fall where the target *would be* when it got there. That took good work on the gun director . . . and a fair dose of luck. Everyone who saw the flash and billowing gout of smoke on the enemy fo'c'sle let out a cheer.

"Silence!" Silva roared, all business himself, now. "No change, rapid fire!"

Haan-Ara's number four gun slammed out nine more ear-shattering rounds in the next minute, joined by the number three gun on the port side of the amidships deckhouse. A kind of controlled chaos prevailed in both places as shell "men" advanced fresh rounds and hot shell "men" chased the big expended cartridges clanging off the deck, all while pointers and trainers checked and adjusted their settings between shots. Together, they achieved another hit somewhere on the enemy ship. Its speed wasn't notably reduced and the last few rounds fell long, proving both target destroyers were still closing the range while commencing subtle maneuvers to throw off their aim. Return fire, however, throwing up bright, sunlit spume, was briefly reduced, implying they'd done some damage to at least one enemy gun. Still, the fire redoubled periodically as the enemy's aspect changes unmasked more of their guns, and *Walker* found herself surrounded by a forest of tall, violent splashes, some of which were close enough to wet the deck and flail her old hull with jagged fragments of steel.

Silva shouted a warning at Tabby. "They're gonna start shootin' holes in us if we don't put on more speed an' start waggin' our tail."

"Caap-i-taan Rodriguez is aware," she called back, annoyed. "And we'll be squirming around like maad in another ten or twelve miles."

Indeed, Silva could already detect a change in the rumbling "feel" of the deck under his feet as the shaft rpms increased, the wake the ship's big screws threw up noticeably growing. Silva nodded his satisfaction. "What's the range now?" he asked Haan-Ara.

Holding the earphone tight, she replied, "Chief Baashear's taalker is just saying . . . Six, six, seero, seero yaards." She shouted the range at the pointer.

"They're half as far as you hit 'em before," Silva groused. "Time ta show me that wasn't a freak shot."

Abel Cook was in the pilothouse with Lieutenant Chiba, mere spectators at the moment, watching the very different islands up ahead grow more distinct. It seemed the "big island" of Raror had somehow . . . broken at some point quite long ago, and the rounded islands between its main parts were either eroded remnants of that old connection or an ancient volcanic attempt to reestablish it. Abel was fascinated by the formations and riot of avian life and actually somewhat concerned that Courtney Bradford might get distracted by the wonder of it all. The important thing was, many of the islands—all somewhat round from the top as well as the side, implying long ages of erosion—had been separated by underwater erosion as well, making the sea between them quite deep. At least that's what the Rarorani said, having fished and hunted big "water monsters" there since the beginning of time.

Reports were coming in constantly from Fred and Kari, and now one of *Shonai*'s planes even higher. Abel and Jack Meek were grateful for how committed Captain Okabe seemed to their joint venture, but had thought it foolish for *Shonai* to reveal her participation. The enemy was aware of her, of course, but for all they knew, she was still hiding in the winding lagoon of the island to the west of where the ghost fleet lay. They knew the Americans and Japanese were at war on the world they both came from, and there was no reason to expect they'd cooperate here. That they did still struck Abel, and probably Chiba, as somewhat surrealistic. But sending her planes on the raid against the League base on Raror had firmly established that *Shonai* and *Walker* were working together.

"I think you will soon agree with our position, Mr. Cook," Lieutenant Chiba said quietly to him. He must've guessed what Abel was brooding on. They'd argued about it enough, after all.

"I hope so," Abel replied.

Chiba pursed his lips. "I know you preferred to surprise them, but think about it from the League perspective. They have been exchanging fire with us for some time. No doubt the destroyers will continue to pursue us, if we do not destroy one another first," he added grimly. "Good enough," he said, holding up a hand, "but why should the enemy *capital ships* keep chasing a mere destroyer?" He nodded ahead. "Especially when it is clearly attempting to lead them on what would be at least a slight detour from their objective?"

"*Walker* is more than just a 'mere destroyer,' and they know it very well," Abel countered. "She's like"—he shrugged—"almost the heart of our Navy Clan, a powerful moral symbol of *all* our victories over them. Add their fury over what she did to them this morning and you might be surprised by the lengths they'll go to in order to destroy her."

"I might very well be, and you could be entirely correct," Chiba acknowledged with a smile, "but what if you are not? What if, despite any vengeful impulses, they believe they can avoid this detour and reach

Fen's Island before us, accomplishing their most important mission, by the way, and deal with your ship at their leisure then?"

Abel had to nod and gestured for Chiba to continue. The Japanese officer nodded as well. "You seem to think that Captain Okabe proposed this course to Mr. Bradford in order to 'prove' our commitment to your cause." He shook his head. "Though this should certainly do it," he continued wryly, "you completely had us already when you gave us hope, then fuel, and then when we saw *Nagato* towed to safety. You more than kept our agreement and treated us as *friends* . . . regardless of our past. I understand 'our' war is more distant to you than us, but it was so bitter . . ." Chiba shook that off and sighed. "I am not certain that we would have behaved the same in your place. Yet, we are all stranded on this world for the rest of our lives. We cannot persevere alone and would prefer to stand by those with honor than those without." He pursed his lips again. "So, my ship, *Shonai*, will soon reveal herself from somewhere up ahead and join your *Walker* in battle, presenting herself as the lure our common enemy now knows is out here somewhere, on your side, and simply can't ignore. There is no question that their capital ships *must* pursue and engage *her*." Now he grinned. "And *Shonai* and *Walker* together? Well, my only real fear is that they will flee."

"Multiple hits on one of the tin caans, aaft!" cried the little 'Cat talker. "It blow up 'an stop!" Like all Lemurians, her English suffered when she was excited.

"Swell!" Ronson said with a grin. "Pass the word, 'good shooting.' What about the other one?"

"Is still comin' on."

Ronson rubbed his tired eyes. "Damn. I mean, we want it to, sure, and we've got to keep shooting back, but what if we sink it? Who's gonna lead the big boys after us?"

Abel looked at Chiba and nodded. "*Shonai*," he said.

In less than an instant, Ronson's question and Abel and Chiba's previous debate became moot when a 4.7" shell from *Bettino Ricasoli*'s single gun forward mount crashed into *Walker*'s stern between her depth charge racks (fortunately unloaded) and the base of the aft deckhouse, exploding in the aft crew's berth, severing all communication to the steering engine room and blasting up through the torpedo-floatplane workshop and sending hot fragments of steel slashing through the thin steel of the aft deckhouse.

Dennis Silva felt the distinctive and sadly familiar sensation of someone slapping his face. He tried to smile. "Sorry, doll, I didn't mean it," he mumbled.

"I is *not* your 'doll'!" snapped Lawrence.

"Doll! Doll! Doll!" Petey screeched insistently.

"Shut it, you ridiculous little leech!" Lawrence sounded genuinely angry, and Silva realized he might find out why if he managed to open his eye. He did.

"What am I doin' here?" he asked, looking up and recognizing the stainless-steel serving counter by the galley under the amidships deckhouse. He was lying on the deck, practically underneath it. "Ow," he added, reaching up to touch his forehead. "Ow," he said again, fingers coming away bloody. "Who hit me?"

"The Leaguer destroyer," Lawrence said. "And they're still trying. You is knocked cold."

"Get me up," Silva insisted. "The number four gun?"

Lawrence shook his head. "Out o' action, lots hurt. Steering's out too. Us're *hand* steering, relaying directions as they try to restore control."

While Lawrence and someone else struggled to lift him to his feet, Silva was struck by how clearly his friend had passed important information and wondered if it was just an unusual situation in which few words required sounds he couldn't make or if he himself was just so used to the way Lawrence talked that he'd subconsciously rearranged and filled in the blanks. Petey jumped up on his shoulder and he winced. The sling was gone but the bullet hole remained. So did the sound of firing, on the deck above and now forward as well. Looking around, he saw what had to be most of the young crew of the aft 4″-50 laid out in the dubious cover to be found here with Pam and a pair of her surgeon's mates racing to stop their bleeding. A fist clenched on his heart when he saw Haan-Ara, though conscious, soaking an awful lot of her fur with blood. "How is she?" he asked.

"She'll live if any of us do," Pam declared, looking up at him. "Now you've woke up from yer nap, why don't you see what you can do about that?" she challenged.

Silva nodded, the motion making his vision swim a little. "Sure thing, sugar pie." He started aft. "Is the gun wrecked?" he asked Lawrence.

"I don't think so. Don't rightly know."

"We'll find out. Scratch up a crew on the way. Where's Fen?"

"Here, Chief Silva," came the voice of the little Lemurian behind him. "I'm not hurt. I went forwaard to take my place there, but I'm still just a 'baack up.' I thought you needed 'baack up' more."

"Good lad. Run, fetch s'more spares, an' meet us aft. Even Marines'll do in a pinch. They've all had a little trainin'."

"Ay, ay," Fen cried, very serious as he raced off. Silva nodded and tried to hurry as well, just discovering how much he hurt. He wondered if that came from getting blown up or if the last couple of days were catching up to him.

"Flit along in there an' keep Earl comp'ny again," he told Petey. He actually felt the little lizard's claws dig in.

"No!" Petey insisted.

"No? Goddamn. You know it's gonna be loud where we're goin'. You'll just get scared an' haul ass anyway. Prob'ly get stomped on."

"No! Goddamn!" Petey shrieked.

"Suit yerself, you little shit. You wanna get smushed? Fine."

Silva and Lawrence emerged in the open on the starboard side, passing the four-tube torpedo mount, emptied at the big German cruiser. Two hits out of four fish fired was actually pretty good considering how radically *Walker* was turning when she sent them. He wished they had some reloads, but they would've been in the aft deckhouse and likely would've exploded when they were hit, blowing the whole stern off the ship and killing everyone there, including him. There were still four fish in the portside tubes but only two were "warshots." The others were only practice fish. Three shells landed nearby to starboard, throwing sheets of spray across them, and Silva looked to see the League destroyer barely four thousand yards off their starboard quarter. It was his first good look at her. *Bettino Ricasoli* was another fairly handsome ship, considerably more modern-looking than *Walker*, if actually slightly smaller. She had a higher freeboard forward and only two stacks, which made her appear vaguely similar to the "modern" American destroyers they'd raced to save at Fen's Island. At full speed now, as *Walker* seemed to be as well, with smoke haze streaming back from all four funnels, the enemy DD might be a touch faster too. Maybe more than a touch. She only appeared to have three of those 4.7" guns, however, one in a kind of turret forward, and a pair in another one aft. *Walker*'s number one and three guns salvoed back at her, missing just aft.

"Extra hard to hit at these speeds," he shouted at Lawrence. "Constantly changin' ranges too." For the first time he realized *Walker* had been slowly turning back toward the enemy, getting closer to the hazy main island coast. He also noted with what could've been a thrill or a chill that a pair of *much* bigger silhouettes now loomed on the eastern horizon. Those would be the old French battleship and the superheavy cruiser with battleship guns. "Oh boy," he murmured. "They see us now. We gotta shake er break that Eye-tie tin can an' get our steerin' fixed before we steam right back amongst them boogers. C'mon!"

The deck on top of the aft deckhouse was covered with blood and debris, but a couple of "old" Lemurian hands were already working on the gun, and Tabby and a couple cadets were still there in the vicinity of the auxiliary conn controls. They weren't using them, however. Instead, Tabby, both lower legs wrapped in blood-seeping bandages, was sitting on a stool brought up for her, listening to directions in her earphones and loudly repeating them. Her words were then shouted down through a blooming flower of twisted steel, where someone below repeated them again down a companionway to the big manual wheel below.

She saw Silva and covered the microphone on a boom in front of her mouth. "You okaay?" He nodded. "We're steering," she told him. "Daamaage control party's below. Haad to put out a smaall fire an' vent the smoke. But we caan't turn awaay while thaat baastard's tailing us if we caan't get thaat gun baack in aaction!" She pointed at number four.

"I'm on it," Silva told her.

"Hurry," Tabby urged as another pair of shells slashed the sea just behind them. The one and three guns shot back, tracers converging and both hitting the enemy between the aft funnel and turret. Debris flew in the air and a fire erupted, but the target didn't slow and almost immediately shot back, knocking a hole in one of *Walker*'s funnels, but the shell didn't explode. Not enough there to set it off.

"What'a we got?" Silva asked the two 'Cats. He knew them both as experienced machinist's mates.

"The gun looks okay," one said, "but the support structure's compromised." He pointed at the deck. "It *leans*," he emphasized. "Wiring's no good, shredded, most likely." He pointed at the warped deck again, where the conduits in the space below would've been directly exposed to the blast.

"It'll shoot, though, right?" Silva demanded.

"Sure, in local control, an' if you remember it's leanin' when you aim it."

"An' it don't tump over when it fires," warned the other. Silva looked at him and blinked. "This one's a duaal-purpose mount," the 'Cat reminded, "for both surfaace *and* air taargets. Taller, more complicated, *heavier* mount," he emphasized.

Silva was nodding. "Which ain't properly supported no more. Yeah." He looked at the distant warships they were now almost heading toward, while the little destroyer dogging them would soon be too close to miss. He looked at the cadets Fen had brought, now scurrying up to join them, then back at Tabby. "Yeah," he repeated. "Out of the way, unless you want on the crew."

"Not me," said one. "I've got other work and I ain't no deck ape."

The other 'Cat—Silva remembered his name as Mulk something, but everyone called him "Milky"—glared at his companion, then looked back at Silva. "I'm a good loader, or breech maan. This very gun at St. Vincent."

Silva had been at the other end of the ship for that one, but he nodded. "Swell. Loader then. Larry? Take the breech. Fen, stack a couple life jackets on the trainer's seat." When he saw the tiny Maarik-Fas climb up on the battered deck, he grinned. "Pointer for you, young lady. More life jackets, Fen." He looked back at Maarik. "If you were two feet taller, you'd be gun cap'n an' I'd have a nap. Just take notice that the sights're gonna look a little twisted"—he eyed the lean—"which means the gun'll throw her rounds right, every time, an' more the farther you shoot. You'll hafta get a feel for it. Ever'body else is shell handlers an' hot shell men. Sort it out, let's go!" He waved at Tabby until he caught her eye. "We're up. Start yer turn an' we'll put some rounds right down their throat." Turning back to "his" battered gun, he shouted, "Load! Three rounds, up ladder, rapid fire. Start at three thousand yards an' I'll correct—somebody get over here an' remember my windage corrections for the different ranges. You'll be our gun director gizmo, see?"

"Gun is ready!" Lawrence cried.

"Commence firin'!"

On the bridge, Lieutenant Chiba was frowning.

Abel leaned over and whispered to him, "I guess Captain Okabe is hedging his bets, waiting to see if the Leaguers come this way on their own after all, before revealing his ship."

"Apparently," Chiba murmured back. "It does make sense, I suppose. Regardless of our nearest pursuer, however, the enemy capital ships are already close enough to engage us themselves."

That was true enough, Abel thought, though *Walker* had finally started turning away, shell splashes spraying high to starboard, alarmingly close to where they would've been. And though they were technically in range of the League capital ships, a hit would be almost miraculous. That confirmed Abel's suspicion, while raising his opinion of Captain Okabe even more. "I know what he's waiting for," he suddenly said with certainty. "The smallest guns the enemy have are the eleven inchers on *Elsass*, but the biggest guns on *Shonai* are eight inchers. Whether they come this way or not, he wants *them* in range of *him* before he makes an appearance." He frowned when another splash landed close alongside and the ship shuddered from a hard strike aft. "If we make it that long," he qualified, turning to see where they were hit. Dark smoke boiled up from beyond the amidships deckhouse.

"Damage report!" Ronson barked.

"Already coming in," called the talker promptly, her normally small voice incongruously louder and understandably more stressed than before, but also firmer. "Staarboard torpedo mount is destroyed," she relayed, the word likely from Ian Miles. She visibly stiffened. "The aaft fireroom waas holed above the waterline. No casuaalties, but Sureen says we're going to lose power and make a lot of smoke."

"Who's working to restore normal steering? I thought Sureen was back there."

"Sergeant Kaik led the detail. Sureen says he's good with machines."

Ronson sighed. "Well, Sureen knows what she's doing, but tell Tabby to get on Silva's ass to scrape that DD off of ours!"

Easy does it," Silva crooned. They hadn't managed a hit yet, but the splashes gave them a good range and an excellent idea how far left to hold. Now, as the enemy ship swung in directly behind them while *Walker* completed her turn, the target was almost perfectly bow-on, and somewhat unexpectedly, Silva called for an armor-piercing round. Now, leaning over to look down the barrel himself, he said, "She's comin' straight on. Make your range two, eight, zero, zero, Maarik. Fen, train out a whole beam width to her left this time."

"On taarget!" the two young 'Cats chorused and Silva stepped aside. "Fire when ready," he growled, "straight up her goddamn nose!"

Maarik stomped the trigger. *Wham!*

A lone tracer arced up and away, just starting to fall when it disappeared right over the jack staff, possibly even hitting it, before slamming into the deck right in front of the ship's forward turret. A cloud of what was probably paint dust swirled, but there was no other apparent effect for another long instant. Then there was. A jet of flame seemed to torch straight up, crowned by large, unrecognizable debris and framed by a giant black-and-white ball of smoke and steam.

"Stabbed her right down to her guts!" Silva whooped, but just as the number four gun's pickup crew began to realize they'd utterly smashed the tenacious little destroyer, there came an urgent shrieking sound of much larger projectiles, and a tight pattern of waterspouts, each taller than *Walker*'s foremast, marched across the wallowing, sinking wreck. For a moment there was only stunned silence, broken by the thunder of the mighty blasts finally sweeping across them.

"Whaat . . . ?" Maarik shouted, shaking her head, but Lawrence was pointing forward in the direction *Walker* was steaming now, past the ship's funnels and superstructure, at one of the big knobby islands covered with stunted trees down to the waterline. There was no beach, and the island actually seemed to have been undermined by wave action, making it look like a huge green ball floating on the sea. Lawrence was actually pointing beyond it, however, where the long, low, sleek shape of *Shonai* had revealed herself at last.

"Daammit!" Fen groused, quickly looking around to see if anyone noticed his language. "Now they'll think *they* saank her!"

"Their shells were already in the air an' they would haave, most likely," Milky consoled.

"Yeah, good dispersion too," Silva conceded. "Even if they didn't hit her square, that many near misses would'a put her down." His eye narrowed. "But dammit, y'all know who *really* got her. Well done." He looked back at the big Japanese cruiser. "But why show herself now? Why not earlier when we really could'a used a hand?" He turned back around. "Oh," he said. Another salvo of eight 8″ shells rumbled by overhead, higher this time, and he watched as tall, hazy stalks of spray shot up around one of the two League "heavies." He hadn't paid much attention to them for a while, being a little preoccupied, but now he saw they were closer, of course, but also a bit farther south than they'd been. "They were just gonna pass us by, head straight for Fen's Island," he guessed aloud, tone indignant. "Figured that Eye-tie tin can would sort us out, but even if she didn't, we weren't worth the effort to rub out for sure." He snorted. "They've turned back for us *now*, though. Damn sure can't ignore a Jap heavy cruiser. *She* can chase 'em down, hammerin' 'em in the ass all the way!"

Sergeant Kaik appeared beside Silva, limping from his leg wound and wiping his hands on a rag.

"Where you been?" Silva asked.

"Fixin' the steerin'." Kaik turned to Tabby. "Steerin's fixed!" he called.

Silva shook his head sadly. "Marines an' snipes workin' t'gether. A sure sign o' the end times. Says so in the Good Book."

A rumbling shriek shook the sky and a storm of huge splashes, some red, others greenish, churned the sea between them and *Shonai.*

Silva frowned. "Well, we're still out'a range for our little guns an' unless we're gonna get smeared off the map makin' a torpedo attack with two measly fish, we need ta get out from between the big boys. You take over here, Larry. I'm goin' forward t' see what's what."

"Me too," Kaik said.

"Goddamn Snipe!" Petey screeched at him.

Silva trotted and Kaik limped painfully quickly forward past the wreckage of the starboard torpedo mount, waving at Miles and his crews on top of the amidships deckhouse and then passing under it, by the galley where all the wounded from earlier had been removed, running and stumping up the ladder to the pilothouse.

"Make your course three, three, zero. Let's swing a little wide before we join with *Shonai,*" Ronson was saying. "No sense getting clobbered by a short round." He looked at Silva and Kaik. "Good work, both of you."

"What's the dope, Skipper?" Silva asked.

Ronson smiled a little, glancing at Lieutenant Chiba. "I thought you didn't hold with plans?"

Silva shrugged. "Not usually, no, but it seems I conjured up one o' my own a little earlier today. Did it on the fly, so I ain't sure it counts, but it kinda worked. Just curious, is all."

Lieutenant Chiba remained somewhat scandalized by the outrageous liberties the big chief gunner's mate took with officers, especially his captain, but it all somehow seemed to work. He laughed. "You mean that if there *is* a plan, you want to know what it is."

"Right." Silva grinned back. "That way I'll know right when it all goes to shit an' it's time ta start wingin' it again."

CHAPTER 32

IN THE SLOT
***USS* TEXAS**

"Fred Reynolds and Kari-Faask haave both reported thaat *Shonai* haas engaged the enemy," Lieutenant Daanis formally notified Courtney Bradford, finding him alone in the open on the starboard side of the navigation bridge by the pelorus. The paint on this side of USS *Texas*'s high, forward superstructure hadn't been blasted entirely off, and the color was more a highly oxidized light gray, almost white, rather than the near uniform bloodred rust almost everywhere else.

"Indeed?" Courtney responded, sounding somewhat distracted. There were certainly sights enough for that. The massive old battleship was idling, slowly circling within what was almost a palisade of bright green protrusions from the depths of a deep blue sea, and the wonders they'd discovered here were unlike any Courtney had seen, though perhaps slightly reminiscent of some Palawan islets or the Phi Phis. Neither were on the same scale or could compare with the variety of avian life. He sometimes almost quivered with the thought of the fauna they might find ashore. But as always seemed to be the case, conflict had doomed his exploratory urges.

That wasn't the chief source of his present agitation, however. Despite what many might think, he remained pragmatic enough to keep things in perspective, and his devotion to nature and science always—if somewhat reluctantly—took a back seat to his dedication to his friends and their cause. He could repress his curiosity to an extent on occasion and it was *almost* enough for him to view such wonders as these from afar, just to know they existed, reserved for later study. He wasn't a young man anymore but was able to prioritize the years he had left, and they would always, first and foremost, be spent to benefit the people—of all sorts—who made up the Grand Alliance. But he'd soon have to fight for it again himself and he was—as always—ill-equipped to do so.

About all that could be said for *Texas* was that she could move, certainly an amazing accomplishment in itself, and Chief Isak Reuben had even restored a fourth boiler to operation. That meant, theoretically, if nothing broke down, the ship might make as much as fourteen or fifteen knots. She could even fight after a fashion. They had enough hands to fire half of her powerful secondary armament (which meant they might have to scamper from one side of the ship to the other), but they'd have to do so in local control. All five of her great turrets could traverse and elevate their massive 14″ rifles, and the men, 'Cats, and Rarorani had been drilling incessantly to feed them, but no one except Gunnery Sergeant Arnold Horn, formerly of the 4th Marines, was remotely qualified to *aim* them. He'd been bringing his team of cadets up to speed as fast as he could, yet wasn't even perfectly familiar with the equipment in *Texas* himself. The layout where he'd learned in *New York* was different. Aside from all that, he'd have to direct the huge rifles by means of a possibly fickle gun director high in an entirely unarmored fighting top above Courtney's head. This by means of what was ultimately hundreds of yards of wildly vulnerable wiring that, while it tested good, had countless potentially oxidized points of failure built in.

If everything held together, Gunny Horn was confident they could hit the broad side of a barn, or a battleship, at relatively close range, and they'd have to fight close for any of the secondaries to count, but tough as she was, with all her vulnerabilities and utterly insufficient crew, "close" was *Texas*'s Achilles heel. When Lieutenant Daanis found him, Courtney hadn't been lost in the scenery, he'd been contemplating the fact that, with the possible exception of the much younger and larger *Impero* still to be proven herself, *Texas* was the mightiest weapon they'd ever been gifted by this strange, wondrous world. Like many of their Lemurian friends, he was often lured to ascribe some spiritual purpose to that. Unfortunately, at the moment and despite all she promised if they saved her, compared to her approaching enemies, *Texas* was a sledgehammer, capable of inflicting immense damage, but her handle was cracked and far too short.

Clearing his throat after the long pause that probably worried poor Daanis, Courtney asked, "And *Walker*? What of her?"

"She . . . took minor daamaage in her duel with the pursuing destroyers but disabled one—Mr. Reynolds flew over and inspected her and believes she is doomed—and Caap-i-taan Rodriguez *claims* to haave destroyed the other destroyer just as *Shonai* fired on her as well." Daanis blinked and swept his tail from side to side. "There is already some . . . contention over thaat."

Despite his mood, Courtney actually chuckled. "No doubt." His tone firmed again. "How much longer? For us?"

"That is a difficult question," Daanis hedged. "*Shonai* and *Walker* are currently playing 'seek me' through the islets east of the main channel while the League vessels draw closer." He gestured at his tufted ears, which were poking out slightly to the side with his helmet in place. "Some of our lookouts placed even above the fighting top claim they caan hear the sound of guns and see smoke drawing closer." He blinked uncomfortably. "To lead the enemy directly paast us, however, as Caap-i-taan Okaabe insisted, *Shonai* must at some point show her stern to the enemy." He paused. "As you are aware, she haas no guns and little aarmor, aaft."

"Yes," Courtney said grimly, "I know. Captain Okabe didn't want to be burdened in the running action by our . . . sedate pace and believed he'd have a better chance employing his ship's speed and agility. He also argued that we'd draw too much of the enemy's fire long before we might effectively return it. He's probably right about that. Finally, and on this point I agree entirely, he maintains that the League can have no idea this ship is operational. Her sudden participation at the appropriate moment may give us our one and only possible edge."

Daanis idly stroked the fur on his chin. "*Texaas* could come as a complete and devastating surprise, particularly if she appears at close range."

Courtney nodded. "That's the plan." He sighed. "I *do* so wish that the inestimably infuriating Chief Silva would stop planting such skepticism about 'plans' in my mind"—he paused—"and heart."

Kari-Faask had slowly learned to love to fly—with Fred at the controls. She was a competent pilot, perhaps a little better than that, but knew she simply wasn't as good or experienced as her best friend and never felt quite as comfortable in the front seat as in the back. That said, she'd probably done more front-seat flying on this trip than she had in the whole last year of the Great War and was confident enough she wouldn't crack the ship up through sheer "dumbaassery" to take cadets up with her. Besides, there weren't any enemy aircraft or vicious flocks of Grik-birds or "dragons" to worry about (that they knew of yet), and her only real concern was avoiding a damaging strike by one of the myriad smaller flying creatures so thick in the air around these islands, or straying into range of enemy antiaircraft fire, of course.

Her backseater today was the little fellow 'Cat, Aalak-Maraan, who'd damaged this very plane and remained more than slightly afraid of her. It was their first time in the air together. Fred told her the "kid" was "okay" and probably had a future in naval aviation. He was certainly keen and observant enough, had only "horked" in the cockpit once, and handled the plane well enough in simple maneuvers with the backseat controls. Fred was going to recommend him for advanced flight training. Still harboring a dwindling hostility toward Aalak herself—never as quick to forgive as Fred, ever since she'd been captured and tortured by Doms, Kari had an even greater tendency to carry grudges—she'd avoided taking him up before. But Aalak had been with Fred when he reconnoitered this far before, and Fred assured her the kid was as good as a camera with landmarks. It was Aalak who'd drawn their best aerial chart of the cluster of weird islands and the main-channel Slot between what turned out to be *two* "big islands" instead of one. Even *Shonai*'s observations had missed that, steering around the little green blobs (from the air) instead of among them.

"Which approach will *Shonai* take?" Kari shouted back at the kid behind her, knowing from experience that, even with the new electronic comm, the noise of the wing-mounted engine and pusher prop above and between them would be louder in the back seat. The big Japanese cruiser was briefly obscured from the malevolent pursuers by what looked like a dark green puffball, and *France* and *Elsass* had redirected their fire at little *Walker* as she chased after *Shonai*. *Walker* wasn't directly behind the cruiser, though, more off her starboard quarter, and the giant colored splashes marched across the sea, towering short of the frail destroyer. Kari felt a chill in her spine, knowing a single one of those enormous shells could be enough to kill the little ship.

"Ah . . ." Aalak replied, slightly hesitant, "I think Cap-i-taan Okaabe means to go around the next cluster of islands and get in some more licks before turning abruptly north for the Slot. *Waalker* should turn northwest as soon as she's out of view. Following *Shonai* from thaat point onward in line aastern would . . . probaably not be best."

Kari nodded, impressed by the kid's understanding of the tactical situation. The two enemy capital ships were doing just what they wanted, so far, drawn in pursuit by the big cruiser that had scored a respectable number of hits with her 8″ main battery, her fire adjusted by Fred as he orbited high above the enemy. The enemy had no such assistance. Of course, both were a lot tougher than *Shonai*. But now they'd complicated Fred's spotting. From their initial line-abreast advance, the faster *Elsass* had surged ahead of *France* to close the range and would be within six thousand yards of the Japanese cruiser when she turned away. She'd only have her three forward 11″ guns to engage her then, but *Shonai* couldn't shoot back at all.

"Yes!" Aalak shouted. "*Walker* just got two hits on *Elsaass*, right before she ducked behind the island!"

Kari banked right a little to get a better view and saw a new column of smoke rising to join another that the German cruiser was already spewing. It looked impressive but might've been nothing more harmful than the ship's boats set afire. It wasn't affecting her speed. Flashes of fire and tall columns of spray coincided with another three-gun salvo from *Elsass*, indicating a few hits and several near misses by *Shonai* as she sprinted into the open and salvoed all four forward 8″ turrets. *Elsass* was mauled this time, taking heavy damage to her forward superstructure. Once more, however, she just kept coming and firing.

"Tough ship," Kari grumbled. The fire from *France* was intermittent now, her view somewhat blocked by her smoking consort. *Shonai* sent another salvo and then abruptly turned to starboard, heading north, the sea where she would've been churned by a trio of geysers. "Where's *Waalker*? Do you see her?"

"No, Lieutenaant," Aalak replied. "I thought I would by now."

Kari blinked concern. As deep as the water was *supposed* to be around the dozens of little islands, there was no guarantee it truly was. She hoped her ship, the closest thing she had left to a home, hadn't run aground or torn her guts out on an underwater rock. "Keep looking. Sing out when you see her."

"Ay, ay."

Looking back at *Shonai*, running as fast as she could and making smoke to confuse the enemy's aim, she said a quick prayer to the Maker on the ship's behalf. *Shonai* was fast, supposedly faster than *Walker*, but the aft third of the ship was dedicated entirely to servicing, launching, and recovering her seaplanes, and there was nothing whatsoever back there that could defend her in a surface fight. She wondered then if *Shonai* had launched her other planes. Kari hadn't seen it if she had, and there'd been nothing transmitted about it. A rag of black smoke flapped in the air nearby and the little Nancy jolted.

"Craap!" Kari shouted, banking right and diving. "I get too distraacted!" The big German cruiser, smoldering as she was, still had antiaircraft capability and had clearly moved, or Kari had strayed, close enough for her to prove it. Several more bursts of black smoke appeared above and behind them as the Nancy plummeted from the sky, trying to gain distance and outrun the enemy's ability to adjust their aim. Kari wasn't sure it was working. She loved her Nancy, and the little planes had served them well in the war against the Grik and Doms, but they were just too slow to be useful in combat against the far more modern League. Then again, this wasn't *supposed* to be a combat mission, was it? There was an audible blast and burst of pressure right over Kari's head. Something barely visible slashed through the wing and twirled away past her forward cockpit, and the engine began shaking maniacally, threatening to tear the plane apart.

"I think the prop broke. I gotta cut the engine. Send a mayday!" Kari shouted over the comm, her hands moving of their own volition to shut off the fuel flow and cut the spark. There was no response from behind her. "Aalak! Send 'Mayday' right daamn now. I gotta set this thing on the waater with a dead stick!"

Still nothing. The engine coughed and died, and the sudden wind-blown silence of the exhaust was deafening. Kari wrenched her head around to look at Aalak behind her. The upper fuselage of the plane was torn in numerous places, the fabric peeling back and flapping, but the kid seemed fine, staring north through an Imperial spyglass. "Aan-swer me, daamn you!" Kari shrilled. "Are you hurt? Dying? You *better not* be dying, you little shit! Everybody'll think I got you killed on purpose."

"*Elsaass* . . ." Aalak finally shouted. "She got *Shonai*. Hit her baad."

Fighting the stick to keep the nose pointed down against the drag of half the prop—she'd been right about that and these earlier models didn't have variable pitch or the option to feather—she took a quick glance to the north and saw *Shonai*'s stern wrapped in flames under a billowing tower of smoke. She thought the ship was still underway, but they didn't have time to confirm it. "Quit screwin' around and send the mayday an' our position—though I bet Fred'll see us go down. I'm gonna try to get around thaat tree-covered bump *Waalker* went behind in case she's still there, but no guaraantees." Scanning the water coming up fast below, Kari already knew they'd never make that. She could try to go *over* the island, but they'd probably just crash into it, and the scraggly trees clinging to its rocky slopes looked as unyielding as teeth. She'd have to try to set down in the water close enough to shore to give them a chance to get there—before something ate them or the plane. "Tighten your belt an' hold on," she snapped.

"I haave faith in you, Lieutenaant Faask!" Aalak shouted piously behind her, between transmitting their situation and position.

"*I* don't," Kari barked back. "Fred's always the one who craashes us. He's good at it now."

"Kari-Faask's plane is down," called the talker back behind Ronson. "Lieuten-aant Fred Reynolds says she's down in one piece and floating about fifty yards offshore, but the plane is chopped up an' might sink."

As Kari had suspected, *Walker* had slowed to steerageway just beyond the island she'd disappeared behind and Kari was forced down beside. And as Kari also considered most likely, *Walker* was lurking in wait for *Elsass*.

"Ask him what *France* is doing," Ronson said tensely and the talker relayed the message.

"Still coming," the talker reported a few moments later. "*Shonai*'s planes attaacked her with bombs. One hit her but didn't slow her." There was a pause. "One of the planes was shot down. *Shonai* is still underway but slowing. She seems to be haaving trouble with her steering, like we did."

Ronson doubted the damage was much the same, or could be put right as quickly. *Shonai* was out of sight past more islands to the north and actually in the Slot when she was struck, but Fred had already reported that it looked like half the ship blew up. Ronson's first thought was of all the aviation fuel she'd taken on from the ghost fleet, but Lieutenant Chiba suspected it had been her torpedoes. She'd actually retained and hoarded one remaining weapon to shoot aft, twelve of them in point of fact: six tubes on each side loaded with excellent and deadly 24-inch-diameter, 30-foot-long Type 93 torpedoes. Chiba explained, "Captain Okabe probably should have used them long before, but we didn't only want *Elsass*, we needed *France* to commit to the chase as well." His face was a mix of worry and sadness. "Now that she seems to have done so, both ships would have gotten a mouthful of Type Ninety-Threes soon enough—if something didn't happen."

Ronson gave the young man a sympathetic look. "We already knew your torpedoes were wicked long-range monsters, but even though we use pure oxygen in our own now, it can be pretty scary."

Chiba shook his head. "Yes," he agreed, "but the biggest danger is in the explosive itself. Shimose powder instead of TNT, like most navies use. Shimose is somewhat more powerful than TNT but uncomfortably susceptible to shock detonation. We learned through costly experience in our old war with your navy that the explosion of one can set them all off. We lost several ships, even cruisers, to what should have been negligible hits. The accepted practice has been to launch them at extreme range to minimize the risk of that. Captain Okabe told me himself that he would risk a closer release if the potential reward might justify it."

"Damn," Ronson said. "Gutsy, though, and a whole swarm of big-ass torpedoes in confined waters would've been a good idea if it worked." He looked at the faces around him. "We don't have a 'swarm,' only a single pair of warshot fish in our portside mount, but it's our turn to give it a try." He shrugged. "Might as well shoot the practice fish too. The enemy might run into a hot one trying to avoid one of those." He looked at the talker. "Ask Mr. Reynolds to estimate when *Elsass* will clear the island and pass ahead of us. Tell him where we are if he doesn't know." He considered a moment. "After our attack, he can set down by Kari's plane and render whatever assistance he can."

"Assuming our attack accomplishes something other than our own destruction," Abel Cook said wryly, "wouldn't it be better if he continues to report from above?"

Ronson shook his head. "'Assuming,' as you said, I expect us and *Shonai* can do that."

"While we are doing what else?" Abel asked.

Ronson looked at him and grinned a little nervously. "Hauling ass."

CHAPTER 33

At a final warning from Fred Reynolds that *Elsass* would imminently appear, *Walker* straightened up on a course of 280 from the looping turn she'd used to increase speed to twenty knots, portside torpedo mount already rigged out at 30 degrees, her aspect sufficient that her numbers one, two, and four gun mounts would bear. And the range would be close enough that her portside 25mm antiaircraft guns mounted in tubs alongside the seaplane catapult, aft, and all her .50 cal and .30 cal portside machine guns would at least be able to annoy the enemy, perhaps disrupting the fire of her secondaries.

Chief Bosun's Mate Carl Bashear had abandoned the gun director on the fire control platform, left the main battery to fire in local control, and taken his place at the torpedo director on the portside bridgewing. He'd once been a torpedoman himself and was the chief instructor on the ship. A number of cadets had shown great aptitude for the arcane art of aiming the wildly complicated weapons, but Carl had decided to take this on himself. He trusted the cadets to do it right—in drill—but this was for most, if not all the marbles, and he was almost too tense to do it. Ultimately, it was probably as simple as his determination that, if somebody screwed it up and got them all killed, he didn't want any of these kids spending their last moments torturing themselves with that.

"There she is! Bow's coming into view!" cried a cadet on the fire control platform above.

"Range . . . mark!" cried Bashear, gazing through the telescope on top of the complex machine as he tracked the target. A number of settings such as OWN SHIP COURSE, SPEED, INTERCEPT OFFSET, etcetera, had already been made.

"One, four, seero, seero!" cried the young 'Cat on the range finder, and another cadet turned a dial on the director to indicate that.

"Target course is zero, two, zero. Speed . . . mark!"

"Fourteen knots!"

About half of *Elsass* was in view by now and they'd soon be seen themselves.

"I haave a solution!" cried one of the 'Cat cadets who, along with Carl, were gathered around the machine like worshippers at a shrine.

"Send it!" Carl snapped, and the torpedo course and gyro angle solution orders were transmitted electrically to analog dials on the mount where torpedomen communicated the settings to the weapons in the tubes. Turning to look at Captain Rodriguez, Carl Bashear took a deep breath. "Tubes two, four, six, and eight show ready in all respects."

Elsass was right in front of them now, firing forward at *Shonai* and streaming smoke from the numerous hits she'd taken herself. She'd been a good-looking ship in her own right, a twin to their own *Hessen*, but the time spent corroding under peeling and blotchy paint in tropical neglect had only been kinder by degrees than what the rust-red ghost fleet had endured. Of course, she was somewhat battered now too, but despite the licking she'd taken today, little if any of her combat power seemed affected, and her slight speed reduction was probably only due to prudence in these strange, confining waters and the fact her target was slowing as well. Once again, Ronson wished they'd had the opportunity to communicate with her crew. They might've found them as disgruntled as *Hessen*'s had been. Even now, Ronson briefly toyed with an instant's inspiration to call her in the clear, but that was impossible. The fight was already on, already too brutal to simply stop.

"Fire torpedoes, Chief Bashear," Ronson said.

"Fire two," Carl called, and they heard the smoky, booming *chuff* of the impulse charge hurling the first 21" brass-bodied Mk-7 Baalkpan Arsenal torpedo over the side, where it entered the water with a steamy, concave splash before racing away toward its target. "Fire four, fire six, fire eight!" Carl shouted, and the ship lurched with each ejection. "Secure the mount," Carl ordered, turning back to Ronson. "All torpedoes expended, sir."

"Very well," Ronson declared. "All guns, commence firing! Helm, make your course three, four, zero. All ahead full," he told the Repub cadet by the EOT.

Fregattenkapitan Johann Maurer, commanding *Elsass*, shouldn't have been so focused on *Shonai*, now somewhat feebly hobbling away under a tower of roiling black smoke less than eight thousand yards to the north. His remaining lookouts were even more negligent, but like him, they considered the savaged Japanese cruiser the only significant remaining threat. Everyone was therefore completely surprised when the same little destroyer that invaded their anchorage and sank *Prinz Eugen* that very morning suddenly appeared close to starboard, winding up to a sprint, guns flashing all over her and streaming smoke. Those shells and bullets quickly found their mark, shaking the ship with relatively small but significant and damaging blasts, knocking out comms and causing gun's crews in open mounts to seek cover from zinging and ricocheting machine-gun fire. Worse, no one even noticed her until *after* the telltale impulse charges caused the big splashes alongside her, so their immediate collective instinct had been to redirect fire at this impudently aggressive little annoyance. The possibility that her brazen, seemingly foolhardy assault portended something far more menacing didn't occur to them at first. It would have in just a few moments, no doubt. The little four-stacker destroyer had torpedoed *Prinz Eugen*, after all. But they didn't have moments. Not even one. The torpedoes *were* seen and panicked warnings were shouted, but no possible maneuver would avoid them by then. Four torpedoes were seen to hit the starboard side of the ship, and a few men later wondered with gratitude (because they were right above the strikes) or morbid curiosity why only two went off.

The pair of towering, steamy blasts were quite enough, however, at least to knock *Elsass* out of the chase. The forward fireroom and starboard engine room were blasted open to the sea and quickly began to fill, swiftly inducing an increasing list to starboard. *Elsass* still had power, but continuing the fight was suddenly the very last thing on Fregattenkapitan Johann Maurer's mind. Having watched how quickly their prize turned turtle after suffering a similar blow, his every thought now turned to saving his ship and her people before they wound up in this terrible sea. He didn't even notice little *Walker*'s winged dash north, though he noted with passing appreciation that no one was shooting at them anymore. He did, after what seemed a very long while filled with hurried, urgent reports and a numbing flurry of grave decisions, each deserving hours of consideration but required of him in seconds, see the determined but equally rusty passage of the old dreadnought *France*.

Maurer knew precisely what his overall commander was thinking, what drove him now. Commandant Francois Messe (the debauched and essentially banished cousin of the "most equal" member of the Triumvirate, Marshal Messe) would never relent. It was no secret his posting to the end of this earth had been a last chance to shine, and the sudden wealth of technology that practically dropped out of the void and into his lap had seemed to assure his return to favor. His first impulse to move the whole League base to the island with the treasure trove of ships might've been best, in retrospect, but was forbidden by the Triumvirate. They were rightly concerned the great blast would attract inspection by the Allies—which it did—but those first investigations were easily contained while a plan to draw off significant Allied opposition to League operations was successfully implemented.

Then, of course, everything started falling apart, beginning with the overly aggressive bumbling of that ridiculous Ames character, who brazenly went to Respite to seek repairs for "his" *personal* prize, USS *Scott*, which ended in the escape of one of his distastefully (probably Dominion-inspired) mistreated prisoners. And the crippling damage he inflicted on the port at Respite had been sure to provoke a response. In this case, the most grievous error had been Commandant Messe's for ignoring one of the strictest League doctrines: The barbarian descendants of previous crossovers must never be trusted.

So even as the grand strategic plan was unfolding nicely, his tactical situation began to unravel at the hands of unimaginably diverse "allied" peoples, many mere *animals.* And now *this* disaster! Their long-secret base in the Pacific not only discovered but ravaged, his great prize destroyed, his most modern ship badly crippled by a meager, ancient destroyer and a half-smashed Japanese cruiser that Messe had long considered of no remaining concern. If he didn't somehow turn all this to his advantage, he might as well die in the attempt. He'd certainly die for his failure.

Now Fregattenkapitan Johann Maurer dolefully watched Messe's elderly, dilapidated, but still mighty "flagship," *France*, boom by up the channel, flying a signal from her halyard: "Complete repairs and follow me." He barked a laugh that drew incredulous looks and he waved encouragingly at his harried, frightened people. He was already bitterly certain *Elsass* would be fortunate not to sink. She wasn't *going* anywhere. Commandant Messe would just have to cope with the shattered Japanese cruiser and plucky—but surely out of torpedoes now—American destroyer on his own.

Dennis Silva and Lawrence clattered down the companionway under the bridge structure and poked their heads through the curtain to the wardroom, quickly taking in the wounded sitting on chairs by the fore and aft bulkheads, lying on mattress cushions on deck, or—in the case of Haan-Ara—lying on the wardroom table. The big light above it had been lowered on its adjustable, jointed, spring-loaded fixture to provide Pam and her surgeon's mates the best illumination to perform their work. Haan was still conscious, though agreeably drunk on a big dose of "seep"—the popular "recreational" but still analgesic drink made from polta fruit. Haan was already swaddled in bandages, but Pam was still stitching a long shaved gash on her shoulder.

"Hi, Chief Silvaa!" Haan slurred. "An Mr. Laawrence! Whaat're you doin' here?"

"Yeah. Don't you have a battle to fight?" Pam groused, snipping a stitch and starting another. Silva ignored her. Pam was doing what she loved, what she felt *called* to do as strongly as any cleric, but she was always grouchy at times like this.

"Came ta check on you, sweetie," Silva gently told Haan, eye sweeping around the space. A couple of those laid out on the deck had been covered completely by sheets, and he frowned. "You an' the rest in here," he added. Glancing up at Pam, he said, "We stuck a pair o' fish in that big Kraut cruiser an' bought a few minutes, rest. She's out of it. That fat French wagon's still comin', though."

"Chief Silvaa called me 'sweetie'!" Haan chortled.

"Sure, kid," he confirmed with a grin, "but only off duty, see?"

Haan blearily waved her hand. "I know you're just foolin'. Ever'body *knows* you're Paam's."

"Shush, now." He chuckled. "Don't spill it!"

"But ever'body *aalready* knows!"

"I can't help what people think," Pam snorted, but her tired, pretty eyes slashed up at Silva in a way he remembered from better times between them. "Dumb ape ain't *my* responsibility," she added. "You"—she gestured at a sick berth attendant standing from one of the wounded on deck—"check Chief Silva's wound. Bend down, Dennis! What's he s'posed to do, climb you like a tree? Check out his new bullet hole if you can tell it from all his old ones. Put some fresh polta paste on it and change the bandage. He's probably not through jumpin' around for the day and he's liable to bleed out."

"Thanks, doll," he said. "That's the nicest you been ta me in I don't know when."

"Nicest I've felt like," she retorted. "Don't read nothin' into it."

"Thanks Doll!" Petey screeched.

"I don't understand her at all," Lawrence said as they clambered back up the companionway and trotted aft.

"You'd be the only one, if you did," Silva assured him. "I don't reckon *she* understands her more often than not."

Petey shrieked "Eat!" as they neared the galley, but they didn't go past it, climbing the ladder to the top of the amidships deckhouse instead. The number three gun was trained out to starboard but there was no target within its arc of fire. The smoking, listing *Elsass* stood out against one of the green islands, this one resembling a leafy anvil from this angle, and *France* was still churning forward but holding her fire. The aft stacks and searchlight tower blocked the number three gun, but its crew stood ready. Number two had suffered some kind of casualty, and Ian Miles and that gun's crew had removed the access panel on the main mount pedestal to trace wires as fast as they could. Number one wouldn't bear, and that left only the badly torqued number four gun just now. Not that anyone was anxious to poke the bear. *Walker* had opened the range to about nine thousand yards by the time she caught up to the limping *Shonai* and slowed to match her current best speed. Barely ten knots. The old enemy battleship clearly knew that and appeared to be running at fifteen or so, closing the distance to finish her prey with the fewest precious shots. Even if *Walker* still managed to escape, a strong possibility, she couldn't do anything to prevent *France* from steaming on to retake possession of Fen's Island and all the treasures there. She *could* hit *France* from here, even with the balky number four, but couldn't really *hurt* her at any range, and shooting at her was almost sure to provoke her into shooting back.

"What's the matter with it?" asked Chief Bosun Carl Bashear, waving at the malfunctioning weapon and huffing from his trip down from the fire control platform and back up here.

Silva shrugged. "Me an' Larry just got here. Ask the *Marine* how he screwed the gun up."

"Why can't you ever just shut up, damn you!" Miles almost ranted. "Always a wiseass, with some stupid crack . . ."

"Sounds like *you're* the one fixin' ta crack—" Silva began, but Bashear rolled his eyes and made a slashing motion with his hand.

"This is *not* the time for the dubious and juvenile 'wit and wisdom of Dennis Silva,'" Bashear grated.

"Did he just say *joo-vin-ile*?" Silva hissed aside, and Lawrence nodded solemnly.

"Joo-vin-ile!" Petey proudly proclaimed.

Miles looked ready to commit violence, but some of the nervous cadets around him smiled tentatively. A couple even chuckled—and that had been Silva's intent from the start. That's what he did.

Miles looked at Bashear, tilting his helmet back and scratching his head. "I don't know what's the matter. If I had to guess, I'd say it was one of those big near-miss splashes that drenched us. Water got in there"—he pointed inside the mount—"and shorted something out. This trip was also the shakedown cruise after practically rebuilding the whole ship. Failures like this would've been reported and sorted in the yard when she got back." He glared at Silva, who was ignoring him now, stepping over to the rail to watch *Shonai*'s battered form struggling along under a pall of smoke. Miles raised his voice to insure that Silva heard him. "*Walker* wasn't *supposed* to even ever *fight* again, damn it!"

"See?" Silva said, turning with a grin on his face. "That's my biggest problem with 'plans.' I got nothin' against makin' 'em, even actin' on 'em. An' havin' half a dozen backups in yer pocket is swell. It's them fellas that lose their shit when they fall apart an' don't know what ta do then that really wind me up." He met Miles's glare with a cocked eyebrow. "Point is, I figger it's always better ta be surprised when plans actually work than when they don't. Got that from Cap'n Reddy himself."

Miles's fury seemed to dissolve and he stepped away from the gun and straightened. "Right," he finally said. "It's just . . ."

"I know," Bashear nodded, eyes flicking around at the cadets as he lowered his voice. "Kids."

Miles nodded, then cleared his throat. "Button that up," he directed, referring to the access cover. "If we have to keep fighting, we'll do it in local control." He forced an amused snort. "It's not like we can *miss* that big bastard!" Now it was his turn to lower his voice, tilting his head at *Shonai*. "But how long are we going to stand by her? She's finished. We ought to either be taking people off her right now, or she should come about and fight with her forward guns."

Silva was slowly shaking his head, a weird gap-toothed grin on his face. "What, now? Why, the 'big plan' ain't even run its course yet. If we give up on it before it does, it *will* fail. Guaranteed."

Flashes lit the cluttered horizon to the south, brighter than before because a haze was starting to filter the bright afternoon sun and turn the sky a murky, blotchy blue-gray, as clouds began to form. It was almost certainly building to rain again, but that merely highlighted the fact that *France* had opened fire. Eight 12″ half-ton projectiles, four from her forward superfiring turrets and four more from her two wing turrets, shattered the air as they screeched in to fall in a scattered pattern of mighty splashes starting roughly eight hundred yards aft and stretching a little forward of *Shonai*. None hit, but a couple fell close enough to drench the men and younglings on *Walker*'s amidships deckhouse and raise a gulp of steam from the wreckage of *Shonai*'s scalding stern.

Silva blew salt water from the whiskers around his mouth. "Which Ronson'll be screamin' bloody murder about now an' I reckon it's just about time."

"Us going to clear out?" Lawrence asked with some concern.

"Lordy, I hope not." Silva grinned all around. "We're fixin' ta see somethin' nobody ever has, an' won't never forget."

CHAPTER 34

Still slowly circling within the screening palisade of islands where she'd lingered since shortly after dawn, USS *Texas*, BB-35, had lurked in wait for *her* primary prey to take the bait dangled before them. Still in contact with *Shonai*'s single remaining scout plane, and Fred Reynolds as well until shortly before, reports had confirmed the "bait" had indeed been irresistible, but was taken more savagely than hoped. Gunnery Sergeant Arnold Horn actually briefly *saw* the ravaged, smoke-roiling shape of *Shonai* creep past a gap in *Texas*'s "hunting blind" from his high vantage point in the foremast fighting top, though he doubted the big battlewagon had been seen in return from the cruiser's lower vantage point. And the darkening sky would conceal the gray haze of smoke rising from her single big stack.

TBS traffic from *Shonai*, and now *Walker*—which Horn hadn't seen—passed the welcome word that *Texas*'s expected dueling partners had been reduced to one (a huge relief for the former China Marine), but her single remaining opponent was virtually undamaged and already firing on the maimed *Shonai* once more. The time had come for the old, battle-worn, even *atom-bombed* USS *Texas* to spring their final surprise and reveal herself, to stand between her consorts and the enemy at last. He looked through the missing window down at the two forward gun-houses, already trained out to port, as was the one amidships and the two more aft, ready to fling ten 14″ armor-piercing shells as soon as they came to bear. Glancing around the confined space at the portion of the fire control team he'd assembled up here, the rest in the plot room and at least two in each gunhouse—nearly all cadets—he did his best to force a confident grin. "I guess this is just about it," he said. There'd be no reason to sound general quarters since everyone had been training at their stations all night. He nodded at the young talker. "Inform Lieutenant Daanis and Mr. Bradford that we're ready to raise hell at their convenience."

Down in the pilothouse on the navigation bridge, Lieutenant Daanis blinked questioningly at Courtney Bradford. Courtney had been holding his helmet in his left hand, nervously pacing to peer out each of the round windows (the main visible difference between this pilothouse and *Walker*'s from inside it), and massaging his sweaty scalp with his right. Catching Lieutenant Daanis's eye, he almost barked, "Yes? What is it?"

Daanis blinked again and cleared his throat, tail straight and still behind him. "Mr. Braadford, I waas ordered to conn this ship for the sole reason thaat I haave some experience with laarger vessels. You, sir, are in commaand and must fight her."

Courtney's eyes went wide. "That was not *my* understanding! I'm perfectly content to point and say, 'Go that way,' but I'm not remotely qualified to command this . . . this *thing* in battle!"

Daanis blinked ironic amusement. "More so thaan I, if I haave heard correctly."

"That was entirely different!" Courtney insisted.

"Yes," Daanis agreed. "You aactually steered the ship." He waved at the "old" *Walker* hand, an unusually tall Lemurian standing behind the big brass wheel. "I haave the conn and shaall give all such directions. Gunny Horn will direct the guns. But *you* must give the order to commence the aaction and tell me how you waant it to proceed."

Courtney blinked, rubbed his face, and for the first time in years, he really wanted a drink. "Yes, well . . . yes," he continued, voice firming. "Very well. *Shonai* and *Walker* have passed. *France* will be approaching and will be quite close when we emerge—that should please Mr. Horn . . ." He sighed. "I suppose the best direction I can give you is to quote Horatio Nelson—a great admiral from my world." He cleared his throat. "No captain can do very wrong if he places his ship alongside that of the enemy."

"Shit!" barked Gunny Horn, part laugh, part terror, when Courtney's "battle plan" was repeated by the talker. The giant floating weapon had straightened on a heading that would take her into the Slot, where it was barely a mile wide. The breeze sweeping in through the windowless frames picked up, sending rust and paint particles swirling as USS *Texas* ponderously increased speed. "Stand ready, fellas," Horn finally said. "I think this is going to be a gunfight, just like in the Western pictures. Whoever draws first is going to win." He was too intent on what he was doing to notice the nervous looks exchanged by 'Cats and young humans who had no idea what a "Western picture" was.

One round from *France*'s third main battery salvo scored on *Shonai*, striking just to starboard of her mainmast, smashing the 25mm mount there and burrowing deep before exploding and flinging everything above it and a large section of starboard-side hull plating into the air or sea. Steam lines were savaged and a gulp of white vapor swirled. Two near misses straddled *Walker*, though they probably hadn't been aimed at her, tossing her violently, opening seams, and tearing at her port torpedo and 25mm mounts with big whirling shell fragments.

"Commence firing!" shouted Carl Bashear. "All guns that'll bear, commence firing!" Only number three and four had a clear shot, but they slammed out rounds almost at once, for all the good they'd do. A lucky hit on the enemy superstructure might take out the fire control or navigation bridge, but that was the best they could hope for.

"*Shonai*'s signaling with her Morse laamp," called one of Ian Miles's 'Cat cadets.

"She tells us to lea' her!" Lawrence exclaimed, surprising even Silva that he'd picked up enough Morse to get that.

"I doubt Cap'n Ronson'll leave her," Silva opined, "but ask him to peel away enough to get number one on target," he told the talker. "We might draw some fire from secondaries, but we ain't big or important enough for main guns—an' we're just takin' damage that ain't even meant for us. C'mon, Larry, let's get our asses to the fo'c'sle!"

"Asses To The Fo'c'sle!" Petey urgently yelped, nervous as usual in action, eyes seeming almost impossibly large as he made the rest of himself as small as he could against Silva's neck.

"You said it, dummy," Silva told the little lizard distractedly, making his way to the ladder and sliding down. The deck around the forward two stacks between the amidships deckhouse and bridge structure was filling with wounded again, and he ground his teeth. The ship had started the fight shorthanded, having farmed out so many people, both veterans and cadets—mostly to *Texas*—and though the majority of the wounds Silva saw didn't look all that bad, it wouldn't be long before *Walker* didn't have enough people to fight her at all. "At this rate, we'll have you haulin' shells to the guns," he groused at Petey.

"Shells To The Guns!" Petey adamantly declared.

Walker was increasing speed and turning sharply to starboard, throwing up packets of spray to port when Silva and Lawrence hopped through the hatch on the front of the bridge structure. Philan Bele's gun's crew on the number one 4"-50 hadn't fired a shot all day, but now they were tracking the target, Susan Raj and Maarik-Fas rapidly winding the trainer's and pointer's wheels as they stared through the optical sights in front of them. "On target!" Susan cried, and Maarik echoed.

"Fire!" Bele shouted. *Wham! Wham! Wham!* went numbers one, three, and four, one after the other. They didn't see where they went because *Walker* was rocked again by a salvo of half a dozen 5.5" secondaries throwing up spume just forward and abeam, water falling on Silva, Lawrence, and the gun's crew.

Bele slammed the breech open and the heavy empty shell clanged on the deck. Turning to Silva, he shouted, "I am not sure this is better than taking main battery fire!"

"Sure it is!" Silva shouted back. "We might survive three, four hits from *these* popguns before we sink. Just *one* o' them others would do it."

Bele looked at him like he was mad. "They nearly just got us with six or more!"

"They didn't, though. Quit whinin' an' count yer blessins."

Bele shook his head and closed the breech on the shell the loader just inserted.

Despite his bravado, Silva frowned as soon as Bele refocused on their target. It wasn't looking good. The last hit on *Shonai* had slowed her even more and might've even wrecked her. It was hard to tell if she was still underway. She *was* finally turning to bring her own forward guns to bear, and at this range, her eight 8″ guns could play havoc with *France*. But the whole point of "the plan" had been for her not to have to face such an unequal duel—neither *Shonai* or *Walker*—so something must've happened. Bele was fighting the number one gun just fine, and Silva realized he and Lawrence weren't really needed here. He wished he'd at least run by the bridge to see what the hell was going on, find out what was holding up their supposed "ace in the hole."

"Plans're for shit," he murmured darkly, just as *Walker*'s three guns that would bear fired again.

"Look!" Lawrence shouted, pointing. "Look there!"

"Look! Look!" Petey squealed.

Silva blinked through the spray in his eye and lifted his helmet to wipe it off his forehead. "By God, there she is!" he almost whispered, then raised his voice to a bellow: *"There she is!"*

The "ace" had climbed out of its "hole" and abruptly steamed into view from the left (east), from between another pair of the weird, almost mushroom-shaped islands, appearing like the red-gray rusty wraith she actually was in a way: a mighty discarded weapon from another world, raised from the dead. She was pushing foamy rollers around her bluff ram-like "Taylor" bow on an almost reverse parallel to *Walker*'s current heading, steering to cross *France*'s bow at roughly ten knots and at a range of less than fifteen hundred yards. She was close enough to *Walker* that she'd feel the wide wake and they could almost hear her blowers and the great mechanical labor of her huge reciprocating engines. A big battle flag, the Stars and Stripes of the American Navy Clan, just like *Walker* flew—probably taken from one of their abandoned auxiliaries—was streaming from her mainmast, aft.

"Oh, there she is!" Silva roared gleefully, capering in a circle on the fo'c'sle. "We're gonna see a helluva prizefight *now*!" He wound up to throw a mighty punch at the air.

There was no question it would be an unprecedented slugfest at an utterly ridiculous distance, the engagement range more reminiscent of muzzle-loading cannon in the age of sail than anything ever imagined for dreadnoughts such as these. Even accounting for variations due to their likely origins on different worlds, the known "stats" of the contestants were similar enough to what one might expect if they weren't. That made the match fairly even. Both had been completed in 1914 and participated in the First World War, between familiar belligerents. It might indeed be only the League ship that came from a different "postwar" history than the one *Walker*'s original crew remembered.

The two battleships had similar displacement, top-rated speed, and could muster the same number of guns in a main battery broadside. *France* had twelve guns to *Texas*'s ten, but her "wing turret" design left the off-side turret out of action. *Texas* had a very slight edge in length and beam (573′×95′ as opposed to 544′×88′) and armor belt thickness (6″–12″ compared to 5.5″–9.8″), but that didn't much matter in this match. They'd both been designed along a similar armor philosophy that attempted to provide at least a little protection to almost everything instead of the later "all or nothing" principle providing even heavier armor over critical spaces and virtually nothing elsewhere, but it had been believed that even this earlier armor scheme should protect their engineering spaces and magazines from most contemporary projectiles at rational distances.

There was nothing rational about the range Courtney Bradford chose to fight, and all ten of Gunny Horn's 14″ rifles salvoed while *France* was still reloading from her last shots at *Shonai*. The noise was tremendous, deafening, and sufficient to shake a short rainfall from the increasingly sodden air. The titanic blossom of brown-black smoke made it impossible to see the result.

"Keep shootin' while ya can," Silva shouted at Bele, working his jaw to pop his ears. "Me an' Larry are headed for the pilothouse. I'll keep my eye on ya," he assured. Slapping Lawrence on the back, he motioned for him to follow and headed back for the hatch at the base of the bridge.

"Make your course zero, six, zero," Ronson loudly commanded the helmsman. "Slow to one-third," he told the same Repub cadet still standing by the EOT. "Silva. Lawrence," Ronson acknowledged as they stepped into the pilothouse and moved to stand by Lieutenant Chiba and Abel Cook. "Bring us in alongside *Texas*," Ronson resumed to the helmsman.

Texas was turning now, probably as sharply to port as she could. "We'll take cover behind her big ass," he added.

"Hey!" Silva exclaimed. "We won't *see* nothin' there! We'll miss the fight!"

Ronson regarded him with narrow eyes, then pointed at the bulky bandage under his shirt, leaking enough blood to stain it. "Haven't you seen *enough* fighting today? I know too many of our people have," he continued bitterly, "and this old ship, this *school ship*, has had more than enough holes shot in her. You want to see better, climb up to the crow's nest!"

Suddenly, Silva, Lawrence, Chiba, and Abel were all looking at each other, but Abel was the first to bolt for the ladder up to the fire control platform, followed by the young Japanese officer.

"Shit," Silva muttered. "I should'a thought o' that."

"You think they'll get in it together? It's . . . 'ery tight to two o' they."

Silva was shaking his head. "They're both pretty skinny. They'll fit." He shrugged. "An' I wouldn't fit in that little bucket by myself." Together, they strode out on *Walker*'s port bridgewing to see what they could.

Gunnery Sergeant Arnold Horn had been shaken off his feet for the second time in the less than fifteen minutes *Texas* had been in action, even here, high above, where it seemed half the enemy's broadside struck the base of the forward superstructure. Rubbing his knee and checking his hand for blood, he stood. Flames still licked out of the 5″ gun embrasures in the casemate from an earlier strike that put most of the ship's secondaries out of action, and now smoke was roiling out of the jumbled wreckage below the navigation bridge. Before he could even ask, one of the 'Cats quickly shouted, "There's casualties in the pilothouse and Mr. Braadford and Lieutenaant Daanis are shook but okay. Engines and helm still aanswer—and we still got the plot room!"

"Thank God for that," Horn breathed, then shook his head. *Not that it really much matters to what* we're *doing at this point,* he told himself. *I doubt we're eight hundred yards apart. The gunhouse captains can practically aim their guns by looking down the barrels now.* He literally couldn't believe what he was seeing. With no other option, the two rusty leviathans had been reduced to just circling each other, clawing and bashing away with barely enough room to manage the turn in the confined Slot without running aground. He remembered what Courtney said, quoting Nelson, and imagined the crazy Australian would have them lie alongside until the hulls crashed together if he could. *This is nuts!*

"There's a caasualty in the number three gunhouse!" cried a 'Cat.

"What *kind* of casualty?" Horn demanded nervously. "Is it about to blow up or what?"

"It won't traaverse. Both electric motors are down."

Horn imagined those gigantic motors, each capable of rotating the whole 500-plus-ton assembly. "The primary and backup aren't even on the same *circuit*!" he cried incredulously.

"I know! Daamage control paarty reports a hit punched through and blew up against the baarbette, shredded everything around it, and knocked out all power going in. They're using baattle laanterns in there, all the way down to the maagazine, trying to do everything by haand, even traverse—but they not praactice thaat."

Horn shuddered involuntarily. It would be bad enough in the gunhouse itself, but just the notion of being down at the bottom of that multistory iron cave with its myriad steel stalactites, passages, and dangerous machinery . . . Everything *could* be operated manually, with great effort, but the very idea of doing it in the dark with little more than meager flashlight beams whipping about . . . He shuddered again. "At least they don't have to move it much," he grumbled.

France had maintained a pretty much constant position off the port beam and the two ships had mauled each other horribly. If *Texas* had any real advantage at this point, it was the heavier weight of her shells that could theoretically smash deeper, and the thicker slope-face armor on her gunhouses. When he could see clearly enough through the churning smoke and rain that had finally commenced in earnest, he thought they might've knocked out three of *France*'s turrets. Two for sure. One looked like they'd opened the top with a can opener, another had never even trained out against them, and he suspected they'd knocked it out with their opening salvo. Of course, with her long-serving crew, *France*'s rate of fire remained better, so she was still getting in just as many licks.

The ship shook again as 12″ shells smashed into her, blasting up a blizzard of deck timbers forward of the number one gunhouse, annihilating the aft fire control tower, and shearing off the starboard boat crane, which tumbled over to crash down alongside to starboard, half in and half out of the water, held by a tangle of cables. The nearby coast of one of the big islands—Horn couldn't even remember whether it was east or west of the Slot—was churned by several shells that missed and blasted up mighty trees like grass clippings. The funnel had been pierced repeatedly and one of the tanks, still incongruously perched on deck, had literally been shot off into the sea like a squirrel off a limb. Its misshapen wreckage narrowly missed *Walker*, steaming close by to starboard, when it hit the water in several pieces. One of the mainmast tripod struts had been shot away and the whole structure leaned alarmingly to port.

The ship was being shot to pieces around them, and probably the only reason they were still afloat and underway was, ironically, because the fight was so close and the trajectories of their projectiles so flat. There'd been surprisingly little critical damage at or below the waterline because most of what might've been aimed there either struck the armor belt above that lethal zone or hit the water and exploded far enough away that it "only" sent jagged splinters into the side of the ship. Her already leaky portside torpedo blister was now a sieve, of course, but the starboard torpedo blister had been flooded to counter the list. The upshot was that there'd been no plunging fire and most of *Texas*'s machinery and magazines were below the waterline as well, and the major caliber hoists were protected by the heavily armored barbettes. She and all her people—cadets, shanghaied merchant sailors, and yes, "wild" Japanese and even Rarorani—were holding their own. Horn just didn't know how much longer they could. Another hit where the armor was already compromised could blow them all to smithereens.

That's probably what happened to *France*.

"All guns report 'on taarget,' 'cept for them in gunhouse three, an' they say they're ready to shoot anyway!"

Horn blinked. He'd unconsciously been wiping the rain off his Imperial binoculars with his wet shirttail. "Okay. You don't need to wait on me, you're doing the job. I'm basically just watching the fall of shot at this point."

"Fire!" shouted the 'Cat cadet to those around him and through the microphone. Firing circuits in the fighting top, plot room, and each gunhouse were closed, and the mighty ship shook once more, raising more damp rust dust to swirl out the open windows like every preceding salvo. The deep *shhhhh* sound of heavy ripping canvas didn't last long at all, and Horn, watching through the binoculars he'd quickly raised, was sure he saw good strikes down the length of the League ship before the rising belch of smoke obscured it. This time was different, however, because even before he heard the distant crashes and detonations, he saw a sharp yellow-orange glare. "Hey," he began, but before he could say another word, the roar of a huge explosion swept back across the rain-drenched team in the fighting top. The gunsmoke swept aft and Horn kept looking. "Hey . . ." he began again, but stopped. *France* was . . . decidedly misshapen, lying at the base of a towering column of black smoke, flames leaping high as she rapidly lost way, already leaning noticeably.

"Jeez," Horn said and gulped. "I was just worrying about that happening to *us*," he said lowly.

"Whaat?" called the 'Cat behind him, and a small rush moved to join him, gaping out the empty windows, wiping rain from their faces.

Horn took a deep breath and let it out. "That," he said before shaking himself. "Cease firing and secure. Inform Mr. Bradford that the enemy's out of it. I guess we blew her guts out." He cleared his throat and spoke more formally. "*France* is . . . listing heavily to port and going down by the stern. Recommend we go pick up survivors." He shook his head. "Won't be too many."

A strange, different sound began rising with the smoke from below, over the noise of the blowers and the deep *shoosh* of exhaust gasses, and it took Horn a moment to realize it was cheering. There wasn't any around him, where they had the best view of what they'd done. "Well," Horn finally sighed, "better them than us. Good work, everybody. Let's get tarps over all the equipment we worked our butts off to make operational. After that we'll go below and give the 'good job' to everybody else that helped us kill those poor bastards over there."

CHAPTER 35

USS *Walker* swept out ahead and was first on the scene near the sinking League dreadnought. She was already nearly gone by then. She'd broken in half and the stern had swiftly plunged to the bottom, but the bow was still floating on air trapped within her relatively undamaged starboard side, almost level with the sea. Crowded rafts bobbed in the roiling water, and many more people were lying or standing on the slipping hulk, crying out in terror at the approaching water. All of *Walker*'s machine guns were manned, not against their helpless enemies, but the real horror that came in the aftermath of naval battle on this world: the wildly voracious fish and sea monsters.

"All stop!" Ronson shouted. "Cargo nets over the side and get all our boats in the water, now!" he called aft to Chief Bashear, who'd already positioned himself to oversee their launch. He looked at Silva. "Issue small arms to everybody not busy with the boats. You know what to do." Silva nodded and, along with Sergeant Kaik and Lawrence, who'd just joined them, took off down the ladder. Men were screaming and machine guns were already firing in the water, which fostered a few moments of panic on the rafts and the still-floating hulk before they realized what the targets were. It wouldn't make much difference, and few would be plucked alive from the sea. Blood in the water would draw predators like a dinner bell. Some who'd found themselves flailing in the spreading, unappetizing oil slick might have a chance. Ronson and Abel Cook strode out on the starboard bridgewing, and Ronson shouted down at the whaleboat and launch as their crews unhooked, "Focus on the men on the wreck before they're in the water too. *Don't* let 'em swamp you!" A veteran 'Cat in the bow nodded, holding up a Blitzerbug.

The rain had tapered off to a drizzle as if, now that the concussive firing had stopped, there was no longer any reason for it to fall. The screaming was constant now, however, as merciless flasher fish the size of tuna that acted like piranha tore swimmers apart regardless of how much ammunition was expended. Silva, with his BAR, and a few others who'd seen this before grimly spent most of their bullets ending the misery of those already being shredded and beyond help. A big motor launch from *Shonai* arrived towing a pair of 40-foot cutters, which were pulled alongside the rafts and cut loose before the motor launch made for the sinking bow as well. Apparently, the big cruiser had gone dead in the water and was preparing to abandon when *Texas* finally interposed herself and had already launched her surviving boats. *Texas* didn't have any of those to send. All she had left were some rafts. She was creeping closer even now, but there'd be no use for rafts by the time she got there. Shockingly quickly, the only men alive in the water were the most thoroughly covered with oil.

As usual, larger monsters began to arrive, swirling the wave-tops with big fins or flippers—huge menacing shapes nosing about, largely content to feed on the schooling "flashies," but sometimes prepared to sample a boat or raft. Long, massive jaws broke the water, exposing uncountable teeth as they yawned wide, the dinner-plate-sized watery eye just behind them glaring at one of *Shonai*'s packed cutters. The eye exploded in a viscous spray when Silva fired a quick burst from the BAR, and the great fish leaped straight up, half out of the water, and crashed back down amid a tremendous splash. Flippers flailed and it spastically jerked as flashies turned their attention on it. Ronson and Abel saw Silva spit a long brown stream over the side of the ship and nod to himself with satisfaction.

France's sharp bow was rising back out of the water as the bulk of its carcass sank deeper, the last survivors actually sliding down into *Shonai*'s launch before it reversed itself rapidly away. "There she goes," observed Abel Cook as the bow slipped away with a rumbling, crashing groan and a last great exhalation of air.

"There she goes," Ronson grimly confirmed, looking up at the growing drone of an engine overhead.

"It's Fred Reynolds," supplied the talker unnecessarily. Fred had asked to be picked up just as the action was ending, saying Kari's plane was sinking and couldn't be saved if they didn't hurry. When Ronson asked if it was possible to fit Kari and Aalak in Fred's plane with his cadet, Fred reluctantly confessed it was. "They're pretty small," he'd conceded. Ronson told him to do it because, at that moment, they were racing to save people without that option. Now Ronson watched as the overloaded Nancy banked around into the wind and approached off the port quarter. With a last look to starboard and the small flotilla of packed boats, Ronson turned and told Jack Meek, who'd just come on the bridge, "Ask Mr. Bradford what he wants to do with them." He jerked his thumb over his shoulder. "Looks like a couple of hundred of 'em, and we don't have room aboard here."

Meek was nodding. "That's what I came to tell you. He says to take them to *Texas*, but he wants as many of our Marine cadets as we can spare to help guard them." He arched a brow. "And not only to keep *them* out of mischief. It seems the . . . rather large Rarorani contingent aboard is expecting their customary post-battle feast."

Ronson rubbed his mustache. "Oh. Oh, shit."

"Indeed," Meek chuckled, noting that Tabby had come on the bridge.

"Permission to—"

"Yeah," Ronson said. "Secure from general quarters. Signal all boats to make for *Texas*. We'll send our Marines over as soon as we can," he added to Meek, then turned back to Tabby. "And tell Earl to fire up the galley and cook something edible for a change."

Stepping out on the port bridgewing, Ronson, Meek, and Abel watched the little floatplane set down and begin to maneuver up under the boom that was already swinging out over the water.

"*Shonai*'s last aircraft will be arriving soon as well. It will have to go aboard *Texas* too," Meek said. "*Shonai* can't recover it. *Texas* lost one of her big cranes, but the other is still operational."

"Yeah? What's the plane been up to?"

"Orbiting *Elsass*. Watching where she goes."

"Goes?" Abel asked, surprised. "I believe we all rather suspected she sank."

Meek shook his head. "She apparently not only stabilized her list somewhat, but got underway." Ronson cast a nervous look south, but Meek raised a calming hand. "Not in this direction," he assured. "As badly mauled as our, um, 'task force' is, *Elsass* is in no better shape for a fight. The Japanese aircraft last saw her steaming back east in front of a long oil slick."

"Their base. Back where we started this morning," guessed Abel.

"Presumably," Meek nodded. "At least for repairs, though I can't imagine she could hope to escape."

Ronson snorted. "We couldn't chase down a one-legged frog. *Shonai*'s a wreck and *Texas*'ll probably have to take her in tow—if *she* doesn't sink. Have you seen how bad she looks from *this* side?" He waved. "Sure, *we* could catch her if we transferred some fuel from *Texas*—we had a pretty long high-speed run—but we're out of torpedoes. What'll we throw at her? Dirty words?"

"That's not what he means, Captain Rodriguez," Abel said, shaking his head.

Ronson sighed and nodded, noting the Nancy swinging inboard, aft. "I know."

It couldn't have been another minute before Kari-Faask came stomping up the ladder, followed by a sheepish-looking Fred Reynolds and a grinning Dennis Silva. Kari proceeded to march right up to Ronson until she was almost touching his chest, looking up at him, blinking furiously. "You never waanted me an' Fred's plane on board from the staart!" she bitterly accused. "You let it sink on purpose. You may not'a known this, but me an' Fred didn't get 're-aactivated,' we *volunteered*, so we're still civiliaans outside the chain o' commaand an' thaat was *our daamn plane*! We better get another just like it, braand-new!" Spinning hard enough to slap Ronson with her tail, she marched off the bridge.

Fred watched his friend go, hesitating, glaring at Silva's expression before looking back at Ronson. "Sorry about that, Skipper. Don't worry, she knows why you left her floating and she's not really even mad at you." He shrugged. "She's a *good* stick," he emphasized, "always has been. But she's never been as confident in the air by herself as she ought to be, and I think she's mostly mad at herself for getting shot down"—he nodded at Aalak—"with a kid in the plane." He chuckled a little uncomfortably. "I bet she was pretty scared too. First time she ever got knocked down without me along, and getting scared makes her madder than anything." He smirked. "At everybody. But give her a day or two and she'll mostly be mad at me."

"Forget it," Ronson said. "I know how she feels. This was my first command, you know, at least that I ever got appointed to, and I got Captain Reddy's ship shot full of holes, and a bunch of kids killed."

Silva's grin went away. "*You* need to forget *that* shit, Skipper. You . . . *we* all done what we had to. Only ones here ta do it. An' ever' one o' these little grubs"—he tousled the fur between Aalak's ears—"learned a heap more about what 'the life's' like than they would have any other way." He shrugged. "An' I ain't even gonna ask permission ta speak my mind. Never have before." He pointed at his captain. "These kiddies aboard here an' elsewhere graduated ta *full-fledged* destroyermen t'day—all of 'em—an' to my mind, bemoanin' the fate o' the ones as didn't make it *just because they ain't full-grown,* belittles the fact they done it anyway, willingly, because it was right." He shook his head. "I'm mighty proud of 'em, an' I reckon they oughta be held up as heroes for it." He glanced down and rubbed his eyepatch before looking back up at Ronson, the grin creeping back over his face. "Last thing I gotta say is this: half a dozen puny little holes in *this ship* won't hardly ever be noticed. A week in the yard, a couple patches, a lick o' paint, an' she'll be good as new. Again."

EPILOGUE

THE AZORES

Captain Matthew Reddy paced alone along the rocky, windy beach of the tiny, nameless, uninhabited island north of the "greater" Azores. The sky was gray and damp, but it didn't seem like rain and it was actually a little warmer than usual. He'd donned a Filpin Lands–made approximation of a peacoat most frequently used by aviators before this expedition to colder climes, and he grimly suspected "his" American Navy Clan was going to have to contract the manufacturer to make a lot more of them. Similar coats were available in the Republic of Real People, but they'd be going to supply that allied nation's own growing navy. *Besides*, he thought glumly, *I'm not just a destroyer skipper anymore; I have to be a diplomat and keep Saan-Kakja sweet.* She wasn't just a friend and huge supporter of the Navy Clan, she was High Chief of the Filpin Lands, an actual "state" in the United Homes, just like the Navy Clan. A lot of contracts were let to their allies—nobody made optics like the Impies, for example—but Matt tried his best to support nascent home industries. Shaking his head to focus his thoughts back on his current purpose, he felt his face heat with wrath. Kicking loose a strangely shaped stone, he knelt to pick it up and flung it hard into the surf.

Matt wasn't actually "alone," of course. One of *Walker*'s numerous "daughter" destroyers, actually copied from her (and somewhat improved) idled offshore, its "dazzle" paint scheme wildly distorting its silhouette against the dark horizon. In addition, Brad "Spanky" McFarlane, Chack-Sab-At, and a squad of veteran Marines had escorted Matt ashore in one of the destroyer's motor launches. They currently lingered watchfully about two hundred paces away. Regardless of the behavior of a sleeker, more modern-looking League destroyer about the same distance from shore and the equal number of Italian Marines watching Ammiraglio Gherzi casually step closer to Matt, "uninhabited" didn't mean there might not be deadly monsters on the little island.

"Good morning, Captain Reddy," Gherzi greeted. "As always, it is a pleasure to see you"—he paused with a smile and waved around them—"though I am tempted to protest the inconvenience of the setting. And this environment is not nearly as comfortable as our last meeting."

Matt nodded, expression stony. "Yeah. This"—he gestured around as well—"is because I'm mad. Not at you in particular, I guess, but at this whole situation and especially what happened between our different sides in the mid–South Pacific." He let out an angry breath. "I guess I wasn't sure what I'd do if our two heavies met again." He shrugged. "At least half *Impero*'s crew are Lemurians, you know. Mighty excitable. They might've even shot at you without orders after what we heard happened." He cocked his head at Gherzi. "And I don't know what *you* know. You might've been ordered to come out shooting as well. Better to meet here with smaller stuff that might not start a whole new war."

Gherzi affected a concerned expression—which might've even been genuine. "You know what I thought about the . . . activities in the Pacific," he said plainly, "and though I truly haven't received word of the conclusion there, I *did* know your beloved old destroyer and other meager forces in the region chose not to abandon the site in question. I assume by your demeanor that you are better informed and the outcome of the confrontation was . . . unfortunate?"

Matt took a deep breath and touched his chin with his fingers. "Yeah, you could say that. I got a pretty complete report and it was bleak reading. Want me to tell you?"

Gherzi nodded solicitously. "If you do not find it too painful to relate."

Matt pursed his lips and nodded. "Okay. *Walker* was damaged and suffered a number of casualties. You knew she was a school ship full of cadets, and most of those killed and wounded were human and Lemurian *kids*." His eyes flashed, but he kept his tone level. "An Allied cruiser"—he wasn't *about* to elaborate on that—"and a ship those *kids* managed to make operational suffered even worse."

"You have my most profound sympathies," Gherzi said, and he *sounded* sincere.

"And you have mine," Matt told him, continuing relentlessly as Gherzi's eyes widened. "See, before that happened, your League base on Raror—that's the name of the big island there, which is actually *two* islands, it seems. Courtney Bradford wants to rename it 'Caprona,' for some reason—" He blinked and managed a tight smile. "Sorry. Distracted. But that base has been fairly thoroughly destroyed, and so has the big German cruiser your people towed there. Sunk in the anchorage," he bluntly added. "After that, the *real* fight started because my people didn't wait for yours to come at them, and at least one of your destroyers was sunk. We don't know for sure about the other. It got hit pretty hard and dropped out of the fight." He spread his hands. "There was a search for survivors but no sign was seen. It's possible she joined with *Elsass* after *she* took a bellyful of torpedoes and slunk away. Only thing for her to do. We don't know if she sank or not either, but we'll keep looking." Matt paused a moment while Gherzi absorbed all that, expression morphing from incredulous to horrified, then Matt pounded his last spike home. "My understanding is that your old battleship, *France*, put up a hell of a fight, practically muzzle to muzzle with the ship those kids fixed up, but they hammered her to the bottom."

Gherzi's mouth opened, likely to object, but nothing came out.

"And that makes me almost as mad as the rest," Matt relentlessly resumed. "I'm told our people tried like hell but only saved about two hundred off of *France*. What was her complement? Eight hundred? A thousand? But she blew up and broke in half, see, and you know what happens to people in the water." He turned to look at the gently advancing waves. "All those people on both sides dead. For *nothing*," he snapped. "More of your people who had no business in our territory are gone.

Dead, hiding, or prisoners. More of *my* people are dead or hurt, and our crummy 'phony war' has carved a big chunk out of more locals too, who didn't have a damn thing to do with it!" He'd started to rant as his fury built, and he forced his voice lower. "And the ghost fleet is still ours," he stated emphatically, narrowing his eyes back at Gherzi, "unless you want to try to bust through us here and go for it now."

Gherzi just stood there, his dismay slowly turning to something else. Finally, he almost whispered, "I could, you know."

Matt shrugged. "Maybe. But we'd tear the guts out of the cream of what's left of your fleet. You *know* that," he pressed, "and you may or may not match us in airpower here, but unless you've got a couple of carriers in your pocket, we'll dog your ass all across the Atlantic, sinking your transports and oilers the whole way. If you ever even made it through the Pass of Fire, you wouldn't make it much farther—and you'd never get back. You might try heading south around Africa," Matt suggested, then shrugged again. "You *might* even tear through the Repub fleet, though I doubt it. But if you did, that'd cost you too, and what was left of your whole mighty fleet would be just a skeleton with a bunch of broken bones. And all that's *before* you cross half the world in *our* backyard." Matt tilted his head back and his voice softened slightly. "No, you're smarter than that. You damn sure don't want another war. I don't think you wanted *any* of this. You're just wondering if those idiots in your Triumvirate will see it your way or not."

Ammiraglio Gherzi turned his head away and nodded with a sigh. "They may not, you know."

"Sure they will. You're the best they've got."

"For now," Gherzi hedged, before meeting Matt's eyes again. "But one day we will meet in anger again. I fear that is a certainty. This will be the *second* time you have bested me, and I can't even say that my own vanity doesn't demand I balance the score," he confessed.

Matt shook his head. "The only part of *this* mess you had anything to do with was drawing me here in the first place. You won that round, hands down. What happened in the Pacific had nothing to do with either of us, so I figure we're even. I'd really prefer that our next big 'rematch' be a game of chess or something. You'd probably kick my ass at that.

Anything short of more killing, and definitely not another fleet action," Matt added grimly.

"Perhaps . . ." Gherzi said, unconvinced. When he spoke again, his voice was all business. "What will you do? If I begin drawing down my fleet . . . and convince the Triumvirate this is not the time for their final cataclysmic clash for world domination?" His tone had turned sarcastic as he spoke.

Matt chuckled. "I'll do the same, hopefully sooner rather than later, then I'll go home to my wife and kids."

"A delightful woman, your 'Lady Sandra,'" Gherzi replied thoughtfully, then his gaze drifted. "I as well. I have them, you know? A fine wife and young children." He frowned. "It is not looked upon with favor to make actual *wives* of the conquered peoples surrounding the Mediterranean, but where else would we find them?"

Matt looked down. "That's nuts," he said. "But you know that too." He continued with sarcasm of his own. "And even if you didn't already have enough women—we've been there ourselves—you could find plenty in other *friendly* nations." He huffed. "But I always figured that was the main reason you went back to the League after St. Vincent. Couldn't have been easy on your family if you hadn't."

Gherzi pursed his lips, glancing back at the Italian Marines waiting behind him, then stuck out his hand. "Until next time, Captain Reddy."

"Next time, Ammiraglio Gherzi."

FEN'S ISLAND

"Oh my! Look at this!" Courtney Bradfood cried excitedly, stooping to part a patch of tall grass high on the crest of the crater far above the surrounding sea and increasingly busy anchorage. His voice was muted by the stiff breeze there, but Abel Cook, some distance below, heard his call and hurried up to join him, panting slightly from exertion in the somewhat unconvincing air. He wasn't the only one short of oxygen. Lemurians from seagoing Homes had the hardest time at high elevations, having spent their whole lives at sea level. None liked being much higher than they were now, and the 'Cat cadet members of Courtney's "survey" party had already rebelled from their role as bearers, barely creeping along behind the rest of them, gasping like they were dying.

About sixty yards away and standing at the very highest point for as far as he could see in the whole world from there, big lever-action repeater resting on his uninjured shoulder to protect against "big boogers," Dennis Silva didn't hear Courtney's call. Entranced by the view, he wasn't really paying attention, not even to his "duty" as guard for the party. Its fifteen members were entirely surrounded at a distance by a band of cheerfully protective Rarorani, after all. They'd kick up any threat before Silva could spot it and had already provided a cornucopia of specimens for Courtney and Abel's perusal. They were much more conscientious about not "breaking the heads" as well.

The sky was crisp and bright without the slightest hint of a cloud and the sea was a deep purple-blue. Unusually, there wasn't any haze, and the islands to both the east and northwest were a crisp bluish green. Silva grunted his satisfaction at the distant but equally clear sight of a trio of approaching ships, one of which was the massive, veteran, SPD (self-propelled dry dock) USS *Tarakan Island*, escorted by a pair of new construction destroyers out of Maa-ni-la. The plodding SPD had apparently been dispatched to Respite as soon as they'd reported what was here, and the destroyers were diverted from their sprint to join the fleet at the Azores when the standoff there was resolved. There'd been other arrivals in the weeks since the "Battle of the Slot," mostly adding hands to the effort to stabilize the damage to *Texas* and *Shonai*, both of which had been in real danger of sinking. *Tarakan Island* represented more than just a dry dock in which to make more fundamental and lasting repairs, however. It was cranes, heavy machinery, endless torch fuel, and rivets and wire and boiler tubes and a thousand other things, but mostly the people she brought that would exponentially ramp up the effort to save even more of the abandoned rusty treasures here.

The focus would be on a few more destroyers, submarines, and transports, of course, but *Nevada* was a high priority and pumps had even been carefully taken aboard the battered and heavily listing *Arkansas*. Some actually whimsically talked of attempting to save the weird, grotesquely mangled aircraft carrier on the cruiser hull that seemed no more inclined to sink than she had when they got here. Much of the rest, even still afloat, would be stripped of guns, mounts, engines—anything that could be salvaged, down to knobs and switches, even tubes and sockets on electronic equipment—and the remainder would become fine, first-class scrap. The Grand Alliance could make good steel now, but nothing like this had been available since *Amagi* and then *Hidoiame* were broken up. Despite all the tragic sacrifice, the true bounty of the mission was almost incalculable, and the League's determination to seize it for themselves or at least deny it to their enemy was understandable—even if the methods of those who attempted it only increased the mutual animosity of the two powers.

But *Walker* was essentially ready for sea, her unexpected work here done. So was the supposedly "secret" aspect of the Corps of Discovery. (Half the off-duty cadets currently accompanying them—Fen, Philan Bele, Sam Jenks, Maarik, Aalak, and Susan Raj, for example—wanted to join when they got their commissions.) When Jack Meek had pointedly asked how they even knew about it, little Maarik had just blinked abject innocence like only she could and said, "Secrets? On a *destroyer*?" There was little he could say to that. *Walker* would steam back to Respite in a few days, then on to the Filpin Lands and finally Baalkpan to complete her training cruise, returning to her "home" port at last, where she and her intrepid crew would be welcomed as the heroes they were. In the meantime, Courtney had been granted those "few days" to do some actual exploring, starting with the immediate environs.

Pam Cross and Lawrence both poked Silva in the ribs, one on each side of him. Lawrence earned a harder poke back, but Pam only got another appraising gaze. Aside from her boondockers, sagging socks, and ever-present Blitzerbug, she looked very fine to him indeed. Cutoff shorts displayed short but shapely legs, and her midriff was bare under a tightly knotted T-shirt. An unbuttoned oversize khaki shirt—one of Silva's—resembled a safari jacket on her and provided a semblance of modesty.

Things had been very good between them, but they always were after a fight. Silva had to wonder how long it would last this time.

"What's up, doll?"

Pam gestured over at Courtney, thin hair swirling over his reddened scalp, spare straw sombrero twisting in the stiff breeze, secured around his neck by leather ties. "He's found somethin', dummy. Let's go see."

"I like what I'm lookin' at now," he said with a leer.

Pam reddened prettily and savagely poked him again. "C'mon. It makes him happy to share his discoveries. The weirder they are, the better."

"Weirder!" Petey gasped. He didn't like the altitude either.

Ambling over, the trio joined the others. Lieutenant Chiba watched their approach with a grin. He'd been chosen as Captain Okabe's liaison to Courtney—and the Grand Alliance—from the newest Japanese contingent to join. He'd be going all the way to Baalkpan. There remained some lingering controversy among Okabe's crew about joining the "American" Navy Clan, and Captain Reddy had signaled that he understood and they'd be honored and appreciated regardless of their decision. Those who thought they'd be more comfortable leaving the Navy altogether and settling among other Japanese were welcome to see how they liked the Shogunate of Yokohama, for example. If they wanted to stay with their ship, however, the American Navy Clan was their only alternative. The Shogunate didn't have a navy of its own and the Grand Alliance couldn't support powerful unaffiliated cruisers running around. The choice was fairly simple. Some would stay in, some would get out, but *Shonai* and eventually *Nagato* would go on with at least partially Japanese crews.

"Whatcha' got, Mr. Bradford?" Silva asked, bending over to view the proud Australian's latest wonder.

Courtney stepped back and declared, "Behold!"

Silva squinted his eye and frowned at the ugly brown elongated . . . thing, roughly six or seven inches long and about two inches in diameter, apparently bumping mindlessly along on six shiny, greenish, chitinous legs. Pam laughed and Silva blinked before he said, "Why, it's a walkin' turd!"

"It *is*!" Courtney gleefully exclaimed. "It truly *is* a walking segment of feces!"

The thing seemed to decide on a direction and relentlessly marched over to bump against Pam's shoe. "Eww!" she said and pulled her foot away, slightly bumping the rather furry-looking lozenge. Undeterred, it continued determinedly on in its new direction.

"I bet that was a chore to push out!" Bele said with mock seriousness before he and the rest of the cadets actually giggled like the youngsters they still were, in spite of everything.

Silva grinned at the sight of these kids being kids again. "Quite a find, Mr. Bradford. Ain't every day you find a turd out rompin' around on its own. Oughta name it after Earl. Favors 'eem." The laughter increased.

"Well, obviously there's a creature *inside* it," Courtney scolded, apparently somewhat put out. "Something like a prodigious dung beetle either laid an egg within the, ah, excretum, or perhaps burrowed in itself, in larval form, growing and feasting on the—"

All the adults exploded then, laughing so hard in the thin air they could barely breathe. Lawrence's laugh was unusual anyway and he sounded like he was choking.

"Excretum! Excretum!" Petey shrieked, agitated by the unexpected mirth.

"Got a new word, huh, shithead?" Silva asked his little friend, thumping him on the head.

"Eventually, they extend their legs and are able to ambulate," Courtney went on insistently, ignoring his companions. "Quite the survival strategy. Few predators can possibly be much tempted—"

"Ta *chase* an, eat turds!" Maarik shouted gleefully and the hilarity resumed.

Silva's single eye lit up. "Hey, Mr. Bradford, you know how dung beetles'll get ta wrasslin' over the same turd ball for their very own? What do you call it when two o' these boogers bump into each other? A turd tussle!"

When the laughter again subsided, Courtney huffed dramatically, but Silva finally saw the glint in the older man's eye and realized he was pushing this on, enjoying it as much as the rest. He caught Pam's eyes on him and knew she saw it too, saw him feeding it as well, for the same reason. For the first time in longer than he could remember, she actually looked *proud* of him, and that was the greatest gift she could give him. He winked at her. "Well, Mr. Bradford, I'm glad you found *somethin'* of interest on this trip. So, what do you think? Is this 'Corps o' Discovery' gonna be a goin' concern or just a one-time thing?"

Courtney nudged his walking turd, or *Ambulans feces* as he was already thinking of it, with his own shoe, and it doggedly continued on straight ahead in the direction he'd pointed it. "There'll always be a *need* for it, especially as long as the League is out there and remains a threat. Or other enemies we've yet to even find might lurk beyond our knowledge," he answered seriously, then looked up, including Chiba in his gaze. "We really know so little of this new world we've been cast upon. A bit about some islands and coastlines. A bit more about Africa and small portions of the Americas, I suppose. Practically nothing about most of the inner continents, and still vaster stretches of the seas themselves." He gestured around. "This island and the larger ones to the east didn't even exist where we originally came from." He smiled at Abel Cook, Pam, Lawence, then focused back on Silva as he gestured at the ground. "And I do hope I'm afforded a greater opportunity to search the world for fantastic glories like our smelly new friend." He sighed. "But my idealism has faded considerably, subdued by bloody reality, and I know my curiosity must always remain secondary to the welfare of the people, lands, and cause we care for. I'd advocate *expanding* the Corps of Discovery even if I knew I'd never find another single new thing."

Silva raised his brow at Pam and then nodded. "Good. I hope it pans out an' I'll put my shoulder behind it—if you don't think I'll jinx it."

"Just mind your manners in front of the brass, for once, an' they might even listen," Pam suggested ironically.

"I can *try*," Silva conceded and looked back at Courtney. "But the thing is, we *did* good here an' even capped it all off with a helluva fight. I might be kinda fuzzy on the first from time ta time, but that last part's always been my thing." He took on a thoughtful expression, as if trying to define it. "Like a hobby." He vigorously rubbed his nose with a knuckle and continued. "Another thing—two things, I guess." He tilted his head at the cadets. "You plannin' on lettin' some o' them scudders join up? Ta stay with us, I mean."

Courtney blinked. "Why . . . I doubt it'll be up to me, but I suppose it's worth consideration." Glancing fondly at Abel Cook, he smiled a little sadly. "The young on this world do often seem required to 'step up' rather early in their lives. And I don't know where we'd be without many of them."

Lawrence spoke up. "And e'entually us—the core o' this Corps"—he shook his head in mild confusion—"us are going to run out o' us to teach they things."

"He's right," Abel said, nodding respectfully at Lawrence. "Especially if you mean to expand this organization, the core cadre in particular, we must recruit from outside it. Who better to choose from than those we have already evaluated? Perhaps it's even preferable that they start a little younger than we'd like than too set in more . . . conventional ways."

"Which brings up my second thing," Silva said, nodding. "'Corps o' Discovery' was fine for when we went a'scoutin' around Borno that time, an' puffed up as it sounds, I guess it still suits for a cover, but you know the Navy an' its ackro-nomes . . ."

"Acronyms, you big dope," Pam corrected, tone thoughtful and without the typical sneer.

"Them things," Silva confirmed, shaking his head. "Just seems that if we're gonna keep runnin' around, sneakin' an' spyin' an' blowing shit up, 'COD' ain't the most inspirational brand ta stamp on our part of it, yeah?"

"Scouts," Pam said suddenly, then smiled at Abel. "'Scout Cadre.'"

"I like it," said Abel, and several of the others looked at one another, grinning.

Silva shrugged. "Fine. Swell. Whatever we call it, it beats the hell out'a chasin' rhino pigs around New Ireland." He smirked and lightly shoved Lawrence. "Turned out pretty fun too. Let's do it again."

Petey roused himself from his perch and stretched, his furry gliding membranes going taut. Blinking his big, luminous eyes around at the sudden silence, he nipped Silva's ear and said, "Do It Again! Eat!"

AUTHOR'S NOTE

(MINE, NOT COURTNEY'S)

Those of you familiar with my fifteen-book Destroyermen series, which came before the four-book Artillerymen series, which *happened* about a hundred years before the Destroyermen series . . . Anyway, some will remember I frequently incorporated "real" ships but had a rule never to use any with actual wartime records. Alternate universe or not, I'd have to *change* those records for them to appear in "my" world and I strongly felt that would be highly disrespectful to those real ships and brave crews who fought them. I might've tinkered around the edges of that rule on occasion, but never, ever broke it. Now, in a way, I have. Sort of—but not really. Although many of the ships appearing in this yarn actually did have major, epic, inspiring war records, I didn't mess around with any *active duty* histories, I just added a little extra to the end. I doubt any old sailors who served on them would object to that and expect most would be amused. One major—obvious to many—liberty I took was the inclusion of USS *Texas* (BB-35) in what many of you have guessed was the "Able" test at Bikini Atoll. Her sister, USS *New York* (BB-34), *was* actually there and survived both Able and the much more destructive Baker test (which our rusty ghost fleet was fortunate enough to be transported away from). My first instinct was to stick with *New York* and give her a new lease on life. So badly irradiated by that second (underwater detonation) Baker test, she couldn't even be scrapped and, like USS *Nevada* and many other survivors, was ultimately sunk as a target.

Prinz Eugen wasn't. She was really there too, but, suffering from severe structural damage Baker inflicted, she was towed to Kwajalein Atoll. The once-handsome cruiser was leaking but was also considered too dangerous to board. An attempt was made to beach her, but she capsized and sank. The center of her three propellers and her rudder remain above water to this day.

Back to *New York*, my problem was that Gunnery Sergeant Arnold Horn was well established as having spent time in her at some point in the past. Not only was that experience a major plot point in the Destroyermen novel *Devil's Due*, it was referenced again in this tale. I thought it might be just a little too convenient to "bring her back to him," as it were. That stirred my realization that—duh, alternate universe—*Texas* could've just as easily been similarly expended and was only saved by the people and State of Texas that wanted her for their own. I wish *New York*—and so many other noble ships—could've received a similar reprieve. But *Texas* was saved and is currently undergoing a major (and I mean *major*) restoration, from the total replacement of those pesky torpedo blisters and who knows how many more tons of worm-eaten century-old steel, a whole new deck, restored aft fire control, renovated foretop . . . I simply can't list it all, and my hat's off with heartfelt thanks to all the great folks who've lavished so much time and effort into a historical icon I dearly love. She's the only remaining battleship that participated in both World War I *and* II and is the sole surviving example of a defining era of naval architecture. She may not have the long sleek lines of the Iowas, but she's just as beautiful in her distinctly determined, no frills, very . . . businesslike sort of way. A quick plug here for the Battleship Texas Foundation (check them out) and that glorious, mighty old lady that will soon be moored at her new home at Pier 15 in Galveston, Texas. Go see her when she is. I can't wait to visit her again myself.

ACKNOWLEDGMENTS

I must thank my agent, Russell Galen, once more. I'd probably still just be tinkering at writing if it weren't for him. Fair winds, Russ. As always, it's my pleasure to thank my great editor, Anne Sowards. Her patience, support, and encouragement are always much appreciated. Fred Fiedler and, to a *much* lesser extent, Jim and Dave (just kidding) deserve my thanks for their guidance regarding atomic issues, which I know less about than the average squirrel. I probably still managed to goof up most of what they told me. Fred is a USS *Ohio* plank owner, a true "nukie puke," and possibly one of the two smartest people on the planet. He's a lot like Courtney Bradford too. Probably taller. He and Jim have spent most of their adult lives harnessing and containing nuclear energy. Dave, on the other hand, has spent most of his life flying around prepared and practicing to release it. Thank God he never had to. The three of them were able to enlighten me a great deal about the perils of radiation and the historical understanding (and detection) of it from various perspectives.